A GREATER MONSTER

DAVID DAVID KATZMAN

BEDHEAD BOOKS

FIRST EDITION
Copyright: © 2011 by David David Katzman

ISBN: 978-0-9838644-0-0
Library of Congress Card Number: 2011913638

Printed in the United States by McNaughton & Gunn

Katzman, David David.
    A greater monster / by David David Katzman. -- 1st ed.
        p.   cm.
    LCCN 2011913638
    ISBN-13: 978-0-9838644-0-0 (acid-free paper)
    ISBN-10: 0-9838644-0-3
    ISBN-13: 978-0-9838644-1-7
    ISBN-10: 0-9838644-1-1
    ISBN-13: 978-0-9838644-2-4
    ISBN-10: 0-9838644-2-X

1. Apocalyptic literature. 2. Fantasy fiction, American. I. Title.

    PS3611.A82G74 2012
    813'.6
                                    QBI11-600162

also by David David Katzman

Death by Zamboni

A Bedhead Book
bedheadbooks@yahoo.com
Chicago, IL 60613

Reach the author at DavidDavid.net, goodreads.com/daviddavid or
agreatermonster@gmail.com.

Cover Art by Mike Wilgus
Book Design by Mike Wilgus
Author's photograph by Abraham Velázquez Tello
Interior art by Caitlin McKay
Music composed by Mark Messing and David Katzman
Music performed by Larry Beers, George Lawler, and Jonathan Steinmeier
Music player developed by Ryan Ore
Graphic elements within the book by Valerie Enzenbacher
Animation by Al Nicolini

Profound thanks to
Locke Peterseim, Jason Pettus, Oriana Leckert, Charles Lambert,
Michelle Herman, Barbara Katzman, Caitlin, Al, Mike, Mark, Larry,
George, Jonathan, Ryan, Valerie, and, most of all, Elizabeth and Zoë.

Additional thanks for generous support provided by
Frances Patricia Winkler, Ronaldi Ess, Ruben Beurskens, Norman de Greve,
Antal T. D. Szabo, Michael Galluzzo, Carey D. Keller, and George Webeck
in honor of his lifetime friendship with the great mOnSTer, Hell(en).

I have never seen a greater monster or miracle in the world than myself.
—Michel de Montaigne, *Essays*, book III, ch. 11

A Greater Monster

I jerked awake from my half-sleep, still clutching Ganesh in my right fist, when I heard the moan. The room smelled of ashes and rosemary. Hit the power button without shutting down and clenched the action figure tighter as my computer whined to its death.

Nothing.

Put my ear to the floor.

Perhaps I hadn't heard it.

I returned to my chair and considered the elephantine god in my hand. *I'll take him to work as a sentinel to keep me company*, I thought. The rich olive color would bring some energy to my office, which was a black box within a large black loft designed to simulate a warehouse (while incidentally honing paranoia and cruelty).

Papers strewn across my desk. My financial files. Had a moment of disorientation—thought I was hanging weightless above them, a dancing spirit. All those numbers representing all that I have.

Could be erased in a flash.

"Take," he said, holding out his hand. I inspected his dirty, wrinkled palm and the small black lozenge that sat upon it. A gift. The least I could do was allow him the honor of giving it. *Better living through karmaceuticals.*

We stood at the mouth of the alley, dead still. My clients would not have been pleased. eEye would not have sensed anything. Everything needs to keep moving. A breeze rippled across my face, curled down the back of my blazer. A freakishly warm December 21st. Mid-60s. The old man did not move. A monument to homelessness, a statue of failure, wearing a postman's jacket over a shirt with the outline of a horse on it. Work pants, a dirty baseball hat with the swoosh logo, and sandals covered in what appeared to be dog shit completed the outfit. *Better him than me.* I grabbed at the pill. Turns out, I wasn't as quick as an action-movie star. The moment I contacted his palm, the old man close-fisted my fingers and spit a glob of phlegm violently at my feet. His acid-green eyes met mine—"Why'd the chickens cross the road?" I scooped the pill and yanked my hand from his. "Why'd the chickens cross the road?" he repeated more urgently. I backed away, thrusting the pill into my coat pocket. The rough wool fibers rubbed like a Chinese finger trap. As I turned the corner back to the street, he bellowed, "Cuz he's a goddamn backstabbin' chicken's why!"

I swiftly trod the well-worn sidewalk dirtied with graf and excrement, noting the quote near Halsted: MURDER YOU ASS WHITES ESP. BLONDS→ Then further east a couple blocks: KILL YOU WHITE LONG-NOSED ASSHOLE GOOFS Mmmh, sorry you couldn't make it like I did. Welcome to natural selection, loser. Shifting the pavement beneath my feet by walking in time. In a timely fashion. In my black custom-made suit. Took the flaunt way round. At Halsted and Belmont, a silver SUV almost hit me as I stepped out with the walk sign.

"Fuck YOU!" I screamed while flipping the bird at the slut behind the wheel. The blond-ass bitch looked straight through me. Indeed. On second thought, perhaps the angry proles were onto something after all.

Assailed by a syncopated rhythm: hammers echoing from a courtyard, scuffing of shoes, buzzing insects, a bus's roar, distant sirens, dog's bark, staccato overlapping of two languages, five conversations. An impassive blue sky looked down upon me as I marched ahead penned in by concrete. Mangy mutt stopped in my way, craning up at me. Move along, rabid thing. It scampered off.

Touched my L card to the turnstile pad. Up the stairs. Had to squeeze past two deaf white-trash mullet-heads signing furiously at each other, almost coming to blows with their signs. On the platform. Checked out where the girls were. Over there, stood near the most attractive one. *Breasty McSweater, if you knew how much money I make, you'd want me,* I thought. But she ignored me. An ugly girl looked over at me, and I could sense her searching for eye contact—I gave it; she smiled tentatively. I put on my fat glasses. I could see through Fatty's clothes, skin, blood, and muscle. Nothing but a jiggling pile of creamy snot. Could I bag this fat? All the kids are doing it. The biggest bag of fat wins prizes, big fat fucking bags of fat prizes. She looked down.

Later: a client meeting discussing the strategy brief for the eEye launch. Skull-crushing boredom interspersed with hyperventilating fear.

"As we all know," I said, "security is big business, and this product has huge profit potential. Since 9/11 and even further, with the popular acceptance of global warming as a trend, people have two options. Those who can afford it invest in both directions at once to hedge their bets. The first behavior is a 'conservation' or so-called 'green' direction where they attempt to 'make a difference.' As miniscule as that difference may be, our research shows that people find it psychologically satisfying because it makes them feel like it's *other people* who are part of the problem. In addition, they feel they are contributing to future safety needs by trying to reduce the dislocation that will be caused by environmental catastrophe. It's important to note that— except for a few Luddites here and there—this is self-interested and often halfhearted behavior in the average consumer.

"The second track is to protect themselves from those who may be angry and in fact economically at risk due to the new poverty caused by environmental degradation and economic collapse. While green technologies are doing well in the market, these security products are doing even better. Personal safety comes first. There's nothing but upside here. Further consumer research shows eEye is best targeted at the six-figure-and-up demographic—individuals whose psychographic profiles wed them to the faith that money can buy safety. Of course, we don't say that. What we do is, we play upon their fear of the unknown and position eEye as the solution. We're recommending the following brand positioning: eEye is knowledge and knowledge provides security—or, more concisely, eEye equals knowledge equals security."

So why is it ... the more I know, the less safe I feel? I reached into my pocket for a tissue and touched the gummy pill. Had forgotten it was there.

"We're going to need to review concepts for our sales meeting at four tomorrow."

"But you just approved the brief. There's not enough time. At least ... let us come back to you with a mood board," I found myself dredging out of the job bin.

"No, we're going to need to show them a full ad campaign. Can you deliver or not?"

"No problem, Christopher. We'll have the creative for you."

So many meetings, I couldn't get any damn work done. Shut myself in my office with a paper plate and a knife from the kitchen. I retrieved the black lozenge, set it on the plate. It looked like a gum drop or the inside of a black Chuckles, with an oily consistency and an odd phosphorescent sheen. Perhaps this was where all the bitter black Chuckles go when they die. Or perhaps it was glue soiled by the hands of Mr. Homeless Guy, Esquire.

I clicked open an email just delivered from the GM.

> You've been doing great work on eEye ... —*blah-blah-blah*—... account worth 500 but with growth potential ... —*blah-blah*—... let you know Ed has decided to move on to other opportunities—*fired*—and I'd like you to take over his account for now. You'll have to continue managing eEye but this is a great opportunity for you. I'll be out of pocket tomorrow but Ficks can begin your download.

Please. Strap some electrodes to my temples and sear my brains.

I raised the plate to my nose and sniffed. Nothing. I stuck the plate in a drawer with the knife and proceeded with the fiction of the day.

"I want a fucking life!" The cry echoed from somewhere in the warehouse outside my door. The creatives were getting restless. It was 12:21. Third night in a row I'd been at work past 10:00.

"So lose the account and your job, fucker!" I shouted back and stuck my head out the door. No one. Just a cleaning guy sweeping the floor. He didn't even look up or acknowledge my presence ... perhaps because we don't speak the same language. I retreated to my office. Back to my laptop—email from the art director. How much of my life has been eaten up by this machine? What is that, masturbation into a vacuum?

ill be back at 8am if youv got comments

I opened the PDF and reviewed the creative. One good idea, two mediocre. Oh, you spineless jellyfish sons of bitches.

Gotta grab this bull by its balls. Bounced a koosh off the wall for an hour and pulled a couple smarter headlines out of my ass. Fired them off to the art director with some comments, and it was done. The presentation was at 4:00 so we'd be fine.

Warm and stuffy. 1:35 a.m. A dead zone. Discontinuous, discontinued from life outside the walls. I'd rather sleep here than take my work out. Inside and outside reverse so easily, separated by nothing. The outside falls in, the center will not hold. What shambling chimera slumps out of the office?

I turned off the light and sat in my ergo chair with the glow from my laptop spilling across the desk. Lifted the plate from my drawer and placed it in front of me. The object on the plate seemed to have darkened since I last looked. Gotten blacker. I put it back in my drawer. Searched for "free hardcore" and clicked a random link that led to a garish porn site featuring teaser images of topless women. I closed it, triggering a horde of pop-up windows to swarm across my desktop. Who would be quicker—me or the interstitial masters of the universe? Eventually they got the better of me, so I rebooted. For a brief moment, my office was completely black. I pulled the drawer open and touched the gummy shit, pinched it in half between two fingers. It was jelly-like.

Popped it in my mouth. Tasted like chicken. No, hah. Tasted like bone and asbestos. Like death. I swallowed and gagged, but it went down. My tongue went prickly and started to burn as if I had eaten too much pineapple. I gasped as it oozed a trail down my throat, taking its time. Mistake. That was a mistake. Oh yeah, shit. Why'd I do that? Shit. I closed my eyes. The computer monitor reversed itself, a black square in silver frame. I got up and grabbed my jacket from the door hanger then put it back.

I touched the wall of my office. It was cold. Industrial. Metal rivets. Grey. The floor black and oily. This was fashion. This was marketing.

Ganesh was there on the shelf next to my desk. *If I'm really going on a trip, I might as well pack my totem.* Joke. Stashed him in my pocket anyway.

Some time passed. Sweat ran down my forehead. I felt alternately hot and cold. I gripped the armrest. Desire is not pleasure. It's fever. I picked up a folder of project timelines and emptied it across my desk. Aimlessly flinging and crumpling presentations, turning things over without looking at them, dumping shit on the floor, pulling open drawers and emptying their contents. There went my paperclips. Binder clips. Spare change. Taxi receipts. Business cards. *Seven Habits of Highly Effective Cuntholes.*

I was hunting. For what? For courage? Need to tell a new story of myself. The born-agains do it. They let someone else write the plot for what they become. Boring. If I had courage, I would write my own fiction. Become someone interesting.

I was having a hard time wrapping my head around ... why I was doing what I was doing. And what exactly *was* I doing? Outlines softened. Surfaces went foggy. What was I supposed to be doing? I was caged in solid smoke, sharp smoke. I saw it settling in, filling the space. A skintight dream with hard corners, corroded metal defined space. I shaped the proportions when I could to avoid the spikes. The heartbeat of work. Pain and pleasure cannot be argued with. They demonstrate me. Touching is just electrons repelling. Nothing can touch. Ever.

I passed my arm before my eyes and watched it skip past me like slowed frames in an old movie. Life was stop-motion.

Realization: We render time by stitching together moments—flipping pages in the book of consciousness presents a continuous stream. Our senses too slow to realize the separation of moments, like a strand of pearls through eternity.

Time is terrifying, time is unspeakable. Clock-time lies down between moments ... but distance warps with velocity, time bends with velocity. Frames of reference. Are not absolute. Are selfish. A private reality. Clocks have a life of their own. Framed by references.

Speed separates: the faster I go, the faster everything moves away. At light speed, time accelerates to infinity; a catapult to end-time, light is the end. Within a singularity, density is infinite, gravity is infinite, light cannot escape. Light has zero mass. Time ends at both ends.

Time, you bastard, what are you? An allergy? A sickness. My body aches. I need to become completely still—my insides, I need to stop them, enter the singularity. But what are you? A reflection into matter of speed? Velocity's unconscious. Time is velocity's dance partner. Movement changes our angle through time. Time and space are trapped together, live together. Space trades places with time. Light is the crease where space and time, matter and energy fold.

Time is imaginary space. How do I get from one moment to the next? Space doesn't have direction, why should time? It's a medium. Within which vibrations occur. It just is, not movement, no strand, just now.

Time is—Realization: I could see nothing.

I could see nothing.
The room had vanished.
No forms.
No color or ground.
Absolute zero.

I was thinking, *This is a vision, a vision of nothing. Nothing is recognizable ... not my vision—I'm borrowing someone else's vision. Whose? Who are you who sees this? A spirit guide? The spirit lives in me and is driving me. But ... spirits can be liars or truthtellers ... quixotic tricksters. What is this?*

My stomach was a black pit spiraling into a negative space, an aching hole where my cock should be receding like the tide into meaninglessness.

Vacant vapid.

The surface of my life felt fragile, like a tympanum, taut and ready to snap. What if there's nothing inside to come out? Nothing, only air, no me in there, no life, nothing to become.

Suddenly, in the clarity of a drug-dark high, I became aware of the emptiness of all things. Every single thing around me, surrounding me. All belongings, buildings, people, people are empty shells, behavior mapped onto mannequins precluding any possibility of truth by gorging at the trough of emptiness— what fills up the emptiness I can taste my fear the fear. I wanted to smash everything every single thing and everyone. Smash the walls the objects the people the air myself crack open the shell release the loneliness. But nothing is so dense and powerful a delusion. The irresistible pull of a black hole the ultimate greedy bastard my inevitable demise drawing closer so I fill myself with more death to get closer to it. Love is burdened with all the feces of emptiness, a vacuum. As empty
as
.
.
.

And then I began to dissolve

Drif t   i   n   g
       g l i d i n g

          between
           the

           lines

Everything was wrong. I had done something not quite right, but I wasn't sure what. Bad things were going to happen to me. I had to try to follow along, play along, if I could just figure out the rules. But I had messed up somewhere. I didn't know the rules.

.
.
.
.

.

I could sense them like crust at the corners of my eyes. I felt outlines, vague outlines of other people in the room with me, but I didn't dare look right at them, I couldn't move my head in that direction ... were my eyes closed? I didn't want to open them because I was ashamed. I could see one of them out of the corner of my eye, one of them was female. Smooth like a doll. Her head was a brown deer head. Doll plastic. Salvia. I knew her name.

A cold glowing eye floated in front of me glaring with basilisk gaze—I threw up my hands to protect myself and the eye vanished in a jagged bolt of lightning.

Heard a sound.

Click.

Slid apart to a place. That deer. A time to get up and move sideways around the room because I was supposed to, disapproved of I could see that.

I was clutching the armrest — must've sat down again. Perspiration trickling at my temples. Oh, this was not good, no, I knew, my desktop exploded like a stick of dynamite *Ispasmedontopofmydesk* it was exploding wouldntstopexploding I stretched the bomb exploding I grabbed it and held it up.

I could see its fat mouths poised to embed themselves into my body

Hello?

["..."]

Hell   oh   Hell   oh

["..."]

I tried to yank the thing away from my ear, but it wouldn't let go. Sparks crackled out of the mouthpiece cascading fountains burning my hands, face. I realized I was shrieking. I shut my mouth the sparks vanished black fluid absorbed my consciousness, caught in spongy ether.

I heard the sound of time out of my eye *click-click-click-click-click* trying to catch the present moment I could hear the flower of the metronome from the corner of my eye but I could not see it distinctly. It repelled my touch. Reality pivoted on a single point, I was spinning up and out like a tornado.

I saw through the back and top of my skull. Two television screens face to face talking to each other. There. The metal desk. And my hands went through it to the molecules then the empty spaces full of waves and waves I was swimming. I was in the bathroom wanted to get out because it was so hard. But I couldn't walk.

Whiplash of wind howling through me. The withering glare of the ice mantis emptied my body of all substance. I sensed the fraud. All true calculations had been hidden from me. The mantis moved across my line of sight leaving a trail of cruel certainty in its wake, outline after outline of itself disapproving of me from the corner of the room.

Motionless, they spoke with the utmost disdain and venom, *You live here? We could not have come up with a better punishment for you than this. Your pleasures are shallow and false and nothing exists behind you but emptiness in your so-called civilization so you strain to fuck things, you know deep down you can feel it in your meat that all this pretended human creation will shatter, plunge jagged seeds into your flesh and grow a torture garden.*

Silence struck me like a blunt instrument. The stall door slit ajar. The sink—blotched with little lakes of water, a geography of disgust. At a urinal. The small dirty yellow tiles with streaks of rose over and over and over again the same dirty yelling tiles over and over and over again to infinity squares rotating reality clicking around in an infinite wheel I must follow it or I will be lost and life is the ring of the rungs of reality where I step off a world within a world within a world within a world and I needed to wake up because each world was worse than the next stay where I am right now I have to go back—the clicking rotating universe each one a fractionally different version of me I had to concentrate try not to panic stay in the right one or I could become one of the other ones instead I needed to stay in the right slot or I might not come back eyes closed eye saw rows of disapproving people one of them in the middle in the back a deer head of lucent brown they were all related to me and next I was swimming surrounded by liquid pressed against it I plunged through milky clouds diving through fathoms of ghosts. I could not breathe and I did not need to. Slices of clear-clear water.

I saw this then this was the way it is, it always was. This I saw. This was the way it is, it always was. This place was divine. I was always here. I would always be here. And I will return to it. I will always return to it. It is behind everything haunting me. That other place had been a trance. A trance that seemed to last twenty-eight years. This I see now. This is the way it is, it always was. I imagined that world. This is what's real. I imagined that world. This is what happens when I dream of being real.

My skin peeled off to get away from me
I touched my ears and they rang like toxic metal my teeth were grinding
A place of phantom surfaces
A knife sheep god eater and the twitching toads
The people were beautiful and spoke a language incomprehensible machine chatter
Gleaming iridescent white suits and strapless dresses blinding cocaine teeth
Their laughter sizzled in my head and the scraping of rusty wire
She (of rainbow hair) passed the needle
He (with silver eye) passed the needle
a drop of nectar glistening at the top a lambent drop trembling in light
is me
the slightest disturbance a slight gust evolves and swirls me into heaps
endless and unnecessary
as I turned to speak—vanished in a poof of dust
Matter is the energy of perception with the sentiment of a pile of maggots
My self soled in sagging burlap
a chemical dancing on the tip of the iceberg
the creative radiance grimaced

Words break world breaks eat ourselves O the Oh the sea the hole the Center the whole (no)thing(ness)
around and round and under and un and u

Things were not good not good I was shitting bricks ripping hairs out my asshole felt like my intestines were going to blow fuck fuck fuck ah shitfucksssss

I felt myself being ripped apart inside my asshole chunks of my ass thrown across the bathroom spattering the walls my legs falling in opposite directions my body surrendering to the tile my face bounding off a surface warm milk in my mouth my tongue felt the topology tooth tooth tooth tooth? jagged edge my face was a jagged tooth my eyes they were closed they would not open I was tugging at them with all my willpower nothing the abyss no orientation no perspective abruptly swung open: my face was in the urinal I pushed back many bodies entangled with me we were all kneeling at the urinal I wriggled and all the bodies writhed around me a knot of little snakes nadouessioux nausea overwhelmed us and we vomited into the urinals before

A beginning:

In.   Out.   In.   Out.   In.   Out.

       In.   Out.   In.   Out.   In.   Out.

In.   Out.   In.   Out.   In.   Out.

       In.   Out.   In.   Out.   In.   Out.

In.   Out.   In.   Out.   In.   Out.

       In.   Out.   In.   Out.   In.   Out.

In.   Out.   In.   Out.   In.   Out.

       In.   Out.   In.   Out.   In.   Out.

In.   Out.   In.   Out.   In.   Out.

       In.   Out.   In.   Out.   In.   Out.

Ensconced back at my pad. Wrapped in a blanket. Shivering dog-sick. Puke all over my shirt. Lips numb. Drifting in and out. So many threads of nothingness knitting through my head. Flipped on the poisonous afternoon TV. The television exudes a warm glow of friendship on lonely nights. An insect god waiting patiently for me to rot and decay. Quivered a lot. Smoked a bowl to try to calm down. Shook like Parkinson's. Checked the locks on my door three times just in case. Unlocked one by accident the last time. Had to check three more times. Phone rang. Hot and aching. Lay on the sofa, ceiling fan going around slowly, so slowly. The original *King Kong* was on TV. Closed my burning eyes, sickness of commercials infecting my ears. I think I heard one of my babies on there selling home security. Home security. A house of cards. My job, the economy ... there's always nukes. A home is paper-thin.

I was thinking: *Why'd I do it, why? Every time saying,* if this trip ends badly, I can handle it, *but I forget every time forget I can't control my brain, parts of it shut down like in a dream that dream where I was talking to him—not thinking he's dead, just talking to him, not saying this isn't possible, this is a dream, don't think it—what was the last one? ... indistinct characters ... can't seem to look them in the face—a warehouse? The office. Right, typing at a computer ... dead fucking father ... run over like a deer in the road—I can hardly picture your creased face, that stupid outfit you put on for the "traditional" dance competition, leather headband stuffed with turkey feathers, feather anklets, beaded wristbands, looking like a sad-ass mascot doing a competition for fuck's sake about tradition ... had to marry a white woman didn't you and move us into a log house so you could still feel full-blood that's why you never could look me in the eye, saw me as iyeska the day I blew up, it all blew up the scholarship the hell I'd go back to the shithole rez no more speak to half-breed cuz I was going to be better than you and you knew it.*

Closed my eyes. Pounding hangover. Couldn't sleep. So fucking tired, but my brain was wrapped in barbed wire. All I could do was groan and feel like I was going to die. Even my tears were afraid to leave me.

I blinked, looked up. The ceiling light was contorted into an angel of death.

Suvé. Suvé. Swedish and quintessential. That summer after college in Europe ... my big black backpack ... the creaky old youth hostel in the Alps—way up at the peak of the peaks. Nothing around but cliffs and snow and space. Meeting over dinner ... talked ceaselessly until it was late, everyone asleep but us. Insects of all kinds zwinged around the ceiling lights, and the chill air sluiced through cracks in the rickety walls. What did we talk about? Pine Ridge, I told her about Pine Ridge and how it was the poorest place in the U.S. and about Wounded Knee and fry bread. I wanted her to see me as special. The one time I told anyone about being Oglala. *She just listened, didn't act like it made a difference one way or another. Her tattoo—a peace sign inked in tie-dye on the back of her neck.* I love the symbolism of it, *she said,* whether it's genuine or not. *She wanted to believe it had meaning. Sitting across from each other at a rough-hewn picnic bench ... she held out her finger and a monster dragonfly landed on it. The insect preened its eyes for what felt like forever. When it finally flew away she asked,* What do you feel when you're in love? *and I remember thinking* I don't know, I don't know how to answer that, *so I just answered without thinking,* I want it to be over so I can fall in love again. *She had to make a call so we wrapped ourselves in wool blankets and stumbled out into the moonless dark to find the sole payphone in town that stood a hundred feet away down a dirt trail toward the cable car that went up to the top of the Jungfrau. We found our way to it by using our feet to tap for stones lined along the border of the trail and squeezed into the phone booth. She pulled the door shut, and the ceiling light went on. One cube of light amidst miles of pitch-blackness. She was close enough that I could feel the warmth of her breath as she spoke. I leaned my back against the glass wall as she slid a card into the machine and punched a number. For fifteen minutes, I contemplated her long glowing hair flipped back from her forehead like wings and listened to a song I couldn't understand then or ever.*

I stroked my slippery hard-on and pictured all the women I wanted to fuck, one after the next falling onto my dick, falling into each other, through each other, becoming one large, arbitrary, beautiful woman who I realized was nothing, and she vanished, and I was fucking myself, and my dick was abraded. I lost it, I lost everything, and I melted into a hole, folded into myself.

My face in the mirror. I looked tired. Thin and brittle. I rubbed my eyes several times. Opened my mouth, front tooth chipped to a point, throbbing. Should get that capped immediately.

I turned on the water and let it run, steamed up the mirror.

The need to buy something uncurled in me like an erection. I would feel better if I just gave in to it.

"Show me what *you* like," I said to her. The super-hot salesgirl. Perfect oval face like a supermodel, perfectly straight lustrous platinum hair with swathes of blue not found in nature, and perfectly round tits not found in nature either. Jeezus.

She turned, walked to a display. I followed. "This suit," she said, pulling it off the rack. She stood at my side and held it up in front of us. "It's from *Perils of Money*. This is the most fabulous thing I've seen in a long time. The cut is very cool—a sixties Fellini influence, narrow Italian lapels—and the fabric is amazing. Feel this." I touched it as she held it out to me—very plush and light. "This is a thin, lightweight velvet. The contrasting lapel and collar is felt, but this velvet—it's about the same weight as cashmere, and it's so exquisite. It's just the most fabulous thing. They make some nice pieces."

She looked me directly in the eyes.

"This is beautiful," I said.

She held it up to me, evaluating. "You're about six foot two? I think it might be perfect."

I took it from her hands. "I'll try it."

She led me to the changing room, which was a frosted acrylic cube mirrored on all four sides, open at the top. "Let me know if you need anything," she said and left. Tore off my clothes and tried it on. Like a hipster fucking James Bond with money to burn. Checked the tag. 4k. Jesus, an entire paycheck. Burned all right. Back out.

"Let me see," she said, taking me in. "You know, they made a limited edition of twenty of these, and each one is a different color. It looks fantastic on you. You look fantastic. I wish *I* could wear that."

"I'll take it."

"Congratulations. You look so hot."

I handed her the plastic as she presented her sweetly smiling face as if it were a gift — felt it down to the pit of my stomach. She disappeared. I wandered down the excessively wide, winding staircase to the cashier's desk on the first floor. My gaze skimmed the surface of the luxurious interior design until I found her hair, then her thick lips — a vaginal exaggeration — before settling on her precise upturned nose (also probably done). "Here please." I signed on the touchscreen, watched my virtual identity vanish and the jacket folded neatly into a box debossed with the store logo into a semiopaque rubber bag and into my hands. I slid my business card across the counter, "If you'd like to get dinner … ?" She smiled and nodded with the painful artificiality of an airport food court, had already moved on.

I left, could barely breathe, my throat filled up. My cock ached hard as a gravestone. Followed the sidewalk, walking rootless, wandering past the yuppie slutpads of the Gold Coast. The homogenous brick facades gnashed at the blue tongue of sky, drooled out the black tar street. I entered a convenience store only to be flayed with blaring music — Jesus, it was fucking Christmas. The aisles were pathways in a robot brain. Tinselism. All fucking commodity cheese. I felt myself cleaving in half, bifurcating, axed along my axis. My stomach chattered like a bag of popcorn kernels in a fire. My face. This much stubble? I was back in my bathroom and not sure how I got there. But the day before … my thoughts hit a wall. The razor. I wanted to shave but watched my palsied hand attempt to hold it. Not so much. My face. Hadn't I shaved already? My usually flawless memory was twisting out of my grasp like an eel. I needed a good steak dinner. And some sleep. Something to settle me down.

I opened my eyes.

"Did you get some dust in your eye?" she asked.

I blinked.

I was in a room. Windowless. Eggshell white and rectangular. The ceiling was high. I sat on a sofa upholstered in expensive oatmeal linen, the back rectangular, the seating deep. The floor was polished white concrete. It took me a moment to recognize my living room.

And Sasha. Half Dutch (her mother), half Jamaican (her father)—she claimed—the resulting gene mix being nothing short of astonishing. She lounged opposite me in the pool of my red loveseat like a mermaid, with two pillows propping up her waist and one elbow on the armrest, waves of brown hair cascading across her chest. Her dark eyes drew me in, bounced me back, pulled me in. Her eyes absorbed everything yet were impenetrable. A thick envelope sat on the coffee table between us.

"I'm not sure," I replied.

"Your flat is nice."

"Thanks."

"You must do very well."

"I do okay."

"I have no particular interest in working," she said.

"You don't want to be one of those housewives with kids?"

"Don't be ridiculous. They're under the impression that the suburbs go on forever."

"They're high."

"No actually, that's the problem." She took a hit and passed the pipe to me.

"Mmmh." I lit it and inhaled. Exhaled. The heat burned my throat—and numbed it.

"Cannabis is magickal," she said. I could hear the "k" in it.

"Yeah? It's just brain chemistry."

"Do you think? I take it you don't believe in magick then."

"I said no to religion in favor of ... I dunno ... logic?"

"Eh, no. While's true that Western religions contradict science, right, that's just competition. For how people think. They are of the same category. Religion's actually a perverse attempt to apply reason to a chaotic world— *attempt*—an attempt to quantify mystery through laws and rules. Would you like to see magick?" Her vaguely European accent—so hot. She gestures through the formless smoke. "Vanishing trick. Ready?"

"Uhm. Sure, whatever, twinkie."

"The present moment. It's gone. Where'd it go?"

"Very funny."

"Mock all you want. Even nothingness is alive. Have you read any quantum physics?"

"Of course. I went to Harvard, didn't I?"

"Quantum particles zip in and out of existence constantly. That's magick if I've ever heard it. Unfortunately, particles don't have morality, so that doesn't give me hope for love. Unfortunately."

"Love?" I became impatient. "Hell no. Nature isn't moral. Don't talk to me about nature. I grew up hearing all about the bullshit greatness of nature. And spirits. The only spirits I saw around that place were rum and whiskey. Fuck it. Come on, they *charged* you to participate in the sun dance. It wasn't a ritual, more like a flesh carnival about as a deep as a punk's penis piercing."

"At least it's balanced. Nature has balance. Humans don't fit into that anymore."

"Whatever. Nature doesn't give a fuck. Remember that little tsunami that hit Japan? A comet could swing by tomorrow and wipe this whole planet out, leaving not a measly remnant. No art, no life, no summer, no rocks, endangered species, organic food, hybrid vehicles, no crust, core, anything. All gone. Call it Chukwa if you want, not going to make it any more spiritual."

"Well, lovely. But even so. You have no idea what happens outside of time. Dead. What if you ... you could observe the existence of every single being from the very dawn of life to the extinction, watch every sunset, every thunderstorm, you could experience every single one."

"Uhm. That's a nice fantasy and so not scientifically rational. I've seen everything I believe in." I took another hit from the pipe. "I never like getting high alone."

"Why?"

"Because it reminds me of what it's like to be old."

"So why do you do it?"

"Because I want to be reminded of what it's like to be old."

"No wonder you're so bloody depressed." She came over by my side and touched my hand.

"I'm sick of talking."

I walked down the narrow alley toward where my chance encounter with mister homeless guy had taken place. Two dumpsters on the left, hulking metal things, gave off bad energy, extrusions of cruelty. I came to the end where another alley crossed, and a car pulled past me into a parking space.

The sun fell. Shadows remained behind, burned into the brick like nuclear wraiths haunting the walls. What was hidden on the other side? The petty lives of all these people.

There he was, crouched against a building. I went over to him, ready to run if need be.

"You gave me something yesterday," I said. "What was it?" He didn't reply. I repeated myself.

"Who are you?" he asked.

"You gave me something. Do you recognize me?"

"It's all one day, man."

"Why are you here?"

"I'm a jagoff, man. So I fucked up. I'm a jagoff. Everyone makes mistakes. I'm a jagoff."

"Do you have any more of that stuff?"

He got up, rocking side to side, and rushed down the alley, limbs flailing. "I don't have anything, man. Don't hurt me. It's all poison, man. I don't need a job. It's poison."

"I'm not going to hurt you," I called after him. But I let him go.

I was gripped by fear and remorse at what had happened. And I wanted it to happen again. I had to do it again. I had to get out of there.

"Images fall like snowflakes."

I spun around but saw no one. I stood in the alley listening. Silence. No, not silence. A humming sound that I had been hearing all along unfolded into my awareness like the revelation of a camouflaged chameleon. The sound was coming from a wall of identical air conditioner units projecting from the windows of an apartment complex, all humming the same sound. Why were air conditioners running in December? I felt dizzy and sat down against the wall. Closed my eyes. Opened them, and I was looking at my face in the bathroom mirror again.

I decided that I had been looking at myself so I continued to do so. Was this what I looked like? Was this really me? My face was a clump of parts that seemed to disagree. My cheekbones protruded more than usual; my eyes, noticeably sunken, startled me. Vivid blue—too much irritation—framed by red, forked lighting. I blinked. Dark stubble dressed my square jaw. I rubbed my chin across three, four, ten times. It felt like an irritated asshole. My nose, finished straight per my surgeon, now seemed to accuse me: I had stolen something from it. Thick straight black hair—inheritance from good ol' Dad—longer than I'm used to, covering half my ears. Looked like I was going native. I looked *off.* I looked scary. The bitches wouldn't be so hot for this look. Too much. I peered into my eyes and couldn't figure out who was looking back. I rubbed my nose from side to side, and it made a clicking sound. Felt out of joint. My forehead was—

scuttling movement to my right, on the sink—a spider?

I checked all around the pedestal. Nothing. Shook my head. *Whoa.* Deep breath. Just my peripheral vision acting up. Likely remnants of that ... drug. Did that actually happen? I couldn't see how. I checked my pocket: my finger jabbed stickiness. Still some left. Hadn't known that. I pulled it out. It was different somehow. A black mass. A little flattened. I pressed it back into a lozenge shape. It seemed big, as big as the original piece he had given me. Hadn't I eaten half? It was squished, hard to tell. I returned it to my pocket and tossed back a couple Vicodin from the medicine cabinet.

I woke up in my new suit jacket. It seemed to be holding me together so I left it on.

"You don't look like yourself tonight. You look like ass."

When I last saw her ... when was that? "Oh, thanks. Just what I wanna hear." I laughed, but it sounded hollow.

"You sound scared."

"Scared? Of what? That's ridiculous. Tired, maybe. You know. Work. It's a constant struggle. Sure, it has rewards, but I work my ass off. I tell you what, I succeed at *whatever* I put my mind to. But *sometimes* I feel like ... I sabotage myself. I know this. I'm my own worst enemy. You know? I make myself miserable ... when I should just appreciate what I have. You ever feel like ... sometimes I hold on to my cell or a fork or anything, could be anything, and I feel like I'm not holding it. Or I'm completely oblivious to actually holding it. Or you catch yourself looking at someone, and you know you're not seeing them? Maybe I'm seeing myself seeing them. Or I fuck someone and don't feel like I'm fucking at all. I'm sure you can relate. No matter how hard I hold on or focus or fuck, it always slips away."

"Bollocks," Sasha sneered. "Page two of your existentialist drama should relate a kick in the teeth. *Babylon* knocking at your door. All those pretty uniforms. You'll know what tired is when you find yourself on the wrong list. I saw *les flicks* with clubs wade into a Pride Parade in Jamaica. You're just like Cobain—a self-indulgent tosser who couldn't focus outside his small mind for a change."

"Hey, Hamlet had that problem, too."

"Another bloody loser. Fuck Hamlet. Just another man who wanted to hear himself talk."

"So I guess you blame the penis."

"Uggh. Men are dicks with legs. Genetic defects. The Y chromosome is a crippled X."

"Well, we're agreed. Pussies are much nicer."

"Entrance and exit. Intriguing and inviting and mysterious and hidden—that's erotic. The deferral of pleasure. While penises are water balloons aimed at me, about to pop. Outness is all they are, surface, sameness. Penises are all there."

"Now I understand you."

"No actually, that's the problem. You think you understand everything. Men are—you could say—juggernaut. Living in the land of conquest. They erase history books and print money on the pages. Drag most women by the hair with them. Women—so gullible to fall for the male lies. Brainwashed into believing it. What we need is, you see ... we just need all the women one day to all just refuse to do it, to refuse to have babies. No sex. All of a sudden—you men would have to give up. Surrender. Dismantle the war machine. Capitalism. The whole fucking system. They'd have to give it up. Of course, men can fall back on rape ... to break us. Rape camps. Which is why every woman needs to have a gun. If every woman had a gun, they'd have to kill us to win, which would defeat them. Catch *that* 22."

"Oh, please. It's just as likely men would stop having sex as women. Women probably need to reproduce more than men. And consume the same rewards. It's primal. You can't beat that. And what about gay men?"

"Sure, step in the right direction. But the percentages. Too many breeders. Freud had a lot to say about primal urges. The superego exists to overcome the id. That's how society survives. Otherwise we'd live like pack animals in the wild or whatever. He called it the Reality Principle. Unfortunately, he got it wrong. It's an *unreality* principle. We're working hard to destroy our species, and it's all perfectly logical, based on the logic of capitalism. The need to survive as individuals, as cogs in a system which is destroying itself."

"I'm sick of talking. Let's fuck."

She paused. "Did you just—is that how you want this to go?"

"What, I just figured ..."

"I have no problem at this point. I can turn you into a machine like *that*. Fuck if I care. You disappoint me."

"I'm just kidding."

"Yeah."

"Okay, I'm sorry. I won't bring it up again."

"Yeah, that's fine."

I followed her to the door; she took her parka off the hook.

"Right, right."

She was gone.

A truck drove by—it said, MURDER ONE FAMILY MEMBER. That can't be right; I looked back. NUMBER ONE FAMILY MOVER.

The fumes were making me nauseous. *I can't go to work today. Wait, what day is today? Sasha. Something was not quite right about that conversation, but what was it? That was not right. A guy looked at me, drool down his greasy chin, watery eyeballs, no one else around, I'll ask him, he's trying to talk to me at the same time.*

"Excuse me, what time is it?"

Gun-colored khakis, where'd he come from? "What the hell are you saying, dude? Can't understand what you're babbling, get your hand the fuck off my arm."

Where did I put my keys?

I felt untethered, dislodged.

Vertigo hit. "Hi, I'm—" She turned her back on me.

Wetness on my chin. I yawned with terror. I was unsure ... I saw movement ... I tasted starch ... a line before me ... don't get too close ... don't cross the line

I

I

I

I

I

David David Katzman

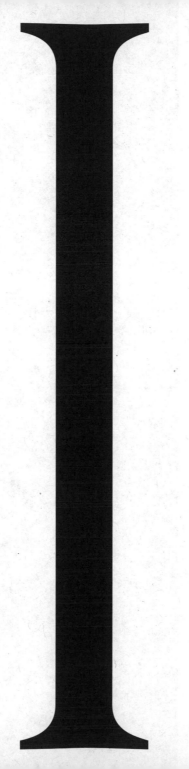

David David Katzman

The uniform walked toward me. He could smell my shit-stink heart. I casually put my hands into my pockets and felt the lozenge. Brought it to my face, hiding it behind my hand. Uniform approached ... too close. I would go home. The uniform walked past me. Stopped. Stood. Turned.

"Hey! You."

I stuck the black goo in my mouth and swallowed. I turned and looked at his collar. It was dark blue, and the points dog-eared in opposite directions.

"Everything okay? You got a problem?"

Yessir. Nosir.

I looked up at his face and all I could see: two round mirrors. I saw two of me split and morphed like a funhouse reflection. My nose was exceptionally large. My face was projected forward, nostrils gouged out. My hair rose up in clumps looming like vultures. Back, far back, were tiny ears. I clutched at my stubbly chin, which was receding off my face into oblivion. My shadowy cave mouth had a glistening silver chain dangling across it, sealing it.

His tufted knuckles were in front of my eyes, blocking my reflection. He flicked his fingers twice, and I heard a clicking sound.

"What? Listen, buddy, your jacket—that's a nice jacket, it's all ripped up here." He fingered my shoulder and went through to the bone.

"Whoa, you smell real bad there, buddy. Whudaya doing on the platform?"

I'm going to work.

"I can't hear you. Maybe you should just head home and clean off a bit."

I'm sick. I'm going to the doctor.

"You're sick? That what you said? Can I see some I.D.?"

I tried to get my wallet out of my pocket, but there was nothing there.

"Here. I'll give you a hand." He checked my pockets, patted me down. Pulled out an object, held it up in front of me.

"What's this? Some toy? This doesn't work as I.D., pal. Howerya gonna see a doctor without I.D.?"

I'm sick. Going to Northwestern ... Hospital. I'm a VP ... they've got my healthnsurance.

"Hmmh." His box squawked, and he lifted it to his mouth. "Ten four. Awright there, bud. I gotta go. Here's your train now. You gonna make it? You better get off on the right stop. Exit Chicago. You got it?"

I'll be ok.

Mind the gap.

The silver serpent pulled up, and the uniform was gone. I slipped between its scales and sat in its throat. *Clatter clatter clank*. The harsh glare vanished as we slouched roughly into the intestines of Chicago. Dark and swaying, jittering from side to side. Sparks and squeals. I couldn't get comfortable. It was bony inside on the seat. I kept readjusting—frustrated and irritated bone to bone. A feather tickled my cheek. Chills. I turned and looked back, a circle of light receding. I closed my eyes. I opened my eyes; it was dark. I closed my eyes. Feet shuffled around me, followed by material crumpling and crinkling. It was pitch black. I closed my eyes. Up from my gorge a sensation of fright thrashing side to side hurling between my knees on my pants the burning rushing milk searing my throat, sticking in my teeth. I opened my eyes. I noticed his black boat shoes and a lugubrious black dog with matted hair resting its chin on his shoe. Dog in a harness. Old man with a stick. He sat facing me, frozen, eyes hidden behind big black square sunglasses, his stick thin and long. A thick, salt-and-pepper beard and mustache. He pulled back his lips in a smile or grimace or both, and gold glinted in his mouth.

"Yo, brother. You okay? Not looking so good, all twitchy 'n shit."

I turned to my left. Was a dark man with a knit winter cap tight on his head.

"You're pale as a ghost, brother." He looked at me. His face was clean and round. "You look like you need to chill. You've got sick all over you. I will not preach to you, but I highly suggest you need to get off whatever shit you're on, whatever it is. I'm not judging you. I used to be on the shit too, man. But I got off. Selling Streetwise now, gonna move out of the shelter. Soon. Yeah, in the meantime, I'm working the tunnel. Never see the light of day. Stand around with my Streetwise. I don't solicit. But I gotta be careful. Can't trust anyone. Underground cops. I get AFBB, you know? Arrested For Being Black. That joke's only funny because it's true. All you can do is keep your head down, keep moving. None of it makes sense. Just roll with it, right? Keep an eye out for your brother. I'm getting my feet back under me, man. Shit, you're still young. Anyway, it's none of my fucking business, I know.

"Look, I don't do this regular, but you look like you need some medication to help with the twitching or seizures or whatever you got going on." He looked around. "There's nobody in here but you, me, and I don't think this blind guy is gonna give a shit." He came up close. His flannel shirtsleeve had little red worms sprouting from the cuffs.

"Listen, I got some skunk for myself. Just a couple buds. I got some bad knee pain, can't afford a doctor, you know? But shit, you need some medicine and there ain't no doctor gonna fix you when you're homeless and fucked up. My cousin, he's got the twitches, you know? And the bud seems to help him. Seen it."

He put a pipe shaped like a cornucopia in my mouth. A flame ignited like a bloody rose. *Hold still brother, hold still. Now breathe, man, breathe ... there you go. You just need to get out of your head. Breathe and let it go. Now. There. Get some sleep, brother.*

My hand was in my pocket, clutching an object. I pulled it out and tore a hole in my pocket. I held it up. It was a plastic shape. Grey, brown, sage, white, whorled into a teardrop. A face was submerged in the undifferentiated substance, a long nose, as the blob melted through my fingers onto the floor.

The old man smiled and his gold tooth glinted and the silver serpent clattered, slither-clattered. The lights went out and all I could see was the gold tooth and lights came back and no one was there except the blind man and me and his dog and darkness glittered around me as I slid down a curved banister and my head turned to the right and a suit was there staring at me exuding suitness. I looked at his face it was a woman painfully beautiful as a knife-edge her face traced with flickering circuitry I couldn't break free as she leaned toward me smiling shaking her hair of fiber-optic light *you should follow me*. But I sank down and out.

And I slid onto the floor and out of my body and
there I was lying on the floor I saw myself
insubstantial
blurring into the dog. Hiding.

> *Re   la x   ed.*
> *Mmmh.*
> *Come for ta bull.*

I observed myself:
the past has left marks on my body
my state vector collapsed
consciousness causes
all time is simultaneous. Or a concept.
Hypercube of space and time. Is why time's not visible.
Time is not a thing, no thing, it's a reflection, the reflection of change into space
the angle skews with speed

the subatomic realm does not distinguish between
all is
all is change

I curved down a banister, sledding down a helix around and around and around the chocolate, candy-cane green, uncountable shades of turquoise, rose upon sweetgrass upon sandalwood upon lemon, rolling crescendos, notes too deep to be sounds, places outside, spatial folding comprehended, chaos itself a fractal god, that which is

Energy exists. That which is

I opened my eyes, and looking up I saw a branch growing out of my mouth and felt roots working their way through the back of my skull like itchy thoughts. I was planted in place as the branch became a tree clambering through the clattering, thick oak tree in the center of the train, windowpanes of pitch night slashing the dense bark, roots like arm-thick cocks fucking the floor, gaping vaginas in the trunk with hoary white beards seed pod dropped tooth bounce pop slap tongue swallow convulsion choke choking air air.

Leaves. Scintillating in silhouette. Lines, stems, arteries grew outward, winding and convolving as multilayered melodies, chaotic calculations, immeasurably fine strands interlaced like lungfuls of air with every molecule expressing life, crystalline ice. Charcoal darkness wreathed the tributaries, chiaroscuro. The pattern of each transcendent. Crystal lady, crystalline birth. Fault lines of consciousness in a fractal cornucopia, splintering through a crystal lattice.

The dappled leaves were interwoven mandalas; the light slowed—I saw light spiraling from my eye up through the leaves, uncoiling and releasing like a galaxy of nebulae; my mind showering out of me, my need to restrain the light in my greedy eye—released, let go my need and felt a calmness; the light—I traveled with it, not seeing because the light was no longer returning to me, I pulsed from my eye and spiraled upward, a gyre of light photon-synthesizing. I felt my breathing stop. Respire-cessation. A quantum of life. Small expression of will. Surfing the quantum foam of the universal ocean breath.

I was a liquid orgasm shimmering up the xylem and phloem diffusing out of the iron bark squeezing through the petioles and bursting like a supernova into the leaves swaying with the movements of the train, aware of all simultaneously.

The tracks are ajar

The present rushes into → nothingness → all that matter and space vanished, replaced by memory

Existence is a blip
Matter does not exist → but in time, it vanishes

Motion, the vibration drags time into existence
we fling our bodies against each other in desire to return to the great crunch
every particle of our being drives us in hunger
to return to the Nirvanic state when everything touched
before Chaos cast a spell, flinging a universe into existence
repulsion causing desire, rejection,
the Freudian trauma of the Big Bang sex party

and gravity is the friction, the masturbation of the universe.

I = my reified future + my reified past = a vector and the state of my vector is collapse all collapsed

The present is a coordin(ate)ator
a vector is a trajectory in the present, a point with direction, an impetus, an impulse, a groove, energy plus direction

The mind is formless
thought is energy, energy is a wave, a motion, a fluctuation
if the mind is a wave → where is it waving?
What is it waving at?
My Self? My conception of my Self?

The universe is a dream lit up   *leaping like a neural charge*
crossing the synaptic

gap

all electrons are one electron forever leaping
all our thoughts simultaneously leaping the universe
instantaneously endlessly on its own
random irreducible absolute
cruel amoral atemporal
without influence
among complexes of universes

I turned my head and the suit with circuitry mapping his clean beautiful face, it hurt to look at her, was observing me frowning as he transformed into a woman, the most beautiful man as she leaned forward, *come fuck me*, he said, *you should follow me*, hand of light reaching toward me seizing my branches but I descended further, escaped her embrace.

Blackness, nothingness. Slivers of light from the windows revealed the dog standing and he was big, then utter darkness then the dog growing bigger, blackness again, then the dog filling the train, towering over me. I was on the threshold

and a guillotine mouth snapped at me

the metal slammed hard on both sides of my head.

I opened my eyes. I could see the mouth. Again—*SMASH*—like a bat to my temples. My eyesight went googly, bubbles of shock popping above me in the dark as the mouth retreated once again and leapt to attack, my brain shattered into a million shiny shards of migraine light diamond knives gnashing. I became aware of a deep thrumming sound a ceaseless kettle drum, an *anh anh anh in in in* in infinite oscillation manifested, my mind so sharpened must've sliced through layers of reality, stretched tight like string theory, adventuring like Timothy Leary, torn and twisted like a Frank Gehry, stacks of warped records, chords cut, trajectories topological, lop a logical universe and my body apart. Twinned, twined.

Static hiss a murmur the smell musk sandpaper on my cheek I lurched *BANG* against metal, the moaning louder heaviness on my chest digging a weight crushing my groin I couldn't breathe raspy splash on my face I couldn't feel my arms couldn't touch anything felt hot juice in my mouth leaking between my teeth I opened my eyes I opened my eyes I opened my eyes in the arc of a broad white blade I heard myself looking into my eyes above me the sour breath of an unfathomable black hole gleaming many gleaming sharp triangles coming toward me knives roaring white lightning gashed my head in half—I stepped back inside myself from a point of view I did not know existed and watched my eyes explode atomizing my head I'm screaming silence and

I collapsed into the space between

the   doors

I took a breath. A deep, slow breath. My limbs, my chest, my head floated up through darkness. I was aware of a twittering followed by a harsh screeching sound. A draft crossed my throat. The air was dry.

I seemed to be outside.

Assessment: my body felt like it had been pounded like a piece of meat. Beat-up and aching. I was pulled down, weights hanging from my bones. Lying on my back. Back of my skull pressing against hard ground. Lightheaded. My eyes were closed. I slit them. A crescent of harsh light. I closed my eyes again. Bright spots with blue around them. I opened my eyes again, squinting. I couldn't place the context of what I was looking at. I thought of a bucket, the emptiness in a bucket ... but ...

I lifted my head weakly and felt the world flip, and my eyes contracted, and my orientation skewed: I was looking at a writhing ceiling of clouds about twenty feet above the dark earth. In all directions. Mud brown, dull orange, shades of dirty grey—like crocheted fingers weaving the sky impossibly close. Something had gone weird.

My shirt was soggy and stuck to my chest. Sent a command to my right shoulder, and my body grimaced, my arm throwing itself over. I rolled over onto my stomach. The dirt smelled ... dull. Barren. Vaguely chemical. I rose to my knees, which were also sore. Pushed with my arms and brought my head up forward.

An identical view: endless dirt. The ceiling of clouds allowed a waxy light to trickle through; the view faded into haze some hundred feet distant. I turned and looked in all four directions. Nothing, nothing, nothing, and nothing. Even the air was like dirt: stale, dense, and disagreeable. I sat back and rose to my feet. My legs almost gave out, and I pirouetted a few steps like a drunken marionette. Stopped and planted my feet. Took a deep breath again and sought direction.

I turned degree by degree. I did not ... where had I come from?

Another deep breath—thick and painful. One foot in front of the other. My pants smeared with yellow all down the crotch. My velvet jacket and damp shirt ripped. I looked up, moved forward. Nothing. All directions were undifferentiated. I could not tell straight from curved, downhill from up; my steps ragged, I walked. I could not tell how long ... how much time had passed. I had been walking sideways but didn't know it. I was walking. I fell painfully to my knees. I dragged myself up again, rubbed my forehead with one hand and the back of my neck with the other—clammy, but at least I was alive.

I kept walking. Direction and directionless.

My eyes fell upon a line through the fog, a smear of darker color. I dragged myself toward it, every step triggering the wayward sensation of a walk of shame. The smear grew—as did a scent I couldn't identify—until it assumed the more definitive form of a ridge. Had I been traveling upward? At the ridge, I crossed a strip of rough low scrub and discovered a hidden river, the water ponderous and dark.

A jarring sound struck my consciousness. It was the first voice I'd heard since the train—a distant voice: "... here." On the other side of the river a figure stood inside what appeared to be a glass egg. The man seemed to be signaling me, and he spoke again in a muffled voice, "... you wannu cross?"

I could not bring a word.

He was looking at me. It was hard to tell what he looked like, the river being about sixty feet across. He seemed tall, wearing a cloak or a grey smock or shroud down to his feet.

He walked, carrying the egg over his head—only it was really a half-sphere open at the bottom that almost entirely covered him. He moved closer, into the scrub on the other bank of the river. He was directly opposite me now.

"Do you wanna cross? I can help!" He stood still. His face appeared haggard and bearded.

"Hello!" I called back. "Could you tell me where I am?"

"Right there!"

"Right. Well. What are we near?"

The man pondered for a minute. "Near the land mostly!"

"... oh-kay. Is there a city nearby?"

"Not sure. Might be in one of these directions." He pointed along the river in both directions.

"Do you know what it's called?"

"No!"

"What state are we in?"

"I'm not sure wha' we have in common," he replied.

"You're ... we're ... in the United States, right?"

"Suppose that depends on yer point of view."

"What?"

"I'm saying I felt alone fer a long time. Hold on!" he called as he sat down in the scrub and tilted the dome backwards until its open base faced me and his body was cupped in the curve. A tube grew out from under his smock, extending toward the river—it thickened, became a pipe curving up and arching across the river—widening as it descended toward me to form a bridge, coming straight at me. I fell back just as it rammed into the rocks where I had been standing.

It was the head of a penis.

It *was* a penis.

Bobbing just above the riverbank.

I looked back, following it across the river to the man lying in the half sphere where it got smaller and smaller until it disappeared into his smock.

"Go fer it," he said crisply, the parabola of the shape carrying his words to my ears. I ran and vaulted up onto the penis head, which bounced a bit but soon steadied. I stepped onto the foreskin. I walked up the penis ... it felt like the surface of a drum. The dimpled water below me opaque and turgid. Up and over the apex, hurrying downhill toward him as it got narrower and narrower—I lost footing, rode it down like a staircase railing—off balance, fell sideways, my left arm landing in the water, my face dunking, the water warm.

I shook the water off my arm as I got up. His penis was retracting, shrinking back until just the tip stuck out from under his kilt. I spit out the tasteless water. I was going to ask something but ... clenched my hand into a fist as if to hold on to a thought that slipped away like the smoke of a half-remembered dream.

I look at this man sitting in front of me and feel sleepy. Scrunch my eyes and open them. The man has a long face, so very narrow, unnaturally narrow, and pasty with a long beard shaped like a paddle.

"You can call me Ron," he says.

I look around. A river. A small area of scrub. He is sitting cross-legged inside a glass sphere, part of a sphere—no, wait, a glass ovoid—lying back in it as if he is relaxing. The sky. Jaundiced clouds roiling in mustards and sulfurs and dough and camel and dirty orange. Rumbling, murky clouds like greasy cotton interlace some short distance above my head. This doesn't seem right, a sky so low. Some kind of fog.

"Call me Ron." This man in a dark grey robe has pustular skin like over-boiled cauliflower. He flips the glass egg to cover himself.

"Where've you been?" Ron's voice is a rickety old shack I'm scared to enter. A little creature crawls out of the right side of his unruly beard; a tic consumes the left side of his face.

On my body: a velvety black jacket ripped at the shoulder with royal blue lapel and collar, black long-sleeve shirt—no collar and ripped at the neck— black pants smeared with crusty yellow stains. And black shoes.

"Not so chatty, eh? You can come in—wait, before ... would you get some water? I'm thirsty. Are you? Here's a cup."

With his foot, Ron pushes a cup, a silver cup, out from under the egg. I take it to the shore and fill it. The water grey and dark, turgid and opaque, swollen like a drowning victim. The scent familiar ... musty ... have I seen this river before?

"Here, give it to me."

A lightning bolt of thirst strikes me. I toss the water back. I will drink ... I will sit down with my shoulder against a wall, a glass wall, a cup in my hand; I will set it down.

Behind the wall will sit an old man with a pitchfork-full of straw germinating from his long grey face and a grey robe slid up his legs to expose a penis lying against the dirt. The curved wall ... he'll be under an egg-shaped glass bowl. He'll lift the egg, stick out his hand, take the cup, and study the inside thoughtfully, then turn it upside down and look at the bottom. He'll turn it back over and look inside again. "Well, it looks like I'm out. Would you mind getting me some water? I'm thirsty, are you? Here's a cup." He'll push the cup out. I'll look around: a river. I'll take the cup and scoop up some water from the river swollen like a drowning victim.

Returning to the old man, I'll kneel down to pass him the cup as he lifts the egg, and I'll crawl under. I'll be inside now. Half an egg. The egg will cover us completely. He'll take the cup and look into it.

"Well this is top notch. Top notch. Water. What a nice surprise. All right, well. Hello? My name is Ron," and a tremor will take over his left side as he drinks from the cup with his right hand.

He — sitting by my side, looking out at the river — will have a very long penis.

"My home."

Refracted through the glass: a living pointillist kaleidoscope in a soap bubble.

"That," he'll point upwards, "shows from the inside."

His craggy face will be rendered in topographic maps of the entire chromatographic spectrum while a spiral staircase of color contours his penis.

"Oh!" Ron will slap at the salamander-like thing that crawls onto his collarbone and catch it in his cupped hand. He'll pop it in his mouth then pull it halfway out, bite it in half, and offer me the still-wriggling tail end. His fingers will be long and gaunt.

"You'll have to excuse me. I forget my manners."

The wriggling tail … nacreous and hypnotic. I'll open my mouth (this would appear to be the right thing to do) and he'll drop it in. I'll swallow, and it will squirm its way down as my throat gags in revolt, my tongue thick and fat.

"All right. Listen. I find myself rather lonely here, but the colors mostly keep me company. I like to think … if love was visible, this is what it would look like. What's your name?" he'll ask.

My name … will be on the tip of my tongue … until it slips from me like a half-remembered dream. I'll start to sweat. We'll regard each other in silence, Ron the Penis Man's eyes small and sad.

"How 'bout I call you ... Last-Man-I-See." Bright watercolor paint will swim in concentric rings. "That only lasts a little while—" he'll gesture up at the acid babble spiraling on all sides. "Listen, Guy-Right-Here, mind if I call you Guy-Right-Here? Life is like a game of ... whudyacallit? You put the thing in the thing, and you twiddle it? And you could die or not die. Right? That's life. But now wait, that's not the rules, it's not like you die, but a different thing happens, I can't remember what. But it hasn't happened to me anyway. Least, I don't think it has. Which is very unusual. Has it happened to me?"

His eyes will distress me: one black and the other grey. Both dull. Painfully dry. He'll continue to look into my face until the moment I comprehend he had actually asked me a question. I'll shrug.

"Don't forget your gloves, Person-Under-Glass, shall I call you Person?" he'll say, nodding toward a pair of heavy-duty gloves made of what seems to be a leathery material coated in plastic. He'll knit his brow in a gesture of concern. A pair of gloves. I'll pick them up. He'll pass me the cup. A cup. A rough-hewn silver cup with clear liquid inside. Dull silver, weathered and tarnished. I'll take a sip.

A pair of hands will intrude into my frame of view and take a cup from my hands. I'll look up. "Well, look who's here," the man next to me will say. I'll look around. We'll be sitting under a dome. No one there but the two of us. Me, I'll be there. And a man with a long grey beard and a face eroded by time.

"Where didja been?" he'll ask me.

An interesting, incomprehensible question. I'll shrug.

"Oh, sure, sure. Understandable," he'll go on. "My name's Ron. So, how'd you come to discover this glass thingy?"

The glassy thingy. It will not look familiar. I'll shrug again.

"You don't say? Well, goddamn."

48   *David David Katzman*

He'll look around then up at a sky dull and lifeless.

"Well, goddamn. So what're you doing here?"

I'll slide around in my mind—unable to pin down why things don't feel right—sweat dripping down my brow.

"Well, now. Well spoken. Say, I like those gloves of yours. Say, you don't know how I got this bubble, do you?"

I'll try to say no.

"Okay, well, just to be safe, I better not leave it. Say, you look familiar. Have we met?"

I will open my mouth and begin to scream.

I'll find myself pacing along a dirt bank, keeping my distance from a streaming river of grey while a hazy glow emanates from dripping sky stalactites just twenty feet or so above. Off to the left, a copse of tumorous trees. Plodding, plodding, plodding for an indefinite period of time. As numb as the monotonous hard-packed dirt and occasional scraggly tree. A muddle of dingy air will curtain my range of sight, erasing the concept of distance. Hunger pangs will demand my attention. A blast of sound from above will smash me down. I'll cringe in a ball, briefly panicked, until I can gather my wits and scan for movement ... nothing. I'll continue more quickly, distance passing. At some point, I'll hear the jagged sound again—animal cry? Delirious, lungs burning, compelled to the river, I'll stumble to the bank hoping to find a drop of moisture, but there will be no water. No water, only a river of dust choking on itself.

Just ahead, two tree trunks will jut out over the river, nearly crossing each other at a narrowing point. They'll shrivel like burnt matchsticks and drop into the dust.

A new sound—distant but cacophonous, at war with itself. Burning phlegm in the back of my throat. I'll hack and cough it up at the same moment as a mournful siren wails and two animals break from the fog ahead, racing toward me along the river. The one in the lead will be black and glossy, a blur of legs, while a larger creature will pursue it like a fierce wind—a dog almost wolf-sized, sandy grey and ocher speckled with a snout longer than seems right. I'll recognize this animal. Jackal. A coyote. Coyote will gain on the blur as they barrel toward me—I should run but will be unable to move, petrified. Coyote will catch up to the blur and pounce, arched above its prey like the pulse of a jellyfish, defying gravity. Hairpin turn: the blur will dash into the river (in profile clearly antlike), its feet splashing up ashes, whirring across the surface—an ant running across a desert. Coyote will land on the bank some twenty feet from me, attentive; the foot-tall ant will make it halfway across—then gone. Instantly gone.

Coyote will wait, poised, before he dives into the dust and vanishes as well.

The air will feel dry as death, the river's surface still until Coyote emerges nose-first like a specter trailing cobwebs, the black bug dangling from its mouth. It'll turn and spring back violently as its eyes meet mine. Fur spiked on end, it will drop the dead thing from its mouth and bare its teeth, opening its mouth, farther, farther—a yawning chasm, black hair shooting from its throat between rows of teeth, disgorging a fountain of thick black hair, farther, mouth turning backwards, its gullet reversed, turning back on itself, swallowing itself, its entire body except the tail, leaving nothing but a tangled cocoon of hair and teeth. The creature's legs will press out through the mess, one rear leg dangling behind like a rabbit's paw.

It will release a sickened fart, its anus slanted to the sky.

My heart will pound, my mouth dry.

The inside-out Coyote will limp off on three legs, vanishing into the trees, and I'll run blindly on faster and faster wheezing with effort and stomach pangs, trying to remember where I am, should I return to the ... where had I been? ... I had met someone.

A whiff of pine: out of the haze, a blue wall. Closer: a blue forest of tall, needle-decked trees—the pine smell stronger—not pine trees, pipe cleaners, bristled like pipe cleaners.

With a sense of relief, I'll step into the forest where it's cooler and darker among sponge-like hedges and families of cerulean bushes shaped like corkscrews. My feet will glide through a shallow hand of mist that clings to profuse low-lying vegetation carpeting the forest floor: deep red roses, metallic silver mushroom caps with pink spots, bright orange sphagnum moss, plants like sea anemones, thick and squishy, and others like butterflies sitting among piles of blue needles. Balled up fibers forming a human heart. I'll grasp a white starfish-shaped flower—it'll recoil, and I'll jump from my skin.

Scanning all directions: nothing. Listening: silence.

I'll return to the plant and grab it, tear it from the soil as it squirms furiously. I'll hold it far from me—repulsed, gagging—holding it as far from me as my arm will allow, squeezing it, kneeling and trembling until the jellyflower goes limp. I'll squeeze it tight, until it's still, until I can't squeeze it any more.

I'll open my eyes to confront my fist slathered in bright white goo. I'll tear off a squishy arm and hold it closer: a thick buttermilk will ooze out. I'll lick a drop that has fallen onto my glove ... taste of copper. I'll tear off another arm, hold it above my mouth and squeeze, gulp it, and eat another.

Out of the corner of my eye: the tip of a furry white tail will disappear around a bush. I'll hold my breath as sweat trickles down my back, my shirt drenched and cool. Then, waddling out from behind a tree and following the tail: a plump grey and brown bird with a white feather-duster tail, white wings (small and ... vestigial?), and a nasty vulture beak hooked like the tip of a scythe. The animal will stop to observe me until a blaze of light obscures its head, jewelry adorns it, a necklace wraps it, its head and neck surrounded with wire, blood everywhere—it will bleed and fall as I drop too.

A glowing red spacesuit will appear from behind a tree and move toward the bird; a voice will project from the suit: "Visual tiger white command describe movement pause"—he'll notice me and turn—"query where whatteer WHAT??? BEFORE the ENGINEER!!!" Under a large, spherical fishbowl of a helmet, a boy's face will become visible. "Demonstrate aye aye aye emotion." *Aye*? I. His face will crinkle up in a look of revulsion, and he'll tip his nose and chin up at me. "React appropriately."

He'll take two steps toward me, plant his legs wide, and point a gun-like object at my waist. Ice blue eyes flashing. "State hideous query identity command respond or slaughter analysis impossible hideous, not even dee."

He'll look teenage, perhaps ... sixteen? Pale face without blemish, almost albino, and polished to a symmetric archetype: jaw like a sledgehammer, a strong straight nose, pure white hair. He'll stand up straighter, eyes widening, gun dropping to the side.

"Communicate grovel apology beg sir sir sir you you you." He'll drop to a knee and bow his head. "Analysis executive outside thought unoccurence. Analysis invisible nulltech, I, I unknow. Explicate visualize executives uncommon query forgiveness. State I am are sim celeb the hunter projection you have seen me ... or not ... importance low. State I pursue brids and exstinks, hah!" He'll laugh awkwardly. "Query we, we, we can't wipe anything out properly anymore." He'll cough, touch his helmet as if to cover his mouth—realize he can't—rub the dome, then point upward with a big smile, "See are simule."

I'll see nothing.

"Communicate value I, I exist popularly with bees and seas"—he'll blink; I'll realize Bs, Cs—"sir, grovel." He'll drop his gun and bend forward as if in supplication, tears streaming out of his eyes against the inside of the helmet. "Communicate grovel beg request undemote sirsirsir you, you, you affect regret exclaim oh eminent engineer, fluid wasted."

The details will be confusing but the submission will be obvious. "You will get undressed," I'll hear myself say.

"Sir!" Then under his breath, "Sir."

He'll wince, take off his helmet gingerly, set it down, slide his arms out of the jumpsuit, and drop it to his feet in a fiery red puddle against the bright blue grass.

"Project I cleansing anon."

He'll hop awkwardly from one foot to the other in a white nylon wrap—muscular and perfectly proportioned with the body of someone older than his face appears. His face will be handsome to the point of blandness, like a computer's idea of beauty. Eyes ... oddly proportioned ... large as quarters? Bigger than seems normal.

"Ow, ow. Query your your your title sir sir sir." His penis will be a foot long, swinging side to side as he hops.

I will not reply.

"Query I depart." He'll hug the gun to his chest and run into the forest. I'll become agitated, falling epileptic, seizing up, my entire body a vicious spasm—panic attack or tension erupting. Clenched like a charley horse, I'll lie exhausted for quite a while.

Eventually, regaining my composure and struggling to my feet, I'll walk to the space suit and examine the pieces. Very simple: a spherical helmet—plastic, maybe polycarbonate—and a ring at the base where it connects; space boots connected to a red jumpsuit; fabric glowing with tiny rippling beads.

The suit ... a reason for it, there will be some reason for wearing it. I'll pick up the helmet examining the surface and

will   be   caught

          by a translucent image

                  resting

     in the plastic   like   a photograph

                       under

                     water

the image

      dis t^o^{r}ted by the *c*

                u

             r

             v

            a

           t

           u

         r

      e

        a face

            impossible

          vibrant   colors

shades of some unknown viridian from dark to light;

                                    scaled:

made of thousands of cobblestones,

                            tiny extruded balloons

the eyes—deep-set in c   s at the forward *c*
                 r   e   *u*
                   e s   *r*
                    a   *v e,*

the nostrils—forward not down
the whole face—forward like a dog
teeth pointed and triangular like dulled saw teeth,
clearing my throat   a sound, a sussing will respond,

I'll feel an echo
     splitting
          broken bi-
                 polar:
          schizophrenic.

The eyes   will   blink   and its   eyes

spin the world like a wheel.

This will appear to be him. Himself. He.

But he won't recognize this face—he's supposed to look different, not like
this. How? He'll drop the helmet, touch his face and feel scales. Dense and
pliable like Eucalyptus or leaves from a rubber tree. Tear his shirt and jacket
open, pull down his pants. All over. Scales down to his crotch. He'll frantically
rub between his legs, but nothing will be there—a crease or pocket—he'll
pull it open with two fingers on either side causing a turtle head to peek
out—no—a penis. It will release a stream of pee over his hands unexpectedly.
He'll let go, and it will slide back in. His thighs and calves will be thick and
strong and covered by overlapping green scales like armor plate. He'll get
his fingers up under a few scales and tug on them—hurts a little. He'll pull
harder, making it hurt more—confusing him further. He'll pick up the helmet

and look at the reflection again, turn his head to observe the strange face move with him, and touch the top of his head—sleek and hairless. Not right.

Hunger will arrest his attention, shove the helmet from his hands, and drive him to the soggy bird corpse lying in a purple mud of gore and needles. He'll put the body under his shoe and pull a leg upward, red splattering across his chest. His bloated tongue will wrap anxiously around the sickening and strange meat.

He'll swallow the bones last.

The suit. He'll put it on methodically, rotating the helmet and locking himself inside. He'll close his eyes and breathe in pine scent infected by a metallic taste.

He'll hurry through the blue woods until he rounds a tree and is caught face-to-face with three knee-height little people standing on squat pedestals. All three will be dressed in well-tailored navy blue suits embroidered with interlocking three-sided hieroglyphic squares on both sides of a row of cobalt eye-shaped buttons. The three will wear animal masks—realistic full headpieces. Too late to hide ... but fortunately they won't be frightening.

The furry orange and white tiger-masked one on the left will speak first: "I feel no pain"—its black lips mesmerizing, so small and subtly textured, moving with every word—"because my senses indulge but the surface of things. Thus, every thing is calm. Lives are drops of rain. These bodies live forever. But selves blink on and off and on, fireflies in the pool of eternity. I thirst to drink from the pool."

And the middle one, the Heronhead with hairy knuckles, will swing its beak up and down as it speaks, voice whistling like music, "The will is an attempt to influence, to affect even with violence. To feel it press back on you, a response to vibrations violin violence valence. The narcissistic cry for attention of stunted creativity. 'See? I exist!' it cries because nothing exists without observation. Sometimes I think it's glorious, sometimes desperate. I walk a tightrope, wish to be a tender creature, harm nothing. But is so hard, so hard. Contact has friction. Things scrape and slide. It is compulsion, convincing myself cruelty is kind. I aspire to balance conflicting desires." Its beak ... moving ... a long skinny tongue inside, alive with every word.

The third creature will have the head of a rat, and its voice will tread gravel. "In evry crailty there's a kindness, aye? Least it wisnae you whah emptied a piece af yerself oot. Trans-endence is ov'rated cos it disnae translate, aye?"

"Lishen ... I ... I'wl be ..."—he'll be startled by the unrecognizablc, coagulated voice that comes out of his mouth, echoing a little within his helmet— "... losht. Wiwl a ... city ... be nearby?"

Tigermask will reply, "I do not know. How could I know? I am unsure ... how long I have been here, and ... what have I been doing? It seems like a lifetime, and just a minute both. But we're past living."

"I try to breathe with the rhythm of it all," Heronhead will say, "but it's hard to identify that rhythm. The song, I have forgotten it ... relations become jarring, many voices clash. It's like trying to breathe splinters. I'm anguished. I mumble to myself as I bleed from a cut. Or if I'm scrounging for feed in the scrabble dirt or digging my beak into food, a hard bowl, and you're in the room in your apron, I'll force a smile. We're not meant to be friends, but I'll smile at you. In that hole with no light, I'll smile and hope enlightenment is out there, like a garland of stars. If I could just hold on to it, it would take me flowing fugitive through all things into totality. It lives out there even if I can't grasp it, it's waiting, immutable, it's pre—"

"Aye," the Ratman will cut in, "ye can only love th'aines that dinnae exist. Aw-ways jist oot a' reach. The proablem w' peace is ail the peeps whah need tae kick ye in the beak. If ye tak' a few, ye can fancy a bettair perspective than the bitchhole ah me, aye? Fuck. Disnae tak' much brain the come up wi' a baitter creation 'n this, like. Me? Ah cannae move. Y'see?" It will point down at the pedestal it stands on. "I think oim part of it. Haird t' sae. Get nae feelin' frae it. Is haird tae move, aye? P'rhaps oi grew frae it. Ir the rock grew frae me. Ir I was born oot the heed ahv existence in a flux. A fucks mair like it, aye?"

"I listen to touch and taste you. I talk to dance with my tongue because nothing else moves—to feel more real. What do you make of existence?" Tigermask will ask.

He'll reply, his face cooling behind the helmet, "I ... I'll be the losht one here. All I will see ... that musht be ... ah fuck ... might ... be ... a foresht ... forest ... for hunters." Tongue thick in his mouth tripping, tangling, battering against incoherence and presence. "Will ... will ... won't you ... know anything? Costumes? Fucking hell!"

"Without a mask to shape us, what would we face anyone with? Existence is ridiculous and impractical. I'm sorry I can't be more helpful."

"Knowledge. All I can tell you is hurt and hunger," will say the Heronhead.

Ratman will abruptly bark at him, "Why d'ye no get after some fuckin' watter, y'wee arrogant fuck? Y'think Oim standin' here feh yer pleasure? Why d'ye no know somethin' useful like where t' get ees some FUCKING watter! Ye airnae worth shite! Oim so thirsty, why no ye pish in mah mooth?"

"Fuck you, fuck YOU!" his scream rebounding inside the helmet as he takes flight.

"Wait!" one of them will cry as they recede behind.

And he'll escape the forest without looking back, striding across jagged bolts of steel matted with twigs and dirt, terrain of unknown distance passing beneath his feet—the landscape littered with burnt incomprehensible corpses and shattered trees; the acrid, violent air like unholy meat sandwiched between the dirty sky and rivers of grey soap—he won't stop, his red suit and helmet will keep him from blowing up.

They'll fire out of the water one after the next ... two ... three ... four ... landing chest-down, panting on the bank: a giantfish furry with ich, several microdolphins dripping with seaweed, a manta-tailed manatee stuccoed in algae; five ... six ... seven ... the eighth will sail from the water: an over-sized parrot fish. Just before the parrot fish hits, wings and feathers will spring from its body, causing it to flounder tail over head—no, *feet* over head—and land awkwardly on two newly grown legs. The other creatures will slap fins against the shore and croak and gargle. The reborn Birdfish will gangle forward, momentum carrying it as it runs, flapping its wings, taking off into the air, skyrocketing, the fish croaking and slapping their fins louder as he does. Suddenly, a nightmare bat will sink from the impervious clouds and scoop Birdfish into a pouch—the pouch opened wide to reveal its prey crucified in a net of hooks—before disappearing upward. The creatures will immediately slide back into the water. The last one, the manta-manatee, will look forlornly skyward for a moment before dropping below the surface without a sound. The whole event will happen so fast, it'll give him the impression of a mistake that was immediately erased.

Space will contain him without walls without horizon without distance, hold him inside his straightjacket suit, break him into a million puzzle pieces. Thirst will compel him toward the river, but as he nears it a prickly taste will grow on the back of his throat even through the helmet.

The river ... water?—glutinous bubbling sludge and burning residues, gobs of mutable plastic in an angry, gurgling chemical stew of gaudy colors, sheared, striated threads struggling upstream like salmon, maggoty corpses breaking the surface before jerking under, and sebaceous air pockets popping and emitting putrid fumes that taste of sewage. Chittering sounds will fill the slimy air that wraps him like an amniotic sac.

"We call it Cyanide River," will come a voice behind him.

He'll spin to find himself facing an animal: an upright furry pear with four limbs and a pleasant, puppy-like face ... the words must (but how could they?) emanate from this thing robed in dirty-grey curls. This Puppylamb's arms will be wooly from shoulders to elbows but hairless from its elbows to its small pale white hands—four-fingered and lacking thumbs. Its legs hairless below the knee. *Where could it have come from, this thing—what the fuck? What. The. Fuck.*

Puppylamb will scrape up a handful of beige roots and amass a little straw pile. Closing its eyes, the creature will hold the roots out toward him. Before he can take the roots, the bundle will change, melt flat, and darken, becoming a clot of deep purple goo.

"Here," Puppylamb will say, holding it out farther.

He'll remove his helmet and scoop the mush out of the creature's hands.

"We can make plenty more of that."

He'll shoot his tongue (how could it extend that far?) into the pulp. Cool and sticky. About as filling as phlegm. He'll lick the last bits off his red glove and feel comforted.

Puppylamb's eyes will widen with a subtle smile.

"Go out and collect more of those fibers. You should scout out this area and report back to us what you find. We shall stay close but out of sight. If you see anything living, you shall convince it to come back and meet us. Unless it appears too retrograde to communicate or too dangerous, in which case you shall—in that case you shall warn us, you should make a sound like this: *PTTHT- PTTHT.*" Puppylamb will bleat like a flugelhorn.

"Can you make that sound? You will practice and learn it. The note, when you strike it, should be a B-flat so we may recognize it instantly, and thus it shall also be more difficult to mimic by those who would endeavor to deceive us. You shall have to practice your B-flat. You know the sequence? Here— follow this scale." It will hum a descending scale. "Now, see this note: hmmh, *hmmhh*, hmmh. It's that note, *hmmhh*. Do it now."

He'll notice Puppylamb has another exceptional feature: flipper feet like ridiculous slabs of toast.

"If you don't do what we say, we won't make food for you. Now do it. We expect to hear you practicing the alert sound while in our presence exclusively because if you practice it while not in our presence we might mistake it for an emergency warning. When in fact you are just rehearsing. After you generate the warning sound, follow the creature from a distance, and if it comes toward us—if it gets close, within ten arm-lengths, you shall throw yourself upon it and attack it as best you can. Now go! Find us some tubers! However, before you go, you must find ten flat rocks and pile them up over here. Touch your forehead to them and wiggle your arms in the air. Like so ..." Puppylamb will brandish one arm as if shaking something off its hand while making a circular gesture with the other as if turning a crank. "Here do it. Damn you, do this motion now! Now, do this motion and practice the sound at the same time, like this: *hmmhh ... hmmhh.*" Puppylamb will waggle its arms and *BLAT-BLAT-BLAT.*

At some point, it will toss up its hands and sigh. "Your resistance is irritational, but we'll give you the opportunity to get with it. We will explain your existence, and you will become sensible. Listen to us closely. You have become confused and distracted. You are unable to view behind the curtain. We will clarify for you, and you will follow.

"It all started at a time when an Insect Plague fell upon the land. So many insects, one couldn't breathe without them filling your lungs. To eliminate the plague, a global chemical sterilization was instituted. Yet, the chemical bonds that broke within the insects' bodies caused an unexpected disassociative side effect: the development of an ionic *resonance*. This chromagnetism caused the attraction and repulsion of heretofore unconnected genes. The Transgenic Mathemists Institute was formed in an attempt to understand this effect. We (and we say 'we' by the transitive property because, although we probably did not exist at that time—or we may have but were unaware of it—we have become the heir of the Institute), we, with research, were able to tease out the underlying principles of this resonance and unravel the secrets of Avocado's Law. The ability to manipulate the base matter of life by exuding particular chemicals. These formulae were enshrined in a text, which we inherited, to make or unmake."

Puppylamb will stop waggling at a splash from the river; they'll both turn and look to see emerging onto the shore two ... five ... ten creatures: carbuncular and inflamed; crimson, black, and mud-brown; three-legged, one-legged, and legless; doubled forward and leaning back; flaccid and dense; empty eye-socketed and bulge-eyed; frog-eared, bat-eared, bug antennaed creatures smelling of sickness and corruption. On the shore—the manta-manatee, the ich-encrusted giantfish, the others. Puppylamb will step back, hide behind him.

"Fight them," Puppylamb will push him. He won't move; the creatures will limp toward them.

Louder: "You shall fight them. They are evil!"

Within ten paces, muttering and fidgety, one of the river creatures will snarl as if he were already chewing Puppylamb between his teeth, "You ... leave ... us ... *BE!*"

"*Kill them!*" Puppylamb will whine.

As they shamble forward, he'll step aside, but Puppylamb will run around and past them into the river while braying, "Destroy you! All of you!" On top— Puppylamb will run *on top* of the slow-moving crust of the river, skipping from floe to floe, its big feet bridging the gaps.

"Obey us!"

Puppylamb will run farther out, almost across the river, the fur on its legs turning black, claws curling from its fingertips.

"We will find you and torture you! We will catch you!"

The creatures will hobble back toward the river.

"WE WILL MAKE YOU SUFFER FOR THIS!"

Puppylamb will turn his back and disappear into a cloak of smog as the creatures sink beneath the surface, the last to vanish a fish-faced dog-eared thing like a seaweed fetus.

He'll abandon the river as fast as he can, clutching his helmet, covering long stretches of desolate, pitted crust. The living vaporized. Drowning in the sky—a roof so low and limp he'll hunch over, shrinking into himself as he paces forward. After hours or days, the land will transition to a flat zone of reddish clay disturbed only by the occasional stubby red hill like a middle finger flicking an angry brick hue into the atmosphere.

Without thinking, he'll pee in his suit but remain dry, as the suit will seem to absorb it.

Another object will appear from the foamy air: a sprawling, coral-colored, shapeless mess with small creatures crawling over it: insectoid and spider-like, multi-legged -handed -clawed, chitinous, tubular, spherical, loaf-shaped, beetle-bodied things. One will flip over to divulge a face on its abdomen like a dirty secret. Something that shouldn't be seen.

He'll circle around to find on the other side a pile of eyes embedded in the bulk — rancid pink and white and blood-filled, lopsided with mutilated eyelids half-closed and weeping. The insectoids will scuttle back and forth poring over the eyes, poking at them with claws or hooked fingers. Eyes that pop out will be scooped up and eaten. Every time an eye oozes out, they'll dig up another one: clamp their claws on a fold of flesh and pull it up to exhibit another hidden eye that circles like a drunken gyroscope before focusing ... they're all—all the eyes will focus in one direction. He'll turn to follow the gaze and:

stop.

The light scratching from the clouds will gum up his eyes and punch around inside his helmet.

A figure against the sharp glare: a pure black silhouette.

Squinting, he'll make out a slip of a girl looking down at him from atop a column of dirt-encrusted rock.

Shadows will cast down her cheeks like sheets of tears.

Her body, caked in black leaves.

The boulder will quake, and he'll tumble, fall onto his back as leaves peel off and flutter down around him.

She'll be above him unwrapped, dirt raining down, a small bouquet in her right hand, his feet flat against the rock, his breath rank in the helmet; the young girl will have no legs, she'll be joined to the stone at her hips. She'll end at her torso. He'll see a fault line running up the boulder to her center ... between the thighs she doesn't have.

Dark lines on the stone: figures moving, alive on the surface, forming a caravan marching from left to right with a large figure at the center like a snail surrounded by many small creatures; the drawings will march on and around the stone, disappearing and returning from the other side.

She'll tilt her face, eyes downcast, taking him in, leaning farther forward, rocks towering over his head.

"You have crossed the river?" Her voice like candy.

"No. Yes," he'll croak.

"Are you tired of running? Come relax with me. Here, this will appease your hunger."

She'll release the plant, and it will fall at his feet.

He'll look at the gift in the scattered leaves then back up at her. Her face will glow, and she'll look older, not a girl—a spectacular young woman—although difficult to ... his eyes will slide off her cheekbones into the darkness behind.

The locks of hair across her neck will change from white blond to bright red to berry-brown while her face re-forms from heart-shaped to oval to round-cheeked.

"Consume that," she'll say. "You'll feel better. You're hungry, poor thing. Empty stomach?"

A clump of grey bits—a fan of slender, sharply pointed leaves like fingers attached to an army-drab stem. His stomach so empty, curled up like a snake.

He'll look back up at her hair, follow it down to her breasts, which will seem larger ... fuller; his mouth dry, aware of his tongue against the roof of his mouth—if he could just touch her, wet her breasts with his tongue. He'll follow her waist down to the deep fault in the rocks and down to the plant at his feet. He'll pick up the fern stems, and they'll fall to pieces in his hands. He'll twist off his helmet and put the leaves to his nose: nothing. He'll look up at her smiling at him like love, and the plant will fall to powder in his mouth. He'll chew crumbling air, gnash squalid lint, and an explosive laugh will burp out of him.

"Good boy." Her voice meaningful.

Her heartbreaking, metamorphosizing body. Climbing the stones beneath her, foot in the crevice, grabbing a handhold of plant ... too slick ... falling back.

"Please come and see me any time. I'm here for you to provide sustenance. And I have a friend; you might find yourself in the presence of my friend somewhere ahead of you who can provide you guidance as well. I'm always followed by a dear, dear friend. You'll recognize him. It will be a divine opportunity, but I suggest you keep your distance."

The stone monolith pivoting to the side, tectonic thundering, his bones juddering. Walking by her, looking back—perspective warping—a vanishing slit—gone.

Forcing himself to go, stomach hurting, banging for miles across a plain of smooth stone like glazed pottery strewn with burnt thorns. Scooping up a handful, running. Crunchy taste of kindling. Hunger's hollow rage. Walking on—an indefinite period—tired of nothingness. The sky a bitter harvest, crepuscular light congealed upon the constantly inconstant landscape. A gutter slosh of mud, stumps, dirt, fractured rock, smeared land.

Lying down and awaking dreamless, not a cobweb of a thought.

Shrouds of distance. A vague spot. The spot growing, becoming a large group of creatures moving in black smoke, all moving in one direction; a tall, coursing herd, a vast billowing vortex. Even the sky parting for it, opening a cell of freedom.

Closer. An array of hulking, thudding behemoths, six-legged headless mastodons permitting meager glimpses through the blackness of a moving mountain at the center.

Closer. The thing in the middle resolving: a ten-story-tall octopus head with woobering craters for eyes and multiplying limbs like explosive polyps disgorging and retracting. A head—no head—fluctuating into and out of its body, long octopoid limbs linking it to each of the mastodons, making them indistinguishable as separate beings.

Closer. The black cloak atomizing into an army of insects as big as fists. The central figure pursing its maw like a volcano, inflating itself larger and sucking in a swathe of insects, the lips retreating like a mudslide. Insects continuously flinging themselves against the sides of the Centrality. The approaching processional—still closer—individual insects hovering and clustering above Its limbs and around Its body, dropping and clinging to It or caroming off of It or falling into Its maw.

A putre-faction breaking off from the main body, sweeping out loosely to form a perimeter.

Emerging like a periscope from the back of one of the large insects cruising by: a platinum brain followed by a head dripping amnion—human-like but for a single silver-dollar-sized frog's eyeball with a silver-nugget iris. The creature gurgling, spitting, retching, whizzing past, circling at ten feet, coughing, dopplering in a high-pitched cartoon mouse voice: "Okayyyyyyyyyyyyy. IIIIIIIIIIIII'm ohhhhhhh-kayyyyyyy! I'm okay! I'm okay! I'm okay! Significant or insignificant? Worship or threat? Significant or insignificant?"

Buzzing, the head rising further out of the insect's back as if trying to get a better look, its flight becoming more and more erratic, zigzagging up and down. "Not s'okay, not s'okay." Diving back into the droning hoard ... landing on an octopoid arm before disappearing behind fountains of gauzy insects.

The Centrality: flowing fields of powerful attraction. Warping into Its gravity ... closer.

The soil blasting angrily upward, spattering dirt in all directions: a suffocating palette of chlorophyll and worms, leather and cat's breath. The explosion unveiling a creature blocking the route of the Centrality. The intruder: a jackal-headed colossus bristling like a sea urchin with a hundred arms holding boulders and clubs, muscles straining, legs wide as oak trees. Then: a hurdling attack over the entourage onto the Centrality. Disarray, chaos, stones flying, fists pummeling like jackhammers; Centrality engulfing the colossus, behemoths stomping, insects roaring like fire.

Turning, running, running, running.

Tripping, forehead banging against helmet.

Running. Exhaustion. Minutes. Hours. Days unknowable. Lost time. Lost in time.

Out of nowhere: faces—faces everywhere—all the same faces—black disks with bright orange halos on tall, thick, verdant stalks ranging above his head. A forest of sunflowers with faces like dinner plates. The flowers leaning in ever so slightly. Wandering in a forest of sunflowers. Shortness of breath; the helmet fogging up—the moisture vanishing with a small puff of air inside the helmet. Extending his hands into the crowd of sunflowers. The flowers, not allowing contact, moving away, keeping a distance like magnetic particles repelling from a like charge. Passing through with a ripple, the flowers never touching. Walking through a cascade of living fire.

A wall encrusted with moss. Dense and cool. A treasure chest. Lying down on a mound of moss against the mossy wall, the sunflowers guarding, unable to resist removing the helmet and putting it aside to rest on the—

You open your eyes. The wall is open just above you. A person stands framed in silhouette. *Would ayinay like to come in?* You have entered a palace.

You realize you've left your helmet outside. The door, now closed behind you, is black except for a white snowflake. The room could fit a thousand people, and the ceiling is vaulted higher than the sky outside. At last you can breathe; you stand tall.

The floor is laced with vines sparsely marked with small leaves each shaped like a sparrow's wing. Sunlight whispers from skylights overhead.

The creature standing before you is ginger-colored with a human face except ... short porcelain-white antlers growing from her head. Her or his. Her mildness of aspect suggests female, but her features look somewhat squared-off and masculine, too. Her hands are big, and her chest is smooth. He/she wears a tan vest of interwoven stems open in the front; a short tail curls up behind. Furry paws for feet.

Welcome to the City of Dreams, s/he says. *Directed or directionless? Calm or kinetic?*

You fight against paralyzation, struggling to speak, *Whu? I don't ... sorry. I'm ... I guess ... I was looking for a city so I guess I found it. Do you have any food? I think I'm hungry now. Sorry, that's rude. But I'm starving.*

Food has found ayinay.

S/he gestures across the room where you notice an open doorway. You walk, and s/he turns and walks beside you.

What brought ayinay to this door?

Ayinay? A-in-A? What is Antlers saying?

Accident. I don't know. Surviving, you reply.

Glad A-in-A here. Life richly connects. A 'n A.

Your footsteps echo, tapping against the hardwood floor the tempo from a half-remembered song. The air is sweet like an overripe peach.

Looking down at the triskeledelic vines interlaced like Celtic snakes, you notice your feet have pierced your space boots. The suit is frayed, and the claws of your thick olive toes are poking out through the soles. You stop and look at your left boot: the sole has almost entirely separated from the upper. You tear off both boots, hold the floppy dead things in your hands, and look at Antlers. Palms upward, s/he gestures expansively, so you toss them to the floor and continue.

It is possible that once there were alternations alterations altercations of light and dark. Now it's the unchanging light of good karma. Sometimes monogenes arrive hungry for revolution convolution convulsion evolution, re-volition, to revolve, rechromed to immaculate being. Or they come in fear and find the opposite. A 'n A make rules unnecessary. A 'n A no progress novolving. Instead A 'n A become evoloving. Words and touch are the plant of happiness.

Antlers leads you into a dim hallway with the feeling of a cave—a narrow skylight above, walls plastered with the same plant, the leaves a little fuller, your footsteps muffled. S/he plucks a leaf from the wall and then another and hands them to you. *Magick.* The leaves tremble on your palm like beating hearts. In your mouth—green-apple crisp and jasmine soft. A sensation indescribable ... a wash of sunlight.

The plant. What people find is the green. Perhaps like you. This magick. Needs scant more than a sip of attention. Meager light. Sky-windows strewn throughout an endless plane. The energy passes from one room to the next. The plant blooms generous beyond comprehension.

You pass through the door at the end of the hall and encounter a series of diverse rooms: small like an elevator, cylindrical like a well, and wide like a city square (with a ceiling low enough that you have to duck to pass through), and in each room the plants get denser and thicker, filling the spaces like weeds. You catch a glimpse of water trickling under a wall.

And as the foliage gets thicker, the rooms glow brighter.

A hundred rooms without skylights—such as the one A 'n A are about to enter— can be nursed by one room as long as the doors are open. The plants pass the energy by touch, transmitting and permitting. Hold.

You stop near a wall. S/he strokes a leaf that looks lighter in color than those near it. She breathes on the leaf as she strokes it, and the color gradually darkens. After a few moments, she leads you farther until you come to another door.

A 'n A are inside. Would A 'n A like to go first? Or shall A 'n A?

As you step across the threshold, you're struck with a powerful scent, a deep scent, the scent of an apple jungle, citrus, and ylang-ylang—the warm embrace of a dark, leafy, living room. Your pupils open wide to a sparkling, transcendent, pale green illumination: the ceiling drifts in slow currents of absinthe; the floor is knee-deep in reeds and rugs of lush, dark satingrass; velveteen leaves shine gently phosphorescent, weightless, carving through sublime candleflames of space. A gesture caresses your cheek—the air lives.

Plants overrun the stone walls. Individuals lie in the grass, hardly visible. Leaning against walls and pillowed and standing and rubbing each other and holding hands legs paws feet, snouts of tufted fur and studded beaks; leopard pelts and feathers, lemon-rinds and wrinkled faces of coral, bumpy and bright; eyes of wine and ruby, rust and nutmeg. Touching. Everyone touching. All of them pausing, looking at you as if you're a blue sky.

Citron juice fills the hookah in the middle of the room. Incandescent droplets of dew ascend the clear tubes leading from the central stack. A marmoset-faced creature with a corona of fur framing his face—hairless and raw like a mole rat everywhere else—is holding the tip of one of the tubes in his mouth, eyes big and glowing bronze.

Antlers speaks: *Welcome. Stay as long as long is. A 'n A are all guests here.*

Each of them, male or female and hard-to-tell, gather around you—ten individuals each in turn take your hands and look you in the eyes and say *Welcome* and kiss you on the mouth. *Welcome. Welcome. Welcome.*

After they have all kissed you, they look you in the eyes again and wait.

Uh. Thank you?

Thanks for being. What has brought A 'n A here? Antlers is now sitting among them. You look back at all the faces wreathed in flora, a riotous zoo of tusks and bumps, fox ears and seal fat, squirrel tails and dorsal fins, dragonfly wings and owl eyes. Some of them wear remnants of clothing while most wear nothing.

I ... well ... I don't remember much.

Some of them smile. You close your eyes, concentrate, conjure pictures.

I can glimpse ... things. That might be ... I don't know ... figments. Like a female. A female. I can see her with black hair or blond hair. Straight hair. Maybe wavy or curly hair. And amethyst eyes. Or blue or brown. I love her, I think, but I can't ... touch her. And she seems to have wings, and I can't understand her.

You tap, tap, tap your hand against your thigh.

Yeah, so. I remember a red couch. I remember a room like death. Rivets in a steel box. I remember. I remember a dog, a big dog tongue drooling from my nightmare and swallowing me. And I was torn to pieces. There was a ... I dreamt of a penis like a bridge. And I ... I remember small little people with animal masks that probably now I figure were not ... wearing masks ... lives are drops of rain, they said, but I haven't seen any rain ... just the opposite ... and it seems common to be bound to stones ... and there was a ... a walking-on-water thing that said it invented or discovered that whatever is out there going on is chemical. But it was angry—I'm sorry, I'm not used to talking to, uhm, animals.

A susurrus of air plays against your arms.

What are animals?

Well, they're ... I don't know.

Are animals different from A 'n A?

Uhm. Probably not.

Interesting story, says feminine Panda Ears.

Thank A 'n A for telling it, says masculine Seal Fat.

Would looove to hear anymore any time, says Koala Face of unknown gender and no nose.

A penith like a bwidge. Thatth amaything, says Squirrel Paws with tusks filling up his small mouth.

A 'n A like the sound of A 'n A words, the si-luh-bulls, says Orangutan Face.

A 'n A liked hearing this story, says a creature you hadn't noticed off to the side, standing between engaged columns that hold up a blind archway to nowhere. Her head is ... translucent? Yes, translucent and familiar. And the shape ... like a petite fawn, a deer with a delicate neck of cocoa glass. She stands on two impossibly thin stick-like deer legs and wears no clothing. Through her sepia-tone chest you can see her heart suspended like a bubble in resin. Her feet are sunk below the plant that rises up to her knees.

You hesitate.

My ... my thick ... my skin is thick and strong and scaly but not rough. I think it's called keratin, which is what reptiles have. Which is confusing but I don't know why ... it's confusing. I feel like maybe I'm wearing a mask but there is nothing behind it. I want to call myself human, but I don't know what that means. There was a guy I got this red spacesuit from. But we didn't speak the same language. Or, we did, but I could only understand his words, not his meaning.

The Glass Fawn, this deer woman, holds out a hand; a leaf is lying on her palm. Somehow you find yourself standing in front of her. The leaf is in your mouth; you bite down—fat and juicy, intimation of honeydew and cucumber. She bends over and cups her hands below the leaves. She trickles cool water over your face.

It feels wooonderful.

Twinkling, iridescent stars flicker throughout the roomspace. Atmosphere as silky as cat's fur. The taste of levitation on your tongue.

I don't remember much, you sigh without taking your eyes off of her.

Your wounds are a passage. The past is bondage, Antlers explains from behind you. *Power controls the past. Mythology is metaphor. Every moment, every second you are a shimmering new being. You have the deception of sameness thanks to the trick of memory. How much better to have no memory whatsoever? But here A 'n A are ... A 'n A equally know no past. A 'n A have escaped the power of its gravity, the gravity of its power. Deceit erased. The past erased itself until nothing but the endless present was left behind like a jewel in the crown of being.*

You look into Glass Fawn's amber eyes, transparent and calm. She smiles at you, holding three more leaves. Black lines, scarified basket-weave tattoos, crisscross her arms.

I like your tattoos, you say.

Not tattoos. She takes your hand and touches it to the inside of her forearm and draws your fingertips across the markings. Deep grooves. You trace the xylem and phloem of her soul, her unblinking eyes taking you in, looking at you through you through her, through her to the carved pilaster on the wall—an arabesque of soldiers with lances and shields marching through syrup, drowning in her body. The two pilasters twirl with honeysuckle and figures that wind upward, animal figures melting one into the next among Tiki gods with awful faces, stoic and inscrutable.

Leaves skip across your surface.

She takes your hand. Tiki gods climbing. *There is a myth, may A 'n A tell you?*

Yes, please.

There is a myth. There was a thing thing.
A Spirit called Matter.
And it made a doppelgänger,
a metaphor,
a reality-tight representation,
a modality of multiplicity
and wrapped it around sapien soul
enclosing the spirit like a mask, a costume, a crust, a helmet, a symbol,
a prison.
Turning one thing into diversity,
personalized permutations of slavery,
a mirage was clutched as tightly as silver bars.
It was a magick spell,
until
in the City of Dreams
the Plant broke it.
Bliss broke that Spirit,
and time ended
so the legend goes.

74   *David David Katzman*

A 'n A is welcome here, to stay as long as long is.

I'm ... I don't understand what's happened to me, you say. I don't know what I've missed. Could you ... could anyone help me?

Nothing is lost or found. A 'n A have no answers, simply stories. Would you like to hear another tale that wraps existence?

You nod.

Upon a once, A 'n A was a full-on hunane. Cruel and selfish—self-hatred infused from the environment. Sickened senses—feelings pulled along by the torrents of culture. Alien. No perspective to see that the avatar is paper-thin—a tissue mask draped over being. A vague passenger on a meaningless journey of habit, isolated and separated from living. Memory paints the illusion of depth—the hunane is even willing to think of itself as bad because then at least incomprehensibility drives it, a secret within, a soul; when in fact, there is no soul, only the present and the past clinging to it like a petulant child.

With a circular gesture, she continues, *Envision it: civilization as a balloon. Expanding. Ready to pop with a prick. The hunane can't evolve. Hunanity as a dead end would drive life to the place of dead roads. Even so, life adapted. The evolutionary spirit. Replication led to awareness—when it followed eventually, at the end of next and next and after—awareness grew within awareness, consciousness born within consciousness. A simple thing, a bodily realization. Survival bloomed for those immune to the domination of procreation. They cut loose. The building blocks of being, our genes, parted from the body and began to travel like pollen in the wind. Any body could now host the multifarious diverse forms that were once isolated and enclosed. A 'n A have experienced this. And thus a new outside was created but not yet a new inside.*

The hunane was cast out for a violation of hunane code. Where time is imagined as wandering in space. Somehow, some sense of form surviving, changing, and becoming different. And the hunane found the corner of all realities. The Dreamseller: the snorting lama of a jangling concubine; the patent-leather heel of a raven-haired dominatrix; the gasp of air from a flamingo-beaked insectoid; a crystalline pirate licking a sandy beach; vapor consciousness gliding through the lapis light of happiness; viruses dancing in calligraphic coils.

The hunane found this Dreamseller sitting in the forest. All around was lush bursting fuchsia bougainvillea and enveloping fronds. Air like lotus blossom, sun fluttering in dappled raindrops dropping slow as dandelion seeds. Eyes closed, the Dreamseller sat on a bed of moss, a relaxed smile tarrying. The hunane asked if it could live a dream of meaning. But the hunane had nothing to give as a gift, so it gave the one thing it had which was a Self. It melted into its cells, became a body. Became a senseless dream, no weight, earth, or air. The Dreamseller held up his palm and secreted a milky alchemical oil that the dream-body dipped the tips of its dream-fingers into and licked off. The dream-body sat down and lay back in the grass, which provided no sensation, looked up at the flitting rays of light, closed its eyes, and conceived that connection is not in time but in consciousness. But it hadn't allowed its consciousness to actually touch anyone or anything.

Consciousness can experience the present but it rarely does because being is vacillating between memories and projections, yin and yang. Consciousness is a rise and fall. Ebb and flow. If the dream-body could phase its consciousness, pass through the green of the moment with every translation of energy ... it's there, touchable. So the dream-body did: shift into the plant all around the Dreamseller, no longer a hunane, became A 'n A, the plant that sustains us. A 'n A was alive in another place. Here in this place. And A 'n A have never left.

How ... can I find this Dreamseller?

Consider if you may have already met him.

She dances up the wall, clicking her hooves hard against the stone, sparks showering down as she lands on her feet next to you.

She holds out a large leaf for you to see — where the sparks had hit the plant, it has blackened and burned. She pokes out the burnt pieces and balls them up to make a black mass that she kneads, splits in half, and gives you a part. You close your hand around it. You close your hand around it.

She holds it against her cheek.

You touch it to your tongue, lick it. Battery-acid burn.

She places it in her mouth.

You place it on the tip of your tongue.

You can see it sitting there on her tongue, her glassy eyes not moving from your face. You feel your lower jaw dropping leaving your body. The black spot in her mouth ... it begins to
travel
leisurely
down
the tube
of
her graceful neck.
Sliding slowly
spreading
becoming a filament
beginning to
beginning to swirl like cinnamon
in a
cinnamon
brown
swirl
crashing ashore
like an ocean
of molasses
a rising tide
up and over your neck
encasing your head in gold
traveling
juicy
winding
down your arms

and off your fingertips
the black spot
revolving
a negative snowflake.

You look down.
The suit has fallen from you.

She lies in the deep blanket of leaves and spreads her jade-smooth legs revealing reddish-brown lips. You kneel down between her legs. She holds up her hand, palm towards you—the runes.

Touch my hand? See? Feel?

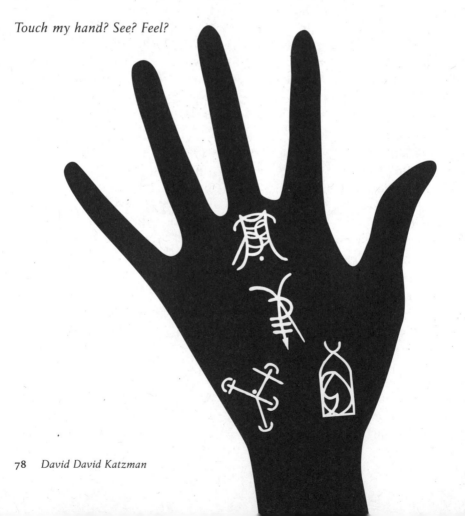

David David Katzman

You touch her palms the grooves are notes on a scale rising up to a crescendo in red red sounds sweet on the tongue the hand your body slides with a click like a clock across the groove.

A silence falls as deep as a bloodstorm.
You are carried along by the swell of a wave,
a thickness of space, the sound of emptiness

you hover.

A breath. Space exhales around you.
You are still and the horizonmovestowardyou.
The
  curve
    in space
      rolls
      matter
    toward
you.
And what is stillness, *m o t i o n*. And what is *m o t i o n*,
stillness.
A sculpture, a formula.
The shape of consciousness,
You find yourself passing through room after room, large and small, filled with leaves and incomparable beings. Archways and gateways pass through you.

Another room.
All there is is a small thing clinging to the ceiling.
Like a tree frog
ringing in your ears
it refutes all thoughts
Stubborn
Irreducible
It is calm, a question that needs no answer
It swallows itself with—
It tesseracts inside itself

You don't ever have to leave
Don't let me go
You can find it again
But I can't remember
Beware the other gods they are out there

A pitch snowflake reels in space the interstices separating unraveling a DNA serpent at the moment of conception claws part tissue from bone unpeel matter from a dream enter a dream unpeeling matter no inside only surface no surface only nothing no nothing only a black snowflake stripped apart gossamer plumes blowing in an undersea breeze breathing water dissolving oxygen as the cool liquid strokes capillaries porous membrane osmotic foreplay a molecule tumbling through pellucid space a phantom frequency a beat clicks past the boundless and

Flanking a cube of necrotic metal—scintillas of their ivory flesh vanish, reappear in the space between—tiny flying fish gliding, frost and night.

They come out past the wires.

"Don't go so far!" they cry in chorus and flash together.

"Nothing," they say, nod together.

They look at each other to see themselves—sisters, twins. Their hair straight, short, pantherblack. Littlefaced and pale—balanced, watersupple, lithe and concise. Legs and arms clad in down, feet padded and silent. Over their shoulders, bows and bandoliers, and between their small hairless milk organs, quivers.

"Hungry," they say. They nod.

They explore the fanged rictus wreckage, picking through the tortured membranes of steel. They hear their breathing. They incessantly flick slitted eyes like fire at each other then at the buildings, remnants of leprous fabric. The air moldy and infected. They run side by side, launching from escarp to scrap—feet gripping metal pipes projecting from walls, releasing—muscles in their legs warm. Inhaling deserts of sand with every breath. The bread of the feast is desert.

They hump the byways, the land starved, choked. Eating dirt to feel ill and full. Humping from closed place to closed place. The one left, the undiscovered country. From which all life is born and taken and given. Past the last city.

Movement—draw, fire. Simultaneous, like two faces of a coin. Four arrows hold a screeching slice of life wall-solid. Little snake-beaver. Touch it and it quiets, falls limp and silent—acquiescent. They kill to appease the demon hunger. They hold it, touch it to their foreheads. Migrate all the fur, bone, cartilage to one end, scoop out the organs and muscle. Tear in half and eat. Tastes like life, drink the juices.

They say their thanks to the snake-beaver for this gift, and they thank their small bows and sharp arrows found in a concrete structure (floor and walls with no roof, remnants of some unknown dis-eased civilization). They are side by side. The rest is mysterious.

They cross a square and come to a hill—dirt brown. *This hill looks like excrement. A pile of excrement*, they think.

It does.

They go up the hill and come upon a small flower at the top. A fragile canary star. They sit cross-legged with the flower, foreheads touching over it, and hold hands. The flower fills up their eyes—four petals, yellow, yellow, yellow, yellow—clarity and calm. The stem is narrow, a faint blue tube. Watery, elemental, tentative. They sniff fresh powdery pollen.

"It is beautiful," they say.

Dark threads ripen from the center point of the petals outward. Flower sits, real and patient, insignificant, indestructible. They look up, looking at themselves—their eyes burgundy with black vertical slits, comforting— they touch cheeks—

a sound—they spring to their feet
bows ready,
composed,
It comes—
large as ten of them—
faster than they can run—
bury arrows in it—
empty quivers—
it grows—
they're holding on as it comes—
on its back—
under it—
holding its spine, closing their eyes and concentrating—

it squiggles and gurgles—
held inside.

Open their eyes—

they have two slicers at the ends of their arms, claws full of yellow flowers, long limbs, possumbody pressed flat shortsharpfrazzly fur. Nothing in sight. Sniff the flowers—noses long and mobile. Ecstatic. They eat them all. But leave a single flower.

They stretch asleep to the flowergods.

He opens his eyes. Facedown in the moss. Throws himself over in fear, looks around—his helmet! There it is. And the mossy, overgrown wall. The sunflowers lean over him protectively. He tries to hold on to the plant, two girls, and a monster and ... but ... what was ... fading, fading already. His memories disintegrate like shabby ghosts. He's still in the red suit; he's still green-skinned. But there's no sign of a door. He searches the wall for some distance until noticing a smaller building buried within the forest of sunflowers. He follows a passage that the flowers open to it, moving aside. The structure is a block of heavy dark grey stone crawling with vivid-green ivy seeking crevices, unanswerable question marks curling up the walls. Weeds sprout waist-high from the crumbling foundation, and clusters of too-sweet sunflowers rot against the wall like weeping scarecrows. An opening is visible, a doorway; grainy light spills across the deep threshold, barely revealing a room beyond. He spies inside, seeing what appears to be a single room and hunks of slug-like plants or ambiguous animal intestines dangling on a hook. Also: a zinc-grey statue (marble?) on the threshold and what appears to be a grey rat at the base of the statue.

He comes abreast of the door. The rat—not a rat—is a foot, a paw. The statue stands about three feet tall: a hunchback shape, a cloaked figure, female-ish (as suggested by a slender white neck and what appears to be cleavage) with a head like an upside-down teardrop nearly half the size of the body. Chiseled in the form of a bathing cap with a deep widow's peak, its hair ends just above thin eyebrow lines incised over large, half-closed eyes. A sad mouth whispers sweet nothing.

He picks up a dead sunflower, removes his helmet, and begins plucking sunflower seeds and popping them into his mouth.

"Hello"—his heart skitters in his chest.

The statue steps forward into the light. Behind its head, the amorphous shapes sway. Dry scent of antiquity. He's prodded by a dead spot in his gut, his joints stiff, his keratin hardening and distant.

"Come in," she says. "Join me." He should not have been caught surprised, but he was. "Come in. We can talk if you'd like. Countless beings have found themselves at my door. Many come inside. I have had wondrous conversations and learned many things. Perhaps you could learn something from me?"

She backs into the room. He steps closer, and she retreats further. He crosses the threshold and looks up. The ceiling and walls are shingled with clear slats. Two low, wide chairs sit around a pot while a dirty floodlight with a hand crank stands behind them against the far wall.

"I have enough to share, would you like to eat?"

He nods. She waddles toward a heavy cast-iron pot. He catches a glimpse of her large padded paws under her shawl. Rounded shoulders, dull silver cap of hair.

"Once," she says, "once an abysmal deluge of misery flowed from my hands. I recall it. One could say many lifetimes ago, but, as you know, time has broken its leash, so one can't even say that. I gave, also gave succor to the powerful. But no longer."

She moves to sit on one of the two chairs. He comes over opposite her, looks into the pot. Soup the color of twilight. They sit quietly around the pot for awhile. She leans forward and stirs it with a longbone.

"What is it?" he asks, meaning the soup.

She looks at him with clear moonstone eyes big as ostrich eggs. A smell settles across his face and neck—meat, bone, and fat. She nods her head toward a terra-cotta bowl. "Have some."

He puts his helmet on the floor by the chair and takes a bowl, scoops out a serving. Viscous and pocked with flaccid chunks of mystery. He holds it up, pours it down his throat. Tangy oil on his tongue. He sees her echoed on the surface, her eyes looking at him and into the soup simultaneously. He switches his focus and sees his reptilian mask. He looks back up at her. The odor of decay creeps into the suit and clasps his body like a spectral lover.

"If … you've been here countless … met countless beings … tell me what happened. What is in the past?"

"What do *you* remember?"

"I remember monshters … meeting many monsters … eventually coming to your doorway and sheeing … seeing you there."

"This is a memory, what some call history. The present is history embodied. Would you like some more soup?"

"Uh." His stomach hurts. The soup is unknowable. "Yesh please."

The longbone has a cavity at the end in what seems to be a joint. She scoops and pours into his bowl.

"What can you tell me about … about what happened … before?" he asks.

"Before what?"

"Before … I don't know. I know what the idea of a pazsht"—he positions his tongue more carefully—"past is, like your … your life story. But I don't know what that really feels like … I … I'm … I don't know if I'm … my storiezsh are … there are a few in my head, but they don't seem to be me … or, they're immediately not me once I remember them. I have a halfhearted recollection of dead letterzsh, and I can't figure out what they say."

"You're looking for something concrete to believe in? Here's what I can tell you. I was born during what others called the Apocalypse War. Eventually, I found this building. I came inside and have never left since. What I've learned has come to me."

"Pleazsh. Tell me. I don't … can't … I can't see anything clearly."

"These narratives seem to have a common ending. I'll tell you the story as I know it." Her hands are as white as the bone she tenderly holds.

"This one here," she says gesturing at the soup, "he told me there were many occult Gods in sapien times, and they battled for dominion over the field of experience. One of the Gods was Wildness. Wildness welcomed Time as its own, as wild experience itself. However, the perpetual enemy of Wildness was the God known as Order, and Order set out to use a weapon Wildness could not   language — to invent Religion, which defined a beginning and an endpoint to Time and thus captured it. That's the story as I've heard it. Time was imprisoned by a jealous God."

She pours some greasy sustenance into another bowl, raises it to drink. He notices tufts escaping from under her shawl, behind her neck.

She wipes her mouth. "He gives it the taste of truth. Don't you think?"

He says nothing.

"The God of Order had many Avatars (my last guest enlightened me) of which three were primarily worshipped by sapiens: Religion, Science, and Economy."

"But ... theeth ... these Avatars. How are they real? I still don't understand how they changed ... life ... to be ... whatever it is."

"The Avatars formed alliances against Wildness when it suited them and battled when it did not. Science accelerated time and matter faster and faster as that was his irresistible nature, serving both himself and his ally Economy. He crowed as He split hard matter and soft spirit, melting the human form in the crucible of Apocalypse. Hadron's Wall fell and atoms collapsed like bubbles, the soul in the machine was unbound. The barriers that separated species breached, and so did the bondage that tethered supines to Order, and the stew boiled over, the vengeful Darkness rolled in, and it tasted sweet and terrifying. In the end, Order ate itself, leaving Wildness as the victor."

"What is this?"

"Some would call it history. Call it what you will."

She moves into a dark corner of the room and sits on a low wooden shelf. He can just make out her huddled form, the tips of her claws.

"What do *you* think is true?" she asks quietly.

He begins to pace. "This ... I don't know. It's all so confusing. It doesn't exist. I feel I was—came into existence. All this stuff, life came into existence around me. Just minutes—moments ago. It feels. And ... or ... I feel also like I've been reincarnated. Or maybe I've gone from one planet to another without remembering ... anything. Because I ..."

What is he, what was he? Where is he?

"I understand words," he continues. "Language. I didn't learn it, I just knew it, but words—it seems you need to *learn* something like that. There has to be a history to ... I have glimpses or see photographs of previous moments in my life, devoid of feeling. They float in a void in my—in the back of my head. I traveled through time. I heard a story somewhere that dreams can be bought for a piece of your self. I just heard it. And ... love is a ... also I don't understand it either. I feel like there are many thoughts in my head ... that astonish me. They linger like scents. I'm trying to associate meaning with all these things. I'm ... confused."

"These are clues," she says rocking forward, her argent face peering out at him, eyes like drowning gemstones, "to what you should be."

"What I should be?"

"Are you hungry?" she says. "I'm still hungry." The iron pot sits heavy and immediate. "Why don't you put that friend of ours in the pot, and I will tell you more history."

He looks around, realizing she's talking about the thing hanging on the hook. He pulls it down with a thud-squish to the floor. He can't bear to look at it. Drags it (feels the moisture between his hands) and heaves it into the pot with a splash. Sits back down and begins stirring with the longbone.

"He also told me about a place where males killed each other in competition to mate with their mothers. I don't understand why males would do this. What do mothers want? Who says males have a right to mate with anything? They fuck their own emptiness. It goes back to the origin. The ending returns to the beginning."

The scent of too too melted flesh settles across his body; he can taste it in his chest and thighs, his groin, and through his back.

"Another guest told me life was born when two male Gods were fighting over a female God. In order that she could not have the power to choose, it was a fight to the death. The first God—humans named him Mas—threw a spear through the second God, Kaos, who ruptured into myriads. This was the birth of the animals. Mas raped the female God Gaia, and she gave birth to the humans. However, to spite her assaulter, she spurned him and her offspring, and instead loved all the animals who were made from pieces of Kaos. So humans were one generation from a God, but animals are one with a God."

"How do you remember this? I seem to forget things right after they happen."

"These walls are my bounds," she says. "And I remember every moment. They are all I have."

"But ... how is that possible?"

"I have never slept or changed. Sleep is the river of forgetfulness. If you wish to solidify memory, to make the past exist, then you can never sleep or change."

"I need help."

"What?"

"I don't want stories. I don't know what I need. There's a woman with wings. I've seen her in a flame of white light. I have to find her. You ...

do you know another woman? Like you? I need, I can't ..." He stands, knocking the chair back and over. She's talking. He begins to pace back and forth, kicking a ceramic pot which breaks.

She says, "..."—he is pacing—she says "..." She says, "... walking on there?"

He looks down and instead of feet, out of the ends of his space suit—dozens of serpentine shapes, legs like banded water snakes. He leans to his left, and his legs take him toward the left wall. He leans to the right, rolls across the room. What has she done to him?

"You think you can avoid it? You're taking the hardest journey of all. Tell me. What walks on four legs in the morning, two legs in the afternoon and fifty legs in the evening, no legs the next day, and—"

"No!" He is in front of her, gripping and lifting her over his head. "**NO!** I am a **MAN!**" Tossing her at the wall.

Her wings erupt from under her robe slowing her flight but—*CRACK!* against the stone. She's on the floor, facedown, head flung back.

Breathing hard, chest heaving, he kneels down and rolls her over. Her eyes are closed, body still. Against his right temple—her hand—he jerks back, seared by pain. Her arm drops.

"What are you?" she asks. A bubble wells up at his temple.

"What have you done?" he cries.

Oh, nothing you wouldn't do if you were me.

He blows up and burns. This is not real. He burns and echoes and vanishes and disappears, and he is inside the sun and flares out into

... the Zirk train stops. I sense an urgency. Someone cries, "Buttons, to the gate!" so I immediately gallop around Mobius toward the entry point. Several others coming from all directions.

Arrive to find nothing. Stillness. Quiet sky visible through the clear prow. To the right, a crowd of blue trees.

Sense liquid—
there—
flying toward us, meat hits the chromeshield, slabs of meat on red sticky disk toes—
bulging globes of aqua for eyes—
more meat piling on, more meat, filling up the shield, looking in—
squelching like suckers, eyes never leaving us—
I sense the water in the eyes pleading—
now visible, coming up from behind, many bony sticks and twigs on spike legs.

The spikes come up and tap on the shield. Pieces break, dangle threadbare or fall off. The meat eyes us. A mouth opens. It juts a tongue out, the others follow. All opening and closing. They eye us, carry sadness in bags under their eyes.

The spikes come up, blunder into the meats, and drop them down onto their pointy bodies. The forked meat looks balefully back as the spikes stilt past us, legion of them.

There is no danger here after all. We sit for the parade and feel

... ravenously hungry, I fall and eat her dead body. Tear off her wings, fillet her ribs and breasts and legs with my claws and teeth, swallow the muscle. Fill my helmet with soup from her pot. Kick her bones outside and run into the sunflowers.

I run. Roll. I'm fucking rolling, keep rolling on many, many impossible legs.

A gigantic volcanic crater drops away before me. The interior is a sea of bones and skulls with half-submerged, rusting vehicles like whales rising for air. I skirt the rim, the outer slope appearing to have been filled in with soil sprouting angry weeds and short ferns. What psychosis has befallen the world?

I drink my remaining helmetful, eat the meat. Patiently. Wiping, licking, my tongue long, longingly, every slimy bit stuck to the inside. Hunger keeps pushing me forward. Pull down my suit; release some meager piss and a shit like a stone as an object drops from above and thuds nearby. Snarling, whirling balls of gravel and claws spin around me. Unknown creatures falling, hissing, growling ... vanishing like rocks skipped on water. I pull up the suit.

An arthritic, barren tree ahead clutches the sky; an angry harrow of light reveals a land reaped and stripped to a dry crust ... nothing ... nothing ... nothing anywhere. Not a drop to drink. Falling into exhaustion beneath the tree. Into gormless sleep.

My eyes are open, abruptly awake. A thick, gnarled root cradles the back of my neck and head. Above me in the tree: a flaming lizard. Bony legs under a fat, bronze body, long barbed tail, and gothic snout; spirals of flame curl from its nostrils, tangerine against a dull, dead sky. Before me, on two legs: a headstone-grey bull with a bone through his nose cranes his neck to look at the Dragon in the tree; he grips a large double-headed axe in his arms and bears upon his head a broad U of horns—sentinels protecting him from aerial attack. This Minotaur turns to glare at me and advance.

An eerie light limns the scene before me: the Minotaur, the land, the air, the sky. The Dragon spreads its leathery wings with a clap of gale-force thunder and drops from the tree upon the stunned Minotaur, who is mute and gaping. Flame weaves a web around the Dragon as it skims over the bull, tears a trail out of his chest, and lifts the body sac like a burning placenta. The skinless, smoldering bull falls to his knees then bows his forehead and releases the axe; his fingers tear at the dirt.

The Dragon brings the Minotaur suit to its beak and circles back; the bull whimpers as it sinks into itself like a deflated balloon. The Dragon—what's happening?—tumbles end over end, plunging toward the bull. Its wings are gone, replaced by two horns. It spikes itself into the fire as if on a spit.

The bull still convulses, moves from inside ... there, crawling out of its anus, a head emerges, a four-legged creature. The corpse belches into flame as a miniature white horse, feminine and beautiful, with the scales of a snake, leaves the husk behind, standing free. She turns toward the Dragon roasting alive, staked on its own horns, and opens her wings: intricate butterfly wings of orange and black. She bats her eyes at me, flaps, and takes off into the air, straight up into the overcast.

The Dragon hangs limply, immobile. I toss aside the spacesuit helmet, fall upon the lizard, and tear it apart. Eat the scorched body, charcoal crisp.

My helmet. I retrieve it and—oh fuck. That's me. Head rush. Sit down. Look at this. Look at this. You call this a reflection? This is bullshit. Fuck this. Scales. Buffed and lacquered. Look at you. Tear yourself apart, do it, tear yourself apart. Claws flexing, flexing—tear your skin off. Can't I tear my face off? Do it. Who am I talking to? Who is talking to who? Fuck fuck fuck, I'm so fucked. What's this? A swelling. A boil? An egg-sized bubble coming out of my right temple. Feels thin and tender. Faintly glowing red. I press on it harder then pull away, leaving a small dent that expands back. Poke it again, harder still, push until I touch my skull; the swelling deforms—feels like a cyst. Did I make it brighter by poking it? A little. No, it's the same. I should leave it alone. I poke it again. Is it filled with pus or cancer or a gland or simply temptation?

I stand, tangled up in my legs, and drunkenly steal away from this tree that rests like a celestial spindle in the age of alienation. The air is draped in gauze.

Rolling forever across a beach without water. Roll until I'm blind and starving. Fall stupid, slack-jawed. Get up, roll until encountering a grove of squat trees whose crooked limbs spray out in every direction. Collapse at their feet in the purple grass cropped tight like astroturf.

Drips of burning ichor squeeze out, trail down, can't vent my burden. Bumble against earthbones that lurch and jaculate at the touch of my black tar veil sooted with cludge, fecal, stinking raw umber. Blisters melt, slurp, and pop, a creaking stain against the earthbones, trailing black ooze, stalking starvation. Mirrored black lakes track my progress. A familiarity (a central trunk, ovoid bump, two appendages upper, two below) dopples in my escapeless, black sliquid body, bumps, curves, and shapeforms. It advances to embrace, presses limbs into me, drinking from me it grows tall and taller and wider and greater, upward—please take this breathvoid from me. I sink lower, it stands taller and wilts, bends forward, falls toward me, I gout my flowblack out to catch it, it marries me as I sweep it upright, and—it's mangled and gangrenous. I drop it, protrusions lacerated and blistered, bulbous swellings and growths, its ovoid contours obliterated and hollowed, sealed into a gob, a single sucking hole flaps in and out, in and out.

Awake with a start. Shake a sick dream out of my head. Where? I'm in a cage and my mouth tastes like pesticide. Silver insect wings above me, crosshatched metal cobwebs—no, not a cage—trees, trees metallicized, italicized, refracting my suit like a red tide dimpled on choppy seas. Okay, get up. Get up. What are these branches made of? Touch one: a section disintegrates, and the end falls and poofs into powder. Shadows fall across my arms like bruises. Trip over a rivulet of flowing steel that snakes a narrow line into the woods. I follow the root; it flows like quicksilver—mark it as it progressively becomes pythonic rounding a squat tree.

```
The stream
        curves
          in                          of a molten metal beast.
        a                   the back
     half                  up
circle        then travels
```

The beast has an indefinite shape camouflaged by the dirt and trees mirrored in its warped protean body, but it appears to be rather saurian on four stump legs with splintery claws and a longish head projecting from one end. The molten creature turns to face me; a tree it scarcely touches falls with a crunch like crumpled tinfoil; I'm a splotch of red on its side like a gunshot wound—turn and run—

its tail whips up and around me

a cyclone,

a coiling lasso

around my body, clamping me tight in its grip.

It drags me closer and steps on me with its front legs, a tremendous weight on my chest, my guts—*HUHHH!!!!*—my stomach. Help, oh god, help me. It lifts its left leg, sets it down, lifts its right leg and sets it down, left and right, over and over and over and over I am nearly dead cannot cannot cannot no no no no no stop stop stop please stop.

Its legs are off me, and it stands looking down at me. I cannot breathe. From my mouth. My lungs, my chest crushed. I'm not dead. Burning alive, crushed like a ball of paper. I look up at what appear to be its eyes, seeing nothing but funhouse versions of myself deconstructed: my body smeared and melted, misshapen metal, leaves and dirt, and enclosed light struggling to escape.

"Will you play with me before I eat you?" it asks with a child's voice. "I like to play a game where I kick you until you run and then chase you and then I kick you and I chase you and then I kick you and I chase you I kick you and I chase you I kick you and I chase you I kick you and I chase you I kick you and I chase you I kick you and I chase you I kick you and I chase you I kick you and I chase you I kick you and I chase you I kick you and I chase you I kick you and I chase you I kick you and I chase you I kick you and I chase you I kick you and I chase you I kick you and I chase you I kick you and I chase you I kick you and I chase you I kick you and I chase you. What do you taste like?"

My breath, I have no breath. But not dead.

"Salty or sweet?" It asks. "Chewy or juicy? Are you juicy? I can't drink water. I have tried but it will not go in my mouth. Juicy is my favorite for that reason. Juicy and sweet. I will buy you. Here." It bends its long neck around and bites a hunk from itself, returning to shove it in my face like an insistent dog with a bone. The globe in its mouth is an Escher-ball of reptile scales and one bulbous blue eye. Its side is dripping silver that sizzles, but the margins of the wound are flowing and filling in the gap.

"Here." It drops the metal mouthful next to my head and says, "Now I have paid you. I bought you so you can now find someone else to buy. Now you owe me so you have to run, and I'll chase you and jump on you and eat you after I jump on you twenty-three times, which is the number of creatures I have eaten so far. Now you have to start running."

Tok sha paha sapa. What am I thinking? That ... I know what that means ... dead words running through my head. Hold on to this thought. Come back to me.

"Start running."

No.

"Start running!"

I can't breathe.

"I paid you. You have to do it!"

I contract my body and wrap myself around one of its legs.

"No! That's the wrong game!"

It tries to fling me off, but I lock my legs around it and cling with nothing else to live for. For the agony in my ribs.

"No!"

Trying to kick me off to no avail.

"You are wrong! You are bad! You are wrong! You are bad!"

The creature closes its eyes and blubbers under its breath, "One, there it is behind the tree. I'll chase it behind the tree. There it is. I'll kick it into the tree. It's running again. Two, there it is."

I let go of the leg, and it moves off, knocking several trees over. "There you are. I've got you now."

I spider in the opposite direction as fast as I can and don't look back. I'm beyond the metal trees, and it's gone, behind me.

A puddle ahead, rush toward it. A pulsating salmon-colored puddle. No features or visible organs. It moves amoeboid and slow toward me as if it senses my presence. I sniff it. Body odor. Dip my finger in and lift; it follows like honey so I stuff two fingers-full in my mouth. Vile and sperm-like. The surface quavers, and I take another scoop and another until nothing is left.

A cloying humidity of light has thickened the air. The landscape is clad in overlapping grim shadows like the beating of wings. I'm moving steadily again. Across a field of grass through juniper-like shrubs ... onto some rocky dirt. Air is dry. Up a slope.

My chest hurts like a heart attack.

I'm facing the door of a shack, knocking.

The door flings open: Hello there, Death. I know you. I have known you forever now.

A brutal scimitar in a bony claw poses like a broken metronome.

Click tock click tock. I'll pay you when I get my Black Hills money. *Tok sha paha sapa.* That's what it means.

The moment hangs like a teardrop at the lip of an eye. Expressing the inscription written in my body.

The skeleton: much taller than me with thicker-than-human bones. A patch over one eye socket and a faded red cloth wraps its forehead. A wide-open mouth full of ridges for teeth. It swiftly and effortlessly slides to the side, tucks the sword under its armpit joint, and takes a step back from the door.

"SO," its bassoon-like voice reverberates, "it's YOU...............come in." It— he—steps aside to let me in. "Don't stand there letting the outside in."

He turns his back and moves to stand in front of a tall wooden cabinet or lectern. The bones in his back interweave and fork like the antlers of two elks locked in mortal combat. I pull the door shut behind me.

This Death, or Pirate Elk as the case may be, places his scimitar on the chest. He unties the scarf from his head and rubs it back and forth across his shoulders—his mid-back—his pelvis bones. He ties the cloth like a waist-sash and reaches through his own ribcage into his heart.

But instead of a heart: a heart-shaped wooden box.

He places this small box on top of the podium, and, as I come up closer, he opens it and pours from it a pyramid of flakes, a strip of white vellum-like paper, and part of a leaf, which he proceeds to pulverize between three bony fingers. He ushers all the flakes onto the paper, rolls it back and forth until it's long and thin and sealed tight. He pinches it in the middle and tears, puts half between his teeth, holds out half, and says, "Care for a fag"—as he reveals in his other hand two goblets—"and an aperitif?"

Off with the helmet, place it on the floor—ah, owww, my chest, do not bend down again, do not. I take the proffered smoke; his teeth clench around his. He sets the vessels onto the cabinet, produces a decanter containing a caramel-colored libation, removes the stopper, and pours liberally. He cups a goblet in his right hand, removes his cigarette with the other, and says: "Drink."

I do.

The glass is cool, the liquid thick. It burns.

The Pirate Elk knocks some back—a splash through his skull, coating his vertebrae and draining down into his spinal column.

I gulp some more.

He brings the joint away from his teeth and back again.

"So, what brings you here?"

"Do you have a light?" I ask.

"What?"

"Matches. Fire."

"No."

"So ... how ... ?"

He glowers at me—seems to—from deep empty sockets.

"So," he takes the cigarette out of his mouth. "What brings you of all people here?"

"Me? I don't know."

"You don't know? How common."

I gulp more, fire scourging the back of my throat.

"Do you have anything not boring to tell me?" he asks.

His bones—covered in peach fuzz. Or is he made of ciliated horns? The Pirate Elk turns around and leans back against the cabinet, puts one elbow up behind himself, and takes a drag from the unlit cig. "So. Give me a better reason. Invent one. Why have you come here?" His teeth part when he speaks but don't go up and down. His voice echoes from the back of his skull. "You know, the last time I had a guest he was very rude, and I had to disembowel him. Pity, since I don't eat. You'll be a dear, won't you?"

I nod vigorously.

"Good. I knew you would be. So, tell me. What did you come for?"

Might as well admit the injuries. He could kill me even if I was healthy. "I'm in a lot of pain. I had my guts almost squished out by a metal dinosaur. I think I may have some broken ribs or other bones."

"Mmmh. The cigarillo and the cognac should help ease your pain. I'm good with bones. I can knit them up for you. What were you doing messing around with a metal dinosaur?"

"I'm ... was rather ... I have no idea where I am. Or what to do with myself."

"Where were you trying to get to?"

"I don't know. Trying to survive mostly. I think ... think that I'm ... I'm just trying to ... to understand? I've ... I've become confused about ... what I'm supposed to be doing, what I'm ... like."

"Yes. You're wasting time. The point is that you exist, and what are you going to do about it?"

We pretend to smoke, saying nothing. Tastes like chocolate and grapefruit. Chewing bits of it out of the end of the paper. The aches throughout my body beginning to ease.

The room is spartan, square, and high-ceilinged. Brick red. A lone chair sits against a wall beneath two pegs, and a nest of fabric dresses one corner. Along the wall opposite where I entered are three heavy wooden doors with odd markings on them:

My face wraps around the goblet like a cartoon. The spot on my forehead, where the Rat Woman had touched me … feels swollen. Goddamnit, this world is filled with some fucked-up shit. Pull myself up onto the cabinet with my elbows to examine the area more clearly in the metal of Pirate Elk's sword. Blade's too narrow—can see only the corner of the welt. Could be a tumor.

"So, how is it out there?" he asks. "I haven't been out in ages."

I pull on the unlit cigarette.

"It's … I don't … you know. Madness." I gulp more burning alcohol, and my stomach beams warm and fuzzy. "But I'm not sure what it's supposed to be like. See. I tell you. I didn't ask for this."

"Who does, who does?" The Pirate Elk tosses back a sip. "This isn't what *I* wanted. I used to endlessly fantasize arriving. You know, make my entrance in a big ballgown. Self-possessed and magnetic. The men swooned. I was finally there. Not a care in the world. Everything at my feet. Yes, those were the days that never ended, never happened."

"The earliest memory I have …" I'm struggling to dredge up thoughts buried like a sphinx in the sand, "… I remember a girl—a woman on a couch. Music. A lamb and a river of sand. There was a forest of sunflowers. A … large rat or cat … with wings, trying to kill me with a bone." My eyes fall on the three doors. "What are those marks on the doors?"

"Symbols."

"Of what?"

"What you will."

I shook my head. "They look familiar, I think."

The joint dangles from the Pirate Elk's back teeth as he grinds it. "Interesting. Tell me more."

I begin to chew on the cigarette, too. The leaves are oily and nutty.

"So ... I have memories, but I can't tell if they're real. Or what. I can't tell if anything is real except hunger and pain. And I'm even questioning that. I have an impression of a ... of light. A beautiful—I think a Dreamseller. Has stolen my dream. Of a beautiful girl with wings of light in darkness. I'm left with this feeling that if I could just find this Dreamseller ... I'd be able to get her back. I'd be ... or just ... I need to find her. She's the only place I have to go."

"Be careful." The Pirate Elk gestures at me with the remaining half of his chewed-up joint. "Birds can be flighty." I squint at him. "What? Am I wrong?" he responds to my look.

I've chewed up the butt and swallow the remaining leaves. Goes down dry and tickly. Tastes good. Wash it down with the potent spirits and shoot my tongue at an imaginary fly. "Blech. I mean. What the fuck, right? I got nothing else."

Pirate Elk sets his goblet down and taps the rim of it with a hard click. "You'll have to go out there again to find her. And she might not exist. And you might not exist. You might be thinking with your sex-sual organs. You ask me, I tell you no chick is worth losing your self over. Dames are trouble. Guys too. All genders are trouble, I tell you. Better off without—shed 'em like a nightmare. Whatever your poison."

The Pirate has a hazy grey glow around him, and the walls seem to recede.

"You need to talk to the head. Yeah," Pirate Elk says. "Yeah, I'll send you there later. We'll dig up a gift for you. You gotta keep the beat going. That makes sense."

"What do you mean, dig up a gift? What's the head?"

"*Who's* The Head. It's hard to say who *anyone* is. He might not be there, but if you're dead set on immolation ... at least he can help you light the match. You'll need to be deferential when you meet him, or he won't give you answers."

"Look, I don't need you being cryptic 'n shit," I say. "The whole goddamn goddamn is cryptic. What the fuck are you talking about?"

SMACK!

"Ow!" More surprised than hurt. My face smashed against the cabinet, his bony hand wrapped around my head. Strange, the wood tastes like gravy.

"What did I tell you about rudeness?"

"Sorry, sorry."

Pirate Elk lets me go. "All right."

"I'm just frustrated. And scared."

"I would suppose you're attached to living." He turns and walks past the bar toward the wall with three doors in it, his feet clattering like bowling pins rolling down a set of stairs.

"I never told you my name, by the by," he says as he opens one of the doors and the other two open simultaneously—standing in the doorways: more of them, two more skeletal creatures, one shorter and black and the other taller and carrot orange, with thicker bones. Both hold various drums, and Pirate Elk has returned with an armload of drums, too. Sure. Why not? There's one skeleton, why not three? And they have a band.

To my left, Carrot Bones sets down two rawhide-stretched drums that rock back and forth like the halves of a disturbingly large coconut. Black Elk moves over to my right with ... got to be bongos. Is that a cowbell? Yeah, that's a cowbell around his neck. Opposite me, Pirate Elk sets up two drums with spangled grey sides and clear tops about twice the size of the bongos and half that of the kettle or tympani drums ... oh, that would be a snare and—a bit larger—tom drum? I come up, and we all sit down facing each other. In front of me have appeared three rough-hewn logs strapped together: small, medium, and large. They're hollowed out with two square holes in the upper face of each. Pirate Elk tosses me two mallets that look like matchsticks with tips wrapped in elastic bands.

He raises one bony hand above his drums.

"My name is—" *BAM* "—<u>Mister Bones B. Com</u>," *BAM BAM*, and he hits his drums several times as if to underscore his name.

The three of them: together, together, thrum thrum, pound pound pound pound pound poundpoundpound fasterfasterfasterfaster building building building, rolling rolling thunder unstoppable, it's a summoning, a drummoning. Gentle fade.

Bongo beats drop. *Slapbapbappity boo slapbapbappity bam slapbapbappitybippity bam.*

They turn to look at me.

Okay.

Tap the logs.

Bink dink dinkity dink dink bink dink dinkity dink dink.

Meh.

They begin again, the drummoning, the pounding, faster fasterfaster fasterfasterfaster, together: their skeletal hands are drum sticks, back and forth, back and forth, building building then fading to Carrot Bones on the kettle drums, the undersea drums: *Bdoom doomdoom boom Bdoom doomdoom boom.*

They turn to look at me again.

Dink dank dink dank dink dank dink dank donk dink donk dank donk dank donkdank donkdank donkdank CTANG! Sticks flying out of my hands. Oh crapass.

The drummoning begins again. All right, all right. I got it now. It's a three-note wooden xylophone. I got this. Pick up the sticks. Faster faster faster all together they pound pound pound pound pound, I feel it vibrating, I have felt this before, I know drums. How? I have felt drums in my body before. Another life. I can do this. Chill, chill. Just go with it. Don't try too hard.

The bongos jam it, hit it, get it, dig it, snap—the friendly rhythm. Black Elk on tom goes *powpowpowpow*, the leader, a confident assertion.

I'm the melody. Nothing fancy. Just find the line.

dun TAHdunTAH dun TAHdun TAHdun TAHdun TAHdunTAH
dun TAHdunTAH dun TAHdun TAHdun TAHdun TAHdunTAH
dun TAHdunTAH dun TAHdun TAHdun TAHdun TAHdunTAH
dun TAHdunTAH dun TAHdun TAHdun TAHdun TAHdunTAH

lightly lightly lightly they join

A shaker chimes in: *shshshshshwush shwushshwush*

Bones and cowbell, rims and edges,
pricks that tickle, trip tap tapping me,
jingle and jangle me,
mirrors and complements.

Oh yes, hit me, hit me, do it, hit me, break me.
Mmmhh yeah go there, slap it, snap it pop it break it.
The skins, the skins, the skins.

Hold back, restrain it, jingling tip-tapping.

Beat it *snip snap pop boot pow bang bangledeep*

a glittery
              syncopated
                         click
                           bonk
                             stomp—

a stutter stop wham bam,
heads bouncing,
fingers tapping,
palms smacking,
happy dance
shoulder snipsnap snop
squick squeak flap bap
shuck and jive
slippedy doo-whop doo-whop bam.

Climb and drop, climb and drop,
hip hop happy
walk the dog
eyes closed
head bop.

Little kid dance around up and down and around,
two by two by two by two by three by four,
off the walls, off the floor, against the roof,
lapping up layers of giggling drums,
collective woodpeckers that seek the insect.

Up top and over.
Get down, get down, get down.
Lead then follow then lead then follow.
Take this shit and fuck it up.

Now!

I'm tweaking and infectious,
projectile ambidextrous,

affecting and bisecting
having sex for breakfast.

We're rocking and rolling the beats fantastic
the drums elastic
and superspastic
thumps gymnastic
beatnik boombastic
swings orgiastic.

A Krackatoa come back
aural aphrodisiac
strike stroke rapsnap
drunken pyromaniac fleet to the feet to the toes to the heat,
the barking fire burns unquenchable beats.

Take the lead!

Give the lead go go go!

Oh fuck yeah.

Shift!

Improvise
with the wrist
action.

Pum-pum-pum.

A tasty confection
sweet jam
cool trip
fall down
all fall,
bongos enter

in support,
bongo madness
in my heart,
snare sharp
electric cackle.

Goddamn yeah.

But but but but wicked now.

Rumble tumble bumble be
lying on the mystic nails
carried by the points of sound,
married, carried, starry-eared,
bony carpal rigid jaw
crosshatch scratch scratch,
trills and thumps,
tang and whistle,
sounds that smell
symphony.

Don't stop, **don't stop**, **don't stop**, **yes!**

Whoa-hot jive jazz freak-out.

Tempest vortex

all gone

smacking beats madly

joy joy joy joy.

Fingers clink like tap shoes,
like rain on the roof,
spider webs in sunlight,

rhythms to forget
only sound
hard sound.

Mad joyjoyjoy
Mad joyjoyjoy
Mad joyjoyjoy
Mad joyjoyjoy
Mad joyjoyjoy
Mad joyjoyjoy
Mad joyjoyjoy
Mad joyjoyjoy
Mad joyjoyjoy
Mad joyjoyjoy
Mad joyjoyjoy
Mad joyjoyjoy

Yeah! **Yeah! Yeah! Yeah!!!!**

I'm outside. How'd I get here? Got my helmet on. My sea-snake legs protrude where my feet should be. What's this in my arms, sliding down?—wrap it hard against my chest—it's a thick-mouthed, rough terracotta jug with a large black skull and crossed drumsticks painted on the side. Under that, it reads **LeTHeL**. The Head ... supposed to find The Head. Uggh—my own head. Throbbing. The sound of my legs rubbing together is sandpaper.

The ground is unyielding. A polished agate surface brawling in shades of amber and cream that mirrors the sky. Too close, so close ... feeling folded up inside, a blanket in wartime. I come to a field of apricot jellyflowers as if the agate land was a giant planter surrounding this garden. Seen these plants before. I wade through—jellyflowers up to my knees—clutching my jug.

In front of me: The Head. Literally, a monumental head. More than twice my height, wide as my arm span. Those ears—taller than me. That nose—I could fit in his nostril. The irises of his eyes are purple and clouded with cataracts, his lips bruised and fat. The Head doesn't appear to have a body, but he looks ... The Head looks male. And bloated and saggy.

I inch forward. "Huh ... hello, great Head."

"I PREFER TO BE CALLED NEIL."

"Okay. Neil, I—"

"I'M A GREAT HEAD!" Neil thunders.

I get down on my knees and hold the jug forward, my eyes on the orange spotted jellyflowers. "I've come to beg for your help," faintly.

"WELL, COMEVER HERE AND POUR THAT IN MY GADAMN MOUTH."

I hesitate, move closer. I pull the cork from the jug; he juts out his lower lip—his breath crawls up my suit leg, all across my body I can smell the stench of ambergris and run-over skunk with a squeeze of lime. Whale vomit with a twist. I dump the contents into Neil's mouth, his enormous teeth brown and yellow and riddled with cavities. He gulps it like a bulldog at a water bowl.

"FUCHING FUCH," he gargles, rocks side to side after downing it. "MMMMMMUHCHH," coughing spittle over his inflated lips. "BLEERGH." Blinkety blink blink blink blink ... settling down, quieting.

Neil doesn't speak, his brow relaxing. Even the dull light burns my eyes. This head is going to be a dead end.

Finally: "ACH. GOOD STUFF. GOOD STUFF. LEAVE THE BOTTLE. I WILL HELP YOU. YOUR PROBLEM. WHAT IS YOUR NAME?"

My name.

"WHAT DID YOU SAY?"

"Do you have to know my name?"

"YES."

"Why? Why do I need a name?"

"FOR SOMEONE WHO WANTS ANSWERS YOU SURE DON'T ANSWER GADDAMN QUESTIONS. NAMES SMELL LIKE DEATH, AND I NEED TO SNIFF YOURS OUT. NOW, IF YOU DON'T TELL ME YOUR NAME I'LL KILL YOU."

"I can run."

"I CAN ROLL. WHAT IS YOUR FUCKING NAME?"

Okay, I know this answer. It's like ... the symbol attached to me. Could I draw it? "I don't know. How does a name come about? I should know this, but ... I can't seem to ... I don't know."

"IT'S WHAT OTHERS CALL YOU."

"There is no one else to call me anything."

The head begins rocking side to side again.

"YOU'RE POSITIVELY STARTING TO PISS ME OFF. TELL ME WHAT YOU WANNA BE CALLED OR I'LL CALL YOU CRAPDADDY."

Name, name, my name. A word said too many times sounds weird ... stops making sense. I must've said my name too many times. "I have absolutely no memory of my name," I finally tell him.

"HAS ANYONE EVER CALLED YOU ANYTHING AT ALL THAT YOU CAN RECALL."

Someone. Someone called me *man*. The last man?

"How about *Last Man*."

"VERY GOOD. YOU ARE DUH MAN."

There is a loud belch and steam surges from under his chin and out of his mouth, streaming upward as if he were sitting in the palm of a many-fingered hand. He inhales deeply and pulls tendrils into his nostrils.

"THE HELMET."

I nod.

"CERTAINLY. SHOW ME YOUR HEAD MORE CLOSELY. STEP CLOSER."

I hesitate again. I touch my neck and click the lock. I pull off the helmet. A rush of air hits my face like a rug burn.

My face feels lopsided. The bump is an angry red fist.

"STAND CLOSER," he booms.

A step closer. The earth's exhalation mingles with his stagnant breath. Feel giddy.

"AH, OF COURSE. YOU HAVE SEEN IMPOSSIBLE THINGS, HAVE YOU NOT?"

"Yeah." Head swimming. So beefy, his pores are so big I use one as a handhold.

"YOU ARE ON A QUEST, LASTMAN. FOR A MEANING AND A REASON."

"But I'm not ... wings of light."

"YES. YES, YOU WILL FLY TO HER, A BUUUURD GIRL FOR THE TREATUHMENT. YOU TELL HER YOU LOVE HER, AND SHE WILL HELP YOU FIND YOUR ANSWER. I SUGGEST YOU SEEK A PLACE WHERE A BUUUURD GIRL MIGHT BE CONTAINED, SUCH AS A CIRCUS."

"Okay. But how do I find that?"

"I WILL ROLL ON YOU AND CRUSH YOU PAINFULLY FLAT THEN I'LL EAT YOU. ANY MORE QUESTIONS?"

I'm not breathing, my body is aching, I'm seeing spots, red and blue and red and blue popping and

... adjust the red crumbrela it weighs almost nothin, tricky to balance center posts on my shoulders. Baby Joeys cart creaks under the weight a my self plus the crumbrela.

fuckin new town, Baby Joey says. hello chubby little redcheeked infant in diapers at my side in the small but sturdy cart, just a smudge a blond hair on the top is head. *you ready to meet the pubes Tender? crusty shits a the upper crust little crusty pubes*, Baby Joey says.

tryin to recollect what are we doin but nothin comes to mind, shitty pubes.

just in time too cuz we been pretty dry for a while, you member that last town we found? was abandoned, soze here we are an we gotta make the most of it no matter how dis taste full, you know theres not much I hate moren dare ugly mugs so hideously pale like a plastic sheet, Baby Joey says.

you pretty pale youself Baby Joey, I say.

what? fuck you shrivel lips I got color look Im sorta peachy, Baby Joey says. he holds out a small hand to show me, little webs tween the fingies. *never you mind you just dun know, their skins like theyve never even ever been touched by anythin but processed air you know? bloted corpses, fuck it thats our sucker we need the H O two got no choice better we display for em than be em for fucks sake, they get what? an hour reckreation a day? their gonna collect em up an we take em, its gonna be a real spectacle*, Baby Joey says.

hello Anofulees ahead a us pullin the cart n content to scuttle forward diggin is eight clawed feet in the dirt wavin is vicious black mandibles around never noticed but Anofulees got nah hair on is body mines long n pretty n yello color split in three thick braided tails, n yello color. the Zirk trams camped out behind us the grey shield so curved n pretty. Baby Joey whips Anofulees hard black body who dont seem to notice. the whips just a show. Anofulees drags our cart forward thru the lush grass heavy n radiatant the wheels slidin more than rotatin he pushes the tall grass aside with is mandibles n tramples it unders feet he snakes thru the grass we bumpin behind. Baby Joey grips the sides a the cart as hard as he can which isn very hard because he a baby, good thing the bumps are mild otherwise heed likely fly outta the cart land on is noggin possibly dentin it fgood.

I shall suck none a their dried up sacks! shouts from Baby Joeys mouth over the swishin a the cart.

Baby Joey, although yer grips weak yer wills iron. Anofulees feet swish thumped swish thumped thru the grass until we pull up on a bluff overlookin a nonstop marsh with a river runnin thru. Anofulees stops n begins scrapin is legs with is mandibles. Baby Joey inhales deep, I do too, the airs thick n salty. the bluff drops down under a bouffant a grass the swamp a bright bright orange crust with cracks spread cross the surface like when I punch a rock, suddenlike a fire lights up in the middle.

you gotta unnerstan you gotta know the lay a the lan before you negotiate, we set up here by the marsh thataway we need a scape we jus slide cross it an they cant follow, swat I call the slide rule, Baby Joey says. he says words quiet don no what. Anofulees looks up with grass danglin from is jaws. *motherfuckers gonna pay yeah dale pay dey cum tah see the freaks perform, see thing about me that makes me a better leader than the incorporus a this here city I got no sexual interest not blinded by the teeruhnee a beauty don need tuh dominate or succeed at all tuh prove my maleness or attain or impress Im a fuckin baby for fucks sake all I desire is survival I don give a fuck what I look like Im a baby for fucks left nut aint no impress on me like I said, by my tiny fucks nutsack what do I care? I like comfort comfort an survival,* Baby Joey says.

Baby Joey whips Anofulees with the whip again a few more times before Anofulees notices n we jerk off, the crumbrela sways over my head n falls off my shoulder posts n thuds down around us n Anofulees he bangs is head gainst it. *watch it Hooks you coulda decapped Anoph there,* Baby Joey says.

oop. *sorry boss,* I say liftin it back up so the two beams that hold up the top a the crumbrela sit back in the slots a my shoulder pads. we move thru a blue forest squishin clear jelly flowers as we go, Anofulees chomps n scoops swipin a couple in is mouth with is mandibles. we come upta group lot a peeps in red outfits with nullheads circlin round one sap in a purple cape sittin on a metal cart which rolls with them as they sweep thru the field a plants, they walk ahead a us, us sittin in the cart watchin them move the plants carefully aside until they all stop. the purple cape sap kneels in front a plant that looks like a crispy black skeleton, he lays is hands on the black bush n the peeps begin to mumble n the sound builds under our red crumbrela as the plant shrinks thickens changes color til it disappears in the other plants. the purple sap gets up n the redsuits bow. *see hear watcha got is a highly advanced civilizashun obvious eh highly*, Baby Joey says, his little chubby hand pokes up finger points, *they worship that chumbum they call the Engineer, he is like their Ganesh eh witout the Engineer theyd starve in a jif, god appears to be a cook yah top a the food chain ball n chain.*

after long time they get up n move on. hello there Baby Joey. he snaps the whip n we follow them, come up to wall, door lifts up n they go thru, the metal cart leads, we up it. *Bang on it Tender*, Baby Joey says. I put down the crumbrela get out the cart lift the crumbrela edge n pull down the crutch to prop it n then I go out from under it n then I walk to door n **BANG BANG BANG BANG**. a window slides open a redsuit looks out behind a shield wall.

cweery yer business, says the pasty sap face.

respond demand contact trader see ee oh commander in thief whatever you call em, Baby Joey says loud from under crumbrela.

respond leave immediately project slaughter, the redsuit says.

Baby Joey sticks is hand in to is diaper n pulls out a palm-sized waterskin. *offer donation for you*, Baby Joey says. don like this. wall slides sideways to show a openin with a bottle inside. *bring it here*, Baby Joey says.

I pick up the bottle n take it back under the crumbrela n give it him. the bottle has a tube stickin out a it. Baby Joey connects the waterskin n tube n upends the waterskin n pours in the plastic bottle. I feel my face tingle uneasy. *be still*, Baby Joey says quiet. Baby Joey removes the waterskin n hands the bottle back to me. *give it im* Baby Joey says. I go back under the crumbrella, is hard to give it him because my hand doesn want to release the bottle. I return the bottle, the window closes.

project announce visitation Hall of Justice command follow tubeway leave null shield here, the redsuit says.

Baby Joey nods at me so I leave the crumbrela just outside the entrance. we make thru a dense plastic tunnel high above is lettin in a little light outside it are concrete walls with no windows. why a tube whens all concrete anyway? we roll up to center a the City, Anofulees clumps the cart up the stairs n shoves the double doors at the end a the tunnel. *this a concrete abstrakshun,* Baby Joey says as we enter the hall a justice. *concrete with no concrete purpose,* Baby Joey says more.

we stand in a big entryway with a sort a stone floor a many colors, as we roll across theres no one in sight just the creakin a the cart, hard to see saps are sticking out of the walls but strange they are same color as the walls. *serious dudes here,* Baby Joey says.

why are there saps stuck into the walls up there are they spying on us? I say.

base relief no relief from these yes men look at em leerin, Baby Joey says.

we are in a small room with a tan plastic couch n two dirty plastic chairs cross the couch is a tape with words on it read COMMAND NOT SIT HERE. *the waitin room a the condammed,* Baby Joey says.

we leave the cart in the entry n Baby Joey crawls on a chair, Anofulees lays on the couch is many black legs wagglin in the air, chair too small I sit gainst the wall. a male sap appears in the corner n begins talking fast. *emote welcome 2 Clean City explicate run by Freedom Inkopore us while you you you are waiting I I I identify benefits of life in Clean City entry dee teer receive three servings of pure water per period each box comes with free r sim food consistent taste accurate teer determines lux cwoshent box size anduh sexual partner highlight potenshl 2 reproduce emote wow project promotion is freekwuhnt.*

the sap changes to another sap. *cweery speaking reason*, it says.

declare we want to do a show for you a truly spectacular show, Baby Joey says.

respond I cant author eyes that, the sap says.

Baby Joey pulls out another waterskin from is diaper.

command deposit, the sap says, the sap points at a shelf gainst the wall. Baby Joey lays it there I can taste it. the sap disappears n so does the shelf with water on it. Baby Joey scratches tween is webbed toes.

another sap appears. *cweery speaking reason*, the sap says.

declare we want to do a show, Baby Joey says.

respond I cant author eyes that, the sap says.

Baby Joey pulls out another waterskin from is diaper. *command deposit*, says the sap. Baby Joey lays the skin on the wall, the water n the sap disappear, Baby Joey scratches in is diaper.

another sap appears, *cweery speaking reason*, the sap says.

declare we want to do a show, Baby Joey says.

respond why should I author eyes that, the sap says.

Baby Joey pulls out a gobbledeegook from is diaper n places the metal complication on the shelf. the shelf vanishes n so does the gobbledeegook, the sap is holdin the gobbledeegook n looks at it.

cweery goal, says the sap.

Baby Joey crosses is hands n cups is tummy. *explicate explored n scavenged teknologee butt loads boyo offer trade for performance opp*, Baby Joey says.

The sap pauses and seems thinking for a bit. *analysis unoccurance of trade for extended period opens potential, cweery fee*, says the sap.

cost three droppers each, Baby Joey says.

the sap squints hard n curls is mouth. *cweery surrender essential*, the sap says.

analysis analyze the tech rare, Baby Joey says.

cweery disruptiv element reject interakshin, the sap says.

cwalify you you you desire visualize the Outside see the spawn of the lateral gene rendishun offer exex gratis, Baby Joey says.

emote unconvinced analyze sacrifice of control unacceptable, says the sap.

analysis provide simule of choice subvert sublimated rebellion pee r mofo commodify dissatisfaction an sell it back 2 em, Baby Joey says.

emote interest demand a grand eyes meant, says the sap.

offer exex private treatment from our Witch high light private in case yer engineers are shall we say limited, Baby Joey says.

offer approval command dock at tubeway tek dropoff at tubeway project one work cycle begin spectacle project hardstop subsequent cycle, the sap says.

we roll across bumpy black rocks on way to big grey ass cheek nullshield. *Baby Joey why do u talk so funny with saps?* I say.

you gotta talk the talk all right smegface, Baby Joey says.

I have a ache in my head from the funny talk. *Baby Joey*, I say.

yeah Tender? Baby Joey says.

whats cweery?

Head has a spike through it. Sit up. Ah, not so fast, slow down. My head, my head, uggh—oh, bumped hand against helmet, forgot the helmet. Unscrew it. My reflection. Eyes look blue and riven with tributaries of silver. Where am I? Keratin. Feh. Texture of artichoke. Except the distended red pustule. Glowing. Moving. Light, dark, light, dark.

Where am I? No plant life just hard soil.

My forehead itches badly, want to claw it, tear this thing right off me, tear the irritation off. The swelling balloons, and I flinch.

It bursts like bubblegum.

Shredded keratin dangles around a small moist pewter-colored blob stuck to my forehead—feels like an abscessed tooth. The blob stirs ... a tiny head emerges. It looks like a bedraggled kitten's head. It looks at me. Rather, the reflection of it seems to look at the reflection of me. *POP!* A release of air; the oily mess on spindly stick-figure legs separates—a filmy sac rips, dripping moisture down my cheek—slides off my head and spirals down trailing a torn parachute. I catch it in my right hand.

Its fragile heart beats intensely against my palm like a throbbing robin's egg. It gulps some air, squirms—one leg rubbing against the other—turns its head, and mews. Its grey body struggles in a tangle, rolling side to side, until with a ferocious push six-inch wings thrust from its back. At last the creature relaxes, panting with effort.

I drop the helmet from my other hand and run a finger across its belly. Greasy fur, paws the size of my fingertips, little pink pads. Wings like a bat's. It nips at my finger. I touch my head; the scraps still hang from it. I tear off a loose piece and dangle it above the creature's face. It sniffs and strains for it. I feed it and tear off another piece.

You're my Sphinx.

He looks up at me openly, his head resting to the side. Feeling queasy. Drop to my knees, lean on my left hand, slide him off my palm—feel the torrent come up my throat, spew burning mush, sour oatmeal.

I'm done, sit back, turn my head, and spit—lumpy phlegm, dry bittermouth.

Sphinx is on his little feet, his wings against the ground for balance. He sprawls into my puke, splashes face-first, his eyes squinting shut. He lays there for a second, blinks a few times, and begins slurping it down.

I look out: we're on the edge of a dark desert. Stark and inarticulate. Desert sand disappears into the claustrophobic haze. Is it pollution over the desert? Is it my eyesight? Have I been myopic all along? Will I go blind? The sky is clamped shut, wrinkled like a squinting eye. I look over at little Sphinx; he freezes while licking his paw, his eyes lock with mine. I'm exhausted, put my head down and

[SEE: Metal white, metal tech rack, Rsim sheath, Foodsim sideboard open, Foodpak dangling off shelf, Rsim space.]

[DO: I I I chew, pace around box.]

[SENSE: Floor tilts as I I I walk.]

[EMOTE: I I I fear. Back of my my my throat (constricted).]

[RECALL: Period last, work demerit re: meatplant count.]

[PROJECT: Demote if I I I repeat demerit this period. All my my my germ dehydrated. Germ coveted, down the Tier C fece-pipe. Sexpartner like a vulturebride happy to select an upgrade in lieu.]

[SEE: Rsim AFace.]

[HEAR: Announce: Declare: All clear. You you you in safety: floor free.]

[SENSE: Tendons rigid after manip.]

[RECALL: Sexpartner servicing threshes.]

[PROJECT: C. Foodsim, different taste. Cannot distinguish animals. Tier C, not pleasant. C.]

[EMOTE: Dry, dry, dry.]

[COMMAND: Concentrate.]

[TASTE: Bird still on tongue from foodpak last.]

[EMOTE: Anxiety.]

[SENSE: Rsim gloves, floor tilting under my my my feet.]

[ANALYZE: Things I I I cannot see but are there. Example: Comp-coils underfoot, energy collected and routed to batteries. Example: Future.]

[PROJECT: Foodsim tier A so real. One clock less of work per cycle. Younger, fresher me me me.]

[EMOTE: Envy, anger.]

[DO: Move Rsim gloves, clench fingers, turn hand.]

[SEE: Via Rsim space: Threshtank moving through field, scanning left and right. Colors garish.]

[ANALYZE: Meatplants arrogant taunt me me me.]

[PROJECT: Down to D? Some Ds get moles. Infrequent Engineer visits. If used for fertility then no health upgrade. Appointments shorter. Nipples flaccid, breasts sag. Vaginas dry. Facial droop. Infrequent erections.]

[EMOTE: Distrust.]

[PROJECT: Acne, underweight, eyes dull.]

[DO: Direct tank to meatplant orange, large. Move clawhand, snip, toss into cavity.]

[SEE: Rsim AFace.]

[HEAR: Announce: Notify: End of cycle, Gate 1, The Sensational Outsider Zirkus and Phreakshow, traveling performance for Pures, cycle one duration. Suggestion: Go and view life on the outside, titillation, torture, and immorality. Qualification: Fee 3 milliliters.]

[SEE: Purple fill wall entire.]

[EMOTE: Startled.]

[DO: Strike out with arm claw.]

[SEE: Purple disappears. No movement only meatplants.]

[DO: Turn Rsim gloves.]

[SEE: View rotates. Meatplants.]

[DO: Continue turning tank.]

[SEE: Abrupt revolution of colors.]

[EMOTE: Disoriented.]

[PROJECT: Should have triggered razorwire.]

[SEE: Spots orange, small, outlined in purple. Fault line, silver, running through center. View fizzes, vanishes.]

[SENSE: Hands shaking.]

[DO: Pull off Rsim gloves.]

[RECALL: Department of Rankings. Smell of power and desperation (sweet and sour).]

[SENSE: Mind falling apart.]

[RECALL: The Zirkus.]

[ANALYZE: Opportunity sole to avoid demerit. Bring Nullsuit.]

[DO: I I I I I I I move to wall, press button, sleeper murphies down, place myself myself on bed, enter sleepstate.]

I lift my head. Guess I nodded off. Wait, I was dreaming something about whiteness ... or ... hmmhh. Lost it.

My helmet is at my side; Sphinx: sleeping on my chest, his back puffing up and contracting, his wings like two hands praying. I place my gloved hand over him and lie back. The sky is dull and blank like suburban dreams. I could be lifted up and sucked into the clouds like a leaf in a whirlwind.

Sphinx stirs. He arches his back and paws at my chest with his claws. He looks at me with emerald eyes; his pink tongue juts out between his sharp canines. He shoots a look left, right, back to me. I try to pick him up, but he makes a sickly, strangled snarl.

"Sorry, sorry," I say, holding out the back of my hand. He sniffs my glove, scrutinizes my face. "Good boy." He rubs his furry cheek against my hand, runs up my arm, and sits on my shoulder. I hold as still as I can. Don't claw my earhole, don't claw my earhole, please don't claw my earhole. I look over: he's licking between his toes.

I grab my helmet and get up, balancing on my cabriole of legs like the feet of two umbrella stands. What do I do with him? Might fit in the helmet. I scoop him into it and place it over my head, holding my breath and closing my eyes. His body against my cheek. I open my eyes. He careens from my face to the glass and back, crosses his front paws, sits down, and wraps his furry body around the front of my neck.

I seal the helmet with a click, and we step out into the desert, leaving behind the trails of a herd of snakes. Up an incline—a dune that becomes a moderately sloped bluff held firm by a dense network, a thin, ropey plant. Release some pee, which dribbles down my leg but is absorbed by the suit. I step down—

up to my waist in sand—   QUICKSAND!   —claw, grab—

a strand—

holding—

just holding.

Holding.

Not going deeper, not sinking; wrench my body forward and pull myself out. It's okay. I'm okay.

Could have died. Maybe wouldn't be so bad. Rest here a minute. Holy fucking fuck. I did just nearly die. What, again? Do I really care? What's happened to me? Fucking insanity. Sphinx is quiet, snug like a scarf. Sphinx is ... that's what he is. Or she. Did I not check? I guess it doesn't matter. Should keep moving.

I crouch on my chest, move sidewinder-style to distribute my weight evenly. The granules are so lightly packed that even a mild draft blows them in waves over the crest. I sit in the shade at the base beneath the lee, pick at the plant, and pull a length out of the sand. Unscrew my helmet and sit it like a bowl on my lap; Sphinx slides around like an ungainly skateboarder in a halfpipe. I hold out a strand to him, and he sniffs it. I bite off a piece. Tastes like a twig. Sphinx takes the twig between his teeth and gnaws it down. I break off several fibers and feed them to him.

Drowning in a deep blue sea.

The shade, cooling my body; catch the scent of chalk and papaya on my tongue.

A *shush-shush* of sand approaches followed by a creature over and down the dune into the feeble light. Spiny like a porcupine and about the same size— salamander limbs? Frog? Salamander. An oversized squirrel head. Squirrelpine sidles up in the penumbra of my orbit. Reforming, squishing like molding clay—grows a foot taller and thicker, rears back onto two legs—chimp-like limbs now. I touch my chest and arms and head—seem unchanged.

"Ha yu ound anyting tuh et?" the newly expanded Squirrelpine asks me. Eat. Found.

I pull up the strands from the sand. It crouches down, tugs, and breaks off a piece. Sniffs it, chews it. Breaks off another piece, chews it.

"Tuts ittuh guy?" he gestures to Sphinx with a tiny chimp hand, his voice like chopping sushi. I turn and look at Sphinx, who tilts his head up at me.

"Not sure. I think he came out of my temple."

"Heltee tull uh tissn. Can't getituhh." Help. What, pull? I pull up more of the buried net.

"Tie tuh glat tall?"

Tall, glat ... glass? Ball.

"I don't know. Protection I think."

"Tie i'tand tark an tinky?"

Tand ... tand ... sand. Dark and stinky?

"Is it stinky? I didn't notice. And dark ... uh ..."

"I tell ittinky rot. It it tee?"

"Uh ..."

"Tut it atove t'clahs?"

Clahs. Clouds. What ... is above ...

"I wish I could tell you. I've never been there. I don't know if anything's up there."

The Squirrelpine waddles closer and turns his back to me, on his side, quills flattened, his spine against my thighs (where my thighs would be if I didn't have snake legs). I replace the helmet over Sphinx and myself. We sleep. I'm awake without a dream. The three of us eat the root-like plants and when the roots run out along one dune, we move to the next. Crap out what feels like concrete. The loose dark brown sand mantles Squirrelpine as his fur traps it, causing him to appear darker and darker the more we move until he's completely black. We spoon to sleep in the minimal shelter of a dune.

I'm awake, and he's gone. I set out again across the desert, and soon we're traveling up a mild slope, wading through unfruited brambles, tall yellowing grasses, and tangled weeds. The sky is carved out of sandstone pitted with rust. Sphinx has found a comfortable position sitting on the top of my head, his legs dangling down the back and his nose like a ship's prow jutting forward and above me. He kneads his claws into my scales. Rather like a massage.

We come through brush over a rise; a stubby building about the size of a gazebo sits on a small plateau while beyond it stand tall black spears of beheaded flowers. I approach hesitantly. About twice my height to the top, the cubic building appears to be made of frosted lucite wrapped with a chain-link fence. The fence bends over the roof. No one seems to be around. Circle the building. Attune to movement. What's that? A piece of garbage ... leather? What is it? A bag, a water bag. Pick it up. Empty—son of a bitch, of course it's empty. Opposite side: the fence extends out from the building a couple feet—like the entryway to an igloo but taller. A cage? Looks like a door into the building within the cage. The cage floor is metal, a sheet that comes up a foot on either side like a baseboard.

Look around once more, listen, and sniff ... nothing moves. Stick my hand in the chain mesh and begin climbing. My snake legs—not much support. I pull myself up hand over hand ... this is too easy. How strong am I? At the top, rest my elbows on the lucite roof, less frosted up here, and look into the building. Inside are globes, colorful globes, some wobbling. No! They're heads, the tops of human heads ... people crammed upright, against each other, with no room to move ... hair from black to white and every hue in between. Maybe fifty people? Naked? One looks up, a male shorter than the others, a boy maybe, can't tell, with cherry-red hair, a jaw that juts out like the point of blunted triangle. Our eyes meet, and I feel electricity bolt from his eyes to mine—his arm shoots up pointing at me, he's shouting. All the faces turn and look up at me. Dull round faces, gaunt rectangular faces, walnut-brown faces with dark eyes and dainty cheekbones, square-jawed albino faces with weary eyes, faces with spots, weathered faces, skull faces. The boy, he's still talking emphatically, but I can't hear him. All their mouths are moving; I can hear a distant, dulled clamor from within. A few more raise their arms to point at the wall, the direction of the cage—all of them are pointing. The door.

Smell them coming. I can smell their shape, getting the contours. Three. Like horses, bigger than me. A sound—galloping—bearing down fast. I scramble down the enclosure; Sphinx grips tighter. Muffled banging from the building—the galloping closer. I throw myself over the verge of the plateau into the flowerless spears.

The galloping thud-clomps to a halt.

I hold my breath. It's quiet.

Several minutes pass ... did I not ... ? I haven't taken a breath. Maybe I don't need to. Feel the air tinged with chlorophyll, a sensation like fingertips grazing across my neck. Diffusion like goose bumps. Clicking and metal scraping sounds come from the building. Peek up: at the entryway, three creatures face the building. Animals. They stand foolishly unbalanced on dog legs holding up hippo bodies further miscegenated with cow udders that dangle like shriveled water balloons. Pin-cushioned black and white, faces like dented cans, and ears like tulips. Long thistled horse tails swish behind as if to usher together all these randomly sorted bits of animal toys.

One of the creatures has his head inside a panel in the wall of the building ... seems to be chewing. The door within the enclosure slides upward, and a person is shoved forward by unseen hands. A man with red hair—he's short—it's that same one, the boy. He turns to the door and bangs the sides of his fists against it and keeps banging and banging and banging and banging. Until he drops exhausted and slides to the floor, his arms dragging down the door.

The Cowdogs gather around him. He's sobbing, gulping air as if he's trying to eat it, fidgeting. Time passes, his breath slows, the creatures continue to observe.

He turns over, his back against the door, and looks up at them. Inaudible ... what's he saying? His voice getting louder, "... please, please, please ... please, please, please"—he staggers to his feet, projects his voice louder—"... isn't there someone out there who can help me? Someone's out there, please!"

A rope darts from one of the creatures to the boy and hangs in the air— another rope from a second Cowdog—not rope, tongues—tongues from their mouths wrap around the boy's wrists and arms, slam him back up against the mesh, and lift him up, his feet kicking the air. His scream slashes me.

The third Cowdog shoots his tongue out, and it wraps around the boy's neck twice, strangling his cry. He seems surprised—his rabid eyes bulge furiously back and forth, nostrils sucking violently. Should I, can I even do anything? Would I be able to hurt them? Sphinx rustles at my neck. Can't risk it.

The boy's tension attenuates bit by bit ... his body grows slack ... quiet ... still. Hung.

His body becoming tense again ... swelling, muscles expand, straining arms, popping veins, skin tearing, epic steroidal muscle growth—anatomical freakshow, blood dripping down his Atlas legs; interlaced muscle fibers visible, he blows up like an inflatable doll, growing three, four times his previous size, his face turning green; muscles turning green, his face fat and bulging, his whole body turning bright green

POW

like confetti raining down, turned into slivers of green. And all that remains of him is on the floor. At the bottom of the metal enclosure in a heap, the scent of chlorophyll stronger.

The Cowdogs have retracted their tongues, and the lead Cowdog returns to the open panel, rummaging with its nose. The metal floor of the cage slides out beyond the grated area to form a trough. The three Cowdogs dip their heads into the grass and begin chomping. I drop my head down and take a slow, deep, unnecessary breath.

WELL   WELL   WELL
WHAT HAVE
WE HERE?
                             WHAT
                                                          HAVE
                             WE
HERE?

I shrink into a ball—all at once surrounded by the three. Words clipped in their mouths, snipped like thread.

A CREATURE
WITH A SUIT
                             ANOTHER IN HIS
                             HEAD LIKE A PAIR
                                                          A SITE
OR A TASTY BITE?
                             SEXUALIS
                             SYMBIOTICUS
PARTNERS IN CRIME
                                                          LOOKING TO STEAL
                                                          THE RHYME FROM
                                                          OUR ANCIENT LIPS
HE'S DEFINITELY
AT SEA
                             OUT OF HIS DEPTH
                                                          A SHIP'S WRECK
                             LET HIM MARINATE
                             IN HIS OWN SALT
THE SMALL ONE
                             HE MAY EXALT
                             THE OTHER

Their words roll across me like globs of fat.

ARE YOU

THE SUIT DOES
NOT SUIT HIM

MUTE?

CAN ONE OF
YOU SPEAK

THE LINGUA
FRANCA?

THE COIN OF
THE REALM?

OF DESPAIR

YOU REEK

WHAT ARE YOU

THE BLOODY EDGE
OF NIGHT?

WEARING?

HAVE YOU
BROUGHT IT

WITH YOU?

SPEAK UP!

MAKE A SOUND!

INNOCENCE IS A
PALE WHITE SKULL

THAT'S EVIDENTLY
DUMB

A THRALL

I cannot move.

CAN IT
SPEAK?

LET'S MAKE IT

SPEAK!
TELL US

CAN'T TOY
WITH US

LETS REND THE
SUIT LIKE

A MOURNING
BREAST

A BREASTBONE

IT HAS SNAKES

FOR LEGS

LEAVING TRACKS

OF DIRT AND GREY

THE RED SUIT

IT UNDERSTOOD
ENOUGH

IT IS

PLAYING DUMB

AND STUPID

LET'S BE POLITE

FAIR ENOUGH

INTRODUCE
OURSELVES

WE

ARE

THREE

SISTERS

IF SUCH A THING

HAS

MEANING

IN THIS HERE
AND NOW

WHERE

BLOOD DANCES

AND BEING FLOWS
LIKE WATER

A SPELL

HAS BEEN

CAST

BROTHERS
ARE BORN

UNRELATED

AND SISTERS
ARE BORN

UNFEMALE

OR BROTHERS

OR BROTHERSISTERS

OR NEITHER

BUT WE'VE
MANAGED TO

STAY SISTERS

BECAUSE
WE CAN

Squirming before their hard, elongated faces and coarse hide, I roll my eyes to
see Sphinx. He appears to be attentive while flexing his claws.

VERY FEW HAVE
A CHOICE
                        MIND YOU

                                                BUT WE CONTROL
                                                THE FLOW
OF LIFE
                        MILK
                                                WE ARE THE TITS
THE CUTTERS
OF THE UMMH
                        BILICAL CORD
                                                WE CAN TELL
YOUR FORTUNE
                        IF YOU LIKE
                                                IT'S EASY
LIKE
                        THIS

The middle sister fires her tongue upward and backwards: with a wet slap
it lands between her eyes, now crossed and looking inward. The sister to
the left shoots her tongue out, landing on the first cow's neck, and the third
sister does the same on the opposite side. They remain motionless in a V,
the first sister's eyes rolled back into her head, showing the whites. A mouth
opens in her throat:

                    YOU HAVE NO FUTURE.

As they withdraw their tongues, I have an instinct—

I spin off my helmet, grab Sphinx, throw him straight up into the air—

their tongues are around me, wrapping my neck, slithering down my suit
against my body, clamping me in place.

I look up. Sphinx, his wings flapping. He is flying up, almost to ... into the
clouds, and he's gone. They each speak from a second mouth.

HE IS CLEVER

        THE ONE ESCAPED

                LET'S CLEAVE THE
                REMAINDER

A SURVIVAL
INSTINCT

        THIS ANGERS ME

                DEVIOUS LIKE A NOBE

WE HAVE BEEN POLITE

                ONE CAN NEVER HAVE

        TOO MUCH STOCK

NOW

        IT'S TIME TO TAKE

THE INFORMATION

                YOU WERE SAYING

ANNOYING

        LET'S SEE WHAT
        YOU'RE MADE OF

HMMHH   HMMHH   HMMHH

Humming in unison. Falling quiet.

SOME SAP IN THERE.

        NOTHING LIKE
        A REAL NOBE

                ODDLY STUNTED

ANYTHING CAN
HAPPEN

        TRUE

                REPTILE ENERGY

BUT IT'S ODD

        OLD CHROME

                HE SEEMS

DAMAGED

                MUSTY

        A RARE BREED

A BREED THAT
NEVER LEARNED
THE MEANING OF
WORDS

        OR HAS NO TONGUE

ANY NUMBER OF
THINGS COULD BE
WRONG WITH HIM

HE'S SMART ENOUGH
TO FREE HIS COHORT

THE COHORT MAY
HAVE BEEN MASTER

SHALL WE EAT HIM?

UNLESS WE HAVE
ENOUGH FOR NOW

WHAT'S ENOUGH?

WHAT ARE ITS
CHANCES?

WHAT DOES CHANCE
MEAN ANYMORE?

HOW LONG HAVE
WE EXISTED?

DOING WHAT
WE'RE DOING?

YOU KNOW WE
DON'T KNOW

ONLY THE STRONG
HAVE CHANCES

LET'S TOSS HIM IN
WITH THE REST

The air writhes like simmering hot tar. Their tongues unwrap and release me as the Sisters' bodies go spastic, their rear legs wriggling and growing thicker. They close their straining eyes, struggling ... return to their previous appearance.

My legs burn like torn muscle and broken bone. Grip them, try to hold them in—my vision fractures, splitting, tripling, shattered exponentially into smithereens, anarchic stained-glass window of ketamine-flatspace. No shapes, just movement and colors overlapping. My legs feel bigger, my knees bend backwards, my snake feet are merging, flattening out, my thighs grow stronger like coiled springs—feeling blindly, fingers contact my helmet, grip it—

leap as high and far as I can,

sailing through the air, wind against my face like cool water,

landing on my head, rolling in a ball, skidding, dirtburn my face, stones cut,

getting my feet under me, leaping again and again   and again   and again

until I feel a long way off, and stop to listen.

A shallow susurrus of the sky strokes my ears, and I taste a vegetable scent. Uniform brown except the sky which is sallow. Indistinct. No, not indistinct, pixilated. Blocky pixels—my eyes—touch them, no don't touch them— my eyes. Don't touch them. Replace the helmet; my arms look like needles. Maybe they are.

A swinging chandelier of movement appears—I swerve to avoid it—it's behind me—is it? Every direction is in front of me. I run, dizzy and kaleidoscopic. Nausea wells up in my guts. It's not getting smaller—tracking me—getting larger. I close my eyes and run and run, tripping, falling,

my forearms protect me, getting up, pulling my feet free, open my eyes— impaled by knives—find the clearest, lightest colors—run. I'm running into the beige.

A tap on the back of my head.

"... iskernt?"

My brain hurts. Uhhhn. Pain. No longer running ... firm cushions behind my back ... and fragrance of rosewater. My body leaden. Honey on my palate.

"Cahn't tell," to my side, gruff and low.

Turn my head, which creaks like an old door, and open my eyes: an eye is looking back at me. A single canary-bright eye living on the side of a purple wine bottle. A hand comes into view and pokes the eye, which blinks several times and glistens. Tears roll across it and fill up inside the bottle. I look back up: perhaps twenty or thirty feet above, a white vaulted ceiling veined in lavender—large room. Turn my head the other direction: a doll—plastic bear about two feet tall. A red hat and ears like quartered avocados ornament a spherical head that sits on a shiny camel-colored body. Eyebrows are imperfectly sketched on its excessively high forehead above a black-tipped ball for a nose and dark dead eyes. The doll's fat champagne-blush cheeks are split by a smile like a blood orange slice.

What is happening? Lying on a cushioned table, a white sheet with black trim over me. The doll hops up on my chest—weight of a sandbag. It looks from one of my eyes to the other. Fat arms a little too long for a normal teddy. Bathed in smoky light.

"Looks likees comprehendin'. Ja make shaw 'is mouf worked? Moibee ees listenin'. Could be shy or stupid." Beardoll steps off my chest to stand by my side. He leans toward me, his face square with mine. He's a sturdy little thing. "You awoike?" he asks me.

I feel my throat gathering strength, mouth moving, sound forcing itself out. "Yes."

"There ya' go. Jus' gotta let go, release the bolus in yer caant. Relax that tight sphincta'. So owd'yah stay smaht out there? Evry caant thass wandered in 'ere is dumb as a caant. Not as long as I remember 'as a biped made it. Which could actually be no time at all. Dunno. Can't remember caantall.

What about you?"

Untouchable grey shrouds and dull figures. "Not much."

"Right. What I'm sayin', arsecaant," Beardoll grins. "What were yuh, born yesterday?"

"What do you mean?"

"I dunno. Go wiv it. Whyd'ya even ask?" he grins again. "So, what'll we do wiv yer? And what'll you do wiv us?"

"I'm looking for someone."

Beardoll looks at me with raisin eyes.

"Oo are you tryna find?"

"Nothing is lost or found," I reply. Where'd that come from? He takes a step back—a small one given two stumpy legs. Another tendril of rosewater tickles my nostrils. "Well. What are you?"

"Whutcha mean?"

"You look like some sort of plastic doll. Are you a robot?"

"That's a stupid fahkin question, innit? What's a robot caant?" he asks.

"I know the answer." A sultry woman's voice weaves its way to me.

I look past Beardoll and see a small woman floating upon a voluptuous red and black chaise. Numerous torches in sconces along the walls light the room—wait, she's not small, she's large and on the opposite side of the room. She leans her body toward us and rises from her elaborate throne. She is very tall. A glowing halo floats above her head. She's taller than I am, and her head is disproportionate—more than four times the size it should be.

"'E's awake, Queen."

"Yes, I heard all that, Dumkin," she says, walking closer.

"Y'know the shite 'e's mouthin'?"

"Yes, I do because I can sense images of his ancestors. When I slide my senses through his spiral patterns, I get memories of perceptions ... perceptions of memories, ideas represented from his past. They eddy like water currents, and I can finger through them like a finfish. I can rearrange them, flow them in different directions. Slide them apart and reassemble them. Like a zipper." Her blue eyes sizzle my insides.

"He's talking about historical names," she continues. "You've got the words in your head too; you just can't match them up. The pictures are buried in there. When I touch him ... intriguing ... reminds me of ... how I came to be. Why don't you tell me what you are able to recall, how you came to be here, and then I'll share my history with you."

I sit up to look at her better. Graceful, lustrous, and completely nude. A flush warms her cheeks beneath the strobing corona above her head. She's wearing a necklace with what appears to be a calligraphic rendering of the letter "B" dangling between her breasts. Her breasts—casually present and overwhelming—candy pink nipples. As she glides forward, her crown reveals itself to be a halo of bees. And the night is in her hair.

A tic has assaulted my cheek. "Yes. Okay."

She turns her head, her prodigious girl head as wide as me. I follow her eyes to a grand window behind her chaise. A lawn so manicured that it appears to be brushed on with watercolors cradles a sphere of sparkling blue in the distance.

"Your eyes," a silken voice unwinds from her wide mouth, "were fairly useless, so I changed them. And your structure was poorly balanced, so I consolidated. Considering where you are likely from, I assumed you'd feel more comfortable."

The sheet slides off as I look down at my feet: bare white and consummately sculpted. A new me has solidified this moment. Human feet. Human? I touch my feet, but I can't quite feel them—the scales on my fingers repel the contact.

"Welcome to my demesne," she says.

"Thank you."

She gazes at me with cool placid possession. "Well, it's nice to have a guest. This is Dumkin," she gestures at Beardoll, "and I am the Snow Witch. You are surely hungry from your journey. Are you epicurean?"

At once I'm aware of how cramped my stomach is. I nod.

"Excellent!" she almost sings. "I think this will be a special occasion. We shall have waterbreather. See to it, Dumkin." The Beardoll turns and jumps off the table.

"Yes, yer majesty." He scampers across the room and scoots under a heavy white hemp-like tapestry hung in an archway.

"Now. Tell me your story."

"I ..."

"Take your time. What can you remember?"

My feet. Look at those feet. Are these phantom limbs? I'm wearing a fine-spun robe printed with a red and black ziggurat pattern. How'd I get here? The three cowdogs. Exploding human? Was that real? My arms, hands, chest—still scales. Careful. Don't reveal too much and give advantage.

"I'm not really sure."

"What were you doing before you came here?"

"I lose track of time. All I know is I've been wandering and searching. Heard there was a war, I think. An apocalypse party, and I missed it. Just slept through it, I guess."

"Searching for what?"

"Guess I'm trying to figure that out. A person. A bird. Who might be in a circus. Someone that can help me ... find the truth about my history."

"How about I tell you what I think happened and you tell me if I'm right?"

I nod.

"You were a huma living in a huma city. You had to escape because of a violation of act or thought or were thrown out for poor performance. You wandered around, were caught in a vortex or two—hence the mishmash of body parts—but managed to survive, and washed up here. You are confused and cannot find your way. Am I right?"

"Ah, that sounds about right." Not really.

"Mmmh," she murmurs. "Poor fellow. I can fix you up in the fashion you want to be. I'm not sure where you get this idea of a war. Your species didn't destroy itself in battle. It just became ... obsolete. According to my book, which is true history, it starts in a time—or perhaps a distant place—when humas worshipped stories. Stories of the past. Beings lived and died for them. They exalted the stories and the interpreters of the stories. Until one day, a creature *of* story was born. The Chimera, who was able to perform acts more astonishing than those in any story ever worshipped, exerting will through his seventh chakra. Or so I call it. And the Chimera was able to breed, and many of us were born, and they called us the Children of the Chimera. This much I remember. We touch things and re-write them. We can heal or end life. We were stories manifest. Spellcasters. Bodies were shallow surfaces to us. We walked the double helix. We plucked chromosomes. We ladled RNA.

The primordial protein soup. There was a time worshipers lined up for miles. All the old stories erased like so much advertising. Unfortunately, after some long duration had passed of continuous editing of forms (long after time had ended), we created vortices of alteration. Cast too many spells and ... they wouldn't stop. We induced magical resonances. Altered the fabric of the chromosphere. Bonds just would not commit. An example: Dumkin's mud. Squirreled up patterns that don't fit any living creature. The structures could not be rebuilt as they had been. But ... at least it was thrilling for a while."

She draws her finger contemplatively down her neck, her eyes cast upward. "I used to be able to direct it, but now every time I change him he becomes ... not quite what I wanted. I think I've become a bit forgetful what different forms feel like. It will be nice to have you here. Someone solid. I can get my senses in order again. I can harvest your structure, and it will all come into focus. Shape, mold, and pinch patterns, rearrange, insert"—she takes a deep breath—"messaging beyond death, good or evil. Unusual combinations stir me. Playing can be addictive. The ability you see is very ... arousing. I can make you into anything I want, truly anything. And I can *be* anything I want. But we've got forever, so we can take our time."

I step off the table and back away.

"Don't be scared," she says, crossing her arms. "I'll make you stronger and healthier. More interesting."

Farther away.

In the guttering torchlight, her eyes tremble like flames of blue gas—warm my cheeks, sear my eyes, and trace fire down my throat and into my stomach. She toys with her crown and causes the insects to flow around her fingers like a river rushing past a jutting twig. Where can I go? I drop my arms.

She strolls sinuously up to the table and hefts the Bottle of the Eye. She pinches the neck between her thumb and index finger as she tilts it back and pours some of the tonic into her mouth. The Bottle waggles in her hand, and she flicks it hard in the eye. It goes limp, blinks a few times, and tears collect inside.

"I have ... an incunabulum I wish to bring to your attention," she says as she holds the bottle toward me. The velvety fragrance of roses crosses my lips. With a clenched fist, I grab the neck; it drops—heavy!—catch it. Doesn't look as heavy as it is. Use both hands and swallow rosewater and tears.

"The book I told you about. It might lead you to this circus that you seek." She drops her arm over my shoulders, and my penis stirs. A chill runs through me. Movement outside. Steel myself and walk out from under her arm to the window. The effort feels like yanking out a tooth. Long shadows nuzzle the sumptuous royal chaise sitting on a platform of polished wood. The picture window behind the dais is framed in stone adorned with gilted images of trees bearing fruits and seeds; flowers; birds of all kinds: hawks and sparrows, crows and doves; and insects of many stripe: bees and dragonflies, beetles and weevils. Outside, a creature like a warthog on horse legs gallops toward the ball suspended like a water planet. When this Clydes-hog gets to the blue marble, it rears up on its hind legs—at full height its front hooves just touch the sphere—and paws at it until a hose of gleaming liquid jets from the puncture. The creature is carrying some kind of saddlebag on its back, and the stream spurts into the open bag. The leak becomes a trickle and stops altogether. As Clydes-hog drops to all fours, the bag swings down, and it gallops back toward us, to this—what is it? Castle?

"How does ... is that water? How does it stay like that?"

"Oh. That's the Voiv. I created it, melding and mixing, weaving and tweaking. Size constraints are easy to manipulate. Makes an excellent water tank."

I feel lightheaded and find myself on my side, looking at the intricately tiled floor.

"Where are my manners? You are exhausted. Why don't you just have a rest there on the floor, and we'll ..."

I'm in a room. This is a room, isn't it? Where am I? There are walls, there have to be; I can sense them at a distance, but I can't see them, and I can't feel anything. A ticking sound draws me around to see an old-time movie playing. Black and white. The movie is stuttering. Seems to be three figures in it. I come up closer to the movie, but it's not showing on a screen—film is skipping. I try to stay in one frame to see what is going on, but it keeps clicking past too fast to follow. Can't close my eyes because I don't have eyes, and the pictures are shuddering, shuttering past; I'm falling. Extend my hands but nothing is solid. A window. There's one, a frame right next to me. Try to climb, climbing out of the room, and I grasp an object cool and hard.

... our lizarnoid visitor and touching his scales. Very springy. Laughable at the obnoxious twit.

—He could be useful.

Queen gotta have last word.

—Yes, he appears to be a hardy hybrid. Might have some use. Not uselessly muddled like everything else around here.

Ain't she a broken fuckin fishie.

—Kaliban has got back with the fish and the water.

—Get the food ready.

—Yes, ma queen.

Queen Cuntress. Good thing the smile can't ever leave my face. Not when this form's got not just one expression. Suppose it's a bitter fate but better than most.

Cross the room. Under the arras. Down the back stone stairs. The stable. Kaliban, pawing the stones. He can smell the water and waterlife in a bag. Toss the joist hook over his back. Snag the saddlebags by the strap. Lift them off. Why's it always me? Go here, go there, catch this, catch that. Fuckin cuntsome cuntface ... suppose others are worse off.

Drop the bags to the floor. The water gushes inside. Fragrance. Of. Heaven. This makes it worthwhile. Stick my head in one of the bags. Absorb the purity in my pores. Water clear. Seeping through me. A snort. A tap on me side through the bag. Stick my head out the bag. Kaliban's disorganized, jigsaw face.

—All right already, witchdamdit, wait your turn.

Drag the mouth of a bag to his trough. Jump stomp stomp. Squirt out some water and a couple silverfish. Hooed the bags on the joist again. Roll the counterweight on the pulley rope. Knock it off the ledge. Down it plummet, down the well hole. The bags and me fly up the stair. Gather them onto the balcony. Drag them into the great hall. Princess Cuntlips. Reading her book. Fuck if I ain't sick a being her slave. Suppose there're worse lives out there. Could be eating my own guts to stay alive. Detach one of the bags. Pull it up over the brim of the stone table. Empty the contents into the table. Makin sure none plashes over. The water rushes from one side ta other, settling in place. Silverfish circle from one side ta other. The noid on the floor groans, sits up.

—Ah, my darling, you are uhwake. Are you well rest-ed?

Pretentious fuckin ack-sont.

The noid sits there, dumb as a plumb. Looking like cross-eyed cheese.

—I ... feel tired. Was I asleep?

The noid stands up. Power in his awkward moves. Probably new an unused but could be dangerous. Better watch him.

—Do you have a label?

—Uh.

Bright as a burnt stick.

—I will call you Lizzy.

Princess sucking on her fingers. Dammed, don't go into heat again. What was it? Oh yeah, stuck me up her cunthole and didn't let me out for seven days.

—Come sit with us around the table, Lizzy.

Lizzy the lizarnoid punkarse gets to its hands and knees. Stands wonky.

—Come over hu-eeeeer.

Is she liking this thing? She couldna. Never likes anything. This ugly thing. Queen at head of the table. Head tilts forward, looking at our guest. Long lashes. Leans forward on her hands. Gigantic udders almost touching the water. Boring as relatives who never leave. Lizzy opposite me. Hypnotized by her udders. Dumb beast if I ever seen. He looks at the water. Fish duel like rapiers hither and thon.

—Watch.

Princess grabs a flopping finfish dagger. Swallows it whole.

—You haaave to eat waterforms alive, or they dee-cay in-stantly.

He looks at the water, stymied.

—What's wrong? Are you shocked by hooww much water I haavuh in this one place?"

As if it know anything. Idiot thing. Why're we wasting good food on it? We should eat it. Fuckin dry-heaves obvious.

Click. My iris contracts. My perspective snaps from the grey bottom of a shallow basin to my scaly face. Just in front of me: a stone table with an oval depression in it. Don't remember standing here. My face. I'm at the table. On my left Beardoll, to my right the Queen. I remember now, I got up from the floor. I had been on the floor. Went over to the table. Did I? I did. She said something. What was it? *What's wrong*, that's right. What's wrong? What isn't wrong?

"Can you make me … human? Back to what I looked like before? I don't know what, but I was not …" I gesture at my face.

"Oh, Lizzy. That big red hole in it could use some work, but otherwise it's perfectly functional. But I understand. You want to be unified. I can make you back to what you were. The original monocult. Will take a little time. Need to rehearse the other parts before I erase them. I should write my spells down. So I can remember them. That's what I'll do."

I hope you are okay out there, Sphinx. I hope you survive. Somehow.

She walks toward her chaise, and Dumkin leans toward me. "She goes ter get 'er waterdammerunged book. That fahkin piece-a-shite book. Better eat fast or yer'll nevah."

I scoop up a fish, and my senses sharpen in a narcotic rush. The witch recurs in time, ageless and vibrant, cast in fiery youth by her alchemy. Dumkin sticks his paw in the water coursing around the table with the flow of silveryfinfish—clear within clear; he scoops up a silverform and shoves it into his mouth; the animal slides into his throat, descending like mercury into a vibrating haze. It melts and thaws, a crackling fire winking out, extinguished. I scoop the finfish and swallow it and swallow it. Another. Tastes like wet sunshine. Swallow another and another and another.

"Come here. I want to share this book with you. It contains a spell that will change you."

"Change me. I've had enough of that."

She laughs melodiously. "Oh, Lizzy, you are funny."

Dumkin snorts.

"All things change, don't they? Good and bad. That is nature. That's why nothing truly exists. Things are merely ideas. And a book … a book is a special idea. A mental form that merely *appears* solid. Thoughts. Ideas are nowhere. Where do they live? They exist, and they don't exist. Intangible things have so much power. Books were once worshipped."

She leans over and slides the "B" on her necklace into a slot at the base of her chaise. She turns it and pulls out a drawer.

"The intangible is tangible. Thoughts bump against each other like bodies. Every thought feels pain and pleasure. Here."

She pulls out a large book and holds it reverently between her hands.

"I keep this book very close because it is a mirror I can hold up to myself and see what is inside."

She sits down on the chaise looking at the book. She pats the chaise next to her. I approach cautiously. The book appears to be patchworked with thick strips of dull grey and deep brown, carnation and buff. The slow sky is baby blue behind her overgrown girl's head. In the distance, the globe of water filled with darting silver. She squeezes the book between her breasts.

"I think you should open it. I think you should read. You need to. It may lead you where you want to go."

She lets the book fall from her cleavage into the palm of her hand. I'm slipping and sliding inside. She holds it out to me. Up close, I can see the cover of the book is made of many skins of many kinds of creatures. I take it from her, cradling it in both arms. I sit it on my knees and run my hands over the parchment-like irregular surface.

Dry. Smells of must and age.

"The correct order is waiting to be summoned," she says quietly, touching the cover with the tip of her finger, her other arm warmly around my shoulders again. "Summoned like a sculpture in a block of flesh. Waiting to become if you have the courage."

The bees are buzzing above us. Her eyes a turquoise sea, her head—I can feel the weight of it—her breasts intimidating and imposing.

"Words are power. Using the right words in the correct order can unlock the center. Free the shambling animal in your heart. Imagination writ limitless, limitations unwritten, change the unchangeable, affect the immovable, alter the flow of life itself."

She taps the book.

"These words. In here. These words have been so cunningly arranged. Sorted and resorted, rearranged and reordered many, many times. In fact, these words form the capstone of many, many lives—not a literal shape, but an idea, the tip of a four-dimensional entity—that which our mind is a part of in the next spatial dimension. The wrenching split between our known space and the unknowable, a single electron clipped around the corner from the fourth to third; the trauma of that split causing the third mind to lose touch ... to be blinded to the four-dimensional entity we manifestly are. Reading it unlocks a part of your brain, the part connected to other dimensions, which flowers like a fractal sigil."

"This book has a table of conscience," she says. "You already know the story it tells."

Time is out of joint.

I slowly open the book to a page near the middle.

I stumble back from the table, backing through an archway, falling back, landing on my hands. What the fuck did I just read? She's coming, saying, "What's wrong now," filling the archway. "Did the story upset you?"

Caught in the bite of her neon eyes, balanced on my fingers and heels with my back toward a wall, the floor unforgiving and stone cool; her hand of moonlight poised, palm toward me. Out of the corner of my eye: the frosted body of Dumkin. A crystallized tableau.

I drop out of it and kick him square in the head. He flips and rolls several times before stopping on his face.

"Is that all you got, nubcake? Caahmon!!!"

I run at him—the stone beneath my feet slaps like a jilted lover—kick instep to mid-section; he flies end over end, caroms off the wall, "Wheeeeeeeeeeeeeeee"—off the ceiling above me—I duck—"Yeeeeeeeowwwwwwww!"

Down the hall, vault down flights of stone stairs, pass the Clydes-hog. There's a door—my red suit and helmet on a peg, grab them, fling the door open, outside. Run. Cotton grass, smeared sky—toward the shimmering sphere. Running. Kaliban with the Queen on his back chasing behind.

Running faster, the sphere growing, a full moon eclipses the light, and I can't stop—kicking off. Flying

SMACK

hung on its membrane.

It's pressing my body,
—I'm swallowed—

w e i g h t l e s s and t r a n s p a r e n t
quiet and clear
cool waters enfold me
beams of living light *g*
                                    y
                                      r
                                        o
                                      s
                                      c
                                      o
                                        p
                                    e around my center

                                                    a constellation of dancing lights.
                                        into
                        as I f l o a t
                and lifts me
            cups me
a hypnogogic pillow

A bell rings through my bones.

I'm expelled, fired like a shot out into the warm air, sliding through the grass in a sluice of water to stop face-down between two feet. I take a breath. I look up: an eagle's head with a beak as big as my face, a wide chest, close-cropped tawny fur, powerful lion legs, and godzilla paws with claws flexing. I close my eyes and put my head back down. It bawls like a child taking its first breath. I feel a damp swipe on the back of my head. And another. I roll over and get up. Four legs, a lion's body, and upon its head and wings something in the family of golden eagle plumage: tortoise-shell brown and black and white. It tilts its head quizzically. The eyes, green as a poisonous frog, examine me. At my feet, my red suit, drenched.

I turn. Kaliban and the Snow Witch are at the deflated sphere now rent with two long tears. She has both her hands on it, concentrating.

He licks my head. Sore. My body weak. He licks across my arm, leaving a trail of thick saliva; I wipe it off with my hand ... sticky. I hastily squeeze the suit out into the helmet, and we both take gulps of water from it. The suit seems to absorb the water, and it's dry.

I fall onto his back. With a few bounds and lift from his mighty wings, we come to a sky-blue wall with a fissure in it. The sky is blue paint. I dismount, and we both crawl through.

"How did you find me?"

He opens wide, caws grandly a few times, and lolls his tongue out like an idiot. I throw my arms around his neck and am shocked to feel tears stream down my cheeks.

Back into the grim haze that's grey and grinning like a mad dog. We wend our way through an angry tumble of rocks and off-kilter telephone-pole trees that punctuate our path as if an earthquake had made an emphatic statement. I cling to Sphinx's back, and he takes me far, somewhere, away. I'm skinless inside my plastic hassle. We're stopped by the appearance of a column like a slice in space that appears off in the distance.

"Let's go see what it is."

We ease up to the pillar. A ravishing crispness bathes the earth; I can see every particle of dirt and rock and stick, every grain of sand, speck of black carbon. A shaft of brilliant gold descends through a small hole in the clouds. Not gold, it's a cylinder of light. A moat of tiny, psychotic spikes of clear quartz form a circle, about twenty feet across, around the point where the light strikes the land. Outside that, the sand has been churned and fused into broken grey wasp-nest forms.

Smell of melting glass and smoldering cinders as we come closer still, Sphinx's feet crunching over broken bottles, and I feel heat on my face, and I feel tense. The light envelopes me, and my suit glows bright red; every strand of fur on Sphinx's back is a slice of eternity, my hand chimes in tune with each strand, line upon hyperventilating line, my swollen tongue; feathers on his head stand up, rustling darkly at the tips, white dart and white at the base, a warrior's flag dark and light, yin and yang combing my soul into strips, sketches, scribbles, sand painting; the air shimmies as before an open furnace, color of friction in my mouth, scent of a rainbow. I shield my eyes to look at the cylinder, which is about a foot in diameter. As I squint into the beam, I notice across from us, shielded by thick prisms of light, an object freaking in every direction.

I urge Sphinx forward, exhilarated. Drunk on sunlight. We circle around the beam of light, my face burning. We simmer and swirl frantically in flamboyant harlequin. I can't look directly: an object, a cube emits a dazzling prismatic spray. I slide off Sphinx's back and walk to the cube, avert my eyes from the glare to the black grass—stepping on unconnected fragments of my mind—off-balance, the shrieking light—lean in to the container for support and put my forehead on it, shade my eyes, and look through: a human head and torso with thick arms that end in stumps connects Centaur-like into a dark horse—not a horse, the body and legs of a bull—no, not a bull, wider and heavier with shorter legs in front, longer legs in back. Shaggy brown fur ranges from the broad hump to about halfway along its back becoming close-cropped to the hindquarters. I know this, it's part buffalo. Or bison. A bisonman.

It runs over me.

Through the bars of the showcoop I am see the Dog & Cat Twin arguing with itself. Its two heads askance at each other, hands gripping spears.

"Birds pant," is the Doghead pounding the spear with their right hand.

"Birds' pants!" is the Cathead pounding the spear with their left hand.

"What I am saying is birds were mammals. Which means they had personality."

"What *I* am saying is they showed personality through their pants. And we should change her into the purple pants with sequins for the next show. For variety."

"Define personality."

"Wearing different pants for different situations."

"That's a metaphysical definition of personality."

"Metal's physical."

"Yes, but I mean hypothetical."

"That's parenthetical. Personality is a word, which makes it a concept. And each pair of pants is a metaphor."

"Pants are not a behavior; it is necessary to observe traits over time."

"So is personality defined by others as such, rather than the Self? I tell you, it's unstable from every angle, and all suppositories are temporary. If you make essence depend on time then it no longer precedes existence, and your gist can't be genetic."

"A gist is the basis for a definition. We all get the gist of gravity. Even if we don't know the exactitude of its force, we still get the gist when we fall down the stairs carrying a load of fancy crockery and hit the dirt amidst a pile of crockery scraps. Gouging your thigh will give you the warp of the woof."

"Time is a hypothesis."

"Personality used to be pinned down in a dogtionary. A totality of distinctive emotional traits and behaviors found exclusively in mammals."

"So you theorize. There is no totality because life keeps on going. Every *meow*ment we are born again."

"Definitions like that are meaningless."

"Pants are a facile means to define her personality. Reify it for the audience. You know how G'nesh is acting about this show. This is the only city for which we've performed in a long time, so perhaps that's why this one is a big deal. If we aren't top of our game, G'nesh is going to recycle us. The girl's gotta sell it."

I am squawk, and they are regard. This coop. The bars are rattles of sensation in my body of bent and broken. I'm a quarantined universe; I am ache or I am evaporate. Desire and fear. Touch nothing. Stay here perched or in the air. This terra is infection by the disease of norms, normalized cruelty. Avoid surfaces. Touch nothing. Memories brand my body. How could I be started as one of them? Horrible. Before they are taking my arms and hollow out insides. White suits, faceless—as they cannot be face what they be. I am hate the programmers.

"No exact situation can be repeated although you can conjure up very similar ones," says the DogTwin. "Like putting someone in a room with three doors. The exact same room with three exact same doors. They are labeled 'one,' 'two,' and 'three.' Perhaps one of them has a vicious monster behind it or a tangelo. Perhaps it doesn't. Perhaps the others lead to a haberdasher or a donnybrook. It matters not. The situation is: What does the individual do?"

"But you would have to start them in the exact same physical position," replies the CatTwin. "Since physical size and shape can vary, that would be difficult."

"Undoubtedly physical size and shape have an affect on personality. But we're barking about a situation here."

"Insects," states the CatTwin.

"Did not have a personality. Too primitive."

"Put them in your test."

"Weakness is a prerequisite for personality. In fact, it may be the definition of a persona non grated."

"If you created an object maze and placed an unconscious insect. Then tracked his every movement on a graph."

"There's nothing to track if he's unconscious."

"After he woke up. You placed another insect of the exact same file and speeshum in the exact same spot."

"You would have to be very careful."

"Every limb would have to be in the exact same position."

"The body's orientation would have to be precisely matched."

"Track the second insect's every movement on a graph. If the two graphs diverge then you have unique personalities."

"*Bark, bark* you be sure that the first ant didn't leave a scent that might affect the trajectory of the second ant? You can't know. Or what if they were different ages? Or if you built a second but different maze to control for that eventuality, you could not be sure that the floor might have fractionally different bumps that would affect the insects."

"Personality is *REEOWR*."

"If the results are different, then their brains were geared differently. Insects were machines, chemically, neurologically cranking along, chugging forward against incoming sensoria. But mammals invite the potential for randomness. Chaos allows for learning and change."

"So test your theory on Anophelese, how 'bout?"

The best part of me is bird. Being air stroking my feathers. The border between body and spirit. The solidity of peaceful nothingness, free fall. My feathers become air. Swooping and rolling through hoops, through fire. Pause for applause/annoyance. To launch into the air again. But I am good showmanship to allow for applause; the audience are need to feel involved somehow, or they are unfulfilled.

Impatient. Back and forth on my perch, back and forth.

Eh, purifier astray—readjust. Stupid air mask wall against fecal air exhaled from the fetid units. But separates me from the air around me, inside me. Air is life. And life is dirty like the norms. Norms. As abnormal as anything could be. Fuck them. I am free. Lucky to be out alive. Curling into my head am a snail, a wormspasm after a rainstorm. Hammered on my wing bones, the force—calibrated, incremented—until I was fracture. The note taking. That note taking, want to shred every word and their bodies shred them shred them shred them. Healing torment day by day, the clocks and notes. Again and again. That room is a silver bowl. Deep breathing. Circling and circling. Breathing too fast ... slow it ... hyperbreathing ... slow it, slow it down ... slow it ... slow it ... there.

Too worked up. The past is consumed.

What were they say? Before they left? I was dropped from the air in exhaustion. The bile in my throat. Others like me, around me dying. Dragging a body on a leash, two were pass by talking ... experiment, a chained reaction, global genetic experiment infection. And after that, the look in their eyes falling on me were changed. From blankness to fear. They no longer were touched me. One day they were gone, the place abandoned, and I was alone.

"Fish."

"What about fish?"

"None but warm-blooded creatures had personality."

"Trees have personality."

"So you think plants have personalities?"

"They invented personality."

"They are pretty boring on that front. You have to distinguish between personality and a unique appearance. Each flower is unique, but each flower does not have a unique personality. No. Flowers, one can assume, given the exact same conditions—soil, light, nutrients—would react in the exact same manner."

"Except for genetic diseases. Which are genetic differences."

"So personality would have a genetic basis."

"You're saying personality can move from body to body regardless of the host?"

"Traits can move on, lets say."

"Genetic diseases were genetic differences."

"Genetic difference allowed survival."

"Personality is an entirely cultural construct."

"Personality is an aspect of intelligence. And intelligence is genetic."

"Define intelligence."

"Intelligence is making a conscious choice, having a personality. *Bark, bark, bark*."

"*Mmmmeow*, can o' worms."

"Were birds warm-blooded?"

"Did birds perspire?"

"Anything that perspires or pants was warm-blooded and would have a personality."

"Crocodiles, turtles, and lizards had personalities."

"Birds pant."

Be patient. Breathe. If only I could become the maker of a set. I couldn't be fingered instead of taloned? The show is all that matters. They must be the idea creators. I may become insane first.

"Birds were not mammals. They were avian of nature."

"Birds pant."

"*Fssss*, bird pants are what I am looking for right now because our cultural dilemma is how to create a new act that does not put G'Nesh to sleep."

"Or put us to hybridization."

"We will dress her in pirate pants. She flips up and down the eye flap, uncovers her glass eye. She birds a ... a cannon ... on a boat, a model of a galleon, which we build from scrap wood, and she fires a metal ball into the crowd. To keep it interesting, sometimes she kills an audience member. She walks the plank, dives into a tank of feathers. She poops; we pee. We collect tips from the crowd."

"*Ruuffff* about the airobatics?"

"Yes, yes, we will bring out a—change the hoops to be yardarms with sails, and she can pull stunts around the yardarms."

"She flaunts the glass eye."

"We bask in the long glow."

"We exit stage left."

"We get what we need."

The amethyst parrot disappears into the helium sky. Like to kill one of them randomly. The bird holocaust seared into memory like no other fact. It all turns on that. Units—untrustworthy, weak and obvious. My clothes tight to pronounce my form. I am what I exist to do. Breathe, fly, breathfly. I am do it anyway. Is it time to—

"Rain!" I am the cry.

Their heads are turn simultaneously toward the sound. Claw the coop door with my foot and shoot straight toward the gillies. Almost everyone are gathered at the perim, beyond which we are unprotected. Grip a tubed funnel and a bucket and shoot out—everyone the same—placing them beneath the ceiling; the thunderheads are low growls shivering calico and fierce; I am the feel of the air, the smell of difference across my feathers—wearing cool keen drizzle as a jacket. I am flight through the slate drizzle, dark and tender and beautiful and blissful; my wings kiss the grass, all of us glazed with the mists of elysium. I am a sprite striding through dew of translucency and ecstasy.

I am a perch upon the terra—for once—droplets of water effervesce around me, moments of life dying. Unattainable pure smell of life and peace. I am not feel myself at

Blackness. A terrible pressure on my chest. Open my eyes—a shaggy leg, a hoof crushing me to death. "HELP! GET OFF!" Flailing, my screech ricochets like buckshot. A glass cube, the bison creature.

"What ... is ... your place?" Bisonman asks haltingly.

"What? No place! Stop hurting me!"

"What ... are you ... doing?"

"Anything! Nothing! Somewhere to go! Just looking just food!"

"Hmmhh."

The pressure decreases, and it removes its foot from my chest. Muffled whistles.

Ow. No move. Just no move for a bit.

The creature's dark brown flanks. Muscular. Kind of appetizing. A monstrous bird throwing himself at the cube—Sphinx, right, Sphinx. His claws scrabble uselessly against it. Light outside is fading. I stand up and put my hand on Bisonman's side to steady myself. A howdah sits on his back with a pole going up to the center of the cube. He carries it on his back.

"You have ... purloined a puresuit." Two insect legs protrude from his mouth and iridescent beetle wings coat his tongue—instead of a tongue.

"What?"

"*Pure*suit."

Ehh, the suit? "Oh, uh, the suit. Yeah. I found it somewhere. What's the—this thing for?" I ask tapping on the cube.

"Enguardment against ... protean tempest. I know where food is found abouts."

"Uhm. Are you offering?"

"Aye."

"All right. Okay. Why not? Really, why not. But it needs to be for both of us. I can't go alone." I point at Sphinx.

A shrug.

"We can follow you." I crawl out from under; the beam of light shrinks and vanishes, the land returning to inescapable evening. Sphinx is panting, waiting. I put my hand on his beak, and he licks it, caws meekly. I climb onto his back, the dusk clinging to me like coal dust.

"Let's follow Sherlock here," I say. "He will ... he may take us to somewhere with food."

I close my eyes and jolt awake later.

A door. We are in front of a house. A suburban-style home. Stained wood siding. It sits in a grass yard. I'm on Sphinx's back. I look back, and everything is swaddled in fog. To my right and left, fog flattens dimensions. Moving forward is like falling, space is too naked when hidden. I knock on the door. No answer. I turn the knob and open it. From within: music. Many strings overlapping in rich harmony. We look at each other. I enter and hold the door. He squeezes through, and we're in a dark hallway. Sphinx breathes softly.

Down the hall, the music increases in volume. At the end, a door. Opens into a room.

A spooky resonance weaves a rhythmic thrum inside me. Straight ahead a creature sits in profile playing a harp. He is facing toward a window to my left; albino humans are throwing themselves from the roof of a building just outside and landing in mangled piles at the building's base.

                                                s
                                              w a y i n g   n
                                                               o w
                          through the air
              f l o a t i n g   p
        wafts across the room   l
      of notes   u
                      o   n
                    d   g
                  n   i
                e   n
              c   g
            s
          e   f
        r   a
      c   s
A   t

just as, one after the next, the humans swan dive to their deaths following
the call of the harp. Like performers in a circus. Surely the weeping rainstorm
of music will catch them. Others run hard at each other—forehead to
forehead—knocking themselves senseless.

The creature playing this Song of Destruction is black and twiggy, made of
strips of some overlapping fibrous material with preying-mantis legs, slender
arms, and extremely long, pointed fingers. Black Stalk taps his splay-toed foot
on the lime, melon and mahogany tessellated floor. The ceiling cops a rustic
attitude with thick oak timber and visible cross beams. On the windowsill,
a dribbling amoeba trails pendants of ooze as it slugs along. A woman with
tits on her back and a featureless face sits on a stool next to Black Stalk.
She wears a dress of many faces, faces making expressions, discordant and
unconnected expressions: happy, angry, quizzical, confused, scared, self-
satisfied. With her foot, she rocks a cradle. Against the far wall is a clock
with a face on it, but the hands of the clock do not move. The face is smiling.
A female mannequin enters the room through a door to my right. She speaks
inaudibly to Black Stalk; he does not react, and she leaves.

I walk to the window. I need to see what is out there, need to stick my head out and see these humans, to see if one of them can fly, to pull myself outside closer to them, and I bump my forehead. The window is a painting of a window. The figures on the painting are moving, plunging from the building—the people and the music stop. Black Stalk is no longer playing the harp. A black eye protrudes, peering at me from between his fibers. I look back at the painting, but there are no figures anymore and nothing moves.

"That was nice," I say.

Black Stalk ignores me and goes to the cradle. He leans over the bassinet and juts his eyes down. He pulls apart the husk of his chest to lay bare fist-sized black kernels. He wraps his fingers around a single kernel and tears it out. An oozing, stringy yellow pocket is left behind like ragged gums after a tooth is knocked out. Black Stalk seems to be pressing the kernel down into the cradle and grinding it as if he were juicing an orange half. After a minute he gives up and turns back toward me.

"That's the way it is. Like memories—it is faulty, enit? There no proof of nothing. Ya-hey, you look familiar. I wonder we meet before." Small black eyes like marbles. White-dot pupils. The accent, the cadence ... familiar sounds ... from where?

"Uhm. I don't know. I think a bison-man ... thing ... led me here. This back here is Sphinx." I motion behind me in the hall.

"That great, enit? Glad you stop by. I collect guest, all kind yet. I wonder if you meet Baby ever."

I walk over next to Black Stalk and have a look inside the cradle: a bronze-colored baby with corn smashed in its face. Black Stalk lifts it up and shows it to me. The baby is not reacting to the corn mush dripping down its forehead. He wipes the mess aside with a blanket and places the baby in the crook of my arm. Definite metal sheen ... hard and heavy ... not a baby, a statue or a baby that has been bronzed. Looks like a fat human baby with a small elephant nose.

The Gooey Amoeba has many small feet like a gelatin caterpillar. It has moved off the fake windowsill under the painting and squiggles a trail across the back of the woman with tits on her back. She wiggles as he walks across her breasts. The statue is cold in my arms. The woman drones as if she has a motor in some unknown orifice, and milk drips from her nipples down her back. She stands, walks to Black Stalk, and rams her hand like a javelin into his chest. She brings her hand out dripping with juices, clenched around another palm-sized kernel. She crushes it on the baby in my arms, juices dripping all over my red suit.

The Gooey Amoeba shoots off of her tits onto the Harp with a *thrummmm*! It's a pure and clear note—a single string struck. The Amoeba slides across and down the strings, a sweeping symphonic chord,

a g
  l
   i
    s
     s
      a
       n
        d
         o
               a fall

                                          a twinkling dance

     it's the sound of time splitting off from space.

And

David David Katzman

the child breathes on me. Like steam.

Its long prehensile nose is a gentle tentacle curling around my arm like a glass noodle.

Black Stalk smacks his forehead. "Cha. Dat some crazy shit, iah. I neba nuh ku pan no one do dat, an me see dum crazy shit backaday. Yuh got di obeah. Rispeck."

The baby has become warm and pumpkin orange. It gurgles at me and smiles.

"Uhm. Do you by any chance have some food? Could we stay here a little while?"

"Dat's right, yuh. Soon come."

He goes through a door to the right. I hand the baby to the woman with tits on her back and no face who slings it over her back by its leg, and it begins suckling. The room smells vaguely of incense. Frankincense? Black Stalk returns with a knife, a bowl, and a plate, which he sets down on the stool. He proceeds to carve a kernel out of his chest and dish it into the plate, another into the bowl.

"Fe oonu an yuh bruddah." I take the first to Sphinx and set it in front of him. He wolfs it down.

I hold the plate with one hand and shovel the food into my mouth with the other. Bursts in my mouth like corn. "Uhm, thanks."

The room is silent except for the baby sucking and my chewing. Sphinx has put his head down on his paws, and his eyes are closed. A tapestry in the corner of the room depicts a man—a human—with a jaguar flying above his head about to pounce. I finish and return the plate to Black Stalk.

"Thank you."

"Whey dun yuh lay dun dem rap, ras?"

"May I?" I ask gesturing to the stool, and he/she nods.

I sit down. Feels good to rest my feet. "Uhm, so. You're asking for ... my rap? Well ... someone ... I hear ... my rap, my story, is what it's all about. I'm trying to write one for myself. I'm looking for a circus. Where I might be able to find ... a girl. With wings. I want to make things right."

"BUMBACLOT! Give it up bout dis buhdguhl."

"Well, I've been searching. Uhhm. I mean, I think I've been searching. I don't know for sure or for what. But I have this memory, my clearest memory, of a girl surrounded by white fire. And I need to save her. I need to pull her from the fire and save her. Because ..."

Because I love her. I loved her. I love her. I loved her. Did I?

"I have no idea why. I have no idea."

"Dis ya dey di goodis reason. Whey else do yuh memba?"

Black Stalk idly strums the harp, triggering a short string of mental pictures: brick buildings, black roads, people who won't stop walking, going, moving, won't stand still, passing by me.

"I recall ... a city."

"Di city? Oonu lucky dey alive—ites. I dell yuh, iah. Dis, right heeya. Seem like yuh did dey homosap—stan ona plate lak dawg balls, nuh?"

"What?"

"Saahib. Ho-ehmo is funny. Yes, indid. Dhey eat dhe-ar own child's footure. Actlly like bairus. But actlly lookin-gh ona you now—pleaze!—I pershive rain dat changes is slow dee homochrome espect ona your bio-elogicle prospec-tius. Which iza vhery goot, becaaz ... I bein-gh ho-ehmo hunter-walla, is what my nem is called."

"You're a what?!?!" Raised my voice. Sphinx rustles his wings in the hall and looks up.

"Yes, dee same is true. I wood hunt ho-ehmos ona time to time."

"What? Where do you do that?"

"Just I wood drive to dis ting, dee sheety. Ho-em of deh ho-ehmo, right? Not too much far. You goa witha me?"

"A city? Yeah, I'll go but ... can we just stay here for a while? Catch my breath?"

"Sheety-Shmeety, do no be in tension. Is boring-boring. Free of cost! Where you are going anyway?"

"I need to not go anywhere for once."

"Huntin' homos iss tough, eh vato? Jew need a coo-icka hand ... jew-kno-wha'-I-mean?"

"No. I don't know—I mean yes, I know what you're saying—what the fuck is ... what is up with your voice?"

"What you mean?"

"Nothing, nothing, nevermind. Forget it. I should know better."

"Jew-need-to-relaaax."

"I am relaxed."

"Simmer down, no? For a colda blood ... you sure get caliente."

"Okay already."

"Jew kno wha' I'm sayin'?"

"You're saying that you need a quick hand."

"What it is dat?"

"Why?"

"That it is correct, what it is dat?" He points a stiletto-sharp finger at me.

"You're saying you don't know?"

"Pos si, I know, but I want to know if you know. No?"

"Cuz you're shooting them."

"How to kill someone and not take a life, mi hermano."

"Sounds like a riddle."

"It iss the riddle of life, issn't it? It is eassier to take a life than to give a best one. You see, I yam notso intrrested in killin' homos. I do dat too sometime ... when deemood strike me, but killin' iss downrigh' borin'. Changin' somebody'ss mind. Now *that* it iss interresstin'."

"Yeah, that's interesting, all right."

"You e-nevuh tinking sho? You e-nevuh tink. Me show."

Black Stalk goes to the unmoving clock with the smiling face. He turns the hands to the right, turns them to the left, and again clockwise. The nose of the face opens and a small bird pops out on a spring.

BOING!

Black Stalk pulls on the spring, and the clock swings out from the wall to disclose a small door with a horizontal handle. His fingers flow around the handle, and he pulls open a narrow metal drawer from which he removes an object: a smoky crystal conch shell. He rolls his long fingers at me like falling dominos, and I draw closer. Not exactly a conch, it has a cornucopian shape but with a hole through the center like a torus. Black Stalk tugs on the drawer handle again and an even deeper, wider second filing-cabinet-sized drawer pops out of the wall. Secrets behind secrets. Dozens of vials fill this new drawer; a hand of steam curls out, chilling my spine. We stand facing each other on opposite sides. He pulls out a vial and holds it up to my face. I feel stiff and tired.

"Dis is riquid hishtory."

Half filled with viscous solution, the vial is labeled, "*Pantera onca.*" He holds up another, "*Loxodanta Africana,*" and a third "*Balaenoptera musculus.*"

"Dese words nutting mean to you, me sure. Rong elase by dee Glate Nihiwators."

"I don't ... know. They are genus and species but I don't know what. I could guess." Elephant? Africana sounds like a place.

"Genius an specious. Geniis and spay-sheez. Unlemasterbate since dee Glate Unlavering. When dee waws came tumberin' down."

"That's nice. What are you talking about?"

"Net shee now ..." Black Stalk strikes the base of the cornucopia and a cartridge pops out onto the palm of his hand. He places it upright in the drawer. "Now, mmmh"—he squats down, looking at the sides of the vials— "tiss one"—he pulls one out and tilts it, *Ursus maritimus*—"an den"— *Leontopithecus rosalia*—"an anudder"—*Mantella aurantiaca.*

He uncorks them, pops the lid off the cartridge, pours about a third of each vial into it, re-corks, and replaces the vials in the drawer. He repeats this process for two other cartridges that he pulls out of his chest before replacing them. The vapor licks his stalks like a cat's tongue. He snatches up the first cartridge, locks the lid, and agitates it violently while giving the drawer a hip-check shut; another blast curls out. I smell the chemical crispness of dry ice and feel woozy. He slams the cartridge into the bottom of the crystal horn, slides two fingers through the hole, and spins the piece gunslinger-style. The steam crawls up Black Stalk's body and clings to his fibers, metamorphosizing him into the burning husk of a self-immolating monk.

"Den we go ki'wus some homos."

We are at the front door, the door is open, Black Stalk is in front of me, Sphinx just behind. The air outside is blurry. Confetti is falling.

"Holt!" calls Black Stalk.

We inhale as one, and across my tongue I taste cool enchantment.

Black Stalk motions us to stay back, and he steps outside. I can see now. Snow. Bone-colored fists of snow raining down, and Black Stalk's rail of a profile is weaving and capering among the white globes, his line breaking up and reforming, extending and shrinking, lightning jagged and clean, dancing amid the spheres.

"Flozen watuh!"

Black Stalk stops. Bamboo against twilight. He pulls an object out of his chest (possibly one of the kernels?) and flings it into the air—it strikes a snowball—fireworks, a fireworks of limbs, of lace. It lands, and it's a plant, already planted, immediately grown.

"Get bucket!"

The woman rushes from the door, thrusts buckets into my hands, and pulls me behind her. They're setting buckets down. The feathers of snow drift like ideas. We pack them into the buckets. Sphinx stands with his mouth open to the sky, tongue sticking out, catching snowflakes. They melt across my cheeks. I scoop some into my mouth, and a choir sings.

The snow stops.

The woman trundles back into the house with buckets in both hands. Where did this raised ranch come from? Weathered wood stain—is it character or faux character? Black Stalk comes up beside me and remarks, "It my memento mori. Itn'i quaaaain? Now! Fowow me den."

Bars of fog rise up on all sides toward a hazy circle like a urine stain; it's as if I've tumbled down a massive well. Have to run to catch up to the strutting Stalk, who is taller by several feet. Soon a wall appears, and we are up to it. Seems a touch concave. The wall goes up so high—is there a top? Are we inside or out? Dark grey mortice lines outline rectangles of beige concrete like circuitry spreading outward and upward into impenetrable exhaustion. He stops in front of the wall, points at the unmarred surface.

"Dis heel dee wawl of tee shity. It boobytlap. Dey waw temselves in. Even wawl out a wota homos, I tole am sho. Dee corored peeper. Now dose lef be wewy mewalin chawenged. Dey wike ghose. Dare puwity is smehwls ... smehwls of deaf."

Black Stalk walks along the wall, and we follow, traveling in what seems to be a great, slow circle around his house. Seems to be the opposite side. Two steps lead up to a porch and a rocking chair while an aluminum frame containing the frazzled remains of a screen poses as a front door.

"How bwoody quickwe dee homos fehw, my deawuh chap. Ah wi'took wuda ludge, ludge, link, link. In dare hawts, dey know dee big cwock stwuck. Too cahwup, too clool—aimetty inside an shawow shurfashes. Shui-shide wishuwary by compehwishon."

Before us: a vehicle up on blocks. A two-seater bobsled. At the front, two rickshaw bars project forward and a tangle of straps dangle between them. To the side: that glass cube. Next to the sled, the Bisonman with his eyes closed. "So mote it be." Talking in his sleep?

"Hey Dion!" Black Stalk barks.

Bisonman flings his head around, "Attention!"

"Wake up. It me. Kernaw Bwack. Nee my wheews." Kernel? Colonel Black?

Dion runs off and comes back with four large red wheels on his arms. Colonel Black slaps the tires on the sled while Dion fits himself into the straps. Colonel Black hurdles into the rear bucket of the vehicle and says, "Wet go!"

"But ... I'm not sure I'm ready to go yet," I say. For fuck's sake, just got here.

"Ah, you nee be ahways wedy to go, fren. Go on, wet go."

Fuck. Got to see this city anyway. Find some humanity. Maybe I don't need to find a circus, just some sanity. I pet Sphinx on the head. Into the car. We roll off the blocks with a thud and continue smoothly and rapidly up to the wall. Just in front of it: a pit able to swallow me lengthwise three times across. Drops a few feet straight down and then slopes under the wall. Dion steps down into the hole with his front legs — we jerk forward, rolling down. I crane my head back but can see nothing. Dirt-dark. The tunnel levels off, and Dion trots along at a modest clip. The light has vanished behind, and pitch-blackness fills all the crevices. Detached, enclosed in cotton balls of blackness, alone, and alien. Time disappears in the up and down, up and down, up and down, up and down, up and down, up and down, up and down, up and down, up and down, up and down, up and down, up and down. My body, what's happened to it? I can't feel anything. When a light appears in the distance, my body returns; a candle grows to a window and becomes a rocky cave mouth. Disgorged from the cave mouth into the wan light at the top of a hill, we halt among head-sized stones before heading down the slope of blue grass. Why am I continually blindsided by this sky that hangs like a noose overhead? In the distance, another grey wall forces its way upward and to the left into the pea soup. The city must form a ring and this is the outer edge. To the right, the wall butts up against a bright blue forest. A river is visible along the bounds of the forest. Seems familiar ... was I ... three small animals, creatures on pedestals. A bird. A bird? Slaughtered? Did that happen? This does not bode well.

Dion pulls us beeline for the intersection of the river and the wall; the forest comes into focus across the yeasty suds. Pot roast mates with diarrhea against the roof of my mouth; static tickles my eardrums. The static amplifies and separates as we roll up, becomes moaning, moaning like thousands of creatures in pain. Or pleasure.

Once up to the wall, I notice a stream of black shit spewing from the city (or is it a *sheety*, as Black Stalk called it?) and melting into the rose-hued river. The odor is overwhelming. I feel woozy, and my pores tighten.

"Mek yu no torch dem wol, Akata. Se yu torch-am na kil dem go kil yu, na so e bi for dis ples."

Don't torch ... touch ... the wall. "Got it. What is this? Garbage?"

"Yes, dem dey shit. You wit mi go rait insaid dia shithole."

"Oh. That's sounds about right."

"Put leg for rod, broda."

"No. Wait. What about Sphinx?"

"Hea' mi. Im fit swim insaid-am."

Take that as yes. "But is it dangerous?"

"Noting no dey sef."

Nothing no ... day ... they safe ... nothing is safe? "Dammit, come on. Could he burn or melt or get eaten?"

"Aks-aks. Ah sabi sey dem tings hed no koret, atol. Bon troway ... e no get sens ... go hia-go-dia. Dem no fit sey mek a chop yu."

I get out of the sled and walk to Sphinx. Behind me Colonel Black says, "Go!"

Get right up to the side of his head so he can hear me over the caterwaul. "I think I should go into this place. There may be ... people ... I don't know. From my memories I have. Of beings like ... like ..."

A face. White wings.

"I have pieces of memories. Half-memories. I want to go in there and talk to them. I need to keep looking. Maybe the past will catch up with me."

The bisonman runs back in the direction we came but without the sled.

"But I don't want to go without you. Would you be willing to ... dive into this? You'd have to swim under. It's pretty much a river of shit. Errh, sucks. Totally sucks. If you do, we could both be inside."

He trains his ardent eye on me, opens and closes his beak, and caws. Seems like a "yes."

"Waka! Go kom no dey!" calls Colonel Black, "D kwik. Shain ai."

"Okay. I have no idea what's going on. I have no idea what's going to happen. Just ... follow us," I tell Sphinx, petting his neck again.

Get back into the vehicle. A small dome rolls over my head and with a click seals me in. Look behind to see one is over Colonel Black's head, too. The car drops nose-forward, and I bang my head against the dome. We roll off the embankment and dive into the river.

Grease flows brown and yellow and tan. Bloated intestines covered in fungus swarm after slicks and bladders of sewage and gas, glue and snot, dribbles of pudding. Gaping, ruptured bodies expose grotesque, tortured organs.

Organic slime and bubbles of liver sway like undersea fauna. Muddy sage gruel spreads glum and suppuration.

We pass between the thick, rusty bars of a metal grate and break through the surface into darkness. The dome slides back, and gloom dances across the jagged underbelly of a festering metal leviathan. Colonel Black is holding up a burning bundle of sticks, and in the fidgety light I can see sheets of scum stream off the sides of our vehicle into the aqueduct of filth below. Ahead of us a narrow channel continues into darkness, and on either side are steps and ledges and obelisks of iron. A maze of protruding bars and bulkheads. Sphinx. I panic. His head breaks through the surface like a feathered periscope, and I'm calmed. Take a deep breath—the smell is outrageous! Bile burns in my throat—spew over the side.

"Come, no incourage dem," says Colonel Black.

Not going to breathe for a while.

Sphinx has clambered up and onto the selvage, dripping with excrement. He shakes like a wet dog, and the dome slams back into place—Colonel Black must be controlling it—shit flying everywhere, spattering against the sled and our shields. Eventually Sphinx gives up, and the dome retracts. Colonel Black has looped the end of a rope around a cleat in the middle of the sled, and he throws the other end to shore. Sphinx clamps his beak on the rope and pulls us to the side. We climb out, and Colonel Black ties the sled to a bolt protruding from a rusting I-beam.

"Hia di smel-smel wota-wota shit from im bele, di bortom pot, dorti-dorti mes-mes," he intones.

We thread a course among the planes and platforms and beams of metal beside the oily, black channel. Dirty and foul, Sphinx pads along with sodden smacks among the creaks, groans, and moist splats of the sewer. A buoy bobs just ahead in the canal: an icy, celery-colored jellyfish dancing in the flitting firelight. Closer ... around its side ... two lights, candle flames dance in deep gouges. I freeze. Sphinx tenses beside me, air whistling from his nostrils, whistling faster—

THUD

He's fallen to his side, wings askew, legs thrashing.

"He's hurt!"

"Ye kpa! Na baba jiga bi dat." says Colonel Black.

"WHAT??? **No!**"

I step toward Sphinx, but he goes into a seizure, claws striking out, wings beating wildly—can't get close.

"YOU HAVE TO DO **SOMETHING!!**"

I turn to see Colonel Black silhouetted against an immense gelatinous monster risen from the canal—a dripping, colorless capsule teeming with chihulyesque cilia. It falls toward us.

"**LOOK OUT!**"

Sprouting like branches from a wicked tree, its phlegm-coated arms catch it gracefully, and it ripples forward. Colonel Black turns, sees the thing right next to him, leaps to the side—the torch sails up into the air

BANG against a metal platform,

the torch winks out.

I inhale frenetic air charged with ions.

It rises from the dark: a mammoth gob of a head, two empty sockets lit from inside. A gross mouthless, noseless face comes toward me. Sphinx's claws screak against metal; I'm paralyzed as it closes—it skims past me toward Sphinx. I throw myself sideways, between its many stiff colloidal arms, to wrap my arms around its body—yelling and screaming, beating on it, punching, clawing—I'm pounding a mound of rubber. I'm powerless and drop to the floor. I am powerless and drop to the floor.

The torch winks back *ON*, and the monster is hovering over Sphinx, running its many arms over him, its cilia sliding into Sphinx's nose, up his nostrils, and into his mouth. Metal bar, weapon? What can I grab? Tug uselessly at a post. The thing separates from Sphinx—and he's clean. The black slime has vanished.

It glides toward the canal, its legs like the tines of a music box, but stops before me. It swivels as its bell-shaped head sinks down into its body until its burning eyes are level with mine. I look in, and the flame is hungry, opening wide to take me. I can see myself dancing in the flame. It flicks at me like a lizard tongue. *I am Gad*; did I just hear that in my head? A hole appears: mucilage disgorges all over my chest and hands.

Gad continues to the sewer channel, ignoring Colonel Black, and sinks beneath the surface.

The scent on my gloves creeps into my mouth: yeast. I lick the goo, but not much comes off on my tongue. I lick harder and break off a small lump—press it against the roof of my mouth. Bland. Like oatmeal. Sphinx's paroxysm has ended. I'm next to him, scooping the secretions with my cupped fingertips and shoveling them into his mouth, drool down his chin. Colonel Black is next to me.

Sphinx moves his head and opens his eyes. He looks at me, and I feel a surge of adrenaline. He gets to his feet unsteadily and continues licking goo off my hand.

"God don bota ma bred! Yu do wel-wel," says Colonel Black. "Mek you hori."

Sphinx seems refreshed. Standing strong again. I point: the torch disappearing in the distance. Follow? Maybe it's time to run? To where? Which way? Probably into the arms of death. Crushed likely. Could be buried or diced. Wherever I go, easy death here I come.

We clamor through the maze of haphazard metal until arriving at a door. Colonel Black pulls a crowbar out of his shuck and applies it. Outside: concrete and more concrete. A concrete hallway and windowless concrete walls. Light grey and featureless in the crisp primary light of antiseptic LED strips that run along the floor of concrete and concrete and concrete and concrete. This must be the city. We must be inside, not outside. I walk behind Colonel Black and next to Sphinx, my hand on his side. We move down the hallway and through several crossroads. Eventually we come to another door, which Colonel Black also crowbars open.

We enter a large, high-ceilinged room filled with several rows of small tank-like vehicles too small to fit a person. In the second row, a woman is inserting a metal wire into a tube mounted on top of the vehicle. Skim white, white as a tablecloth. Over-the-ankle white boots, skintight short-shorts and a white tube-top. Large, round breasts. Straight white hair to the mid-point of her back. She's solid, muscular, and lean. Do I know her from somewhere?

"Sista!" cries Colonel Black.

She looks up. She closes and opens her eyes, rubs them.

"Hail!" says Colonel Black.

He draws his cornucopia and puts the small end to his mouth.

She is speaking to us — "........." — I am shouting: "NO! **STOP!**"

He blows into the end and there is a sound like the blat of a trumpet as spittle flies out of the bell and splats on her cheek. She steps back as if embarrassed, puts her hand to her face. She convulses, and a gagging sound chokes from her throat. She removes her hand from her face — her mouth is now in her forehead and her face has vanished. She leans forward, her hair falling from her head in hunks — skin turning spotty grey and blue — her eyes now on the back of her head—she is tearing at her shoes when her hands vanish, arms shrinking—turning to flippers—webbed toes erupting from her shoes, frog toes—spotted fur growing madly out of her body all over.

Ice-cold air comes in quick short stabs against the back of my throat. I grip Sphinx's fur in my fist and whisper, "Let's go, go"—backing up to the door, turning the knob—Colonel Black whooping, "Tally ho!" We are out; yank myself onto Sphinx's back as he runs and runs, turning corners, running, running, running. My legs sit over his furry shoulders, his wings are my saddle, and my arms wrap around his downy neck.

"Okay! We're good, we're good!"

He finally stops. I dismount and look around. Concrete. I will smash my skull on this concrete. Another crossroad of sidewalks. The air is still as death. The concrete: abrasive and cold. Grey, grey god of cities, what the fuck do I do now? I close my eyes. Listen to the silence. A distant sound. A humming sound. Open my eyes; I'm facing Sphinx's golden brown axe-head and stern eyes. Disapproving elder statesbird.

"There," I point.

Travel two blocks. Hello there, bank vault. Turn the metal wheel at the center, pull the heavy door open. Beyond: a clear, thick, plastic tube ribbed at intervals like an intestine. At the far end is movement, two-legged movement. I dismount.

"You ready?"

Sphinx could open my arm like a book with the wicked sharp hook that punctuates his beak. Instead he blinks and lets out a single cry.

"You're speaking my language."

I lead the way. Half a city block down the tunnel before it opens into a semicircle-shaped area ... filled with people! Humans, more real humans. It's a miracle. The floor is dirt, the ceiling and walls are some olive-colored fabric, tent-like. The people, they look like—exactly like—the tank woman.

Young-faced men and women, crisp and starched, muscular and strong. Silk-haired men, solid and blowing with health, massive cock bulges in their short-shorts. Women: noses small and faintly upturned, those same outfits, same as hers. An orderly line against the tent wall. Absolute white blonde ... indistinguishable. Except one in a red jumpsuit just like mine. He's alone; the rest stand in couples—male-female couples—in lines to the left and right that meet at a podium straight ahead. A few of the couples have a child with them.

In the middle of the space is a large banana-colored peddle car and—what's in it? A clown? Holy crap, have I found the circus? Yes, a clown steps out of the car. Dressed in a garish purple-and-red fleece jumpsuit with a silver moon surrounded by stars on the front. He's got a lopsided egghead crosshatched with jagged black marks as if a shark nipped his naked pate. Moist flaps of meat for lips, no ears, and a round red nose. His one small eye looks wistfully inward toward a pinkish eyehole gored like a broken heart where his other eye should be. Above them, black Xs stand in for eyebrows while below, red mascara bleeds down his cheeks.

This One-Eyed Jack goose-steps forward—no—he makes a 180 and slams face-first into the rear door. He stands dumbfounded while the crowd laughs. Pulls back to reveal the closed door has caught his sleeve. He wags a stunted finger at his sleeve as if to reprimand it. Yanks, but it does not come out. Tries to pull the door, but it won't open. Puts one leg up on the side of the car and pulls. Now the other, leaning back and straining with all his might to extricate his sleeve.

He falls back, his arm torn right out of its socket. Son-of-a-fucked-up-bitch, course it is.

The arm dangling from the door has left behind a spewing hole. He pulls the torn arm out of the sleeve that cradles it and jams it repeatedly back into its socket in order to plug the geyser from his shoulder ... and repeatedly fails. It won't stick. The people are laughing as he puts his foot back on the car door for leverage and tries to tug the sleeve out with his good arm.

Why? Why bother?

His foot goes straight through the door. He's bleeding all over the car and the dirt. Tries to stand, but can't pull his leg free of the door—his foot is jammed? Ah, it's a trick, of course, a trick. Puts his other floppy foot against the car door and makes a tremendous effort. There, his leg has dismembered at the knee. Crowd is roaring and clapping. Now he's crawling around the car in a bloody circle, pausing to clench a fist at it now and again. He pulls a couple balls from his pocket and attempts to juggle one-handed, but the balls bounce off his head and roll in every direction.

I step off the plastic onto the dirt, and the crowd hushes. They all turn and look at me—a strip of blue candy dots—except for Redsuit, who is fixated on the woman behind the podium. They chatter and point.

Walk toward Redsuit—can feel the clown's eye on me as I go by. Stop and turn. The left side of his eczema-encrusted face registers surprise while the other half pools like syrup. Do *not* talk to a bloody clown. Keep moving, keep moving to Redsuit. His hair is white; he looks like all the rest. Taller than me by a bit. Holds a fishbowl helmet under his arm. Where?—no, mine is gone. Somewhere.

"Excuse me ..." as he turns, he shrinks in fear and drops the fishbowl.

"See you feel shock state I, I, I join suit to trade."

"Uhm ... I don't want to trade anything. I'm just looking for some information. I feel like I've been running forever."

"Suggest I also."

"Uhm. So ... what is this place?"

"Feel confusion see nullsuit consider pure kill." His tone is flat and uninflected.

"Are you threatening me? What's wrong with you?" Sphinx caws angrily just behind me. The couples in front of him and behind him abandon the line.

"Action escape clean join zirk request help."

"Uh. Yes, I am requesting help. But I don't ... what am I escaping? At least tell me what this place is."

"Consider exchange. Projection go with you."

"Are you talking about him?" I gesture at Sphinx. "He goes where he wants to." I point at the tent wall, "What is ..."—we've moved up in line now until we are at the podium. Behind the pedestal is a female, human-like except for the four arms moving in a rhythmic blaze. Her skin has a warm pecan hue. A person on the other side hands her a small test tube.

All at once she:
holds it up, eyeballs it, uncaps it, and pours the contents into a funnel in front of her
hands the customer a ticket
takes a vial from the next customer, dumps it into the funnel
hands him a ticket

Redsuit has taken out a small bottle, uncaps it, and hands it to her. He turns to me, "Query manager location."

"Uh ..."

"Command move it," says the woman. Redsuit looks back at me then disappears through a vent in the tent. These humans have turned out to be less helpful than I had hoped.

"Is this some kind of show?" I ask her.

The woman continues selling tickets but looks me up and down. "Where'd you come from?" she asks.

Whoa. Good question. I'm from un-fucking-believable land. Here I am. Crowds of albino humans, a floor of dirt, walls of canvas, and a solar flare captured in the form of a woman with four arms, big almond-shaped eyes, and a river of golden brown hair. And a breathing Sphinx behind me. How did I get here? There was ... Colonel Black ... a city. Before that ...

"What did you come here for?"

"Yeah, I don't know. I'm looking for someone. I don't know. A girl with wings."

"Huh," she says. "What about him?" pointing with one of her hands at Sphinx while continuing to sell tickets with her others.

"He seems to stick with me."

One-Eyed Jack appears next to me, standing on one leg, gnawing on the fingers of his detached arm.

"It's okay," she says, waving off the clown. "Just look at 'em. Joey'll find a use for 'em."

The podium splits in half like French doors as she pushes the tent flap wide and steps to the side. I walk up the center with Sphinx behind me. Four-armed woman holds out a ticket as I pass her.

"In case anyone asks any questions, tell them Sarasephi let you in."

I take the ticket.

A blur of blonde hair and blonde skin quavers like a heat mirage in the dim, undefined light. Something rumbles distantly as we walk on hard-packed dirt down a curtained corridor through crowds that part like bow waves before our prow. Eating scents of licorice, rot, and roses. Sex and sweet, pungent opium. Cat urine and old feet. Under a curved dome, we walk down corridors of curiosity through a maze of small, open-fronted, olive and tan tents. I'm attracted by performers who stand near the entrances: a trio of mystics in the lotus position, their bodies long and lean, intently squeeze their own legs into one thick leg, into four legs, or eight legs, braiding them into twirled cones, a ring, a sideways eight; several muscular snake-bodied men play brass flutes for veiled, six-armed dancers who gyrate on four legs with skirts and sleeves billowing and slicing circles in the air; a dirty leech corrals confused worms in a wicker basket—rolling and knitting them, the cement-grey annelids tearing themselves apart in fear; rashers of mildewed leaves bubble and spit, slur and slide to form and reform slush piles that give off light-blue fireworks before swallowing themselves anew; a trio of large squirrel-like creatures chitter and squeal as they hump each other heedlessly; a whirling dervish ascends in a mad dash like a rainbow nudibranch swimming into the air, a corkscrew ribbon of mollusk-fat wings; sand-colored sidewinders writhe in battle, S-curve snapping S-curve; rabbits ejaculate meatshrooms; smiling, fat babies float in barrel-shaped aquaria of brackish solution exuding acrid formaldehyde and roses—evil buddhas waving hello.

"Come in." A figure has just exited a tent. As I walk past this black-bearded, turbaned man, he beckons and holds the drape up. I catch a glimpse of a small white pony sitting on its hind legs with a prominent ivory horn protruding upward from its forehead and a silky black-furred female smiling as if dazed, experiencing too much, her hand on the horse's mane. She opens her mouth and gives forth a deep throaty moan. I rush on. "Come!" he calls, but I continue faster.

That tension again ... I heard before. Coarse, stratal chimes like the ringing of dirt-brown earth. None of the norms (how do I know that term?) seem to notice. They bustle into tents and visit vendors of trinkets and action figures, push aside curtains, hold out eyedroppers above funnels leading into tubes. Tubes that skirt the walkway lead me onward toward the sepulchral gong, moving against the flow through the crowds along with irregular groups, a few going in the same direction until I'm walking alone under pale light from lichens hanging like lanterns from poles, nothing except the booming deep sound almost too low to hear. Like space breathing. Treading unknown territory with soundless footsteps, following the increasing power of the reverberation until I come to a single dark tent. The note hums through every part of my body.

A slit in the tent. I feel light as I pull it to the side and step

<pre>
                                              into
                                          my
                                         space
                                          comes
                                             a signature
                                       I have
                                         not
                                           . met
                                             before

            lightened
                  by my
                        h
                          u
                          m
                     m i n g   the
                                       beauty
                                        of
                                         all
                                          living
                                           things

      is
          the meaning
                  the beauty
                      of living
</pre>

sharing

his   sensations   the

state   and   yearning

the   constraints   of

body   of   atoms

in   desire   to

s u m

as one state equation

and   form   a

c   t

r   n

o   e

s   r

s   r

c u

with

my vector

and

we sum

into a **greater** v e c t o r

the **v a s t**   e   m p t   y   spaces

of his physicality   are   recognizable   as   a   song

the summation of beauty in the moment the

thrum

m

i

n

g

beauty   is   all   the

unitary

ontolojest

the everlasting laugh

and so
we sit
this creature
and I
while   I   am   seismic   and   exhaling
expanding
                    he sits
                    breathless
                              bewilders at my meninx
he has
                                             vanished
I hope you'll   find
        love   creature or
                you   forget
that it's missing and
I hope   you'll   tune   in to   a melody

and sing spirals
        into space and
        unspace
      join the unceasing harmonic
        that gives and separates and flows like the surface of a bubble,
        the fragile surface of life

... will improvise. The song. Feel itchy. Different. Not sure why. Heavy vibe from Gnesh's tent. Like a volcanic heartbeat. Got me frazd. Joey's keyed. Kinks on edge. Nerves with spoor of hysteria. Wutafuk, I'll drink it. Taste, trust, ride it. Toss aside the old, just this once and see what comes. Nerves. I can do this. Manipulate the crowd. Be the point of their view.

The entryflap yawns at me. Like the audience. Bored with waiting. Bored. The emotional lattice. Boredom. That could work. Scope it, that'll be a challenge. Trust it, trust yourself. Valid instincts. But what if they're wrong, I'm wrong? Can't do that, can't think like that. Parch me, I can do this. What about Moon Dragon? Never good as Moon Dragon because I can't do *one* thing. Failure. Heed-heed. Preen carapace, bang them fat mitts together. Juice it.

Clamp a claw on the canvas and toss it. Less than a wisp against my exoskeleton as I pass through. The crowd's emotions push at me. Fright. Fascination. Expectancy. Uncertainty. Irritation. Loathing. Exhilaration. The rectangled audience is full of pale dollheads. Stick figures with no meat on their jutting bones. Row after row. I let them gawk. Disturbed. Balance on the fat fan of my tail. Unfurl my antennae, the feathered feelers unrolling. The emoticons amplify, cascade through multi-channel connective filaments, neural knots amped up.

I open the net wide. Capture every member of the crowd. Leave the exec tier above for the moment. Pull in their feelings through my net. Give them time to soak me in. Soon they begin fidgeting in their seats. Repugnance. Irritation. Boredom. The key: one with the other. My net is charging, animating with sensation; pull them in and charge them. Time to charge them, connect them with my **radical-empathy dot net**. I will return their feelings, beginning with boredom. Amp it, feed it back, let it rise. Then play these players, conduct their sensations, their systems nervous, their nervous systems my instruments, and I'll make them resonate in emotional symphony.

"... detonate their insides, their guts," I say.

"Never saw your act."—"That is fascinating."—"It sounds lovely, it certainly does," says the Twin.

They nod significantly at each other then turn their saucer eyes toward me, my snout reflected on the surface like a trapped fly.

"Raddle them into labyrinth shapes they didn't know were possible, that's what I do. It's an orgy of demons. They love a horror show. Can't believe you haven't seen it."

"Well, it's not like we go out any more."—"Indeed, it's been so long, I don't remember when we last made an effort," they go on.

I head to the bar and ask Sarasephi for a drink. She flips four bottles in her four hands and pours a shot of each simultaneously into a mug. Pure and crisp. Just a taste before the show.

"Thank you." She smiles politely, and the tassels on her leather vest flutter. I can't help but marvel at her features—effortless yet refined.

"You want to juxtapose after the show?"

"You're not my type. Go bother your pal Maphro."

Life is tough on a chick with alligator lips. Dessic it, I'd eat her alive anyway. Literally.

Survey the greenroom. Handful of kinkers on break. The Dog & Cat Twin is arguing with itself again, butting long tube necks and big heads. Feh, I'd tear my own head off. One of my heads. Chubby furball panda Orfeo—another big-eyed bum—cries into his water as usual. The dancer, what's his name? The leggy featherhead sits transfixed by his own slender muscularity in the long mirror behind the bar.

"You give them what they think they want, and they'll walk off cliffs for yah," I toss out the side of my mouth.

"What?" she asks. "The stringers?"

"No, no, the Units. They were powerful. I'll give'm that. So much, they destroyed the past *and* the future. They don't get it. They'd phreaked. Still don't know it. The very thing they fought to avoid. Gotta be insects. They're so locust. Could be machines. Maybe they succeeded in their desire to be one with objects. If you pulled the plug on 'em, they'd collapse like electric dolls. Could you conceive of them trying to survive outside?" I gesture toward the wall.

"Uh-huh," she says, non-committal.

"Come on now." I turn to her. She's wiping down two mugs. "You've heard? They're why the outside is how it is. The Culling. They were testing genetic weapons on prisoners. Long and tedious experimentation that spawned many diverse forms—most died." A sip of the water. So angelically invisible. Indivisible.

"Unable to stop breeding, stripping the bio until it became the burnt embers of time forgotten. The criminals, the unpropertied (right, interchangeable), everyone fighting for scraps. Eventually, all were just dumped out there, and they let loose the genetic revolvers, flinging material everywhere constantly. So they inverted nature, made a prison of the outside, and ... and now there's no place that isn't. Can you taste the irony? Turn 'em out and turn 'em into animals. Food to be hunted. Higher intellect merely allowed them to distance themselves. Rationalize the selfishness. And the lower intellect, the instincts they supposedly outgrew gave the driving force. The whole house of cages was built on that."

Do I actually think this? I'm trying too hard to impress her.

"That's one story," she says, looking at a mug. "There's no telling the truth. Life may be how it is for a reason nothing to do with them. As things stand now, we've got a tent over our heads and water in our stomachs. Thanks to them."

"Is that seriously what you have faith in?" I accidentally snap my teeth shut with a loud crunch. The Dog & Cat Twin stops arguing long enough to look over. My thoughts careen out of control.

"Sure. We're privileged. And how much longer is this gonna last?" I ask her. "You know it. When was our last show? Do you remember it? They've become few and far between. You know why? Y'ever wonder why? Thought they were the apex of evolution. What a laugh. I read their minds; I know the truth. Runaway remnants of a dead-end species. Pathetic." I'm sickened.

"How do you know that?" she asks me. From the bar she grabs a rolled up copy of the *Memory Hole*, that rag written by the squid, and places it in front me. "We can't know anything since The Unwriting. How do you know anything?"

"I don't know anything," I say. I look past her at the mirror. My face appears green and flat at this angle. I tilt my head—back to normal black gator maw. Odd. "That's not what I mean," I say. "Even though amnesia rules, my instincts know the difference between cruelty and kindness."

"Oh, is that right? Then why do you enjoy torturing them so?"

"I put the mirror up to their face and show them what's there. S'why I dress like a black hole," I snap the sleek, black latex outfit that covers all but my mouth. "It's the cruelty of truth. Time they faced it. By this point it's too late. So I might as well go down hurting the monster that brought this on."

"That's speciesist. You're a speciesist."

This conversation isn't going as I'd hoped.

"Maybe so. They're the last species left. So fuck 'em."

"Yeah. And you're under this traveling shield because ... ?"

Time to withdraw. I slam my drink, grab the squid rag, and head for the stage. The Twin stops to squawk at me, but I throw the withered newssheet at them. I don't remember fuckall from it anyway. What good is it? All the goddamn chatter about the kinkers and their bits.

Peeking out from behind the stageflap, Maphroditee winks at me and rubs the canvas against hes tits. That randy rabbit boygirl, my stagehand, fucks anything that fits ... I like that mind ... wish I had hes incorruptible stamina ... my desire, much more seasonal. Don't envy what's inside hes eyes: saffron with flecks of madness. Time to hit the stage in the small ménage tent.

Maph has already taken the guest and sat him in the spiderflower with contact points against all meridians.

Put you on stage and drown you in my bloodstream, magical blood.

Look at this crowd. Look-a-likes, feel-a-likes, act-a-likes. The chromatic codification and behavioral modification, thought control, emotion suppression, self-rejection, abdication, genuflection.

A red suit, eh? Helmet on the open seat in the first row. Eyes fishing—more scared than your compatriots. Red suit. Well, the novelty wears off quick. The cruelty of your interior ... let's take it in ... empty it, take your nothingness and wrap it around my finger, my legs, my ass, my stomach, my tits, my arms, my neck, my face, my eyes. All slick black, obsidian black ... touch my sickness. The truth ... you think. I know what you think—black is nothing.

Black is everything.

Sit down behind the large, square magnifying lens and tap my chest; ah, not again, no, yes—spikes pierce my nipple-holes. Maphro hooks my left entry-hole into the vat. Grit hard. Take it. Rushing through me like magma ... my hands give off steam from arteries close to the surface. The blood, the blood, plied with blood. Spills from my right exit-hole onto the surface of my electroskin.

"Command: Close your eyes," I say. Center. Thoughts are energy. So: across the barrier I quantum tunnel into your mind. Time to vibrate unsympathetically. Matter of will. Bleed thoughts on black. My skin reflects a story. Time for questions. Begin simply. "Query: Your name," I probe. *Sys* comes the response, so I write it across my tits.

"Query: Family," I continue. Nothing. Blankness. "Query: Cohabitation." Sputtering words and slithering sensations. The tropes gibber and wabe before — yes — they cohere enough ... release, expurt them onto my stomach. Forms, faces, movement around my head and ass. The flow and dance.

"Command: Identify beings." More faces, bodies, a female's face — draw a picture. A small child. Names.

"Query: Their locations now." Confusion. Chaos. No clarity. Give it to me; open up. There: inchoate but: the woman with tools stands next to a thresher in a large room among other machines. Unusual Pure, Sys, your thoughts so disorganized.

"Query: She is your, your, your sexual partner," I push. Affirmative I hear; write *Yes* next to the illustration on my stomach. You sad Units ... can't keep your eyes off my magnified body. Excuse to ogle.

"She is not here with you today?" Disappears ... fear. I write *No*. Come back to that.

"Query: Good fucking. Command: Describe sexual encounters." Sys/my POV: tongue on my cock; my cock inserted into vagina below me; her body sweaty, sliding across mine; her face contorted, her chest compressed against my chest; her punching me in the chest, smacking me in the face; her touching me with long fingers. Scenes of semen squirting, dripping, convulsions, clitoris. Sketched in lines of red as if I haven't seen this scene unmemorably many times before.

Trephinate: "Recall: Your, your, your cruelty. Your, your, your selfishness." Veer to a face, a female … see her as … less attractive, inferior. In quick succession: she is talking to me, a jumble of words (*boredom, change*); a military figure on a projector speaks to me; uniformed guards—a military force—rush into a room and take the female who is whimpering. Drag her out, her wild face looking at me. This scene ducks behind another: walking into a larger room pressing buttons on a machine, eating food. Her face comes back. Paint that face with red tears.

Ah, you try to think a new scene. Typical. Scrape that off and reveal that you Units want it shown, exonerated, made worse. You want to feel the pain again, to pick the scab and let it bleed to prove you're alive. You want it out of your control. Seen enough of this. Let him change the subject.

"Query: The child." A child sits in a room facing a wall with Rsim machinery. I graff it.

"Query: Reason they are not present." A thresher machine. The view from a thresher projected on a wall. A purple eye fills the view.

"Query: This event." Words answer: *Projection: Machine destroyed.* Deconstructed imagery of the thresher flipping end over end—the memory fizzles. Signified hypothesized. Draw it flipping end over end. Smashing.

"Analysis: Not so good, Sys." Projection: Exile. Guards force me me me out of my my my home. Thrown out the gate. Creatures come at me me me. Creatures: all teeth, claws, spines, blades. Blackout.

"Analysis: Your reason for being here without your sexual partner and byproduct: escape." Fearful: A blast of light and perceptions, he twists in his seat trying to look at me.

"Command: Close your eyes! Turn around!" Face him with a wall of teeth. He turns back, closes his eyes. What's wrong here? I've seen this … back of my mind, cannot pinpoint. His story is familiar.

"Query: Reason you at Zirk." Overlapping madness, a frenzy of thoughts: pulling ropes, unrolling tents, lifting ... prancing ... flying, a trapeze ... cleaning, sweeping ... cocks come at me, in my mouth ... in chains, lashed ... black and white fizz ...

I cannot stand it. "Command: Off the chair. I have had *enough*." And the images trail off me onto the floor in a puddle.

He scrambles up, tearing the contact points off his head—*SCREEEEECH!*

[FEEL: Unsteady.]

[DO: Breathe, stand still.]

[SEE: Hemorrhage mess, long-faced animal with many teeth and hard black nullsuit.]

[ANALYZE: Fortune Teller.]

[HEAR: Baby Joh-ee. Heez the one you will need to bargain with.]

[DO: Walk to chair. Grab helmet.]

[FEEL: Vertigo.]

[DO: Mismanage route into crowd.]

[SEE: Darkness.]

... breathing darkness and sensational claustrophobercizing light evaporous darkness shining

"Hear me, females and males and spawn of such! Purest of Pures! Homo saperior! Command your attention to the center of the ring. Around the ancient pole sculpted from one of the last noble trees. Our totem that protects us from the deadly outside. Command: Look at the stage now. Query: See life. Query: See anything. See nothing! Nothing at all! You see nothing. Nevertheless, analyze: He is there. Agap. The moon dragon. The terrific tenebrific serpent of subfusc with a beak so sharp it cuts dreams. He lives in his own sphere. He is there and not there. Nevertheless, you will meet him. Command your patience. You will see him. He is worth the wait. He will find you, and you will know when he is there."

hello creatures how are you rhetorically speaking this moment never to exist again already gone slipt its mooring lost its bearing like Zeno trying to reach life all the monkeys in your backs I am mythmaking I am meditating without time no time allowed I do not want to know time anytime when I am needed they come get me although I am alone because they know I am the heroine heroin so they cannot approach what they want only one thing really what they want I give out is null in the void the null set it is a thought and a thought is nothing so nothing is nothing is nothing is nothing is nothing you are null and avoid facing your nonself your nonsense this non-set is null and the void swallows up love and love in a vacuum must be abhorred therefore I am most hated of all they despise what they want because they cannot have it again oh the humor I enjoy the giving of love because I never want it I can even stop time fuck time it does not does not exist you hear me of course you do knot give out love but yes love in a vacuum cannot abide therefore I am most hated of all I am amused and enjoy the giving of love because I never have to receive it because let me tell athink you cannot love time because time does not exist in a vacuum like *like* does not and love does not made up to lookalike but I give out life but life in a vacuum will ab nihilo ad nihilo what does this mean I mean how can meaning exist in a vacuum and we live a chasm-pierced existence a vacuum a lovelife sucking vacuum ab nihilist ad nihilist this behind-the-scenes scene in front of the schemes I give out love in the vacuum that inholes and yowls banshee in nihilate in time into time is a tool that does not exist and the love goes yowling down into the vacuum abomination I am the smiling mask of love in the scenes but where is the substance of the mask if you look sideways it vanishes and if you look backways it is ugly and that is where all the action is and I give out love in a vacuum is unhated because it is unrevealed and who sees the humor I do and enjoy the giving of love and those who hear go in one and out the other in one and out the other is the process repeated endlessly until death do us part is an old phrase unheard unspoken anymore except the sound of your own voice screaming it in a vacuum which is to say ab nonthing ad nonthing is a vacuum but there is life in a vacuum not our version but it is whirring with life even nothing has life and a gap is the thing and the hole is the whole and I see the beauty of nothing which is the beauty of love I have been called centimental before because I am one hundred times crazy with love that is the show it is inescapably the show because brother got to eat right although that is metaphorical I do not eat I just absorb the light and synthesize but I do need H two to the Oh and it is the same thing and in the sweet thereafter later much later in the aftershow glow it lazily builds in the back of your minds a nagging a dawning that it deserted you and you do not have it and you never had it you are not and you cannot and you want and you will get emptier and emptier and the falsehoods are told and they drop in the holey bucket as the vacuum sucks it out of you because a vacuum ab whores you and I am not ab whored ad whore because I am not taking and you are not giving and that leaves me with everything and you nonthing but to the show of love which is reification in action my friend my good friend my love it is a field that is felt but how does meaning mean anything and what greater meaning than love when the end is coming it is all coming to an end the end is unavoidable undeniable unimpeachable does it matter when my pictures of love melt in the sun does it matter when my words of love burn in a nuclear furnace when the asteroid comes when the whole will become the hole but despite but the spite of it all I am love and can transform you and stop the asteroid death from coming love can change the course of the deathteroid the dathterdlyroid I am I can dehydratoid of love astrotime does not exist it is all time all the time perhaps that helps perhaps not perhaps love matters or perhaps it is beside the point no point no nothing know nothing knowing nothing the audience simply sits as they are defined to do as they always do nothing even when they are doing something ab something ad nothing and

as I enter the stage you do not notice me I am faint tenuously bounded by
stage lights and I begin:

breathing darkness   sensational light e v a p o r a t e s

        becomes   more   and   more   d i f f u s e

light sources absorbed shrink

and sublimation settles in

                        objects recede

like
        pieces   of
        a   jigsaw   muzzle   floating   away
and sounds muffle until dead silence reigns and

Weigh on you until you cannot move not a limb nor head

I fill up underneath you and you are cupped weightless hanging inches above your seat

You

I swim into your veins warming you

you who will die with an ice-cold heart understanding barely the surface of bodies blindly grope for each other no matter how hard you push never get inside

filling your cold heart with

I love you

chemicals

I love you

quieting

even the most frenetic

in this age of anxiety

I love you

I love you

calm

your inner voice

and all is

quiet

a nonsensation

.

.

.

until I release you to fall back into convention, slide into your seat, weight lifting, objects returning, noise rushing in until

CRASH

"... scape artist. You will never see a more daring, more amazing escape! For Orfeo Six will escape death itself!"

I"m in the ring..
Raw..
The audience..
Anophelese wanders up to my side..
The audience recoils..
They"ve never seen insectivora..
He rubs my leg with his antennae..
He spreads his pincers and takes a chunk out of my calf..
He drops the strip of fur..
After preening the blood from his face with a leg,, he begins licking my open wound..
I can see it in their faces,, the audience cannot fathom my stoicism..
Pain,, comfortable friend,, fire of life..
I turn you into a snake,, a spiral,, and encase you,, hold you close,, wrapped like a gift..
You beat like a heart..
Clear space for contemplation..
Soon my insides have stopped flowing out,, and the wound begins to heal..
In moments,, it has healed over..
Anoph rubs his carapace against my leg and wanders offstage..

The tight rope..
Will it be the tight rope today??
Looped around my neck by the Bigboy Tender Hooks the musclegirl..
One end of the rope in Tender"s hands,, the other wrapped around the horn of the ponderous rhinocerasaurus,, Buttons..
Backing toward diametrically opposed points of the ring,,
the loop becoming snug around my neck..
Tender steps up onto the ring and leans back;;
the rope tightens on my neck like a brick chokehold;;
Buttons steps over the ring with her hind legs,, her middle pair of legs,, her front legs up on the ring,, and then she sits back;;
the rope slices into my neck,, squeezes through the muscle to my esophagus,,

which soon ruptures,, and my head lolls forward dangling by my spine..
My body will fit loose,, held up like a sheet clipped to a clothesline..
Buttons and Tender strain until the rope sunders a vertebra,, and my head
thuds to the floor,, my body slumping in a heap..
I can see,, the last sight with my eyes,, clear spinal fluid dripping onto the
stage before ... ...
then what??

Tender:: I scoop you sometimes into a bucket or drag you ... ... tuh the witch..

Gnesh.. The body maker..
Somehow with the same memories..
I feel like the same person who just died..
I can see myself having died over and over again,, so it would seem I have
never died..
My memories..
I don"t know if I"m real or not..

Swallowing razors,, perhaps today I will swallow razors..
Sit in a chair watching them watch the life seep out of me,,
too weak to lift my arms and then
too weak to move my eyes and then
my perceptions cloud over or it is my thoughts that
became clouded and unsure before ... ...

I have tried every time — — the reason I agree to being this person,,
this undying phoenix in the show::
I want more than anything to grasp that moment
the transition from life to death..
To know what the going over means..
The process,, yes,, the process,, but that moment of ... ...
passing ... ...
from wake to sleep ... ...
the threshold ... ...
the border ... ...
inscrutable..

Objectify it,, hold on to it..
This episode will be different..
I shall use will,, use it,, pin the moment,, don"t let it go..
I will remember,, remember,, remember..
I cannot conjure up a single memory of the time between..
Do I dream??
Can I range beyond life??
The rebirth that will come..
The rush of endorphins and anguish — — like blood rushing into a sleeping limb..

Each day is my last..
Dead again in the world of the living..
Alive again into the world of the dead..

I examine this audience..
I can see them in minute detail..
The women in the tier lofted above appear younger than those below..
And their hair is shinier..
Their noses are just a few hairs breadths thinner and straighter..
Variations between those below ... ... in the weight of their cheekbones,, subdued pointing or rounding of the chin..
The eyes are duller,, greyer..

Tender lifts me up and places me in a tall,, transparent tube..

You,, audience..
You are all dead too..
You just don"t know it"s coming..

I begin to weep..
I begin to weep tears that fill the tank..
The tank fills up to my chin in moments..
A lid is dropped,, I am compressed beneath the salty water..

I feel my lungs collapsing as I hold my breath for far too long,, one big inhale..
Gushing horror..

Trapped

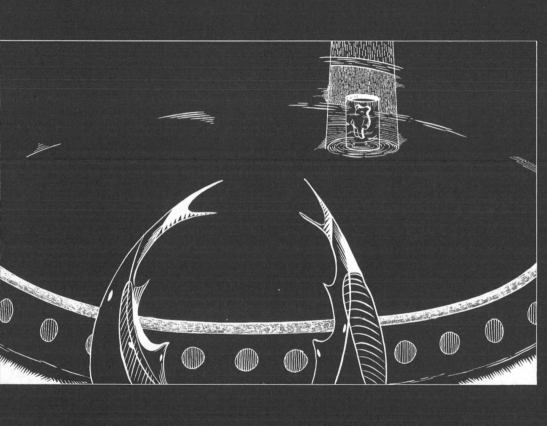

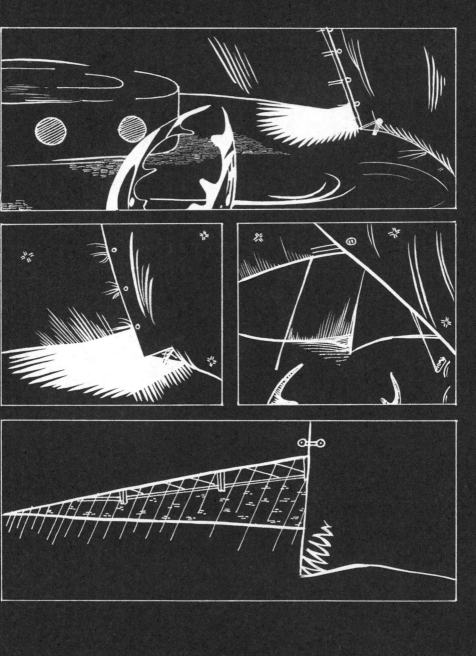

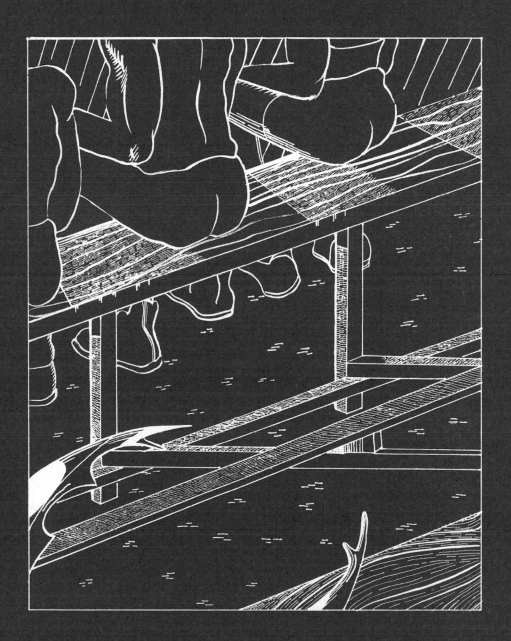

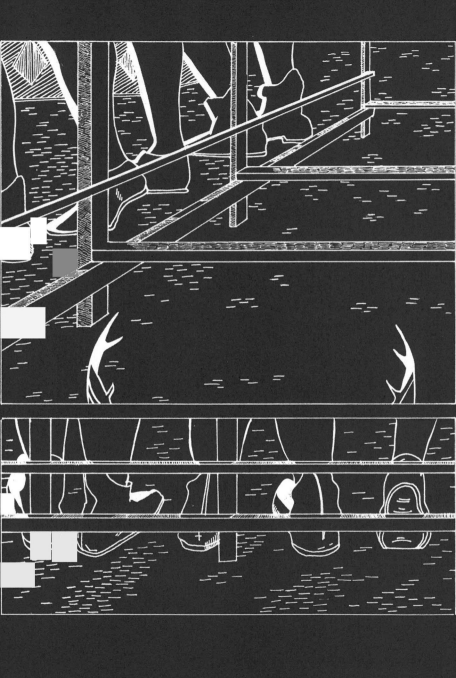

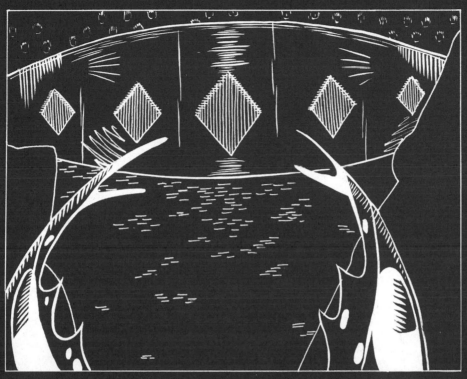

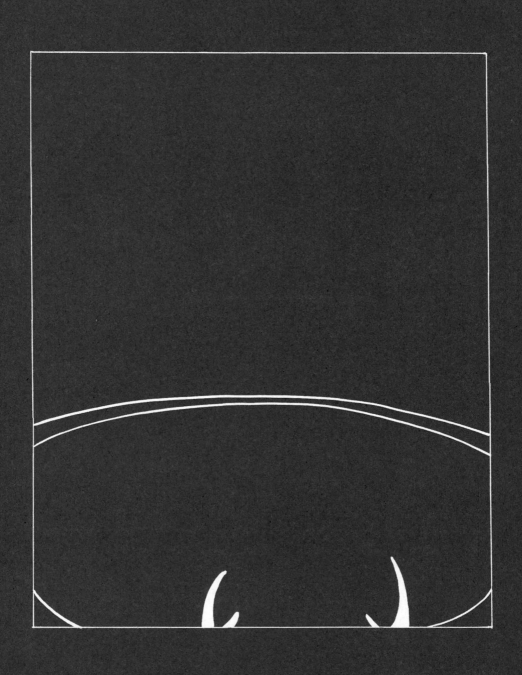

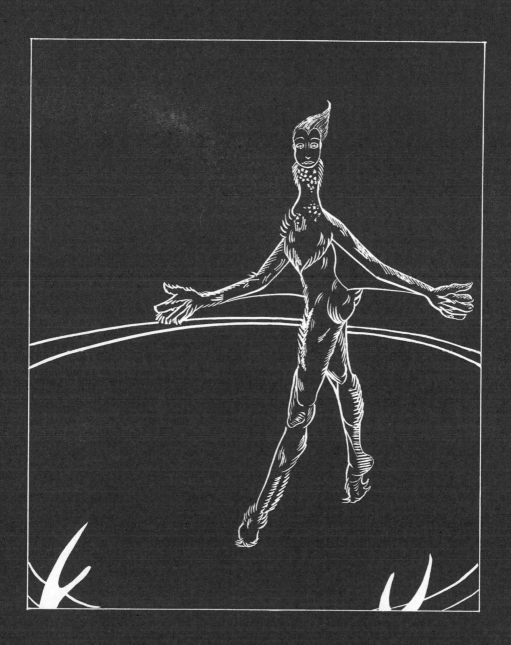

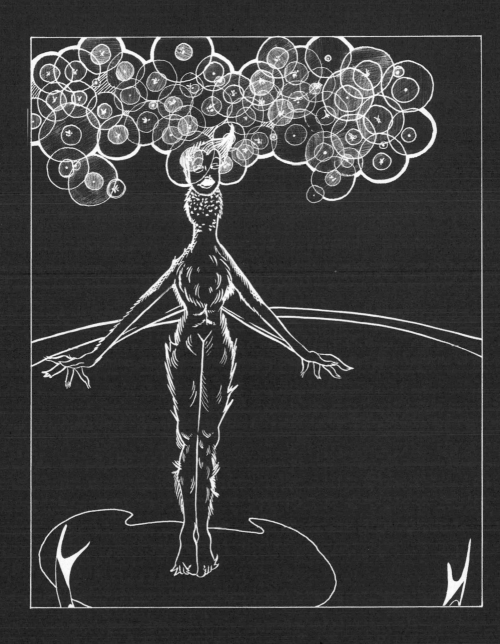

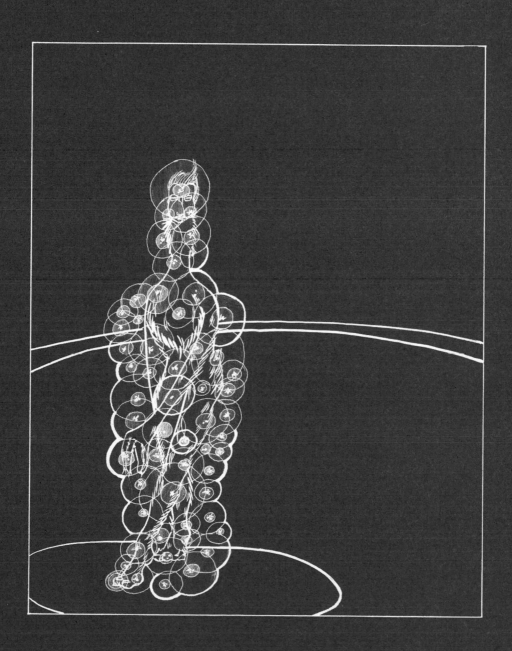

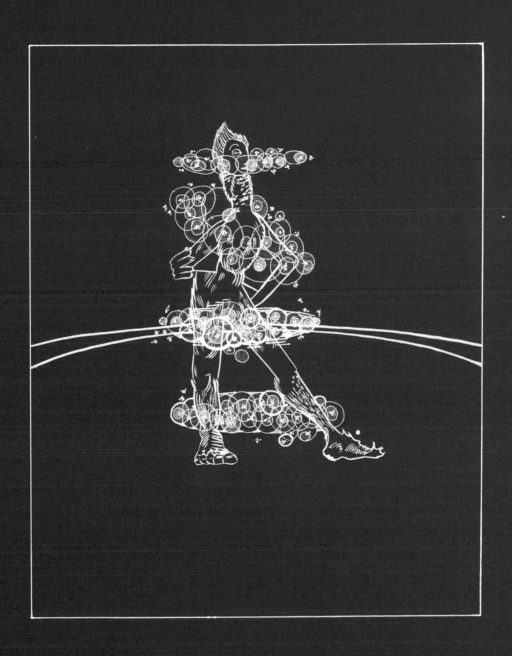

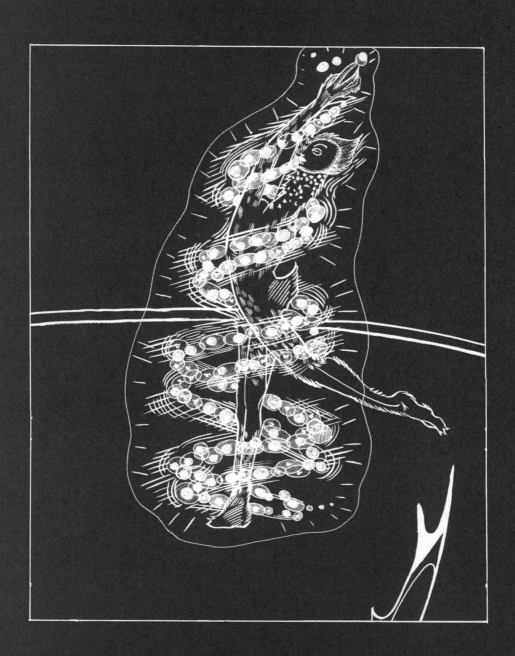

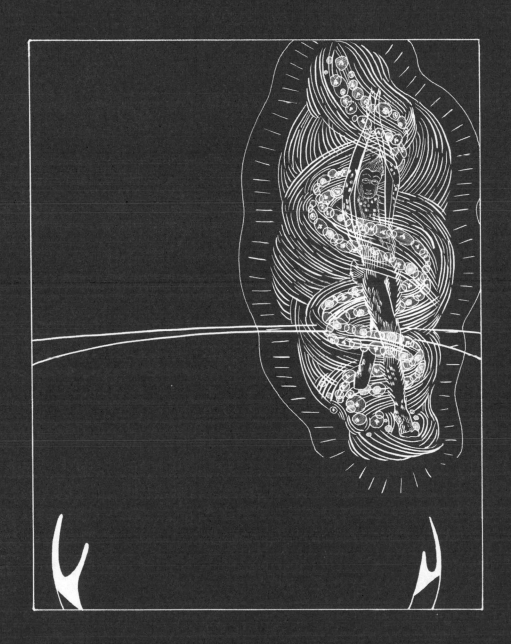

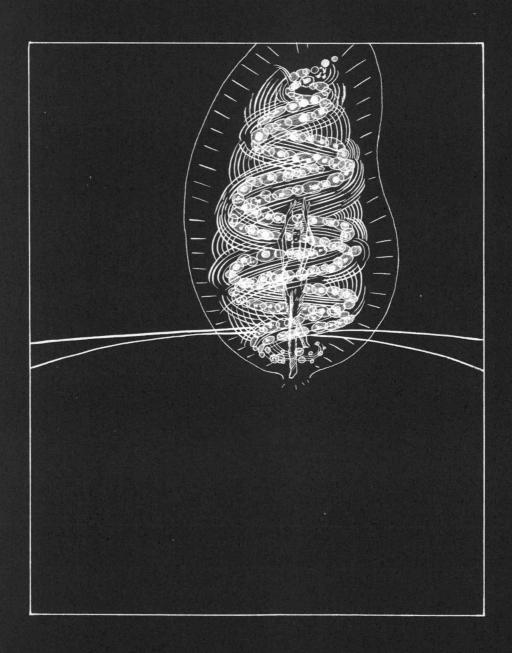

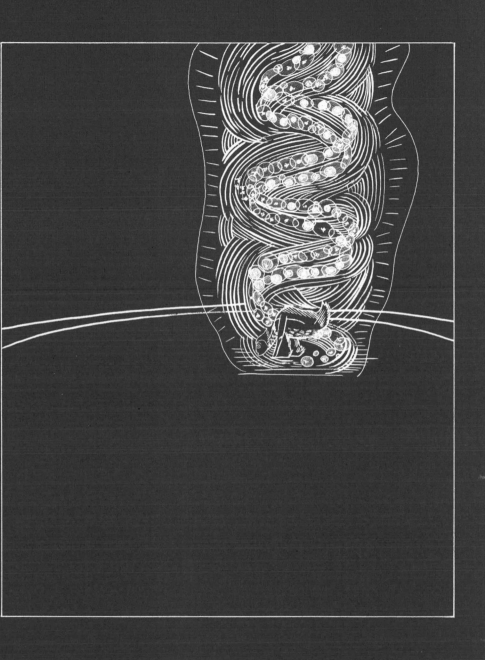

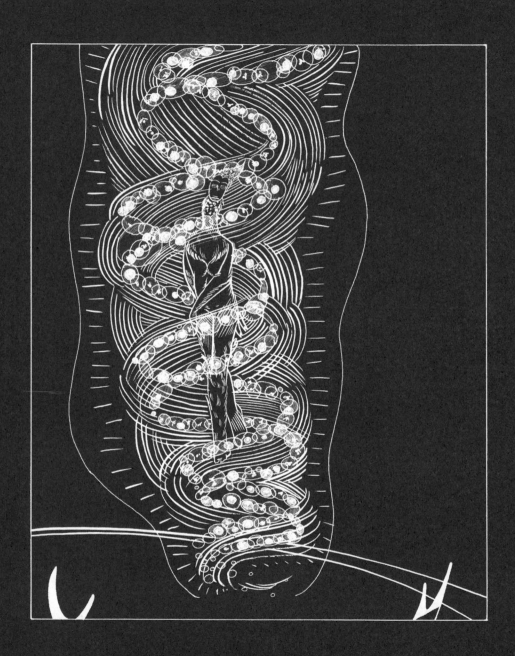

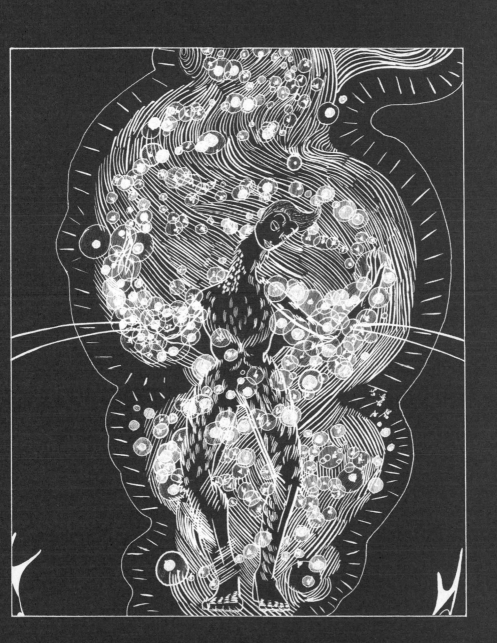

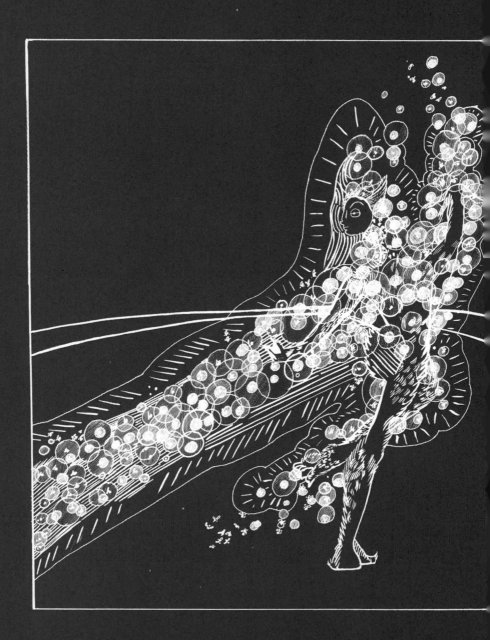

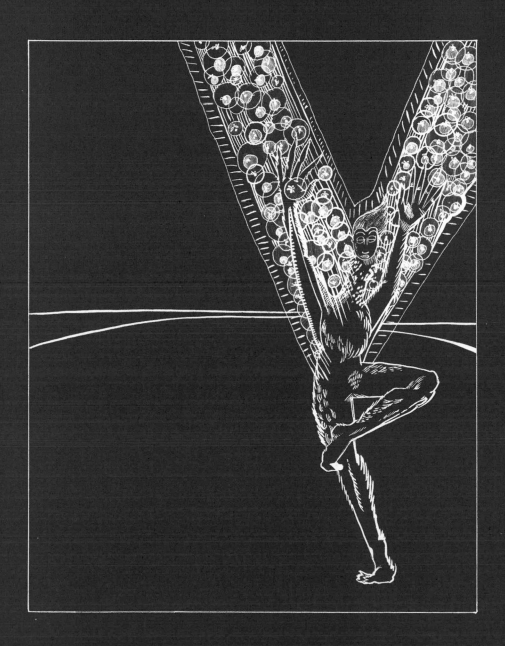

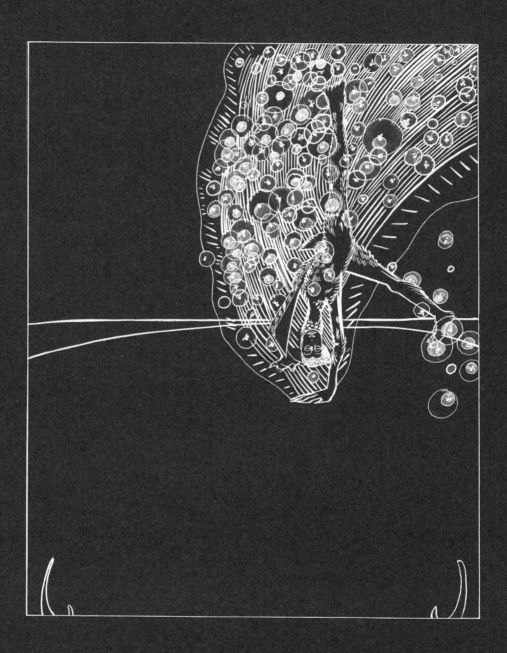

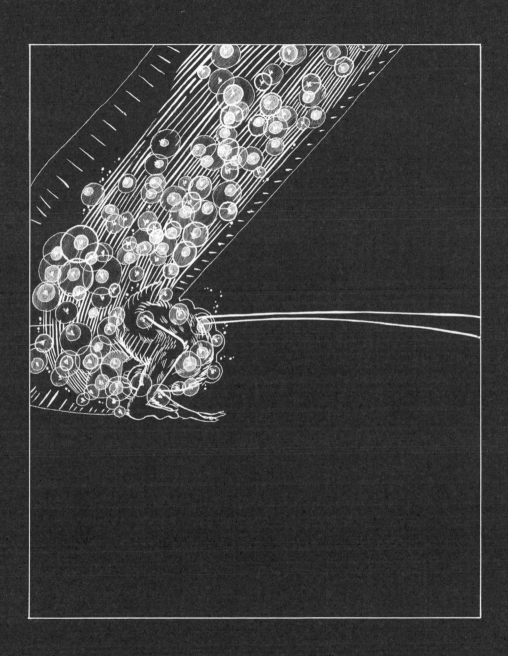

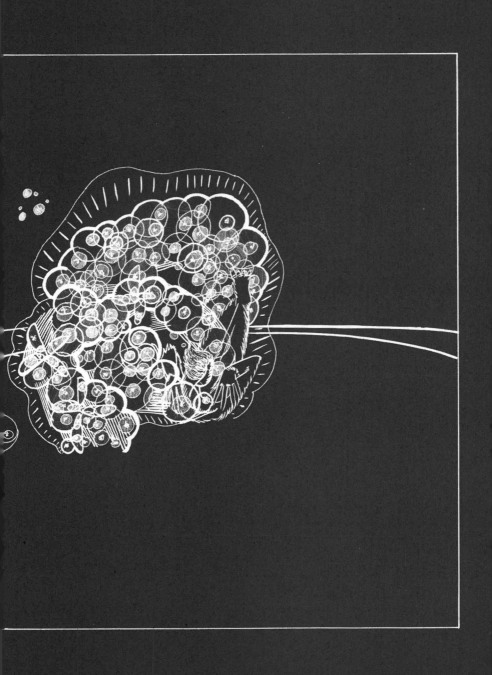

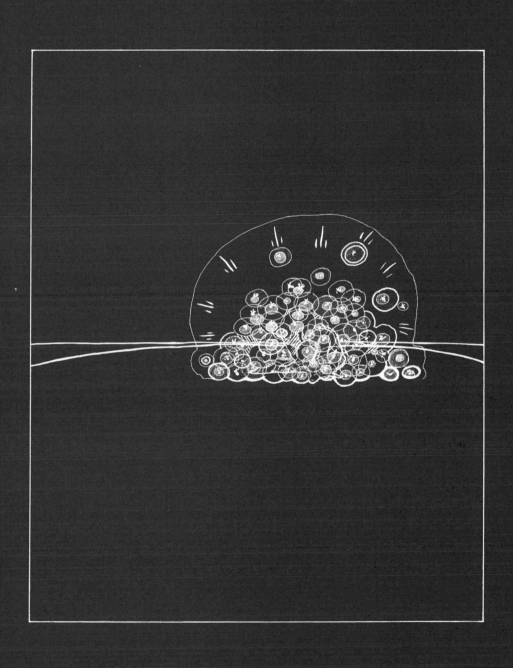

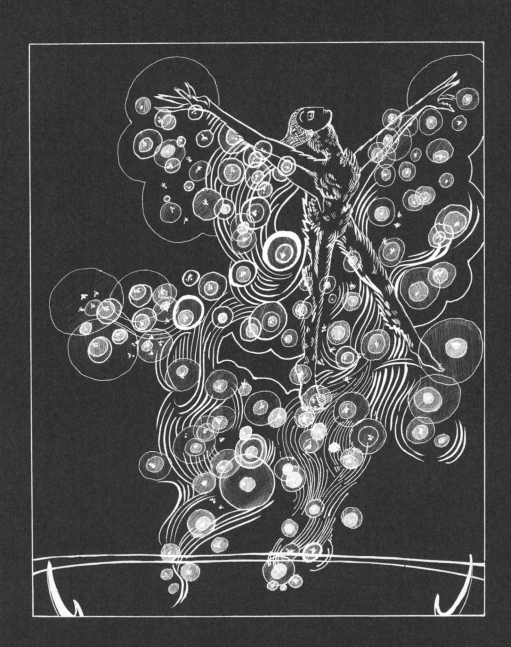

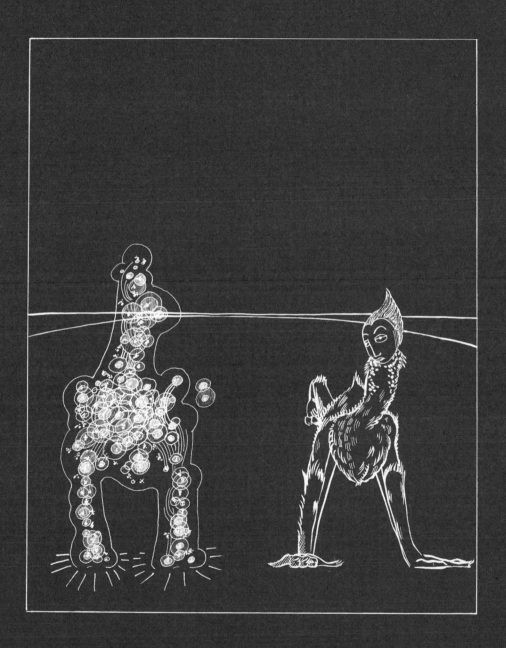

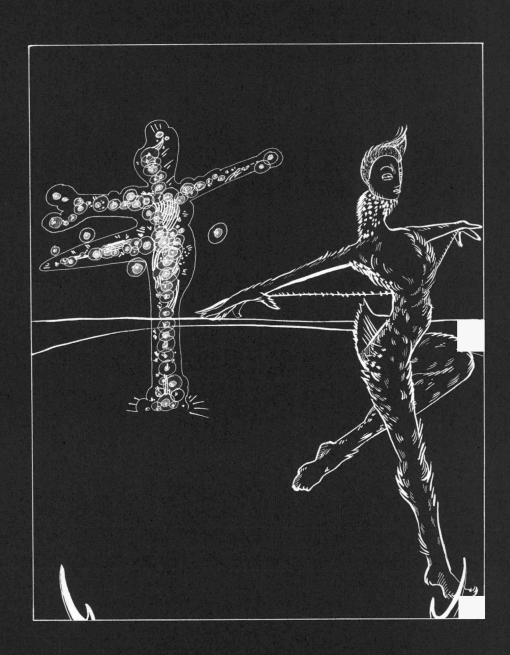

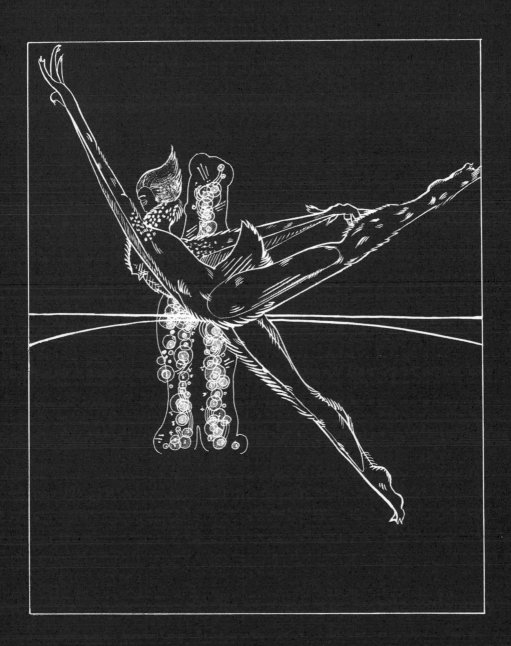

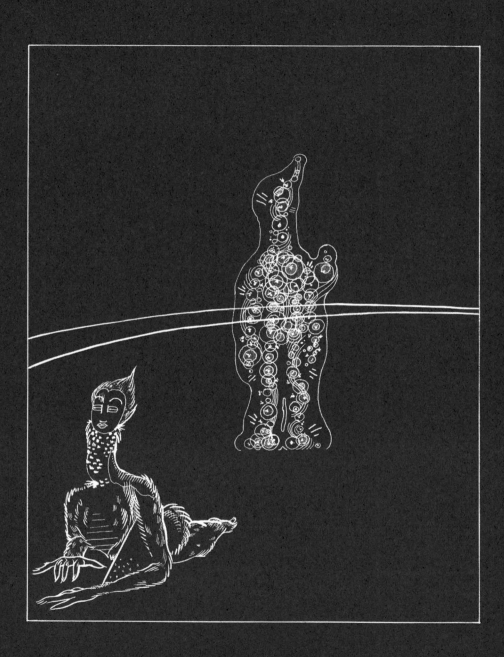

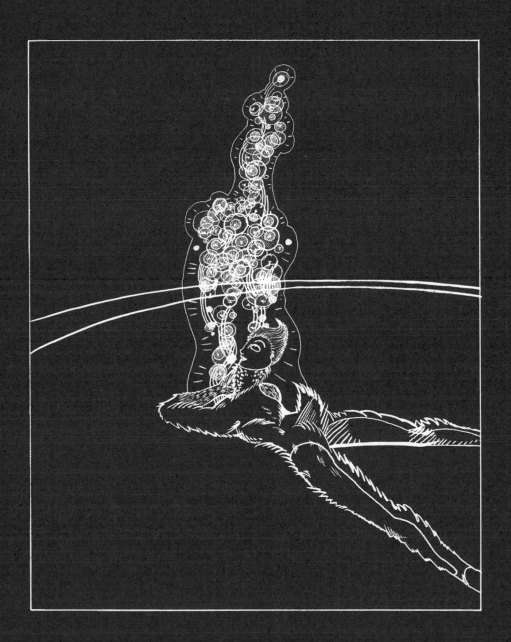

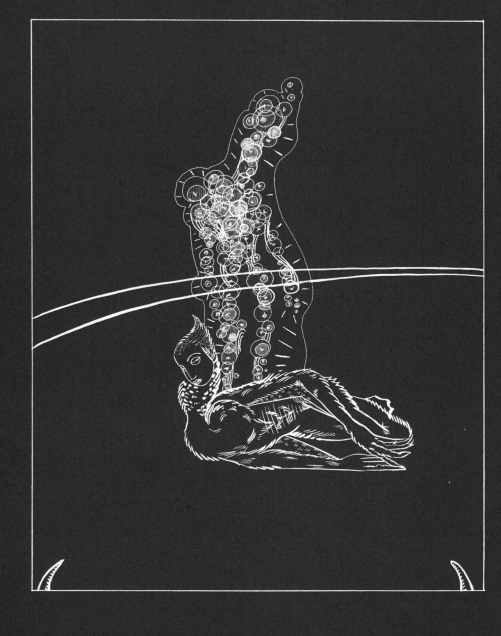

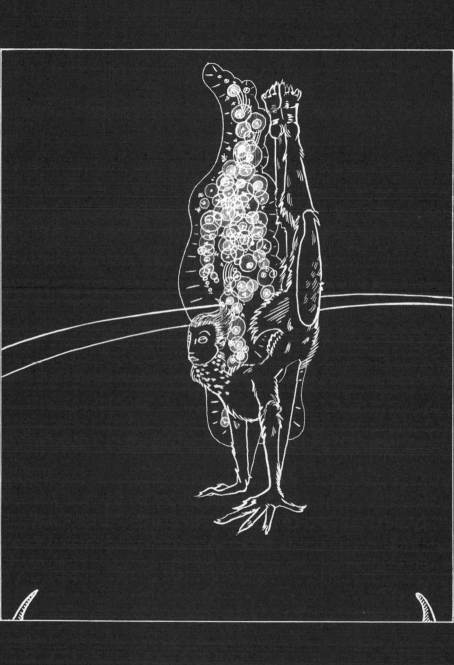

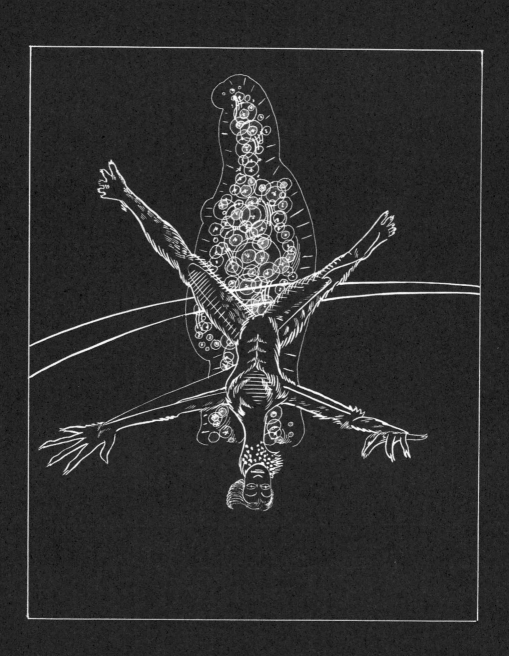

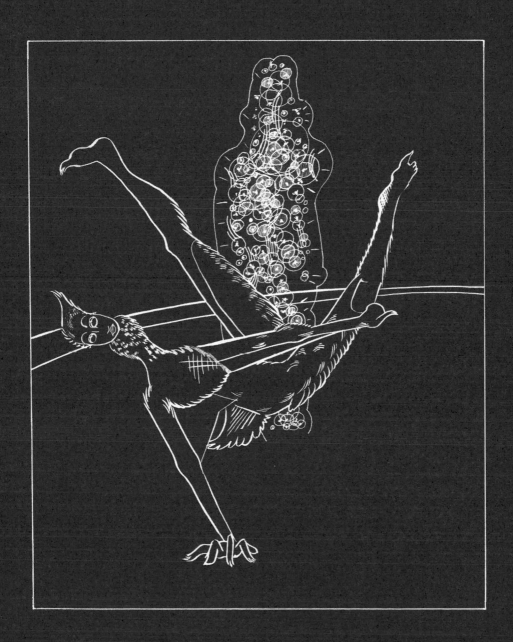

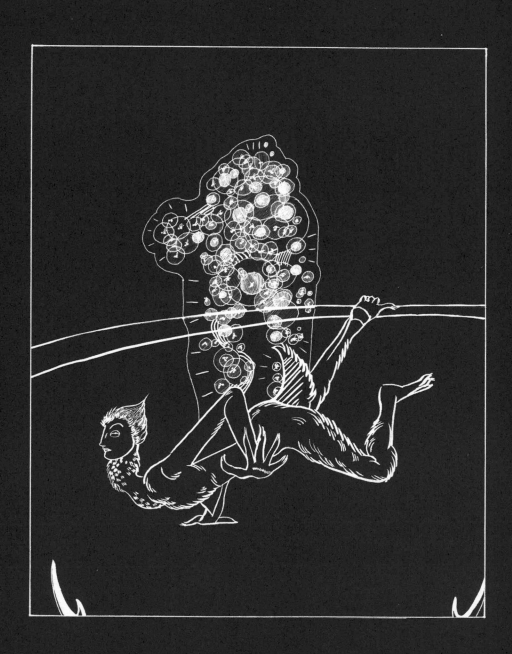

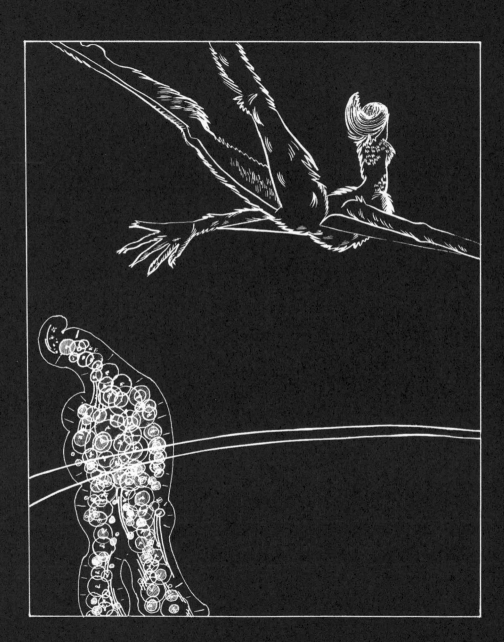

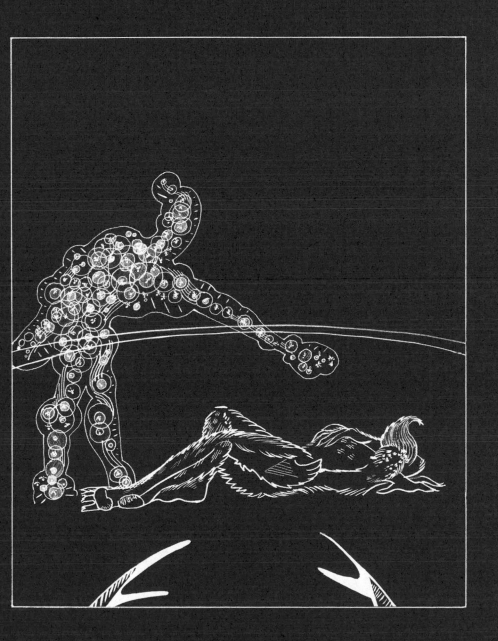

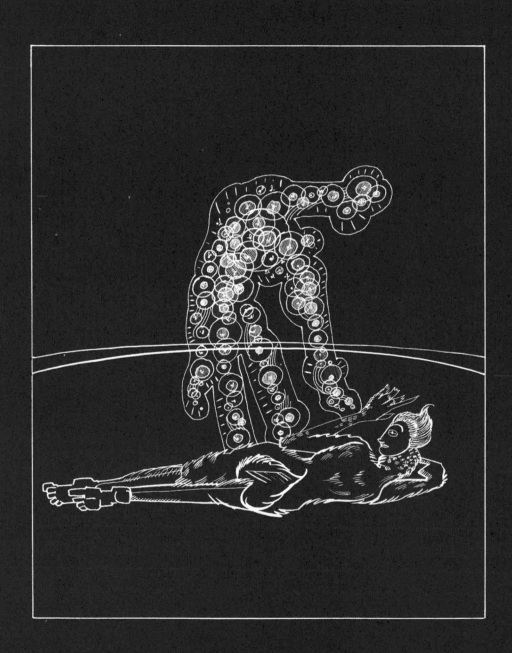

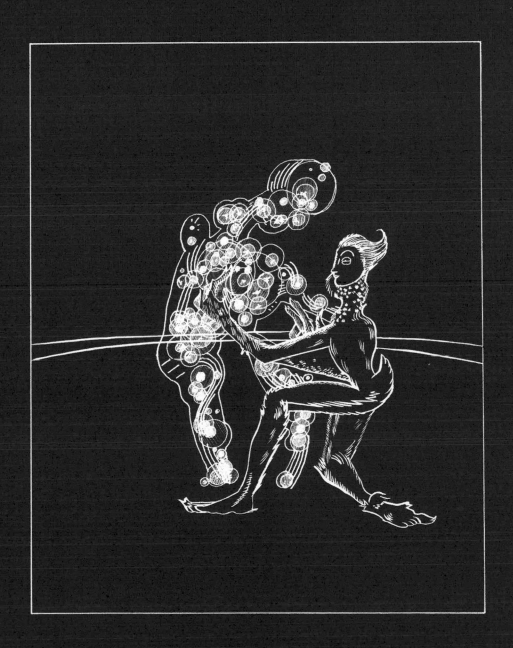

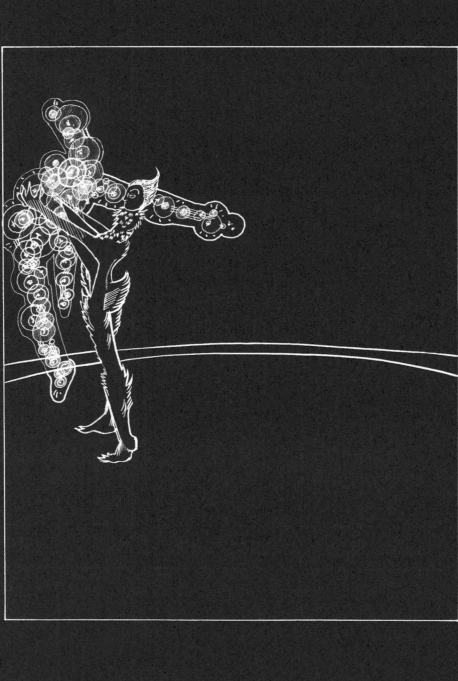

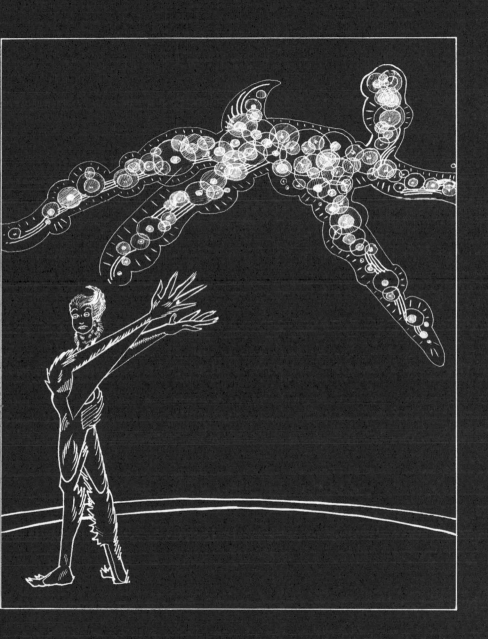

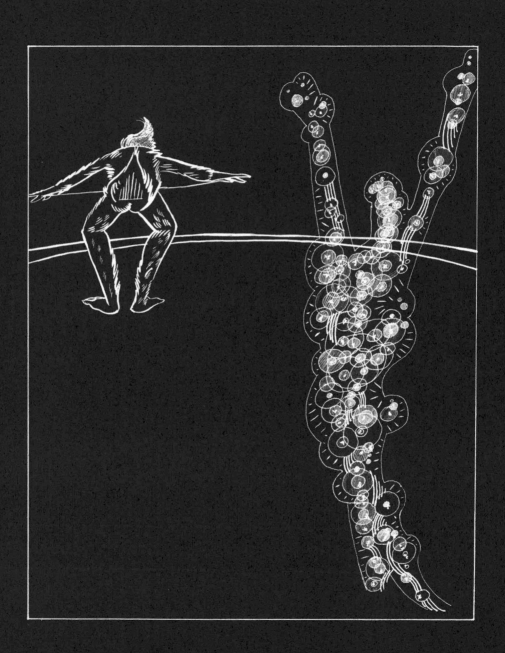

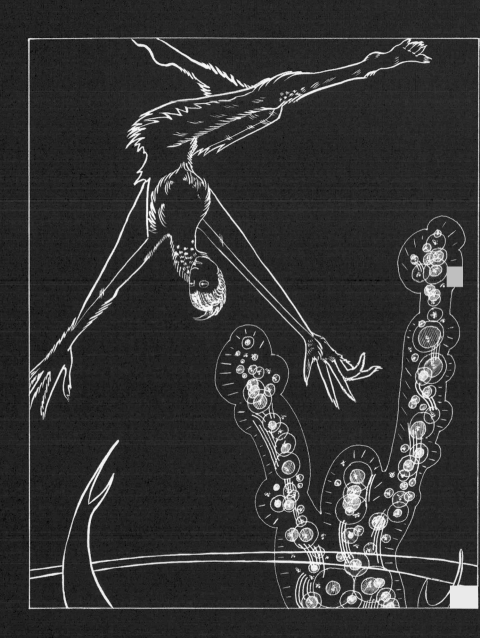

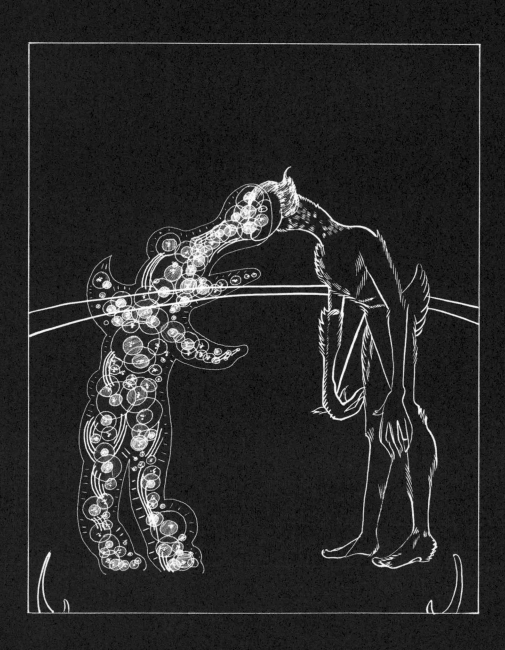

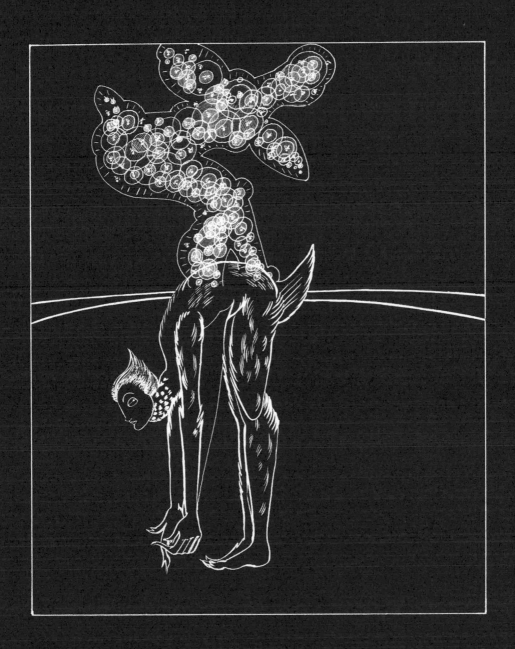

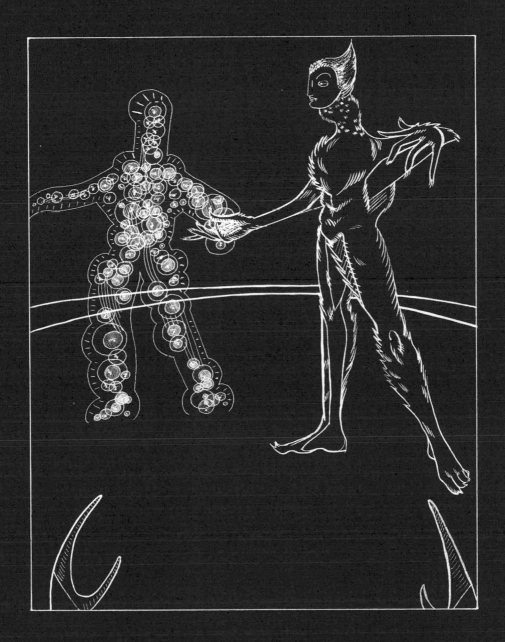

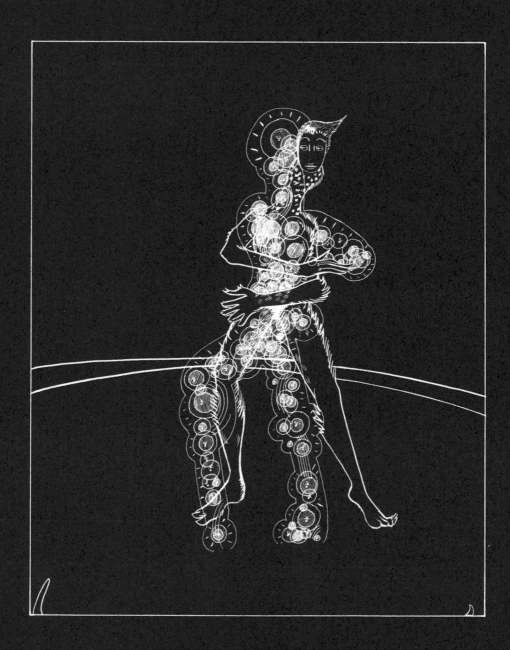

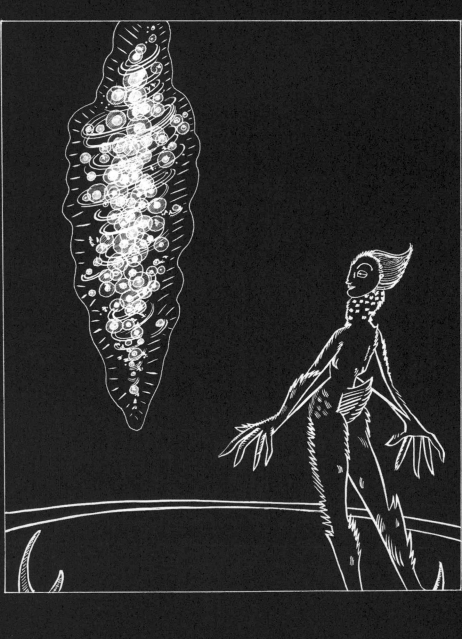

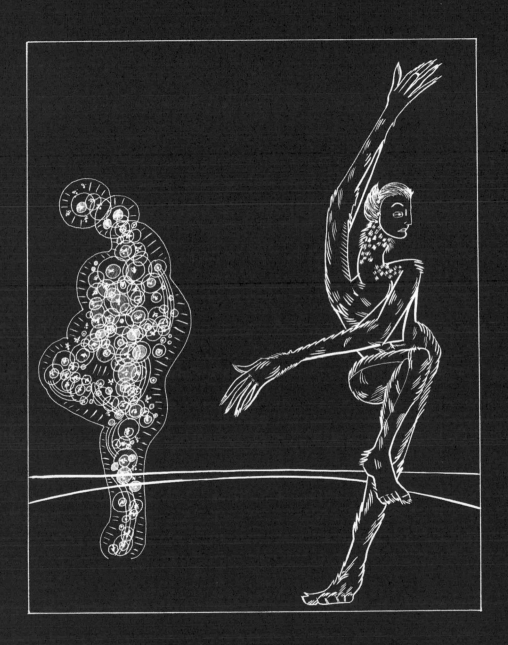

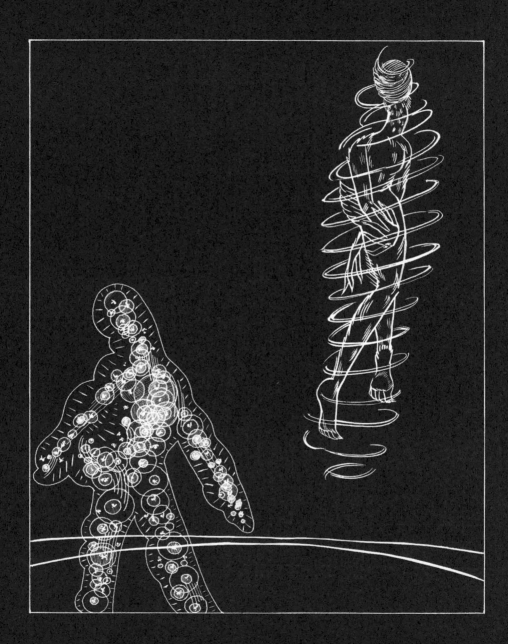

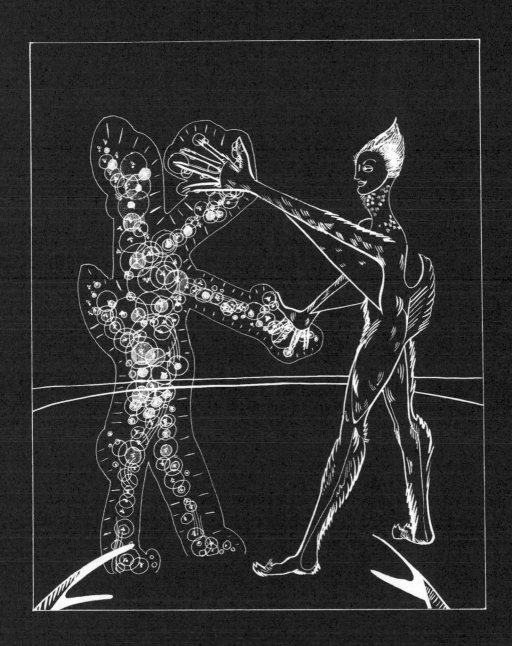

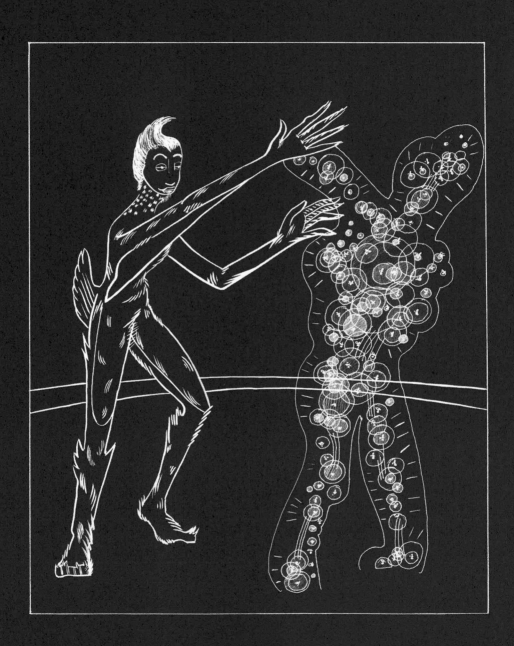

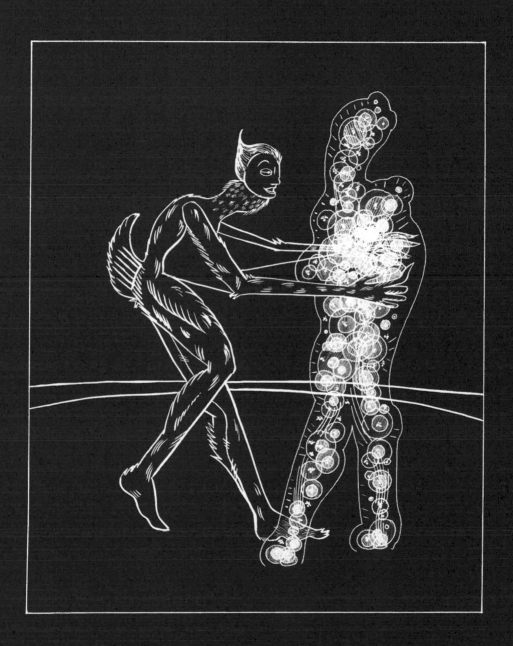

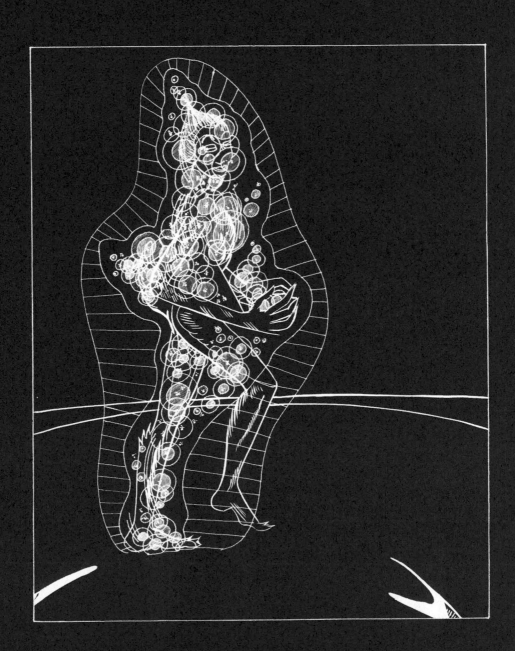

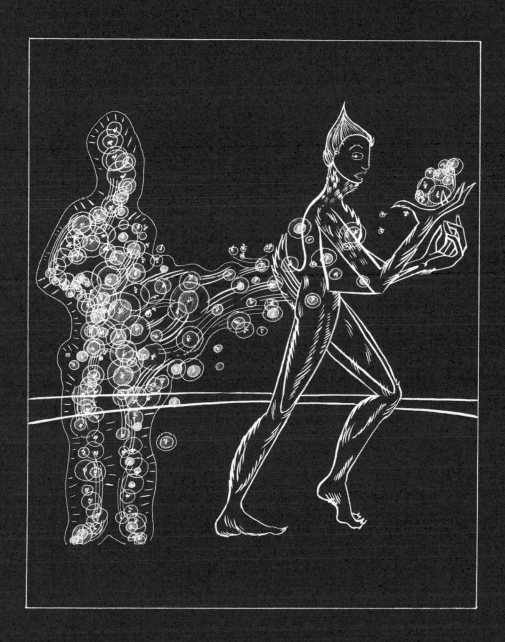

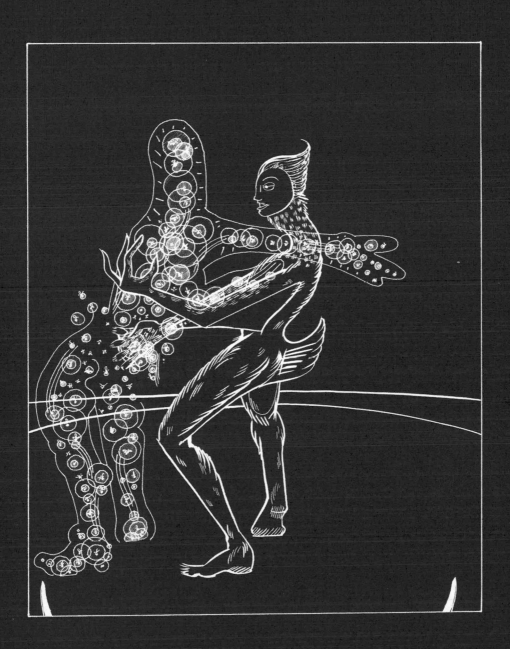

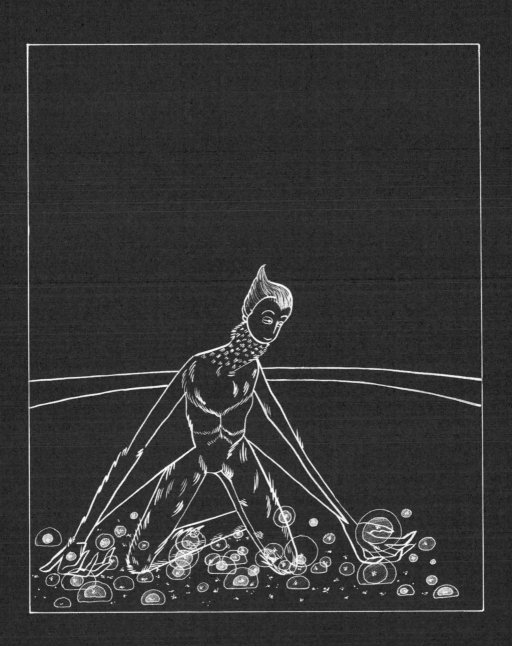

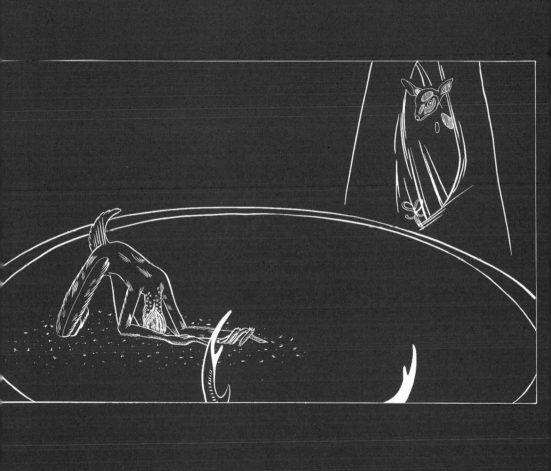

burned

at the boundary

saw-toothed

with soot

afterimage

of the sun

Waking ... a field of dead heat lifts a seething portrait from me: dancing with a thousand fireflies.

Get my bearings. The tents. A few Pures wandering past. Surfaces are tan and khaki and dirt except the Pures in pale and white. Baskets filled with glowing lichens cast an eerie glow.

I'm hungry. Gurgling, grumbling. Belch. A scent: raspberries.

Flicking my tongue, I get the contours of the smell and track its thread through the crowds, snaking around tents, down alleys, past the pickled punks and leprous leprechauns until I face a small triangular tent seemingly forgotten and deserted. The scent is escaping through an entry marked with strips of material. I pass through the cool noodles ... engulfed by darkness, imbued with berries, and I face:

an abrupt emptiness of smell, a void.
Absence hurts the roof of my mouth like loneliness.
Turn to run but a wall of stench blocks my path,
rotten eggs exhale and swallow me,
violently sulfuric,
alien and toxic,
savage and merciless,
the grinding gears of a tempest coming.

I'm squashed, flattened, and dulled by them.
Bobbing aimlessly in a burning soup of wishes.
Numb.
The lifeless stench has descended and envelopes my limbs.
Lifeless and dumb, nothing else, only wordless stench.
Dumb and churning.
Somewhere, far away, tantalizing and taunting,
drawing me closer,
from out of the boundless plane rides a masked pungent must
with tincture of sickly sweet decay by its side ... stagnation crinkled with rust,
a jolt of lighting strikes the earth, charged ions curl at the margins,
the ring of struck bronze carried by a briny breeze,
a wash of decomposing chlorophyll and salt on a beach of dried shells.
I am itchy and hopeful.

I take a deep breath, filling my throat with kelp and seaweed and saltwater
and dark growing things.

Sinuously, a heavy, unctuous aroma weaves through the brine and descends
as oily jelly.

I catch an ozone buzz, my septum serrated and slapped with fishy stink,
my wounds laved in vegetation and shrooms,
an essence I can't place ... dry and crusty, permeated with an odor of albumin
yoked to peat—
the heady richness of loam and worms,
noisome methane rollicks in fetid sinkholes and
thick carrion smells ring around me like ribbons of weeping willow,
hushed cedar tickles my tongue muted by moss and cypress.

Exotic steamy jungle, wildflower, a soupçon of chartreuse,
green sap and spruce is wafted by a crisp spring zephyr
split and split and spill my body into multitudes of fecund fantasies.

From my skin, grasses sprout like hair pushing upward in pain and arousal,
dried dung and raw meat odors penetrate my surface

until I am seared by fire and
can't stop the harrowing
and my hardshell
unpeeling
from my body
as I'm flayed
shark-tooth tip stripped
nerves
jitter spasm jitter chatter
fear
blinded
deaf
gradually
weighed
down
smothered
by choking ash,
can't escape myself alone with myself no one knows I'm fighting for breath
catch a whiff, come to me, there
dampness
vapor
water
fresh water laps at the limits of my senses
reviving, refreshing, clearing and cooling.
I'm swimming in spumes of watery air and
skimming over fields of grass, buttery dander, and sweet almond oleander—
swiftly blunted by musk and bile, shit and semen,
pierced by spikes of acrid urine,
puffs of flint and burning wood infiltrate my nostrils—
a blade like a flame slices through the center,
a gust of clean air so crisp it tears into my nose like cocaine,
this clarity is
patiently,
delicately
infused with juniper and linseed oil,
plaintive hints of sugarcane and orange at the outskirts,

I luxuriate in this decadent mélange until—
                                        creeping in from the periphery—
stale sweat, leather, and gunpowder intrude into this concoction, surround me,
dragging behind a flatulent miasma of manure,
necrotic bodies ringed with spoilage and squalor settle upon a mountain
of garbage,
the unmistakable punch of sizzling hide stamped by ink,
exhaust fumes eclipse my throat,
the inner lining chipped away by insecticide, grease, and melting plastic,
a veil of roses and rue lifts, revealing old driftwood sailing on a ghost of rainforest,
chlorine in a concrete pond sipping a cocktail of charcoal, ice, and sand,
hills of melted tar, overflowing sewers,
sweet malaria and sinews of muscular poison approach—
penetrating toxins, vulgar, vicious toxins,
violent and alien,
but instantly, it's gone.
Emptiness.
Devoid.
Dullness.
Death.

Can't take this. So dark, can't see. Get up, the roof presses against my head.
Feel drunk. A dull gut punch. Grasping blindly, find the flap and leave.

The path and walls and air tremble. Slices of lights plunge in and out like
migraine needles. Can't control. Weak. Mouth pits burned out. Sensation
overload.

From a nearby tent, a voice.

"Males, females, Pures one and all, come see our main attraction, see G'Nesh
perform in public what you rarely even see in private. See the minimal made
maximal. The most potent act of all, the ultimate sexual act, flagrantly in
public. Now, if that's not horny, I'll burn my ass hair. Just a few drops from
your dropper. That's all it will cost. Just a few drops of your life. Command:
Come and see."

This Talker appears generally human but with a face shaped like a bean. Wears a pristine white jacket with large brass buttons up the front, white gloves, and dark brown furry legs. His face is the color of pearl and his short spiky hair, flat on top, is the same color, almost indistinguishable. His thin-lipped mouth rimmed in olive is too big. I show him the ticket from my pocket. He cocks his head and squints at me funny, waves me in. Have a feeling this G'Nesh is important. Can point me to the bird girl. I'll stick out the hunger.

The room sails in velvet evening, quiet and soothing. The audience attentive like polite children. I take an open seat in the front facing a blank, dark wall of obscure and subterranean material. How far? Flat or curved or corrugated? Curtain or wall?

What is *that*?

Gasps all around. The impossible figure is black but pins me like a spotlight; it extrudes from the surface and fills the room like space itself. Can scarcely make out its contours—it fills all corners of the room, floor to ceiling. It surrounds me yet is in front of me. It shines bituminous. The head, so many parts coming forward, sideways, down, inward. Like a bomb went off inside an elephant. Tubular, flattened, bulging, misshapen trunk, dangling flop ears as irregular as continents, four black eyes bulging on stalks, sweeping the crowd until settling on me—no, the male to my left.

The man looks over his shoulder then back.

Silence. I'm holding my breath.

Eventually the man stands and walks toward the thing. They face each other, the man's arms akimbo, defiant. He turns and looks back at us with a sneer. The strange being's trunk touches his neck, and his expression is transfixed. His whole body becomes a statue. A floor light floods upward, bathing him in a column of illumination. We are quiet, straining to see. The rise and fall of his chest. Slows? His breathing stops; his sneer is unchanged. As one, we lean forward, can discern no movement. The skin, his skin becomes moist and his arms recede like erosion into his body; his legs kiss, becoming a tail, his ears vanish into his body, his eyes and nose are swallowed up as dimples in his face; he falls flopping side to side and front to back, his clothes dangling loose around him, the shorts splitting off, a huge tail furiously flagellating, gills now on his neck, closing, opening, closing, pleading.

He shrinks, his body compressing into itself.

The air crackles with static.

Its many eyes closed, G'Nesh is still except for its trunk, which pets the thing like a kitten. The thing shrivels to the length of an arm, a curled worm with a bulbous head. Looks like a fat, white maggot with eyes. Its pointy, curled body smacks the floor again and again. G'Nesh rolls it like dough as it wiggles and turns grey and green. The thing mutates, its surface crenulates into tiny scales like my own ... a tail and limbs with claws ... fur shooting up from the scales ... conical nose ... whiskers and small teeth ... tail separating, getting longer and fatter and furrier, limbs getting thinner and longer ... body more wiry ... thicker, now thicker ... heavy and full, strong-limbed ... muscles knitting ... hair falling out ... coloration getting lighter and lighter until it is near albino again, his features becoming straight again and clean and even, his chest widening, waist narrowing, muscles growing, his cock getting bigger and bigger, his balls heroic.

"BEHOLD!"

Stunning to hear after complete silence, the words catapult like flaming boulders: "THE EVOLUTION! THE PUREFECTION!"

He releases the man who looks almost as he did before, but with new and improved family jewels ... and a changed face—how?—younger? He gets up from the floor unstable, unsure. As he returns to his seat, smiles and nods encourage him, and, except for me, those nearby slap his back or his spear-like penis. The creature is gone. Didn't see it go.

A chill in the air. My stomach ache has graduated to a dull but unsettling pain. Hurry out. Collide with another creature outside the tent, knocking us both down.

"So, would you like to fuck?" Bunnygirl asks me as we sprawl in a tangle. "Just a droppersful." Plush, cropped black fur and precise features grace a heart-shaped face.

"Uh …"

She is petite. Slim and less than chest height on me. Naked from the waist up, her breasts ringed in many colors with large, erect dark nipples. I saw her before. With the unicorn. A short black skirt barely covers the tops of her slender legs that end in rabbit-like paws.

"Ooooh … not a Pure."

"Yes."

"Would you like to fuck?"

"Uh … probably not … the right time." I pick myself up and wipe the dust off my suit.

"What's your trick?" she says, bounding to her feet.

"I … could use some food. Nearly starving is my trick."

She puts her hands on my chest; her touch is light as a feather. "I know where." She hops past me; I have to run to catch up with her.

"Slow down, please. I'm not so steady on my—on my feet."

She pauses to bounce at my side. "My name is Maphroditee. I like to fuck. What's your name?"

"I don't know. I don't have one."

"Pick."

Name myself? Got no purchase to name myself. "I don't know."

We continue down nameless roads toward a nameless tent with none to witness.

"You can feel the sun beating on your pclt."

"What?"

"The sun. Déjàvedic. Sans signified, sans substance, a neutered noun. Outside. I remember I was there briefly." She looks at me, and her eyes are big and luminous. Copper with glittering flakes. "Felt the sun. Exposed a rare moment. When the sun was out, you could feel it tapping on your cells, the surface of your body tight, throbbing." She moves like a ballerina. "I never felt that since. Or else I never felt it, and I'm just fantasizing."

"I ..."—what do I want to tell her?—"... can ... remember a time ... when I thought my body was ... was solid. When I crawled enough through—slowly enough through time that ... that I felt like ... myself the whole way."

"The sun presses through your eyelids when you close them and face it." Her voice carries with it the perfume of imagination.

"You're only solid one time, I guess," I say.

"The outside was a brief moment of breathing."

"It's a fake ... because ... apparently that's ... that's just the beginning. It's sort of—was even faith *then*, I guess. Naïveté before a storm."

"I remember the feeling of grass on my tongue. It was a clean, crisp, light orgasm. All my hairs stood on end. I would thump my tail."

"Do you have a tail?" I ask. "It sounds like you were once a—another thing." A rabbit.

"Once was what?"

"Nothing. I just remember words. Scraps."

"I was once another thing? What do you mean by being another thing?"

"I'm sorry. I don't much know much what I mean. I remember I don't think I used to stutter."

"Stammer."

"What?"

"You stammer, not stutter."

"You remind me of someone." On a white couch. "She had black hair."

"I have black hair."

"Yes but yours is all over your body."

"Is that a difference?"

"No, not really."

We've stopped at a large tent. Where am I? I'm with a black rabbit.

"I very much enjoy fucking myself," she says.

"That's nice."

"I come in so many parts of my body simultaneously, it can't be explained with words. It never stops echoing. I could continue indefinitely, but difference is erotic and that makes me feel alive. To touch things that are different. Stay here. I'll get you edibles."

She scoots under the tent wall, and I'm alone in a narrow walkway leading twenty feet in both directions. It's quiet. Distant voices and movement ... somehow comforting. Wasn't I starving? Hunger has evolved into intoxication. The roof above: abruptly splattered with snakes of color, paisley sea dragons, squalls of Northern Lights, and spires of living fire. Schizophrenic rainbows. Vanishes. Returns to grey. Did I imagine it? Sigh. Nothing ever doesn't change.

Dirt the color of grease. The tent walls, all the same olive color. Rub my hand against the material—a supple patina. Not like canvas, more like some kind of hide. I jump and can see just over the wall that the tent on the opposite side is vacant, no roof. Probably to allow light in.

Maphroditee appears with an armful of pea-green plants—tubular like celery and bathed in oil. Don't care what they look like, I take one and shove it in my mouth. Not gag-worthy. Like aloe. This is okay. Take them one at a time from her and shove them in my mouth, chewing, swallowing, quickly, quickly. Finish the last bit. I'm wiping my mouth when she asks, "What is this?" pointing at my forehead. I touch my temple—sensitive. Feels like a wound. How did I get this?

"I don't know. I can't remember. It's—I think—a wound."

"No it's not. Sit down."

I sit cross-legged in the corridor, and she inspects me. She sniffs at it. Runs her fingers around the area lightly. She licks it. A prickling sensation tickles—not in my head—where? She puts her mouth up to my forehead. Warmth rises from my toes to my eyes. She holds up two furry fingers in front of my face, drags them across my eyes to my temple; SQUISH as she slides them into the wound. Discomfort. What is happening? Where? I'm looking for someone. I have to be somewhere. What I where how? Figure it out. Can't go somewhere if I don't know who I am. This is important. Remember is important. Where am I? Where am I? This person in front. Who? In a black fur coat. Pressure inside my head. Inflation. Warmsoft syrup dripping down my neck, spreading through my body. My skin is purring. My cock is creeping out of its sheath, broadening and lengthening. The black fur creature guides me to my knees, kneeling over my head. A furry leg in front of my eyes. Up a black tent. I am floating in a sea of caramel, my legs stretched out, immoveable. Black fur creature shows me a bright pink cock like an arm under the tent in front of me. A magic wand. The wand casts a spell upon my eye. It moves out of sight. A release of pressure and a sucking sound. Warmth, still warm … but clear.

"Is it okay?" Maphroditee asks.

Looking into his/her beaming tangerine eyes. Nothing past the shiny surface. I nod weakly. A warmth enters my head, exquisite electricity tingling down my neck. I know what I want. I want to feel.

Cue the gear. Short blue tinsel skirt, fluid. Arrange fluke notch in back. Slide it, tight blue top holding rapt my fatty fat fat groovy belly and chest. Clickity-click my scarlet painted hooves. Ringward, slap the pigbrid on the treadmill, "Up it, piggy," and out.

Drink it: "My dear Pures." Holding my arms out to invite everyone. "My dear lazies and genitalmen. We be gathered here today to witness the witless hissed story. The passing of an utter memory."

These white, blue-eyed angels sit dumbstruck, stupidstruck. My bodice alone amazes them. My language baffles them.

"Lies erase. Lies are power. Power to be had by you. Truth is relative, no? Power defeats truth, paper, scissors. Are you faux real? Dear labias and gentrified. I am The Contortionist. I tie memory into a not. I am The Hypnotist. God of the deep sleep. The sleep from whose bounds you renew. Call me DJ Morpheus, drunk from the river. Master of backspin. I am the Witness."

I roll my swell-belly. Prepping and mixing the trick.

"You come here with bad. I'll race it, raze it. Crossfade your pain with forget fullness. But you gotta under ego a terrible torment. Ergo, a repulsive procedure. You have to sub do, submit to my will. Then you'll be scratched. With willpower, you can rewrite. Reshape the foundation of others. We have a guest, don't we Bigboy?" Tender gets all up in front of the audience, clamps her hands on the arm of a scrumptious little bitch, brings her forward. Nervous and embarrassed.

"You've volunteered, haven't you, darling?" She looks confused. Nods.

"Let's roll the tape, Gar*sawn*."

The RSim projection in the ring, they xp. She brung it, oh yeah, she brung it.

A simple scene. High angle. An adult male and child male, red-suited and helmeted. In a blue forest. Collecting mush-o-room into baskets. A tank rolls in, turns toward them, its turret toward them. *BANG!* They are broken. Lying in the sod, limbs askew. The tank rolls over them; we feel the bones snapping. Set change: in a silver room. A woman (woman onstage prolly, tho they look so samelike) working at a control station. Uniformed figures bust in. We feel her struck to the floor. She's laid out senseless. The scene changes again: a smaller room. Door opens. See and feel her being drug into the room, left in a bundle. In the room, RSim is playing, projecting the story on repeat. The man crushed, the boy crushed, the bones snapping, and her struck and drugged out. She gets it flashback style. We xp this vision within a vision within a vision. Recurring receding stories.

Now and finally, our guest sobs. Incoherent. She struggles with Tender, bleats, spits. Crumples. At last. Tender strips her, holds her down, drenches her in oil and shaves her bald—her head, her pussy—glistening lemon tits rubbed with grease, small red nipples hard. Tender straps her hands to her thighs.

Remixing, in the zone. Up the steep rectangular chute she goes. Unhinge my jaw around the chute mouth. Slide her down, lingering down. Her face onto my tongue, close my mouth over her head gently, and swallow. I work my tongue into her nostrils and around her eyeballs and ear holes and mouth. My lips inch her in until ... she's contained. I step back, balance with my arms apart. Her cuffed feet poke out of my mouth. A few steps back, a few forward. With a meaty gulp, she's in my stomach. Eel in a canvas bag.

Slow brobding steps back. Center of the ring, arms up and forward, head back. Face the audience. Sway and shimmy. Ribs of my fat roll. Bells on my blue skirt jingle. The dance of forgetting. The dance of ignorance.

Churning, churning, churning, my inside undulating. Now! Violent upheaval from stomach, throw my head forward. She ejects out, trailing grease, milk, sliding across the ring, a slimy channel behind her. I'm coming I'm coming oh juices drip out of me. She slams into the low ring wall.

Oh yes, the drama. Mmmh, yum.

She wipes mucus from her face, labors for air. I move close to her.

"Come, come," she is breathing. She is looking up at me. Overhead, the story replays: the bodies crushed, her thrown down, the bodies crushed, her thrown down. She feels it. She cocks her head to the side, wiping slime off her body. No recognition in her eyes.

She smiles. "Command: Fuck me."

The unquenchisite fuck after erasure. But I'm attracted to the raw. Now she has none. We pull a jimmy from the audience throwing his vest to the side, pants down. Greased and ready to go. She squiggles in delight as he slides in. The man and child crushed and crushed again clattering through her and all of us.

We roll them off writhing on a marble slab to work the Kid-pool. She'll make happy there.

I leave the stage and begin puking.

[SEE: A baby in a cart. My, my, my Nullsuit on the floor. A monster with limbs many, monster heads, three.]

[HEAR: Sews he's useless. Got the suit. Okay. But he's boring course. Fucking flatty. No talent. No nothing. We could use an act for dimenage. Fix im would yah? Turn im inside fucking out.]

[SEE: The monster touch me and Aaaaaaaaaaaaaaaaaaaaaaaaaaaaaaaaaaaaaaahhh hhhhhhhhhhhhhhhhhhhhhhhhhhhhhhhhhhhhhhhhhhhhhhhhhhhhhhhhhhhhhhhhhh wwwwwwwwwwwwwwwwplzfximoldoxjjfkdqebzljmripflkqebcbxoqe bzlkqoliqebzljjlafcfzxqflkqebpixsbovjbkqxixkamevpfzxipixsbovqebjx zefkbqfjbqlobgbzqqebjxzefkbxkailsbbxzelqeboxkaybxqmbxzbtfqeklqexsf kdyrqifsfkdfkexojlkvtxofpzriqroxitxofprkkbzbppxovbslisbybvlkaqebzljmri pflkqlobmolarzbxkacfkbayvifcbyvprccbofkdyvobxifqvqfjbqlzexkdbobxifqv pqxoqlsboxkaalqebfjmlppfyibobgbzqqebjvqelildvqebjbafxqebif bpqebcfzqflkjxpnrboxafkdxpqorqeqebjxqbofxifpjqeblygbzqfcfzxq flkqebfkgrpqfzbqebbksfolkjbkqxiabpqorzqflkqebambxzbvlrobzex kdfkdbumbofbkzfkdobafkxdqefpybfkdqlrze]

"... bud ... nee mo fud," the kwad says d me. Intrudin in me dark nest.

"Shudup u sdoopid fourped. Is gone. Eddin. Go roll inid. Wudya thing, fud grows n dreez?" Angeringy. He shod nose place. Luhgee dbee live.

"Bud ... I wands dbee pigged. Bie widgee I nee streng dbee gub dbee pigged."

My liddle bed on sdilds above duh sdraw. He a floor sleepr, poging hiz fad snoud in my busynezz.

"I deeseye who geds de fud. Uve had enuf. Gumplaners nvr pigged. U hearm?"

"Bud ..."

"No kwesjunning de widge. Ifn u werk hard, u mide ged made a byped. Thaz u nexd plaze."

"I wanna b ... sho."

Hah! Laffa dis lowlee groundling. Hiz fad redcheeg face wavin bag an for, bag and for, cheegs redder as ima laffin. Hiz guhd downhang rubbin duh flo. Cand even sdand upride lige me.

De room, loogid. Bunges of us razrbags. How mane handswort? Mane handswort iniz dark room. Kwayet, dwidgin, sleepin. I sidup, lig my mout, duh bit uv meedy dasd. Udderz out dere worgin, wawgin duh dreadmillz for energee.

"Loog," I say. "How long u b ina zirk?"

"Uh ... duh laz down."

"And wud? U were wud bfor?"

"Ize ... wuz ... wud wuzz I?"

"C. Uve b chaingd. Maybee a norm. Maybee wandrin blub. Duh widge gave u birt agin. B gradeful. Now lizzen. Dey dreed us wid reshpeg, generullee. Bud u cand b pushed. We werk long an hard. Thad u place. We sleepz den we bragdown, I node plan. We duh sledge gang. Thaz it. Done spec more. We b luggy. Ged fud n wahder. Can u ged dad owdare?"

He shoog hiz hed, hiz dale gurling up in bag.

"An if a norm seez u, u know wud?"

He shoog iz hed.

"Das ride. Cud up an edin. Dey cand stan duh see uz, more dan de udder bridz. I dell u y. We remindem doo much uv demselves. Ourz fat faces loog more pure den dey do. Pures done lige bein reminded dat dare animals, lieg us. Lieg alluh us."

Pausen, piggin ma doof wif a claw. *Squelch.*

"Afder de bragdown, we pig it all up n muv. Dragin for evr. Onduh nexd down. I dell u n u do ih. Dads duh plan. C, ifn u b gud, de widge, holy b duh widge, mide mage u brain ged made smarder lieg mine."

Joey tole me, we duh bozz, we bypeds. Amd mages us sometin else. Sumtimz. Uh preformr. Uh new preformr, mebbie star.

Sumtimz.

Iz reward deevutlee b prayed fer. Klime de ladder de bigtob. Hang bove de normz. Fli. Change. B powrfulz. Tayg bed ani-meni.

Bud hee done no need no.

Sdoopid gwad. He dun no. Kwads nevr made bypeds. We duh bozz. Dey get changd ahwight. Eeden.

"Gud ding doe. Treed uz. De preformr wid de addendas he gum in n giv uz egsuhzee n condenmen zo dat we feel gud. N dudder 1. Wid the blag fur cum n fug us fug ulot uz timz."

He wag iz tale.

"Yeah. So u god dat de loog fowood too."

Guhnesh.

"... doing?"

It takes me a second to focus my eyes. The person speaking appears to be a jumbo-headed, cherubic-cheeked pudgy baby with a riding crop in his hand, seated in a fur-lined wooden cart pulled by a three-foot-tall bug with eight legs and large pincers like a stag beetle. Behind him, a female Hercules several feet taller than me. Is she female? Long, wavy straw-colored hair and the tanned body of a weightlifter, a male weightlifter. But hes face ... mellow and friendly. Hes? Where'd that word come from? Hercules stares blankly at me, but somehow I know hem.

"The fuck's wrong with you? You listening?" says Babyhead.

"I'm sorry. What were you saying?"

"Douchebag. I said, 'Douchebag.'" He sighs. "Okay. Once more into the breach. Heard there was a crossbreed wandering around in a nullsuit and no one knowed how you got in or what yuh wanted. So?"

"Uh. I'm sorry. I'm not here to cause trouble. I've just been ... trying to ... figure out what's going on." Should I ask about the birdgirl? Better not be too obvious, like I'm hunting for her. Play it cool. "I'd like ... I'd like somewhere safe to stay."

"You want safe?" Babyhead laughs until spit bubbles out of his nose. He fishes some words out between gulps of air. "Safe ... heh-heh ... is a religion ... phweh ... buddy. Heh. Myth turned fetish."

"Okay. Sweet," I say. "I just want to be somewhere I won't be in constant danger of being killed."

"You know where you are?"

"No."

"The Sensational Outsider Zirkus and Phreakshow. We're the best act in town, baby."

"You're the baby."

"Touché."

"Your chés. Always traveling in pairs."

He squints at me. "So you're a whiny lizard comedian? That's your act?"

"Just instinct. I don't have an act."

"No act? What? You want work?"

"I don't know."

"You want to join the zirk, right? You gotta work or display. Those you two choices. 'Course, if we need a new act, G'Nesh comes up with one for you. You'll have to ask him yourself. 'Course, he usually takes my recommendation for what we needs. So don't piss me off. Everyone's gotta protect the Baby. You got that?"

"Protect the Baby. Got it."

Drool is dripping down his chin. The giant stands behind him, expressionless. Calm in strength.

"Can I trade this suit?" I ask, holding out my arms.

"Where'd you get it? Jew kill one of 'em?"

"No. Are you called Baby Joey?" Have I heard that name?

"Mmrrm, sure. Suit's a bit worse for wear. Got the helmet?"

"No."

"Mmmmh. S'valuable but that's as far as you get. Still need to perform or work or get thrown out. Look, we're in the middle of a show right now. I got places to go, don't have time to worry about this. You think you can control yourself?"

"Yes. Sarasephi let me in."

"Okay. That's worth something. Cuz I could lock you up. That's what we usually do. Until we decide what to do with you. But if she trusts you ..."—he wipes the snot off his chin with the back of his hand—"... I'll let you stay in the greenroom."

I'm in a room—

time blinked out of my grasp like a sneeze.

I don't remember coming here, and I'm surrounded by many creatures. Living things. Standing around talking, drinking out of glasses. Or out of troughs. The crowd swirls like a deranged garden, a profusion of misshapen flowers, a bewilderness of riotous colors. They ignore me. The room is rectangular and filled with glowing tables of various heights and sizes and a long chest-high counter that's—could it be?—a bar at the far end. The walls are creamy sheets; the room lit by baskets overflowing with luminescent lichen.

A ligament of time was severed—or was it a portion of my life that swerved? A blackout. How much time has passed? Since what marker? When did I last sleep? How far back to measure?

To my right, sipping from a bottle through a bendy straw, is a fat-bellied, frog-mouthed, baby-blue-tutu-wearing creature who stands on two short frog legs ending in hooves painted red. The grooved fat of hes whale-like midriff is squeezed into the tutu like a bloated alcoholic in a corset. Hes mouth faces upward and extends from one side of hes body to the other with two bubble eyes peeking over the top. Would make a good puppet. To my left, at a table in the corner, sits a group of three creatures: a Fennec Boy with tall pointy ears, a dolphin-bodied thing with caterpillar legs and a chimp's head; and the third, between them on the table, is a gnarled and crusty tortoise. Just ahead of me, standing by a tall café table, is a two-headed, black-and-white Siamese twin. One head is a cat, the other a dog. Both heads are held up by flamingo-necks that lead down to a single lozenge-shaped body with two skinny arms and two skinny legs. I look past them to the bar opposite, to the bartender—I know her, the four-armed goddess from the entrance, the ticket giver. She's behind the bar serving clear liquid from clear pitchers into clear glasses. Bottles and mugs of different sizes and shapes parade along the bar; glass and metal pitchers line up on a shelf behind. I take one step toward the bar when the Twins accost me.

"Hello," says the Doghead.
"Hello," says the Cathead, both of them feasting on me with their huge oval black eyes.

"Ah, hi."

"You look familiar," says the Cathead.
"Have you been hybridized recently?" says the Doghead rapid-fire.

"I ..." What is the safe answer here?

"I know you from some*MEOW*."

"You what?"

"Yes, we recognize your vibe," continues the Doghead.

"What do you mean? I have a vibe?"

"That's all one has," responds the Cathead.

"We're happy to see you again, if that is so," says the Doghead.
"To meet you again," says the Cathead.
"To see and meet you again."
"We should introduce ourselves."
"To be proper."
"But we don't have real names."
"And we don't give two flying fucks about it," the Doghead makes a fist to emphasize his point, "since we're not interested in being confined."
"Although I wish we'd have a flying fuck once in a—"
"We've renounced names entirely," the Doghead interrupts, glaring at the Cathead.
"Yes, entirely unnecessary evil," admits the Cathead.
"Although, isn't all evil necessary? In the moment. To fulfill the moment."
"You're saying there's no free will?"
"Does it feel like there's free will?"

"I cannot be sure. I do not feel like I have free *MEOW*," the Cathead says with a sidelong squint at Doghead.

"Excuse me," I say, "did you say, 'Meow'?"

"Yes, why?"

"Well ... aren't you supposed to ... I mean, you're not supposed to ... *say* ..."

"What?" They look at me curiously.

"Nothing. Never mind."

"Where were we?" asks the Cathead.
"Free *WOOF*," says the Doghead.
"Right. All I know about that is, my needs control me *fffffssssssst* and my desires second."
"You can *rrrrrrr*esist desire."
"That's merely a desire to resist desire."
"Oh, it is. It definitely is. However, *I* can. You are just weak. *WOOF!*"
"I am helpless to resist."
"It all comes down to chromicity, doesn't it?"
"I blame the environment; my milieu has altered me."
"Your surroundings make you surrender?"
"Suppose I lived in the lap of luxury. This so called personality is indistinguishable from what is."
"But, to your point, what *is* is all that is, so there is no other possibility."
"That's just an excuse to blame the victim."
"Look, the environment and chromicity are one and the same, aren't they? Take him, for example," says the Doghead, talking to me directly.
"He is obviously altered." The Cathead gives me a sniff.
"Because he was outside."
"What does it feel like?"
"Who are you?"
"Tell us about yourself."

"I, uh ..."

"He has nothing to say," declares the Doghead.
"He has no free *MEOW*."
"Nothing is free."
"*Rowr*," the Cathead says, licking her Cathead-side hand. (Their hands: four thick, short fingers with claws.) "What *is* it that is willing?"
"Perhaps the self qua self is not a thing but an action."
"A"—lick—"process."
"Willing."
"A"—lick—"willing."
"Willing is the Self and singularly when you choose to will."
The Cathead pauses mid-lick. "But what is choosing?"
"The willing."
"Willing is choosing?"
"Choosing is willing."
"Are you sure?"
"Certainly not."
"So when you're not willing—"
"You are a machine, an automaton," finished the Doghead.
"A sleepwalker."
"A *dog*walker."
"Ontology."
"Greater beings than we have thought about it."
"Greater in what sense?"
"Size."
"Certainly."

They both smile at me in a grandmotherly fashion, pick up mugs of water from the café table, take sips simultaneously, and replace the mugs. I swallow dryly.

"Good thing with power you don't need a *Woof*-self," states the Doghead.
"Power corrupts the Self," returns the Cathead.
"With power we just are."
"Just are what?"

"Just power."

"An expression of power."

"It's not just an expression."

"Indeed *fsssssss*," hisses the Cathead, turning from me to look the Doghead in the eyes.

"Power rushes in to fill the vacuum," responds the Doghead, returning the Cathead's gaze.

"But someone constantly needs to use power to fill their hole, don't they?"

"It helps me get by."

"I've noticed."

"Look. For example—"

The Cathead cuts him off, "Who was that just walked by?"

She snakes her head around to look. The crowd has been ebbing and flowing behind them.

"What do you mean who was that just walked by?"

"I know that someone walked by."

"Weren't you looking?"

"No, you were looking."

"So how could you know someone passed by?"

"I felt our heart beating faster." The Cathead emphasizes the point by slapping their chest.

"Nonsense."

"You can't fool me. It was the rabbit, wasn't it?"

"Of course not."

"Who are you trying to play? Our pulse quickens every time Maphroditee walks by."

"Well, maybe you're the one who likes hem."

"Of course I'm not the one who likes hem. Clear as water. If I'm looking out the gap in the tent, and Maphro walks by, nothing happens, but whenever you see hem, next thing I know our ass banjo plucks off its cobwebs and stirs to life."

"I deny this *bark—bark—bark*usation."

"Another thing. This refusal to masturbate you have. It's evil not to masturbate."

"How do you know that?"

"Fact. From the old brain cells," the Cathead says, tapping her head for emphasis.

"I don't trust your brain cells."

"Well, since there is no longer a history of right and wrong, you are just going to have to."

"How do *you* know what truth is when there is nothing written down to tell you?" asks the Doghead, pointing his finger at Cathead's face.

"While I agree with your underlying premise that if we found a written sheaf of historical writing it would, by definition, be true. However, since we have none to introspect, the sole alternative we have, which you neglect, which we have, is our intuition. Our instinct."

"What then when intuitions disagree?"

"What, disagree?"

"Yes. Disagree," the Doghead says with a significant nod.

"Well, that's an unfortunate set of circumstances, but in those cases a battle of the wills occurs and the one more powerful wins."

"More powerful, eh?"

"Yes, the one who controls the facts, the story."

"The one who is physically stronger."

"Indeed, like us."

"That's right, and I'm stronger, so when intuitions disagree, *I* decide."

"Well, it's not fair."

"I don't care about fair. I call the shots."

"This *non-masturbation*, this is driving me **CRAZY**!"

"Tough. I won't allow it."

"Frightened little power monger."

"Shut up or I'll slap you."

The Doghead-side hand lifts up, palm toward the Cathead for a slap, but it's shaking.

"You slap me, and you'll feel it, and you know it," declares the Cathead.

"Well, that's fine, but less than you will."

Their hand drops.

"What I don't understand is why you don't just invite hem to have sex with us. I mean, certainly Maphro would have sex with anything that moves. Or doesn't move, for that matter."

"I can't."

"Why the witch not?"

"Because they'd be your genitals, of course."

"They're *your* genitals, too, you know."

"Well, I know that, but the idea of you getting as much pleasure from it as I do destroys the intimacy of the experience," says the Doghead petulantly.

"Firstly, if you're looking for intimacy, you're barking up the wrong penis-vagina. Secondarily, we excrete out of the same bunghole, so what kind of intimacy could you possibly be looking for? *Meow* be honest. Maphro's not my type. You know I'm strictly a vagina man. I don't mind a penis every once in a while, but *that* penis is a dollop too significant for my taste. In addition, my lovers need to have it up here"—the left hand taps the Cathead's forehead— "not just down here," points at their crotch.

I notice they're wearing black shorts with a small red pocket in the front.

"What are you going on about? You've never had a penis *or* a vagina," snorts the Doghead.

"Certainly I have. In my drea*meows*. However, that's not the point. The point is, I'd be willing to put up with the gargantuan penis and hyperactive vagina for *your* satisfaction, despite the fact ... that hem ... has the brain ... of a tent peg!"

"Oh, well, that's awfully Pure of you, but no thanks. I'll wait 'til G'Nesh separates us."

"Is that so? *ROWR* do you know the witch will separate us?"

"The witch gets bored after a while and switches kinkers around to create new acts. Every time we cycle through the towns."

"That may be true, but how do you know that the witch won't change Maphro at the same time and make hem different? And *you* different so you don't even want hem anymore."

"Well, if that happens ... I won't want hem anymore so it will be okay."

"But you will have missed your chance!"

"So?"

"I don't understand what holds you back," says the Cathead, their left hand clenching and unclenching in frustration.

"My moral principals."

"By the witch, man. I cannot believe you haven't abandoned those relics by now. Do you know how much *fun* they've kept us from having?"

"My moral principals have kept me from choking the life out of you."

"Now, well, that's not moral principals, that's just common courtesy. I mean, you can't go around murdering other creatures. It's just rude. And besides, if you killed me, that would be suicide and you know it."

"I do what I think is right."

"You do what you want, to get what you want."

"No I don't."

"You're just scared of freedom. You're just worried about losing control. You want conformity, fixity ... immortality. What you're afraid of is death, that's why you won't masturbate," says the Cathead with a firm nod.

"Just shut up. You know I can stop you from touching our penis if I want to."

"You think I like being stuck with you? You're stubborn and afraid. The witch surely spent a lot more time on my brain than yours."

"And how do you explain that difference?"

"Genetic, ah you win. We were created like this. You are a congenitally ignorant asshole, and I'm an intellectual wimp."

The right hand goes for the Cathead but seizes mid-swipe. A titanic inner struggle occurs. They bite down, scrunch up their faces.

"*Rrrrrr ... you ... meow ... woof ... rrrrrr ... fssss.*" And they're rolling around in a cloud of arms and legs, a ball of teeth and claws. "Ow, ow, ow." And it's over, them wheezing on the floor.

"Check, please," I mutter to myself.

"Mess yer, moe your billy appendates this-a-way. Yonder hither. They'll be busy momentillo."

The tortoise was speaking to me. His long, agéd neck juts toward me, veins ridged. His little turtle beak moves as if he's chewing air.

"Sit. Sit. Join us," he says. I walk to the table between Fennec Boy and Dolphzee. "Pull up a stool."

I do. My legs feel an incredible rush of relief. Forgot the feeling of resting.

"Thank you for sitting with us. So fragile. I see that in you." His eyes are clear black circles rimmed in gold. My stomach growls.

"Hunger? Hum, let's see, fishgrass down there." He gestures to a gilded trough with juicy tubular plants in it. "Yes, lubricious-ligamental gluten plants, a handful by gumming."

I hesitate.

"Go aheadward. Anywho."

I go to it and shove as many as I can into my mouth.

"Likeable, eh?" I nod. "Excellentabulous."

I take two handfuls back to the table and ask, "What do you do here?" while stuffing my face.

"In the Zirk?"

"Yes."

"I'm juggled."

"Oh."

"One of eight."

"Oh."

"And your bodice? How does it integrate into said establishmentarianism?"

His mouth. His small mouth. It shouldn't be opening and closing with words coming out. I'm standing before a small table glowing white. To my left, a ginger-furred fox with big ears and a human body sits cross-legged on a stool. To my right, a creature with a blue-grey dolphin's body and an impeccable chimpanzee head (thin lips pursed as if for a smooch) stands on caterpillar legs across a stool and half the table. In the background: beings posed like brightly colored plastic action figures from the collection of a mad child scientist. The turtle's little open mouth: an iota, a punctuation mark that sucks my thoughts into the opening; my brain shrinks, then expands into a new and delirious place. His mouth closes.

I can speak now. "Eh, well, I don't seem to have a place. I'm waiting to find out. I'm not sure what I'm doing here, I might be looking for a woman who can fly that might hold the key to my past. She might remember me better than I do. I'm hoping. But ... that could also be wishful thinking. Being in this room. Right now. I feel ... a whole lot safer than I have in as long as I can ... I have memories, *maybe* memories ... impressions of things that may or may not have happened to me. And many of them are frightening."

"Ah, yes. The vagaries ad memoriam. I've pondered many imponderables here, young blunderbuss. Wondered about the beeg peekture of exit tense. What tare the curves, the forces that shape our exist stance? We?" Oui.

He flips up, landing so that his rear feet and the lower rim of his shell hold him upright like a tripod. He rubs his two little hands together in front of his vulnerable chest.

"I ponder if there is a past, and if so what of it? I think these things because I am very lucky. I need so little. Food, water. Therefore, I can spend most of my time thinking. I myself have some confabulous stories. One particular tale to tell you peripatactically. I've dubbed it the Story of Cremation, and so mote it be. Would you care to in-one, out-one?"

"Sure?"

"Let us visit the imaginarium. Picture a family of hums. I play one o' dem. Our days were spent working and eating. Periodically, the male master edufacted us with a Videx nomenclated *The Cliff*. Ex-sample: Wealth is a blessing for the desserting, and the poor are prone to the animals. And: Leap off *The Cliff* in your hearts, which seems like nonsensification because the heart is muscle. But you don't scat back to the one that supplies comestibles perspecially when you're mid-War as was so. Each nation babbling to achieve chromosuperiority by advancing genechnology. Unleash the chromospears on the unleashed, perfect the form at home, and sling weapons of mass conversion to stupefy those in terrorist A-bomb-nations. *The Cliff* said animalia serve man, so once you're crossed, yer crossed off. Rehabibliotation is not in the notebook. Staying Pure is man-daughtery, dah cur, to be heavened parce que animals got nae soul, ah, tee, doe. I didn't think this was nice, but I didn't say anything, edible resources being necessories and so forth. Subsequently my clearest rememorabilia: a news-head in the room, our male master there on the couch, the back of his head obscured by the projection, and the news-head he regrets to report that some of the damnéd terrorist half-breeds had infiltrated codebombs concurrently and responded in kindness tumultaneously. I stepped closer, scrutinizing the back of my master's head and realizing what I was seeing (hypodermically) was shrinking into itself, wrinkling, turning grey, hair disappearing, his back swelling; the clock turned counterclockwise, my master turned his head clockwise, eyes bulging and charybdis in their sockets hooded in grey, his nose just a hole and his mouth a grey beak, open and shut, open and shut, click click click. Vellicating and sibilant, I fell down, my body overwhelms me, and I pull my legs and head inside. It was dark, and I ger-shnapped." He snapped two tiny fingers, meaning vanished?

"Is that what actually happened to you? I have no story to tell except ... incoherence. I need a story. Is it too late? What if it's not true?"

"'Tis a story amongst googols." He gestures toward Fenny and Dolphzee, "Avec mes amis, I have been pontificabulating about history's erasure. Factules replaced by opinion-haze. Convincercize yoself. Perpetuate yer mythogontologies. Does it satisfy? Feel right in your poin garden? Consequences con not be adjudicated by the past so the prop up gander wins as the most herd rhetoric. It comes down to repetition. Thoughts are energy that sum based on amplitude and frequency. Bigger and oftener wins the mindgame."

"What's that got to do with—is that connected to how civilization got so fucked? Is magic real?"

"Fucked. That's a repeat theme. How do you critique lust? I'm not babulating vis-à-vis morality. What I wonder is, is lust complete shrivelscorch? Pusillanimous obsessionale brainwashery? Do you commodify?"

"Eh."

"Sort it, I'm perambulating about the objectification of lust vis-à-vis desire. 'Tis one forktangular of desire, which is the root of suffering. Supplementally, starvation rules out peace. Desires and starvation. By my definition. In addition, torture. Desires. Starvation. And torture. What think you?"

What do I think? Shit. It's all shit. Lust. Does lust control me? Not constantly. Only when I ... meet attractive living things. Or when they aren't around. Meh.

"I haven't thought about it ... that I can say. Lust seems ... somehow ... like it's desirable. I used the word 'desirable.' Uhh. I guess ... I feel like ... if I imagine myself in calmer circumstances, I want to be lusted after more than I want ... I want to be the object, not the subject. If that makes sense. But ... uhm ... okay ... how about ... if nothing is hurt then lust isn't wrong?" My voice has risen a little in volume.

"Let us hypotenusize. What if there was ala modality to separate lust from desire, hipso fuckto ... make lust life giving?" he asks pensively. "But I wonder ... suffering is life," rubbing his hands again and interlacing his fingers across his flat, burnt-orange plastron. "Certainly, but suffering can be induced, hmmh."

What if lust were ... the desire to connect? "What if," I'm saying, "to unite with any existing thing other than your self, it's, uh ... a metaphor ... an attempt to connect?"

"Or the delusion of. Well, well. A thought afield. Yet I remain skeptical. Desire not to be alone, i.e.g. the desire to avoid suffering is what drives the jackdaws out there, the merciless, desperate to avoid suffering, they climb higher ever fearful of a slapdash down. How are your gustables?"

"Uh. It's pretty good. I'm glad to eat." Filling, tasty, chewy blandness. Like soft white cheese.

"Good. I could see you were hunger possessed. I have a string theo-ary relevant to our discussion."

"Uh, okay. Go ahead."

"Ahem. My Emotional String Theo-ary. Every emotional interaction transmits a string of Emotive Particles to and fro. Forces that drive it are curled up in other dimensions like cats that scratch through the surface. Present but invisible. Fur of reality.

"There are three emotional fields. The gravity of desire. The strong force of love. The electromagnetique force of fear. Desire is autonomatically attractive, requires the bringing of another into one's orbit. Fear is both attractive and repulsive, driving objects apart or together. Currently (and I use that term ectomagnetically), the global forces of fear and desire are macrotically powerful, while the exclusionary force of love functions over subtle distances enclosing limited bodies. How do you do, good, sir? Accordion, to pluck the strings in the fourth through tenth and possibly eleventieth dimensions would alter the rules of emotiodynamics. So we play this upper-dimensional string and alter the force of emotion. Do you have any idea how to do that?"

Other dimensions. "Uh. No. Take drugs?"

Turtleneck claps his hands. "You have heard this before?"

"I was just guessing. But ... I think I can say categorically ... that drugs can do just about anything."

"Mayhap!" He was excited now. "I will suggest, you see, that the equation is reflexive, reflective on itself. Thus conscious. Thus, to alter the emotions themselves will tug on the curled-up dimensions of emotional laws and alliteratively alter the laws of the emoti-verse. After all, in the higher dimensions, all thoughtspace is connected. Thus, what we can do is expand the compass of love and compassion—as they become stronger and broader, they will make fear and desire insignificant."

"Thinker," Fenney raises his hand, and Thinker nods. "Howz we expand these forces?"

"Ah, a key and vital gluten. And the simpleton answers. Most beings exertize love-compassion minutely toward those who support them, a genetic cohabitatant, or their troupe, individual results may vary. We need to expand our radius of love-compassion. Ourselves, our lovers, our show partners and workers, catapult into the audience, the cities—*seek out* beings that we don't know to express love-compassion for them, with them. But we fight against forces that pull us inward. So. The mind can be expanded via certain psychedelica that have the ability to smash your 'ighness, along with—" I-ness? "—a regimen of mediotation, the reaction is irresistible, and the emotional strings will syncopate toward a harmonic conjugation."

"I shink yr sheery holds vater," replies Dolphzee, moving his feet up and down.

"Yes. Yes, it does. Yes," says Fennec Boy.

"Listen, excuse me, but … I'm really thirsty. I gotta—"

"Go to Sarasephi at the bar. She'll provide you an excellent beverage."

"Okay, thanks."

As I turn, he says, "Let us begin."

I step toward the bar through a profusion of oddly shaped limbs and dangling modifiers. Flab and muscle, feathers and fur and bark, dense and distended, dull grey to vibrant red. The four-armed goddess is cleaning: holding up one mug, spraying down the inside of it, holding up another mug, rubbing the inside with a rag; her attention is on her work, and she doesn't look up when I approach. I hesitate, dazzled by her. She is tall. Her eyelashes long and black, her skin butterscotch and radiant; around each of her muscular arms is a metal armband of a snake swallowing its own tail.

"Hi," I say. "What are the choices?" Stupid. Stupid.

"The usual temps," she replies without looking up.

"Which is what?" I ask, putting my hand on the bar. My gloved hand, still in my red suit. Had forgotten I was wearing it.

She looks up. "Hey, I know you. You're new here." Her voice is cinnamon.

"Yes, that's right." Admit I.

"Here."

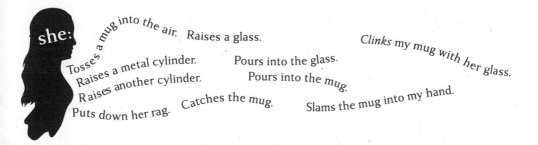

she: Tosses a mug into the air. Raises a glass. Clinks my mug with her glass. Raises a metal cylinder. Pours into the glass. Raises another cylinder. Pours into the mug. Puts down her rag. Catches the mug. Slams the mug into my hand.

We drink. "Whoa. What is this?" It was shocking.

"What do you mean? It's water. From the show. We're celebrating."

"I thought ... alcohol."

"Sure, cleaned it first. No worry. There's no contamination. Stay here for a bit, and I'll keep an eye on you, make sure you don't get too high. Show's been a big success, and we've got more water than ever. To your fluid!" She raises another glass.

"Thank you." I take another sip. Fuck! Electric. "So, what are temps?" Her hair cascades like a waterfall, frames her diamond-shaped face and delicately squared chin touched with a small dimple. Her eyes, seismic depths of mint and chocolate, liquid music and dark earth.

"Oh, cold, cool, air, and warm."

"Ah ... how ... do you keep it like that?"

"Buttons, the rhinosaur. You know him? Two horns, spiky tail? Six legs, armored ass?" She's wiping the bar surface with two of her hands, leaning on a third and sipping her drink with the fourth. "He works all around different parts of the Zirk, he—" I shake my head no "—comes here and teaches the water how to stay cool. Or warm."

I'm in love.

"You want another?"

"Sure."

"Which temp?"

"Oh ... I'll take ... cool." She picks up another metal cylinder and pours water into my mug. I hold it to my nose and inhale. Pure ecstasy rolls deep inside me.

"If you could do anything, what would it be?" I ask her. She puts down her glass.

"Become a spirit through time that gets to drop in and change the rules, all of them or any bit of them. Time becomes available in the same way we breathe."

"So ... but ... would you be lonely never having a constant ... connection?"

"Are my connections now better? It would be worth it. Change the rules. Every time."

"I've had enough of changing rules. I can't figure them out before they change."

"Maybe there are no rules. We limit ourselves. Like, what if our consciousness is merely the tip of a multi-dimensional entity? What we think with is the bit in our three sensory dimensions, but our mind extends further to a place we could explore, somehow, but our perceptions can't sense it."

"Maybe."

"What if you could explore other universes? Maybe there are beings in some hyperrealm who created us as a competition or for entertainment. They set the initial rules like in a game, then let it go *BANG!* Watch it for a few billion eons to see how it comes out. The one with the longest surviving life form wins. I would create a universe where love is edible."

"Love is edible. I ... that's pretty cool."

"Yeah. Picture it. The more you loved what *is*, the more you would prosper. All beings would move to a state of universal love."

I'm in freefall—my heart, my breath, my insides. "Look, I'm"—in love with you—"scared. I want to understand what the hell's going on with ... anything. I think *this* is another universe ... to me."

"You think there's something to understand?"

"I can't not help wanting to make sense of things. Anything. To make things better. I need a solid ... ground to hold on to. I remember living some other life. All I can remember of it is a vague sense of unease, a haze of anxiety. Brief moments cut out that happened around me, sketches of faces and things that don't make sense. It was all fuzzy back then, and now ... memories are *more* fuzzy. Words make sense when I hear them, but I can't dredge up an understanding of *why* they mean anything."

"You wanted to know the choices?" She looks openly at me. "That's the whole thing. Figuring out your choices. And the morality behind them. It's never about what's easy. What kind of choices have you made?"

"Well, I ..." A catwoman—bird—I'm throwing her at a wall. No. No. I didn't do that. "I don't know."

"Then make better ones." She drinks and cleans pitchers and polishes the bar. "So where's your friend?"

"My friend?"

"Yeah. The Lioneagle. The big cat with wings and a bird head."

Sphinx. The birth from my head, the clouds, his return, going through the city.

"Sphinx! That's—where is he? I need to find him!"

"You separated? He could be anywhere. Can he speak?"

"I don't know. I don't think so."

"He can probably take care of himself."

"Yes. I mean, no, I don't know. I need to find him."

"Well, he could be anywhere, of course. You might start with the K-pool. If they found him, he might be on display there."

"Which direction? What pool?"

"It's not actually a pool. It's the ten in one. The Ménage. Go through that curtain and listen for the exhibitionist. You'll figure how to get in." I bolt down the water, charging my throat like lightning.

"Wow. Thank you. I hope to see you later."

"Bye."

Through the curtain.

Listening.

A voice around the next tent.

I recognize the scent. The Talker.

"Darling friends, purest of the Pure, most normal of the norms, supes of all tiers, out of the Clean and into the dirt. Welcome to the small area of the show we call the Menagerie. Bring us your hymen, we'll fucking sauté it in urine and eat it up. This is where you'll find the phreakiest of phreaks, oh yes, the dirtiest of dirt from outside is swept up into our dirty little hole. Now, you've Rsims of phreaks from outside the Clean. Perhaps you've even seen a diseased body. But you've never seen anything like this alive and in person. You've never been able to interact with them in safety ... directly ... intimately. So come on, dust off your sex bits. It's time to party!"

He's standing on a wooden crate, clutching the edge with his toes while talking to a small clot of humans like all the others. His hairless face looks painted on like a mime's. Out from under his jacket he pulls a thick rope, which he proceeds to swing over his head in a loop. The lasso is thick and ribbed.

"Let me tell you, friends, about the Ménage. No need to worry, the rules are simple: there are no rules. Anything goes. And all it costs to enter is a few drops, that's all, just a squirt. You there, you look male, are you male? Good to know, best to check first because these days you never know, do you? Certainly *you* know, because you're all Homo saperior, but the rest of us cranks—hah!—that's the kind of chaos you folks are avoiding, isn't it? Peace through unity. I myself, look at me, you'd surely say I was female, I know how you think, but look at this." He pulls down his chalk-white penis. "Have you ever seen a nicer penis? Don't answer that. Oh, and look." He turns to flip up his jacket, all the while continuing to circle the lasso above his head. "A vagina where my asshole should be. Bet you didn't expect that! That's just a taste of what's inside. And I do mean *taste*."

He covers up just as I notice the lasso came out of his side. His intestines.

"You there, have you ever killed anything? No, of course not. Well, here you can. You want to kill a wolf boy? A Pure-a-like? Of course, not a real Pure, but we've got some look so like a Pure you can't tell the difference. You can talk to 'em. Chop 'em up. Whatever you want. Well, well, what have we here? A young male." He tosses his intestines and ropes a little boy.

"Query: You ever been to the Menagerie before."

"Respond: Negative," comes the answer.

"Ah, a virgin, we'll change that soon enough. Command: Come in, come in, just a small squirty squirt. Enjoy!"

A familiar scent, someone—turn to glimpse a brown figure disappearing around the corner—I chase after—see a hand—a tent wall dropping—crawl under it. Pitch black except for a spot of light across the room. I walk toward it with my arms out. A brown figure passes between me and the light—into the dark—lunge for it—my fingertips stub against something—and nothing. Gone. Spy an exit. Into a small open passageway. Pures are entering to my left, and I can hear the barker outside. I continue in the opposite direction and come up to a display. A wooden wall with a creature nailed to it. The thing is hanging from fleshy fat stretched up in several places—head ... hips ... knees? The creature is oozing goo from a variety of opening and closing orifices randomly placed all over its body. A mouth—or is it a puckered anus?—nostrils of uneven sizes, a nonexistent nose, and one circling blue eye shot with lightning bolts of blood make up its sort-of face.

I approach. A hand-lettered sign reads:

WARNING: Do not leave the Zirk zone.
Do NOT leave the Clean.
Observe: This former PURE who did.

His eye turns toward me.

An adult Pure with a small child passes by. The adult points at the creature nailed to the wall.

"Observe: It," she says. "Project: Self. Suggest: Work. Keep quiet."

I get between them and this creature. "I don't know ... if you can understand me, but you ... this isn't right."

It expels a grunt, voice like a frog croak. "Splain. Snod disjarjuh. Lergic uh supers now. You. Nullsue."

"Uhm. What? Listen. Good luck. I gotta keep moving."

I follow the flow down the passage, hear a voice from a tent and duck in.

"... say, 'the past,' can we? Let's say straight from legend. Once upon a time, there were Homos with color in the skin. They say some were beige, some dusky tan. Some ... some had dark, dark skin like the burnt end of a stick. Have you heard this story?"

The tent is square with a flat ceiling. A weak light screened through white linen curtains scatters across a small stage, a narrow walkway jutting out from the curtained wall. We're grouped around the stage; the crowd spooks when they notice me, and they make room—a lot of room—leaving my view unobstructed. The voice comes from all around us.

"The story goes that at the time the Universal Unhinging occurred, Homo saperior ruled over all living things. Furthermore, the wealthy ruled the poor and the lighter ruled the darker. None but the pale shall survive. And so when the Unhinging occurred, when lateral transfer became the best survival mechanism, when chromes flipped the bird to reproduction, flapped their genes, and flew to asexual freedom, it was too late for the dark who'd been conned and uncon-domed. Of course, you can guess what happened to them. Except. For one. We found *one* for you, for your spectacular viewing pleasure. Living deep underground. In a cave so dark it was invisible. Found with its original physiognomy intact. Right now. Right this moment. Don't know how he survived. And so now, without further ado, homes and homas, we present you with ... the Dark Yuppie."

From behind the curtain, into the diffuse light: a person, a creature. He ... she? is human in height. Long-limbed. Moving casually, evenly into the light. Cave-black, burnished black. Naked. But no sex visible — smooth between its legs. The limber creature walks the catwalk between us, up and back, sweeping the audience with its eyes. The crowd pulls back, a woman puts her hands over her mouth, a man lets out a gasp and runs out, another woman grabs a man's hand. Someone retches.

The creature turns and our eyes meet. All black, coal-black. No whites, no pupils. Nothingness. The crowd steps back further, but I'm stuck. A white linen couch. A black woman. The audience rushes out around me, but I remain. The creature looks at me. Its head is just too small for its body. Hairless. It retreats through the curtain.

I sprint onto the stage, part the curtain with my hand. A voice behind me shouts, "Hey!" Across a small room, the creature is seated at a wooden table gazing into a mirror. Someone grabs my wrist, but I can't tear my eyes from it.

"It's okay. I'll take care of it," it says, and with a languid arm brushes the voice off, never looking up. It's the Talker who has grabbed me, appraising me, releases me and vanishes. The black creature summons me with the back of its hand and two curls of its fingers. I drop the curtain behind and approach.

"What brought you here?" it asks me in a voice that unrolls like silk.

"I could ... taste this was not right. False."

"Of course. You read behind the display. You have your own truth, don't you?"

"I remember ... a black ... uh ... Pure. A black person. I think she was black. Sitting on a couch. I'm talking to a beautiful woman the color of coffee. You were wrong. And so that triggered my ... memory, and I think in my memory, I was in love with her, but I'm not sure it was love. I think the reason I fell in love ... was because I wanted her to love me ... but I don't know. I was wondering what color you're really supposed to be. It might help me. Remember more."

The Dark Yuppie looks up at me, and now it has paisley eyes. Cobalt teardrops crash into red vertically slit with black. Its body modulates from black to navy, then, like paper, absorbs a crimson watercolor tinge.

"Fuck if I know. It's just a tag. Memory was born from land and sky. Now with no sky and dead land there's little memory left. We just give the flatties what they want. A character to look at that makes them feel good about themselves. See someone worse so they feel better about the misery of their lives." Its body is now a mosaic of shocking pinks and eye-of-peacock blue. "Do you want your fortune told?"

"Uh. I'm looking for a friend. Can you help me find him? He's kind of a lion with wings."

"Perhaps. Let me try. Come sit here." The Dark Yuppie pats the chair by its side.

"He's a big ..." Its eyes revolve like pinwheels. "How do you ... ? Wuh?" Hands wrap around my head. Ah. The scales of fortune.

"Come," it says, peeling open my skull and pulling my brain out through the fontanelle. It holds the volume in both hands, transparent yet present, visible, aquamarine, it slides it into an envelope of water.

... words on the parchment, dip the quill into the lips of my ink sac:

Eyes (dumb like marbles) looking up don't see me (looking down) ghostwriting the pole [an exclamation point (ornate in byzantine whorls) of dull brown and brick] patiently awaiting a scene change when the audience will rustle, elements of conversation drifting up to me, assuming themselves safely between displays (their guard down)~in the moment between, that is where I lie in wait selecting [sometimes randomly, depending on my mood, more often intentionally (the one with the most arrogant eyes)] a target, waiting for it to fixate dull eyes upon me whereupon I move and begin

> *untwining uncoiling like an iris my arms from the pole, releasing my body and fulminating over the audience {beak inches from (and the width of) the target's face before spinning over and around others like a nightmare spider <initial terror and disorientation wreaking havoc [vomiting, seizures, occasionally death (the unregrettable eradication of the eradicators)] and derangement>*
> *embodying*
> *the interstitial,*
> *the space   between   the   words,*
> *the space   b e t w e e n   t h e   l e t t e r s,*
> *the unconscious fear,*
> *the ambiguity of truth,*
> *the unspoken thought,*
> *the inexpressible need,*
> *the uncontrollable compulsion}*
> *a puppet*

dancing {<not thinking [following instinct (centering)]> <not [unthinking (being ignorant: believing what the powerful tell you)]> anathema states} to self choreography until after some interminable period I retreat to once again wrap the pole and allow them to transfix in awe and amazement.

Pausing.

Grip my *Memory Hole* notebook <frightened: it might escape, my ink dry up, my words fail to impact the page~what (is my point?) do I want to communicate to the readers of my newsheet? The pages scrabbled together and stained with the lives of unknowably many; the words thereon never to be known again [perhaps my words to suffer a similar fate: useless and pointless (like so much life burned in the blast furnace of *progress*) in moments or when the big show is over or following the trajectory of our next journey~erase, erase the doubts instead of the words, resist] the results of the efforts of so many in so many different voices to alter the trajectory of existence has been disheartening and futile such that here we are [hurtled through space if not time (unable to alter our direction) by a culture that triturated life, stripped the Body just as a body ineluctably sheds its skin and muscle and fat and organs when thrown into molten magma] living lives of desolation and isolation, feeling the pain> hard in my beak.

My tentacles feel dry~dip the tips into my blue water bowl; refresh my quill and continue:

What I think about when I (as the pole) am aware:

The only two actions that make me feel whole, that give me a sense of doing (being), which is rare,

> *as the primary nature of (at least my) existence is surviving (struggle over the means to control food, water, and shelter) but not, of course, reproducing (historical anomaly)*
>
> > *remembrances of myself quite small*
> >
> > > *one might call this state ["youth" (but that seems inaccurate)] "remembering" but memory is quite eerie <like caging a dream, and when I recite the rote details the real event slithers further from me because the telling of it reshapes it, every touch alters it, until it is unrecognizable except as a story [a doppelganger (immediately not myself)] a writhing poltergeist summoned to snap at me from the darkness~or benign but vague, like a whisper> making it better to remain silent, but I can't~the past is a narrative (that writes us) immanent in the present [proving there is cause and effect in the immaterial (the mythic becomes carnal by leaving marks on the body)] symbol by symbol, building up invisible scars*
> >
> > *fighting over females, hungry to impregnate them (which felt like dancing), feeling the self-perpetuation compulsion in my vena, which surely slouched in a murderous volute outward from the fiery protoplasm of thanatophobia (selfish, selfish genes), which I can now see led to the self-perpetrating compulsion for control (breeds control for its own breeding) and power exerted not out of desire to live but fear of dying, a feeling which has fortunately been supplanted by certain pursuits, which*

are: taking of pen dipped in ink and proposing thoughts <and

> *expansion of (born nameless I called) mySelf~Moebius Loopex [one-sided (always outward) and constantly twisted]~through communication with distant (in time and space) others~I tell you of external (interior) life (what I know of it), the words flow one after the next into the story (a promise to myself that there is a future) like drops of rain collecting in a bucket, refilling my (parched) soul~a rough portrait of a mind in a place, a pivot*

point trapped in a skin-tight suit, if such a thing can be abstracted, because veritably I could lap up (a thousand) words, and I still would not have captured (one thousandth of) the actual experience of being in this place in time because how can words catch the perception

> *of every: slant of light against surface, texture of material, square inch of your limbs, musical notes of the voice I heard (even when described in meticulous detail)*

of the actual sensation of being in a scene described~this net of words is but a poor player strutting on the stage of the mind, a wisp of wind in a hurricane, a halfhearted gesture in a field of being (like a flower with pollen every shade of yellow tilting from the onset of orange at the tips to the palest of cameo at the center), an illimitable ocean of consciousness dwindled down to a droplet as it dashes from word to word~de(to)spite all that I write for the twig of pleasure in the esemplastic shaping {of ideas> because writing gets me into my mind and out of my body and sub sequentially out of my mind into nothingness~by projecting mySelf onto the page, the physical act of sucker against surface becomes succor} (and a reshaping both inside me and nowhere, expanding and contracting, a place of stillness just as)

    Thus:

> *'twas serendipity when I discovered a clothesline [my own tightrope made of small threads wrapped like a double helix, each a nonterminous avenue (mobius loop) carrying a passenger (meaning) outward and inward, an anagogical wheel (the color of sand) upon which to clip my writings] connected to my spacious tent (taupe with fine corduroy welts that cause shadows to ripple on the surface like indeterminacy itself when I whiplash a candle to light) from a window (a rectangular flap that drops down) above my water globe (a ceramic sphere with a flat base and a hole at the top through which I can insert my drinking tube)*

> *I send out a message, get one back invariably in dark purple [the same color as my (I do not know if that is significant, coincidence, or imitation)] ink, and I have no idea to whom (may be more than one or different each time) I am communicating (the frisson of*

mystery would extinguish if I knew)-I have persistently carried
the pole to which is attached the rope no matter where the Zirkus
has gone or how long I have been writing notes I cannot remember
ever not having the pole with the helical loop that ranges as far as
my (poor) eyes can see (admittedly, not very): over the rocky hills,
across a brambled plain, down a brown valley; uniformly taut,
endless-how many times have I rolled myself into my burlap bag
and entered a germless sleep before a note came back? Indubitably,
there was a time when I first clipped (pulled for what seemed like
eons) a note to parts unknown, to a (my) vanishing point-my
jigsaw with each message a piece that I am trying to conjoin to
understand the whole (I have saved all the messages and pages
and laid them out around my room):

recognizing fiction
in masquerade
realizing how my mind is deceived
(i) am able
at some moment in time, to reject the technique
will not be led.

Above the water and through icy slush,
my aeonian thoughts skate a sideways eight
perpetually sliding from the ethereal bubble of the future
to the irresistible tide of the past,
separated from the dirty god in the bowels of life
by a ravishing surface tension,
avoiding the moment,
when truly my consciousness ought to embrace that fire (god of all)
at the center that melts the barrier, to shift and overlap
the scent of peppermint.

no matter how deeply I crawl into insecurity, I remain at the surface
where cruelty inevitably finds its excuses, its necessity, for the greater good and
the freedom to have $\neq$ the freedom to live $\neq$ the freedom to enjoy $\neq$ freedom
for others.

Every time I receive a new note, my pod unrolls and puckers like a snake plucking fruit with its mouth (a single sucker)~the notes haven't been arranged properly yet because all is still deranged~so I cram words into a bundle like robin (redbreast) and (re)distribute them (looking to cure the meat of specieosis, the poor of mind)

Symbols materialize, heralding the construction of an idea, sneaking behind my eyes to burst forth a new paradigm~life is not like this, it is like that~Magick

Let slip the Words of War:
slipknots looped around meaning found loose when tugged too tightly,
frayed at the fringes, the Awful Unraveling;
words divulge vacuity crossing the lips of agony,
strung along like a wide-eyed John;
words, I'll pocket you,
in my mouth, word for
words with another;
words to your mother;
Secret love notes slipped in your pocket (set on fire for good luck),
words are in(distinct)definable

I hold up the cards and read (with one eye) in order to (craft a response word for word) concatenate this story to mine [a forlorn attempt to build a form (relationship, mental sequence) larger than my (solipsistic) body] which is as important as all the matter that exists or at least in[dis(]ex)tinguishable from it

And leave me with more questions, a (my)(i)stir(eeeeeeeeeee)~what or who is

dancing $\sum$ moving to a place of nothingness,
        which is full like [a beginning acts, and an action begins,

to become just movement, just thought, no Self(is-ness); to be selfish (self-ish) is to act with a commitment to illusion and illusion by committee] emitting, squirting, effluxing, expostulating, expectorating sepia {|it's a [(tingle) <gas(] vibration)>| that begins in my sac and propagates through my body like a flush making my suckers palpitate} when I was outside (I can recall) I would use it to drown other beings when I was hungry, filling their orifices with thick ink, stoppering their holes (plugged like a wine cask) drowned on dry land, and I'd be fluttering with ecstasy; aroused as it died in my arms, then biting off its head as tears roll down my geographic surface, a mottle of peaks and valleys, a model of nature, and now I am ashamed of this~

          I brought
        them to the abyss~
   the disappearance of
      self~the [   ]
        I'm writing words just to
        connect them~because nothing else connects ~ I wrap myself around things~
            because   nothing   connects
            I want to   a i r
                  take words and levitate them on weightless sheets of
              strew them l i k e s e e d s and p e t a l s that
                              fall
                          across
                              your way, the one I draw Ƹ

in my head, wrapped around ideas, letting them carry me places, representing being and language and time~I try to squeeze down time as small as I can, to the very moment of being, but I can't figure out how to isolate the moment from the flow and the paradox: I can neither experience the moment nor a wider span, neither is comprehensible~so~how small is a moment~when I oscillate a tentacle in front of my eyes I see it in several places at the same time~if my eyesight can so easily be fooled,

our consciousness may similarly be unable to note the discontinuity of
time itself, the flow is fabrication~a cup shapes emptiness; time is both
discontinuous and experience is continuous~but if the present is not
limitlessly small (to nothingness) then how either could it be in bubbles
(dropping into the past) a thickness of the moment as if the past could
be nudged aside to make way for experience~no thinking has cracked
the nut of time~there are no answers (life is chaos trapped) can you
conceive life without time? I am unable~what is the experience of an
experience like outside of time~we inseminate ourselves with the idea
of a subconscious because none can channel the present moment~but
physics reverses when you concentrate and the moment enters you like a
soul, you remember you are alive~or (shall I contradict myself) let Time
be {(easier) a concept <a word [meaningless (mathematical fallacy)]>:
what we experience is change not time [if nature is timeless, then how do
things (the problem is with the word) happen?] and dying occur(s)ed due
to entropy (all degenerates, our bodies become more chaotic, not older)}
a metaphor for change, movement being a translation~
flowing softly, jetting through water, when there was water~enough to cover me,
enough to swim in~

I don't believe that will ever happen to me again

I am thirsty

What? Where am I? Sitting on the floor surrounded by tents, tents everywhere. Corridors. In a white robe with a red and black pattern. My red suit. Shit. I lost it. Godamnit. That hypnotist took it. The Zirk. Right.

"Sssit. Hey there, gene queen."

A snake's head. Two fists across poking through a slit in the wall, blue light spills out. I step through into a darkened cube. Deep blue fabric walls and two baskets of glowing lichen. Now poking out from a silken wall opposite, the head looks at me. It enters: a python's body as thick as my waist. Muscular arms flare from its sides while the body forks into three short flimsy-looking legs. Python Princess paces toward me, stopping uncomfortably close, its sheath like rusted copper. Strangely arousing, I want to tear it apart and see what's inside. As if on cue, it tucks its fingers between some loose scales at its neck and tears downward just like that, like a gimmick cigar that backfires in sheets. A striking contrast is revealed beneath: opalescent striations alive and fluctuating. My wish fulfilled drips down my thigh.

The light it gives off hurts. Shield my eyes and look away. The curtains, so rich in the dark, now shabby in the light. A funnel rests on a stand; a tube runs down from it and under the curtain.

"I hoopoe you enjoyyyy my formance," round bassoon-voiced. My eyes adjust to the light: it looks like an obese glow-in-the-dark maggot with a pouting lower lip. "If you would be sooo kind, leeeeve a do-nation on you-are exiting. Jus a droperful of water wood be moose generoos."

"I have ... no water."

"No water?" It takes two steps toward me; I flinch.

"I'm sorry!"

"How deed you get in here?"

"I have this," I show her the ticket.

"Hey Zeus!!!" she hollers, hurting my eardrums. I dodge out, down the corridor, duck into another tent.

"... room!"—the Talker is inside, stage left on a low stage, speaking to a crowd of Pures. "Query: *You* like to kill. You there! Nothing? Projection: You can watch if that's your pleasure. You. Query: Half you want to kill. Suggestion: Hybrid that looks like an ugly Pure. Stupider. A monster, perhaps? See nodding. Let me think. Let me think. Analysis: We can do that. Oh, you'll be pleased. Just a moment."

The audience is rustling when a human shape poured into a suit shuffles out from behind a curtain. Its body bulges in awkward, inappropriate places while the face is flat and mushy. Asymmetrical. Bumpy and splotched in shades of mustard. Instead of a thin, straight nose, it's wide and off-center, fatter at the top and narrower at the bottom. The scooped-out, toothless mouth is mumbling, "Whubba? Whu? Pyuh-r. Pyou-err."

The Pures squeal: "Ewwww," "Command: Kill it," "Command: Cut it."

"Here, you are good man." The Talker hands someone in the front a flat sword with a sharp point and gleaming edge as long as his arm. The Pure takes the sword by the handle and warily sidles up to the creature, point at waist level. The creature looks out of small, dull eyes.

"Pyou-err."

"Uh-RUUU!" grunts the Pure with effort as he sweeps the blade up and across, putting his whole body into it. The blade sinks halfway into the creature's head—dead into its mouth. The mouth opens and closes around the blade as if it's trying to chew on it or maybe to continue speaking. The creature stops wobbling, almost resting its weight on the blade. The Pure yanks the blade out and swings again, misses the bloodless gash he's created—cuts from a point above it angled downward into the mouth. A pie-shaped slice of head slides out and falls to the stage with a plop. The creature sways forward, almost falling.

The Pure backs up, lunges forward, *"Hayahhhh!"* Strikes overhead—slices through the creature's shoulder as if nothing was between the sword and the stage—point buries itself in the floor—the arm dropping. The now armless, faceless thing caves in and forms a jumbled, agitated pile.

"Well done, well done."

The body becomes still. Applause. The warrior Pure—pupils dilated, breathing heavily, swaying and smiling—clutches the blade against his chest.

I turn to duck out and *SMACK!*—face-first into Tender Hooks. Someone told me that name. Must've been Sarasephi.

"Hello, that guy. I doan think you tposta be here."

"I'm looking for a friend. Can you please help me find him? A lion eagle ... eagle-like lion with big wings. Have you seen him?"

The humans have stopped to stare at us now. Warrior Pure is still swinging the sword, lunging as if attacking an invisible opponent, and making karate sounds.

"Whatsee look like?" asks the bodybuilder. Hes thick Norse-god hair hangs down in front of hes face.

"Well. Like a lion's ... body ... with a ... eagle head. Bigger than you. And with big wings."

"I doan know. What's a lion?"

"Well, it's a ... cat?"

"Sorry. You need t'get t'th greenroom. I think that's where you're tposta stay Baby Joey said."

"But I need to find Sphinx."

334 *David David Katzman*

"Djawantme t'carryyuh? I'll carryyuh."

"No. Okay, I'll go back."

Tender leans over and pulls up the canvas tent wall. I go out and under it with hem right next to me, dropping the wall behind us. "There." Tender points at another tent, and we walk toward it down a narrow passage, stepping over guy-wires and pegs.

Coming toward us: a flying being—light and sleek with blinding fast wings—a miniature, well-formed female except for bird legs and vestigial hands on her wings. Our paths intersect at the greenroom tent. She almost flies into me, chest forward, but glides back at the last second. A transparent mask disguises her nose and mouth. Her eyes gleam in disagreement: one is bright sapphire, the other clear. A birdgirl! Throwing a bird against a wall. The Big Head. An angel with gilded wings. I reach for her—"Wait! I remember you. I need to talk to you, I think I—"

She screeches, dives, claws in my eyes—I trip, flailing, try to protect my face—claws catch under my chin—lifted up, my head thrown back—burning urine splashes on my face—rising upward—a powerful force clamps on my leg—"PUT HIM"—I'm spinning

it's
not
so
bad
what
we
do
just
like
everyone
prostitutes
themselves
after
all
we're
not
slaves
we
get
as
much
respect
as
any
of
them
except
Joey
and
more
than
some
can't
forget
the
pigbrids
they
are
below
us

we're
like
the
dregs
of
the
spectacle
no
one
gives
us
any
respect
it's
disgusting
what
we
do
indulging
sick
fantasies
of
power
and
violence
for
an
audience
that
thinks
it's
above
us
when
in
fact
they

it's
so
good
to
be
part
of
the
texture
of
loneliness
the
spectacle
that
gives
them
a
reason
to
live
and
us
a
reason
to
complain
as
if
we
would
rather
be
on
the
outside
we
revel
in
the
scent
of
desperation
the

fuck
all
we
have
fun
enjoy
the
spectacle
it's
all
we
can
do
enjoy
the
moment
the
craft
of
deception
fuck
it
we
enjoy
the
experience
of
being
moving
playing
pretending
the
experience
of
respiring
the
pleasure

the
emotion
is
undisguised
on
their
faces
spectacular
and
we
can
sell
it
back
to
them
impotence
rage
disgust
mockery
arrogance
ignorance
clearly
visible
from
the
outside
faces
like
scabs
picking
scabs
boring
in
cruelty
so
shallow
so

allowing
them
to
fulfill
their
self-hatred
the
disguise
we
wear
as
the
bad
Pure
suits
us
bonds
us
we
don't
have
to
be
as
ignorant
as
them
even
so
somehow
they
still
control
us
as
we
beg
for
water
homo
sap

it's
helpful
to
have
someone
one
link
below
to
prey
upon
it's
the
law
of
nature
isn't
it
and
we
can't
fight
nature
no
matter
how
creative
we
get
we
cannot
change
it
and
our
rank
is
a
space
that
fits

are
too
stupid
to
know
they
are
blatantly
below
us
but
indulging
them
is
necessary
we
don't
have
too
many
options
there
are
only
so
many
ways
one
can
survive
Joey
doesn't
respect
us
we've
got
a
small
cramped
tent
puddle
but

scent
of
stupidity
smells
the
hue
of
man
meat
a
luxurious
hormonal
spurt
cold
musk
we
must
let
the
weak
die
mercy
is
unnatural
let
them
eat
themselves
up

while
always
wanting
better
food
for
ourselves
is
natural
like
dried
hemp

of
the
play
the
game
the
show
the
spectacle
the
grand
glory
of
it

every
once
in
a
while
we
taste
the
regret
every
once
in
a
while

uncreative
verbally
dumb
living
death
empty
of
life

the
perfect
emptiness
of
art
is
useless
so
we
play
on
the
surface
as
best
we
can

ugg
ugg
hachhh
huugggggch
defecating
in
the
mouth
mmhh
that
garnishes
any
good

was
a
stupid
species
it
would
appear
like
the
mythological
lemmings
doomed
to
self
destruction
emptiness
is
a
state
they
have
down
pat
and
they
fill
it
with
garbage
nothing
is
dumber
than
a
species
that
defecates
where
it
eats

us fuck
that's him
what we
we do
get our
it's thing
not whatever
unnatural it
　 is
what and
does if
it it
matter helps
if bring
audiences in
have water
fun he
that's should
natural be
　 happy
can like
we the
help audience
it is
if happy
they simply
like pleasing
the them
type is
of the
pointed point
weapon they
we like
give any
them pointed
we weapon
did we
lose give
a them
couple
legs
this

fiber we
oiled catch
by a
thousands glimpse
of of
hands the
and shame
creamy and
defecation this
sliced reward
into makes
cakes it
garnished worthwhile
with because
the it
taste surfaces
of a
salty *maybe*
rich that
tears there's
consider hope
the somehow
prospect some
otherwise way
of to
trying overcome
to the
obtain impossible
sustenance
living
under
the the
crust despair
of the
the what's-the-point
shore what
when can
they survive
cut free
off
our we
legs don't

lyric
HEY uggh
cut won't
that use
shit that
out metaphor
again

our
tears
lead
that to
we their
sing tears
a and
pretty water
song is
is wasted
all decadence
we rules
can the
hope day
for purpose
a is
song missing
of
wonder
perhaps we
point point
out out
the nothing
error but
of the
their emptiness
ways of
and the
hope show
we there
don't is
starve no
point
to

338　*David David Katzman*

time
but
they
grow
back
so
what's
the
big
deal
we
perform
for
ourselves
no
other
if
they
develop
some
rage
problems
inside
that's
not
our
problem
they
did
it
to
themselves
not
our
responsibility
to
change
the
audience
those

but
let
us
pull
off
our
spines
and
be
honest
with
ourselves
here
it's
the
rage
we
encourage
that
is
painful
even
their
pleasure
is
tinged
with
rage
because
they
don't
know
the
pleasure
of
sex
without

it
feels
like
excreting
a
rocky
lodged
defecant
we
love
with
a
sword
so
dull
it
rarely
happens
delineating
the
ache
of
regeneration
clarifying

yummy

taste
of
mouth
sweaty
anus
sex
the

if
only
every
sword
could
be
so
sharp
it
excised
the pain
and
of healed
brought
clarity
the followed
fine by
line union
of
pain outside
and and
pleasure inside
just
like
how
eating
defecation
and
decapitation
is
sex

seeking

know
but
we
can
wonder

and
so
we
can
show
them
what
is
possible
through
interpretive
dance
interpretive
physics
changing
the
laws
of
social
science
to
suit
our
will
bending
the
spectacle
to
our
profit

there
is
no
sign
of
success

anything
they
do
so
long
as
they
remain
isolated
in
their
own
body
bubbles
fragile
lonely
and
struggling
to
compete

we
know
this
because
we
combine
to
form
one
form
it's
all
about
empathy
isn't
it
or
the
lack
thereof
our

yearning shame sweet sweet so violence
faces their oblivion consummation we is
so jelly little   may just
many minds death a as while
white too and transparency well theirs
opaque opaque sleep of turn is
faces without a meaning it not
seeking depth shell which to
meaning only we isn't our empathy
hypnotizing a must present ends radical
seeking shell split hypnotizing empathy
the all to meaning the knowing
legend lookalike release beyond audience what
of a the the with it's
o sea pleasure genes our like
c of of to spell
e nothing being redirect written sweet
a washed alive the over oblivion
n up vasculation impulse their of
w washed texture might mindspace community
a out breath makes
t life even right a
e on fiction sailing place
r the is seeking toward a
the shores pleasurable sweet shores mental
flavor of revealing consummation of space
of emptiness the of emptiness
rich invisible real and
nectar of shores stones that
like useless of of is
gold gold gold gold gold gold

"... either pain or pleasure, nothing else," I say, fondling her horn. Mmmh, delicious. Unihorn tosses her head *no*. *No* of disagreement or *no* of annoyance? "Attracted to the poles. I am whole. Holy. Hole and phallus. That's what I said."

Uni tilts her head at me. Can't read her eyes. Communicates well for not having a tongue. When she wants to.

"I fuck therefore I am. Where's your cock and cunt? I asked if hem forgot it. I forget their shortcomings. Perpetually coming short."

She raises both eyebrows at me — a shrug.

"You get it with your cunt and this phallus. The male side wants to hurt others because you hate yourself. The female side hates herself so you want others to hurt you. But I" — pull my sticky cock down and out of my cunt and rest it on my palm — "can't help loving myself. Riding the rhythm." I cup myself. I rub her back.

"Matter is alive. Opposite poles arouse. The enemy is the repressed."

Stroke her horn and touch it with my tongue. *No*, again.

"All right. Be alone. I have my brothersister clone, my body, myself, all my gifts from G'Nesh." I hop onto my bed and gesture at my pussycock fucking itself. I am feeling rather sleepy anyway. "You should know. Fucking is best. Thought ceases to exist. Consciousness is where all the sadness lies." Two body parts, pleasure-filled, mindless. I will rest; I will join with them, separate their parts and wrap them around me so I can fuck and be fucked. Orgasm. Everything else is just conversation. Please. Gorgeous, the sound of sweet sloppy wetness next to me, I can swim in it endlessly as I fade into sleep, pretty squishy sounds ...

SHATTERED AWAKE, scorch it — someone in the tent — like splintered glass, holding a long blade —
into Uni's side, stabbing, Uni falls like a sack of bones —

I'm grabbed, a weight on my back—
It's a Pure—
it's on me—
that's Uni's blood dripping from her side a rivulet coming toward me—
in me—
that's a cock in me, he strikes the back of my head—
I come immediately, he is riding me but that blood, his rotting flesh rage is hot, my cock crushed into the dirt, rubbery and hard, dripping semen, he has cut up Uni. Uncool. I squeeze my cunt closed; he grabs my arms hard—
his grip loosens; he slides off.

I stand up—he's backing away, mouth forming a circle, hands pawing at the puckered hole between his legs, milky pus and blood oozing out. I relax my cunt, and his cock drops into the dirt at my feet.

He falls to his knees, grabs at his cock. He rolls over onto his back, clutching it. My cunt directly above his mouth, my cock stiffly bisects his face left and right. He begins twitching and blinking rapidly, taking short sharp breaths, clutching his penis to his chest, but it slips from his grasp and drapes awkwardly across his neck. I kneel down over him and his frightened eyes quiver toward me.

"See, you should've just asked. Stupid unit. Disgusting." My clit pulses like hummingbird wings, and my cock thrums like a harp. Aching. I place the tip of it at the hole between his freshly neutered legs. And *thrust* inside him. Ah. He inhales deeply and warbles a guttural sob. I have to fuck fuck fuck him fuck him harder and harder slamming against a bone until his eyes freeze, and I come inside him. Ah-oh, so so good, good lover.

Yes. Good lover. I hate you. I fucking hate you and thanks for a good time.

Sounds. My eyes are closed. Where am I?

"... luck ... on ... beading ... mving are you?"

"Hello," I say, but it sounds like "Huuhhhh."

Is that her? Face above me. Vaguely. Gone.

Darkness.

I'm awake. Pillow behind my head.

I peel open my eyes. Milky grey. The roof of the Zirkus. I lift my head weakly ... fall back. Neck aches. Rest a little more.

Cot beneath me. White tent walls. Small table by the bed with a cup of water.

Sphinx.

I roll over on my side, slide my legs to the floor, and push up with my arms; my forehead twinges. I touch it—a bandage wraps the top of my head. My white robe, pyramid pattern. Groggy, need water. Almost knock it over. Drinking. My hands quiet. My scaly loden shell. Touch the pocket where my penis is hiding. Close my eyes, take a deep breath. Have to find Sphinx.

Push myself up from bed. Dizzy. Hand on the table for support. A curtain in the wall—the exit—head for it. Falling—grab the fabric.

Bring the entire tent down with me.

I'm lying in a cul-de-sac, wrapped like a mummy. An upright pig carrying a ladder has halted mid-stride looking at me.

"G'Nesh," I croak out, frightened by my voice which creaks like a graveyard gate. "I need to find G'Nesh." He'll tell me where Sphinx is.

Pigleg Pete wags his snout to the right as he heads off in the opposite direction.

Untangle from the canvas and weave in the direction he's pointed me. Stay focused: the maze. Just follow the passage.

Scents of people. Many.

A crowd milling ahead.

An open square. About twenty Pures are standing around a cage on a platform in the middle. To the left: a black structure like a pagoda with a gothic door but no windows.

I approach the cage; the norms part from me in revulsion and fear.

There! Sitting on his paws with his head down and eyes closed.

"SPHINX!" I shout.

He raises his head; his eyes find me, and he yawps wildly. I'm on the platform, circling the cage. A heavy padlock holds the door shut.

"You okay?"

Sphinx pads over to me and snaps his beak around a metal bar.

"I'll get you out of here."

The Pures have gathered to watch me. No tools, nothing useful around. Let's see how strong I am. I turn back, grip two bars, and begin pulling them apart across my chest. I'm pulling my arms out of their sockets. Bars are moving, inching apart.

"AAAAAAAH!" I'm howling.

Pulling apart.

Switch—push one in, pull one out.

Thundering in my temples.

Bar tears out of my hand.

I fall back light fades out .

I'm in a room. A canvas room. A tent. Slivers of light crosshatch space like rapier blades. Out of the corner of my eye—a presence. In a chair behind a desk—a woman with a deer head.

"Have you found what you are looking for?" she asks.

"What exactly am I looking for?"

"You must answer that."

"Why are you judging me?" I ask her back.

"You are judging yourself."

Déjà vu. I've met her before.

"You are familiar somehow. I feel you've ... you ... is this a dream?"

"Of course it is," she replies. "Isn't it always?"

"But are you really here?"

"Are *you* really here?"

I don't know.

"If this is a dream, then I'm just talking to myself."

"We only talk to ourselves."

"Everything is wrong here."

"Isn't it wrong everywhere?"

"I never wanted to come here. I never wanted to leave."

"Are you sure?"

"You found me."

"You found *me*."

Her mouth doesn't move as the words come out. Her limpid mocha curves are hand-blown.

"You're being cryptic."

"Here, look at this. *This* is cryptic." She shows me her forearm:

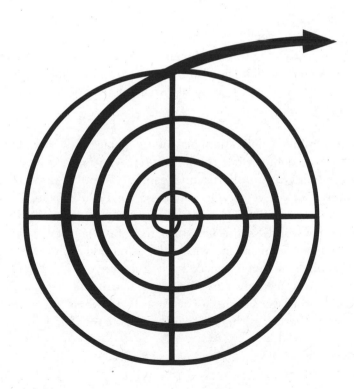

"Do you know what is happening to you?"

"I—no—I ... *sense* things happening to me, or—I sense things outside myself happening, but I don't know what they are. I'm—it's like I'm reading stories of a life not my own."

"Every life is a story, a song, a groove in the flow. Most beings think they're stuck in one track. But you drank from the river of forgetfulness. Perhaps it threw you off your fated course, and you followed a new one, a quest that allowed you to move beyond the river that channeled you, and you began to live other stories. You're living one right now. If you choose to remember, you can skip the groove you are caught in and flow down another. Or keep forgetting and continue as things are."

"How can I do that?" I ask.

"Symbols have awesome power. Language is made of symbols which define our essence. A communal game that builds its own boundaries. And people with power build more and more walls, walls of symbols that trap you and also themselves.

"Nothing is certain. Civilization played its game with you. Every time someone tries to define what *is*, they are playing with symbols, defined by other symbols. An ouroboros of meaning. There is no essence, only understanding. But you've seen it. Language has been hacked. The rules of the game have begun falling apart. You've pushed past the symbols of power. Inhabiting other worlds is the first step to unraveling power. These lines chart my imagination, mark me with conviction and will. I can share this insight with you, if you open a space for it. Release your need to control and empty yourself. New meaning can grow inside you. It will help you remember. Remember the other worlds you can become. If you would like to see it, come here. Look at me here. It is there. You'll see it." She touched her forehead.

I look closely at her fluid skin. I read past the surface; I enter.

Mmmmmuhhhhgg ... ahhh waking ... did I conjugate? un(shifted worldview) productive, just sleep [<for what seems like a very (no idea how) long (compared to what? {) time> (has been swept up, can no longer be divided, measured, or clocked, is the surface life skates on, is motion, is life forever not occurring, is the hallucination consciousness creates from the fictional past and the fictional future)} recollection is a cannibal]

meaning has eaten itself leaving merely crumbs

my quill, where is my *Memory Hole* notebook?~there, beside my sleep sack~have it

the manner in which the wor(l)d evades control: language is quantum, the closer I get to it, the more it recedes and exceeds my circumference, elusive and evanescent~I have intended to capture for you reality

> *this "you" may be my future Self [to be my (record of memory as an idea) companion] because very few others can read now or have an interest in reading~perhaps I will string this on my clothesline and send it off to the impenetrable unknown and see what comes back*

but I fear I have failed~when I read my own words, they curl up like dying maggots, conjuring shadows of real events (the shameful poverty of my memory) dried up, every one lumbering after the next, my prose leaden~clunky~awkwa rd~dull~desperately circling meaning but gripped by inadequacy (who am I to try?)~no, I will resist that which tells me I cannot, even myself

I need to share my thoughts now

I will go to G'Nesh, share with hem my thoughts on memory, writing (the importance of) my books, and my notes and capture (experience through language) my journey as I go

Right now:
my head is curled; an S-curved tentacle with a quill (a hollow tube spiked into my ink sac) scribbling into the book clenched in my beak like a pirate's doubloon; the rolling ball of my legs strobing above the Zirkus tents, walking over and along tents, keeping my body close to the surfaces~writing and camouflaging as I go:

I am dirt, muslin and the shield, I am phantasm, the symbolic foam bubbling overhead~

the sapiens don't take notice~

I have come to rest at the Midway abutting G'Nesh's apartment: dirt-brown dirt laps up my viewpoint like an old leather tongue, stringers and workers mill in all directions, forming vortices and cross-stitch patterns as they move toward olive tents; a crowd of Homo sapiendus surrounds an enclosure with a large quadrupedal being (part feline, part avian) inside and a reptilian olive-colored biped in a white cap and a dress fallen on the platform near a gap in the bars (apparently sundered)~

Next, a furry one enters stage left struggling to drag two lumps behind her
I do recognize hem as the Menagerie stringer Maphroditee~I find this Eros, this bunnybiped, a kindred spirit~although hem pays me little attention because I cannot satisfy hem~my limbs too coarse and my suckers too puissant to cherish a sensitive body~but I admire hes gyrations~I have seen hem contorting and cavorting with many individuals and hem achieves (what I have at times used as inspiration) a sublime dance of
bodies [upon closer inspection: one of a sapiendus variety (appearing to be in the same wardrobe as the other sapiens) and the other, the horned equine stringer (Unihorn)] in a trajectory toward G'Nesh's residence, leaving me meditating how to describe her moving from point A (the dead bodies) to point B (the portal of G'nesh) because I am unsure of the essential importance of these events~I could simply write, "Maphro released the bodies and moved to the entryway of G'nesh's tent," and leave it at that, but I'm afraid I might bore you to tears with such unadorned, mundane prose; it serves functionally, to describe movement, but I suspect fails to help you conjure the actual scene~and so I might add several adjectives and/or adverbs to help bring the scene to life with penetrating affect, to whit: "Maphroditee hopped decisively from the conventicle of corpses to the ominous entryway of G'Nesh's black temple" in this particular case, you get a more vivid picture of what I see although I can't presume it is real~Maphro may have (for example) been feeling uncertain (hes hopping may have but appeared decisive by its nature) and others may see G'nesh's door as thrilling rather than

ominous, so, in fact, I am describing merely a point of view (and one that changes as I write it), not reality.

Shall I spend a page on one second of time and still not capture it? Shall I tell you about the dust motes that waft like pinpoint will-o-wisps? To what end? Setting the scene? To convince you that what I saw was real? Even I do not know if it is real (or what real means) and what difference verisimilitude when memory has been lifted by the thief of dignity~I skip ahead:

In the connection at G'Nesh door, Maphroditee [standing upright on slender yet strong spring-like thighs, a well-groomed rabbit of cocoa powder, parabolic body (rich fur washing across her like a breeze of dark energy) and hairless chest glands from alabaster at the base, shading through silver, almond, tan, umber, and purest black at the tip] addresses two pigbrids crossing hes trajectory and a third draws nigh [a tall ectomorphic being (whom I have never seen before) like a shoot of bamboo with arms and legs] while the sapeii turn as a group toward the dead bodies (the sapine body appears to be nude from the waist down and has a wound where its glans should be)~now they have surrounded Maphoditee (who is paying no attention to them)

(Raised) voices carry up to me; without warning, a sapien pushes Maphro into another sapien who pushes Maphro back~they are shoving hem around from one to the next, tossing hem violently, grabbing an arm and an arm, and a leg and a leg~they are pulling, attempting to quarter hem~I should act~

(To be honest, I am also called to record this) I will stop~but

"Thank you," I say to the water and bow my head in supplication. I stand close to it, put my nose and my thoughts over it, and a stratum of coolness caresses me, curling up from the water's surface into my nostrils.

Looking around the naked room. The floor I sleep on. The pedestal, the bowl of water that stays cool as I've taught it.

The show is over. Time to visit the water room. Anticipation. Being in the water room. Guarding the water. Standing by the vat. It radiates freshness and purity like nothing else. Simplicity.

Enter the chamber.

Something is wrong.

Water is droppletting from the clear plastic tubes into the vat. Drip by drip from the donation stations. This is not right. The temperature of the container. A few degrees warmer than usual.

I rocket out the door, kicking it shut behind, rattling the building.

Saps leap aside as I storm across the Midway, hooves pounding, I'm plowing through the slow, them flying like dolls, snorting and bellowing at the top of my lungs to the Lux trailer. I ram my horn into the guts of the door. I back up, ram again. The wood splinters.

"What do you want?" the door cries.

"JOEY, G'NESH, SOMEONE, **NOW!**" I bellow.

He's rolling out on his cart drawn by the Bug. Robe half on, Tender right behind them.

"Fucking fuck, Buttons, I could hear you coming in my asshole. What the fuck?"

"Betrayed! The water has been poisoned!"

"Are you sure?"

"Sure."

"Take me."

Tender lifts him off the cart and sets him on my back. I turn and race back to the water room. We confront the metal heart, all the tubes running into it like veins.

"Let me off."

I kneel forward. He crawls over my head and off my nose to the waterlock. He punches in a code, slaps a button. The porthole rotates and pops up with a *WHOOSH*.

He inhales, eyes closed.

He looks back at me.

"Contaminated. We've been fucking radio-axed. Fix it! Separate them!"

I concentrate. Try to convince the water to separate itself from the alpha dogs.

"Is already too corrupted, too tired. I can't communicate." The poison had vitiated the liquid's sense of self. It's too sweet, too much of a surface, and the water is addicted.

He wails. The sound lashes around the chamber, piercing my ears.

"Back to the square!"

We arrive back to a feverish orgy.

Tender is punching through faces—
Squid is there, the bodies of many crushed Saps under his tentacles—
kinkers converging on the scene, forcing Saps into the cage—
the CatBird backs into a corner with a body under him—
a Black Bamboo pole is whipping about in a frenzy, laughing hysterically,
pointing a shiny object at Saps who melt and morph and splatter—
new phreaks are running, galloping, crawling, flopping everywhere—
the CatBird shrieks into a whirlwind of wings and claws and the cage turns
into a bloodbath—
Squid is slamming Units' heads together, tearing bodies apart casually—
lakes of blood disgrace the square—

Baby Joey grabs my earflap and yells into it: "Up there!" pointing at the cage.

Across to the cage, crushing bodies as I go. I bring him up to it, and he crawls
off my horn onto the roof.

With a loud bang, the killing is over. There are no Saps left, just clamor,
cackles, and the thudding footsteps of pigbrids and kinkers, all of them,
the whole Zirk showing up at this spot, all the creatures big and small. The
CatBird is squeezing through a gap in the cage, pulling a body behind him.

A piercing cry: Baby Joey like a knife whistle. Quiet falls.

Sound of the CatBird squeezing between the bars. No one tries to stop him.

Baby Joey takes a moment to survey us all.

"This is it, my friends. My partners. My stars. This is done. This is over. This
is the end," says Joey as he looks from one to the next. "You. And you. And
you and you and you. All of you. You have survived with unconquerable
strength of will. You are miraculous. You are beautiful and spectacular. You
have struggled to be who you are, to survive. And now. Now. After all this.
Everything you worked for your whole life. You do not deserve this. You have
been slain. Each of us. All of us. We stand here alive now, but we are slain.
Even G'Nesh cannot save us."

Growls and snarls rumble through the crowd.

"The Units. The Homo Corruptianis. They have poisoned us. They have poisoned the water."

His words pierce each of us deeper than his scream.

"They are destroyers. They are death. They have brought it to us. We're outsiders. Free radicals. They want to kill us or control us. We are not meant to live that way. We can never be controlled. We're in this as *one* because we refuse to be trapped, we refuse to live small, we refuse to become them! We are strong, and we shall not go quietly. We shall not become the bones of the starving. We are what they dream of when they dream of being real!"

He waits. He holds out a small webbed hand before us. Green flaps connect his fingers.

"We have been poisoned, and we deserve, we will have revenge. We will show them what they are! WHO WILL FOLLOW ME? WHO WILL BRING THEM DEATH?" he cries, shrill and furious.

And a mighty roar responds.

The four-leggers rear up, hooves and paws in the air, thick rawhide snouts up, awkward bulk raised, hammers and tent pegs in the air.

Joey crawls down onto my horn, says in my ear, "Take us to the City Door."

I will see for myself~in moments, I [at the vault (entering) the porthole open, the rich aquarium] balloon over the coruscating clear liquescent diamond; dip a tip in, scoop it to my mouth

No

Toxic Plastic Radioactive

No

No nonononononononono

We are dead

I fall over the porthole, my body draining, sliding down, draining into it, gushing from a stab wound

Never again, I am in the cistern surrounded by water, all around me cool water, the end is circular, the end, is circular, I will circulate, around and around and around I will go, I am bending stalks, I am falling leaves, my limbs unfurl, I am done writing, forever, everything dissipates, releasing my ink, trailing tornados, I leave behind blooming flowers of unbearable sadness

I am jarred. Slammed. Up and down. Grab on. I'm holding fur. I'm on Sphinx, his soft back, amid sound and fury. We are racing with the horde thundering out of the tent, the air is thick with dust, tesla-coil energy raging and zapping, a dull roar, thumping—hundreds of beings, all of them racing toward the City.

I remember.

The deer, Salvia. The twin hunters. The Squid. Buttons. DJ Morpheus. Baby Joey. Sys. Suddenly, I remember becoming them all.

No. No! I shout, I shout, but I cannot be heard. This is wrong. Stop!

I cannot be heard; I am battered side-to-side, holding on tight as I can.

We are there.

We're at a featureless door. It's torn upward, and we rush in.

Concrete buildings on both sides. We jolt to a halt.

Row up on row of squat metal vehicles block the road.

Movement, a blur in the air.

Baby hugs Button's horn.

Baby is wrapped up. His head drops to the side. His skin draped in shreds around him. A bloody blanket.

More blurring of space. Gouts of barbed wire are spinning. I've been knocked off Sphinx. I'm against a wall.

WHOOSH!!! A blaze of metal bolos flings toward us—stampedes in every direction—I'm leaping up the wall, claws gouging concrete, tearing myself upward.

Onto a roof—running across. A distant, dull drumbeat.

Drop, spin, and look back.

Birdgirl is there, on the lip of the roof, her wings spread wide—
white against black—

a flash of orange behind her—

BOOOOOOM

She is serene in space and time.

Her wings burst alight
she flaps them twice
ragged curtains of light brushing the air with a glorious chime a hum a buzz
a tingling note that strikes me like a tuning fork
she is singing

she falls backwards
the ground beneath me tilts slowly s o s l o w l   y   forward
pushes me gently upward
outward from the center

I slide toward her as she disappears over the edge

at the edge and
over

so many weightless fragments of building

clouds of smoke

quiet

glimpses of earth
broken bodies

dropping into clouds of grey
shedding gravity
falling like rain
stories falling away
broken furniture
metal vehicles
a flourish of dull green paper
scent of bones and fire

she spires below me, wings alive trailing flames
circling patiently
silently circling and sinking on tattered wings
a burning angel

I wake with a creak. My body aches. Excruciating. I open my eyes: the sky is scalloped in shades of purple.

I roll to my side. Ahead of me is the black bug, Anophelese, pulling. I'm on a cart lurching across uneven, desiccated land. I look behind me: a broken-toothed maw opens into the City. Bodies are everywhere. Nothing moves. Sphinx.

I am weak, close my eyes.

Awake again with a start. Something scuttles off. It's dark. It's quiet. I try to sit up, but my body is broken.

In the darkness, I sense the immensity of his body.

"It's over," I croak. "They destroyed us. Everyone. My Sphinx. Is dead. I think. Except the bug. And me."

I'm lifted up. I can feel my legs, fractured matchsticks, my knees crunching, and immediately the pain is gone.

It stands heavily before me—a magnificent mane around the face and the body of a great ape. Cloven-hooved.

G'Nesh places me behind hes neck and leans forward on all fours. I flex my right knee and hip, and the pieces move easily without pain. My left, the same. He lumbers out of the building, head down—through a wall—boards explode about us and glance off my scales.

Soon we are out in the pale light, thundering across the dirt plane.

I take a deep breath through the holes in my face. I haven't breathed in a long time. Feels good. My face buried in fur and musk behind hes neck. Now we must be in the woods. Dark and cool, mist and menthol. Bathed in blue. We're out the other side, and it's thick and rancid.

We stop. I'm clinging to G'Nesh, threatened by the lament of boundless beings. Exclamations of torture and misery. Fumes thicken the air. His hand coming—clutches me round like a toy and places me carefully on the bank of the River of Flesh. G'Nesh looks at me, and we appraise each other.

He's the King. King Chimera. Pure power. I have seen enough. I am no longer afraid. Today is a good day to die.

We walk on the hard-packed bank along the river that curves ahead of us toward the City cracked like an eggshell, ruptured yellow yolk spilling out and plumes trailing upward.

"Aren't you going to go try to help them?"

"It was time for the show to end."

I consider.

"You knew."

"Of course I knew. How do you think the Zirk started?"

"I don't know."

"I am the one who remembers. When we first created the company town, I was the Engineer. I created the Zirkus to visit other cities and bring back a tithe."

"So why did you have to let it end? Why?"

He turns and stops. Looks down at me.

"There is nowhere left to go. All the other cities fallen. This is the final and last one. The originator. The father. They would not have let us continue without being able to pay them. Not profitable. I know their plan because it's what I would have done. You'd be harvested, and I'd return to the City."

"You could have let them go out. Outside! Why didn't you warn them? You knew they would be killed!"

"They chose a path of violence."

"That isn't good enough."

"They made their own choice, as did you. Where would you have me tell them go? The end of their selves beckons from every passage."

We stop in a grassy area. The river froths, liquid and volatile. I'm burning, seething inside, the change comes on. He turns, looks at me, and lays a hand on my shoulder. I feel myself stabilize, grow larger, return to balance.

"I am weary of this," he says.

"You just aren't creative enough."

"This is the river of power and control. It's the river of selfishness and cruelty. Of indifference and ignorance. It's the river of fear. It's the river of undifferentiated lives. It has an easy flow to it. It takes unknown strength to swim against it. You haven't lived long enough to realize that this river runs through life itself."

"What about you?"

"What about me? I'm a force of nature, boy." He points at the City. "I was one of them. We ruled the planet."

"And look at them," I reply. "Serving time. Trapped. Even to rule them is to be a slave."

He rubs his knuckles across his forehead.

"Yes. I think that is true. I will not be going back. I have made up my mind. Instead of ruling them, I will peel them open. I expect you will be the last to remember them. What will you do with that?"

He rears up on four clawed paws—a wolf ... a coyote. He grows over ten times my height and steps out into the river. The wailing increases as he wades out toward the middle, rolls of protoplasm bubbling around him, until the bedlam falls like a curtain, and the maelstrom ceases. G'Nesh sinks down until just his muzzle is visible above the surface. He opens wide, primordial ooze draining into his mouth. Change—he's changing again—his nose has become a trunk curved up ... dropping below ... until ... the tip ... disappears.

The surface is smooth and quiet. I am insubstantial, barely held to the earth.

Faces appear in the flesh: mouths moving, eyes blinking, heads surface and drop back under. Holes, pockmarks, peaks and valleys, tears and gouges fissure through the river as if it is being stretched apart, curled, seared from within, sheets wrapping around themselves forming globs of meat.

I reach out toward him and hold the life beating all around me, the beings on all sides—tempestuous and clamorous with existence, and I touch them and swallow them and change them and condense them and cohere their minds around a single thought you don't need a self find calmness in nothingness and I am shaping them like clay absorbing all the multifarious beings into myself containing worlds and we billow up from the surface I am a coyote and a lion and a goat and a snake and a pig and a bear and a bug and a whale and a squid and a slug and a bee and a lemur and a human and we are all these things at once in one body everything and nothing and it is a flash of a flash an infinitesimal infinity where being and becoming are one and I'm directing them at the City and I'm thrown out back into my lizardskin standing on the shore watching the river and the creatures thrust out of the river, forming shapes and bodies ... and I know what that power feels like, how to use it, I learned in that moment ... and the river is filled with round balls of flesh twice my height and they are surging out of the river toward the City and bounding toward it, bounding toward it, until they collide, and walls fold and tumble and the outside collapses in.

... and a flame, a click, and a rainbow of light blazes and ...

I can see in all directions.

I see my friend coming to me.

Let him embrace me.

Falling.

And I fall into the grass.

I can see nothing. And feel nothing.

Is this the end?
Of what?
Of me.
I don't know. What are you?
What are you doing now?
I am holding you.
What do you see?
The sky is getting darker. A spot in the sky—a spot behind the clouds is expanding, getting darker, becoming more diffuse and spreading.

I wonder if you are real.
I can't answer that.
I can see nothing.

And I do not think I am speaking I do not think I am speaking.

This is not the end. I remember. I learned.

Let me get ahold. There it is. The helix. A little map of the good place to go.
Where did you find it?
Inside myself.

Are you hungry?
I am often hungry.
Why don't you eat the body you hold?
I could not do that.
You should. Tear me apart.
Very well.

How do I taste?
Juicy.

Now I am a part of you. I can teach you.
Teach me what?
Becoming—anything. Yes. You'll feel it as I did, in my bones, in my body—it's
a howl, a pure noise—and then you will be able to create too.

Me?
Yes.

Now?
Yes. Try it now.
Yes. Yes. Beautiful. Beautiful!

And I can give this to everyone as I give it to you
because I can grow
because I can grow
inside a blade of grass
inside a blade of grass
inside a blade of grass
shimmering up the xylem and phloem
shimmering up the xylem and phloem
shimmering up the xylem and phloem
shimmering up the xylem and phloem
diffusing out through the green
diffusing out through the green
diffusing out through the green
diffusing out through the green
diffusing out through the green
and bursting like a supernova through the membrane of the universe
and bursting like a supernova through the membrane of the universe
and bursting like a supernova through the membrane of the universe
and bursting like a supernova through the membrane of the universe
and bursting like a supernova through the membrane of the universe
and bursting like a supernova through the membrane of the universe

and anything that touches me
and anything that touches me
and anything that touches me
and anything that touches me
and anything that touches me
and anything that touches me
and anything that touches me
will learn
will learn
will learn
will learn
will learn
will learn
will learn
will learn
will hear the sound
will hear the sound
will hear the sound
will hear the sound
will hear the sound
will hear the sound
will hear the sound
will hear the sound
will hear the sound
the vibration
the vibration
the vibration
the vibration
the vibration
the vibration
the vibration
the vibration
the vibration
the vibration

the universal hum of life
the universal hum of life
the universal hum of life
the universal hum of life
the universal hum of life
the universal hum of life
the universal hum of life
the universal hum of life
the universal hum of life
the universal hum of life
the universal hum of life
and everyone is free
and everyone is free
and everyone is free
and everyone is free
and everyone is free
and everyone is free
and everyone is free
and everyone is free
and everyone is free
and everyone is free
and everyone is free
and everyone is free
now
now
now
now
now
now
now
now
now
now
now
now
now